Misdeeds

By Kathryn Kelly

Edited by Crystal Cuffley

Cover by Crystal Cuffley

Manufactured in the United States of America

This is a work of fiction. The characters, incidents and dialogue in this book are of the author's imagination and are not to be construed as real. Any resemblance to actual events or persons, living or dead, is completely coincidental.

Blurb

John "Johnnie" Donovan is determined to make his relationship work with Kendall Miller, the attorney he met during his cousin's birthday party. Before he can move on with his future, however, he still has loose ends to tie up from the past in the person of a rival MC's president who is also Kendall's ex-boyfriend. As Johnnie tries to balance his club life and personal life, another tragedy forces him to make a choice between the two. Will Johnnie be able to live with the choices he makes?

Kendall Miller is trying to pick up the pieces of her life in the wake of her ex-boyfriend's assault. She's ready to move on with her life and the man of her dreams, the sexy VP of the Death Dwellers MC. She demands his complete attention and isn't willing to share her man with all the baggage of the MC. She doesn't want to be an afterthought to him nor does she want to live her life in the midst of the clubhouse, especially with the competition taking place between Kendall and the club president's wife. Then, catastrophe strikes and Kendall's life is once again altered. Can she and Johnnie have a future together or has their love been doomed from the beginning?

Dedication

To all of Johnnie's fans, those who wrote and
demanded his HEA and those who are just discovering him.

Every minute you are thinking of evil, you might have been thinking of good instead. Refuse to pander to a morbid interest in your own misdeeds. Pick yourself up, be sorry, shake yourself, and go on again.

Evelyn Underhill

Chapter 1

Chrome gleamed in the breezy day, a never ending wave undulating beneath the sunshine. The roar of the hundreds of motorcycle pipes set off a few car alarms, but no one cared, least of all the citizens who lined the procession toward the church.

Kendall Miller laid her head against the back of John "Johnnie" Donovan, her arms tight around his waist, his Harley idling beneath them. His white-gloved hands gripped the handlebars, his body tense, his heart beating hard.

Johnnie had gotten released from the hospital three days ago, having been shot less than a week before by members of Kendall's former boyfriend's MC. Or, maybe, even, Spoon himself.

No matter. She wished Johnnie wouldn't have to be here, in front of the church, his bike parked between Outlaw, the president of the Death Dwellers MC, and the club enforcer, Mortician. Sadness and somberness hung from them, but they sat in stoic silence, awaiting the arrival of their road captain, Val, delivering the body of the club treasurer, Kaleb Paul "Kitchen Patrol" Andrews, on a motorcycle hearse.

Next in the processional, the lone vehicle, a limousine containing K-P's daughter, Bailey, and his recently-acquired and very distraught old lady, Dinah. Behind the extra-long car, the surge of bikes, the rumbling pounding through Kendall's brain.

Val rode into view, stopping at the edge of the rapidly growing double-sided rows of motorcycles as, one by one, riders backed the bikes into the places, spanning outside of the church parking lot and into the blocked off street.

A moment passed. Then another. And another. Grief threatened to overwhelm Kendall and she tempered the urge to scream at Val to ride to the church steps. He continued to wait, revving the engine at times, too far away for Kendall to detect his state of mind. If his emotions mirrored Johnnie's, K-P's death devastated Val.

Finally, the reason for the delay appeared. *Bailey.* Dressed in black leather pants and a black shirt, she stopped next to the hearse, her intention to walk alongside, clear.

Kendall glanced at Mortician, who turned away from Bailey's direction and allowed Kendall to note his internal struggle. The club enforcer cared about Bailey, visible by the sympathy in his eyes, his hunger for her noticeable despite his grief. So many emotions played across his face, Kendall couldn't decipher most of them. If he went to her now, he'd be claiming her as his. While Kendall understood the dynamics of such an action, she wanted him to ignore the stupid codes just this *once.* Bailey needed him right now. Later, Mortician could set her straight.

Val started forward at a slow speed, keeping pace with Bailey. As they passed each brother, the bikers throttled their engines in honor of K-P. After a minute or so, Bailey stumbled and the road captain halted again. He glanced at Mortician before returning his attention to Bailey, staring at her, understanding softening his pose.

Shivers raced through Kendall at the sudden, oppressive

silence. No one moved, all focused on Bailey. Kendall willed her to regain her composure but they wouldn't rush her. They blanketed Bailey—the daughter of one of the fallen brethren—with their protection.

A gust of cool wind whipped around them, the affirmation of life twisting Kendall's heart and sending tears to her eyes. In a couple of days, she'd have to face another funeral. Her sixteen-year-old sister's. There would be no huge showing for her. Caroline had been one, small girl with only Kendall and their mother as relatives. She'd been popular in school, so high school kids and teachers should've been able to attend, though it would've been nothing close to this overwhelming ceremonial rite.

Due to shattering circumstances surrounding her suicide, however, Kendall intended to opt for a private funeral. Any other way and too many other questions might be asked. Questions Kendall had no logical answers to. Caroline had been happy, perky, smart, and popular. Teachers would want to know what drove her to hang herself when there'd been no signs of distress brewing.

Caroline had never been troubled or trouble, so an alert school administrator might suspect something.

As much as she wanted to, Kendall couldn't blurt the truth of her sister's death and confess Caroline had been as much a victim as K-P. He'd been murdered by Logan Donavan. Caroline had killed herself *because* of Logan Donovan.

Kendall despised him. He'd taken so much from all of them. Worse, he was *her* biker's grandfather, which made it doubly important to remain silent. As a result, her little sister would be buried with little or no fanfare.

Bailey stepping forward and Val moving the hearse a fraction drew Kendall's attention. Bailey drew closer, her tears and heartbreak easier to glimpse. Her mask of composure slipped with each step she took toward the entrance of the church. Mortician straightened and closed his eyes, his shoulders heaving, his big hands tightening on the handlebars. He'd queued his dreads and the diamond studs in his ears glinted in the sunshine. He glanced in Bailey's direction again, hesitated and threw a scowl toward Johnnie and Outlaw, holding out as long as he could. But Bailey looked so distraught and fragile. Kendall wanted to offer her a hug of condolence herself, although she'd only met Bailey in passing. Finally, Mortician caved and broke rank, pausing his Harley next to the hearse to converse with Val.

Bailey stared at Mortician, blinking away her tears. Swiping at her own tears, Kendall tightened her hold on Johnnie. This was so hard. If she could change anything in these past few days to take away everyone's pain, she would.

Mortician sped off, roaring back into sight and stopping next to the limousine. Once the limo driver backed up, Mortician slid his bike behind Bailey. Palming her cheeks, she peeped over her shoulder, starting—as did Kendall—when the club enforcer held out his gloved hand to her and gave her a small nod.

Not hesitating, Bailey rushed to him and threw her arms around his neck, her body shaking. Mortician waged another resistance—another losing battle—before he wrapped one arm around her waist and whispered to her. He thumbed away her tears, then indicated the spot behind him. She mounted the seat and rested her cheek against his cut, her arms embracing his middle.

Johnnie glanced over his shoulder to Kendall and winked at her, the smile breaking through his grief like sunshine breaching clouds. Approval gleamed through the sadness in his silver-gray eyes. At Mortician's actions, she knew. Her heartbeat picked up speed. They hadn't spoken in a couple hours, not since they'd started from the funeral home and rode through town to get to the church, pausing twice for moments of silence.

The noise increased, closing in on Kendall as Val neared. Mortician skirted around the hearse to take his place before Val rode past.

"Kaleb Paul," Mortician yelled, revving his engine, his face filled with grief. His shout started a tide that Johnnie took up as Val reached their spot.

The big Harley vibrated beneath Kendall with Johnnie's revving. The calls of K-P's name and the roaring Harleys symbols of their grief and anger. She tightened her hold on Johnnie, kissed the back of his head.

Val stopped the hearse at the end of the steps and the roar of the bikes abruptly ceased. As one, Outlaw, Johnnie, Mortician, Digger and Stretch rose from their bikes. Outlaw adjusted the white gloves he wore—identical to the others'—then grabbed his wife, Megan's, hand, guiding her behind the motorcycle hearse with K-P's remains. He nodded to Johnnie then did the same to Mortician, the cue for them to escort Kendall and Bailey to where Megan stood.

"In the middle, Bailey," Outlaw instructed, frowning at Megan's high heels but not saying anything.

Kendall supposed he didn't want Megan wearing stilettos while pregnant. Kendall carried a child, too, but no one worried about what she wore.

Flanking Bailey's left side, Kendall grabbed the girl's cold hand and squeezed. Death was never easy, especially a violent, unexpected one.

Val dismounted and took position at the coffin, second row, right side, behind Johnnie, who stood at the head along with Outlaw.

Worry for Johnnie's health consumed Kendall. The gleaming mahogany casket *without* K-P's body weighed a lot. With him in there...she shook the morbid thought away, focused on Johnnie. True, the gunshot wound had been superficial, but he'd needed surgery to remove the bullet. He shouldn't strain himself carrying a coffin.

Undertakers were supposed to do this task. Kendall swore pallbearers loaded a casket in the hearse—or in this case on it—and then carried it to the grave site. On the other hand, these men lived by their own rules and damn anyone who didn't like it, so she shouldn't have been surprised they did something out of the norm.

The slow march into the church and down the aisle took forever. The sluggish passage of time didn't help Kendall's fretting over Johnnie the entire way toward the front of the church.

Bailey halted, a half-sob and half-laugh escaping her. Kendall followed the girl's line of vision to the floral arrangements. The three unusual ones—a spoon, a *stove,* and one that looked suspiciously like, of all things, an *onion*—stood at the foot of the coffin.

A blown up photo of K-P straddling his bike, the sun glinting off his bald head and silver beard, sat amidst the myriad flowers, the sickly sweet smell turning Kendall's stomach.

Mortician stopped next to them, some of his dreads now dangling from his ponytail, his red-rimmed eyes tired. "Bailey, girl, c'mon. I'm gonna bring you to your seat."

Bailey glanced back and her shoulders drooped. "Mom isn't here yet and neither is Uncle Arrow."

"Arrow isn't far off," Johnnie offered, joining them in time to hear Bailey's words. "Your mom…well, sweetheart…I don't think she's coming."

"I don't want to be on the pew alone. Not now."

"Is there a problem here?" an authoritative voice broke in.

"Of course not, Father Wilkins." Megan's voice drifted from Bailey's other side. "We're just deciding seating arrangements.

His jowls flapping, Father Wilkins pinned an under-eyed glare on them. "This doesn't take much brain power to know family goes on the first pew, Mrs. Caldwell." He smirked at her. "Ah, yes. In order to have brain power, you need a brain. I simply forgot who I'm dealing with for a moment."

His contemptuous words brought about various reactions. Johnnie scowled at the round, little man, and Mortician scratched his jaw. Bailey bristled, narrowing her watery gaze while Megan stepped toward him, huffing out a breath.

Before Kendall dredged up a feeling one way or the other, Outlaw tapped the priest on the shoulder. "Yo', Father Wilcunt, you ain't gonna have to worry 'bout your fuckin' brain in a minute. Insult Megan one more fuckin' time, motherfucker, and your brain gonna be on the *outside* of your ass. Then you can tell us how the fuck real fuckin' brainlessness is."

"K-P's funeral, Christopher," Megan reminded him in a tight voice.

Anger flickered in Father Wilkins's eyes. "Since putting you out isn't an option—"

"Not if you don't want your ass beat—" Outlaw interrupted.

Johnnie took Kendall's hand into his own and led her to the second pew, leaving the argument to Outlaw and the priest.

"How are you?" he asked, gorgeous in anything he wore. Dressed in full colors and leather turned him into a sexy rogue. Dropping next to her, he caressed her palm, his touch sizzling along her nerve endings. "You've held up well this morning."

Kendall kicked up her mouth in a forced smile,

determined to be strong for him, despite the tenuous place she had in his life. Grief dulled his silver-gray eyes, his tempting mouth tight with sorrow. "I'm fine. Worried about you."

"Don't be." He squeezed her hand, the edge removed from the words with the gesture.

She stroked her fingers through his blond hair. "I can't help it."

Instead of responding, he laid his forehead against hers. "How's Baby Biker?"

Baby Biker. Her name for the child growing inside of her. Hearing *him* murmur it melted Kendall's insides.

"Fine," she whispered, lowering her lashes in shyness, her nerves speeding her heart. During the past few weeks her life had become a series of irrational events, so why shouldn't butterflies flutter in her belly and heat sweep her body at Johnnie's words and close proximity?

For the past three days, he'd been overwhelmed with the goings-on of the previous week. Now, he worked with the others, planning retaliation. He never discussed with her the club's intentions against Spoon and the Torpedoes for all their infractions with the Dwellers. Mortician didn't discuss it with her, either.

And neither did Megan Caldwell. Kendall wondered at the extent of her awareness about the Dwellers' activity. Kendall's guess? A lot more than Kendall knew and a lot more than Megan let on.

Johnnie dropped her hand and stood. "Excuse me for a minute."

Tracking his movements to the back of the church, Kendall noted a frail looking, graying blonde woman. Dinah Nicholls. Megan's mother and K-P's old lady. Gripping her arm, Outlaw whispered to her just as Johnnie reached her other side.

The disagreement between Outlaw and Father Wilkins had been solved because the priest approached the altar. Bailey sat on the first seat with Megan next to her.

Grief and hurt—too many emotions to name—assailed Kendall. She stood from her spot in the second row, needing a distraction and making her way to Bailey's other side.

"Meggie, your mom is in the church," Bailey choked out.

"Okay. Kendall is here if you need anything until I get back." Megan released Bailey's hand, popped to her feet and headed to her mother, who'd made it halfway down the aisle.

Immediately, Johnnie tugged Megan between him and Dinah. Meggie's arm slid around her mother, then dropped away a moment later. Johnnie draped his arm around her, fisting Dinah's coat. He whispered something to Megan and she smiled. Together, Outlaw and Johnnie flanked the two women, not knowing the effect on Kendall of seeing Johnnie with his arm around Megan.

His chest burning, Johnnie swallowed back tears and handed the bottle of tequila to Val. Almost time for the final goodbye to K-P. The pain spread to Johnnie's gut at the knowledge. He wished the ache related to the still healing gunshot wound, but he knew better.

He'd met K-P on his tenth birthday, a couple months shy of twenty-four years ago. One day, Kaleb was alive and at the clubhouse, daring anyone to fuck with Dinah and threatening to hack Mort's dick off if he touched Bailey. The next day, K-P was gone. Human like everyone else, not the invincible man Johnnie had chalked him up to be.

Christopher stepped forward, bottle back in hand after it had been passed around, and took a final swig. He raised the bottle up. "To Kitchen Patrol," he began, his voice breaking. He paused. A tear slipped down his cheek and he heaved in a breath. "Fuck me."

"C'mon, Prez," Mortician encouraged, under his breath, standing next to Johnnie. "Get this shit done."

Yes, get this shit done. If Christopher broke down, they'd all break down. Each one of them held the other up, so if one fell, they'd all crumble.

Kendall squeezed Johnnie's arm, a silent sentinel at his side, observing how close he was to losing his shit. Wrapping an arm around her waist, he pulled her closer to him, glad for her presence. During the past three days, she'd been right at his side, caring for him, fussing over him and worrying about him.

He appreciated every kindness she'd shown to him and every tear she'd shed on his behalf. But he didn't want her stressed out. It was his job to worry over her and see to her happiness and comfort. She and their baby had been through enough. The little scratch that grave mite had given him—Spoon or *whoever* from the soon-to-be-wiped-off-the-face-of-the-earth MC—shouldn't have distressed Kendall so much, and guilt that he'd caused more fear for her, prompted Johnnie's self-avowal to heal as soon as possible.

Still, he didn't intend to rush their relationship. He had to make sure they were compatible in all the ways that mattered. He cared so much about her and felt more and more possessive toward her with each passing day.

Yet, he needed time because, in spite of her declaration of love, *she* needed time, too.

"Why don't you help him out?"

Her soft question snapped him back to his surroundings and he glanced at her.

"Outlaw," she urged, her warm breath fanning his ear. "He's faltering."

Johnnie loved Kendall's height. In her bare feet, she stood almost eye-level with him. He turned to her, nosing her hair. "I don't know if I'll do any better at keeping my composure than he is."

Christopher had yet to speak again, frozen in place and staring at the casket. Megs stepped next to him. She'd been lagging back in the crowd, for once out of her husband's sight. He bent, so she could speak to him, always standing at Christopher's side no matter what.

She'd been suffering with extreme morning sickness, but ever since Johnnie had shouted at her, she'd been acting strange. Johnnie couldn't help but wonder why. They'd straightened it all out in the cave, hadn't they?

Christopher snickered at something Megs said and she responded with a tender smile, standing on her tiptoes to kiss him before stepping back.

"Never thought I'd be standin' at K-P's grave," Christopher began slowly. "He was one of the finest brothers I knew. Even if the motherfucker liked you, he gave you shit. Next to him, we was all runts." He glanced up at the green tent ceiling before squeezing the bridge of his nose. "He loved onions. Never met a motherfucker who could eat raw onions like K-P." He smiled again and nodded like he'd worked something out in his head. "You free, Kaleb Paul. Free to fly. Free to ride."

Johnnie blinked in a futile attempt to stop tears determined to flow, Christopher's heartfelt words, unleashing the dammed grief.

Eyes and nose red, Christopher emptied the bottle of tequila into the grave, then handed it to Megan, removing his white gloves and tossing them into the gaping hole. One by one, they followed suit and flung their gloves. Johnnie.

Val. Mortician. Digger. Stretch. And the rest of the brothers who'd attended.

By the time Johnnie led Kendall to his Harley, he couldn't wait to get away from the cemetery. He had to accept the inevitable. K-P was gone.

K-P was *gone.*

K-P. Was. Gone.

He slid into place on his seat, comforted by the heat of Kendall's body against him, the beat of the sun on his face. The memories of K-P he'd hold close to his heart for the rest of his life.

Johnnie's gut twisted and he despised Logan to the depths of his very soul. He had to let it go. He had Kendall and their baby. As long as hatred consumed him, he'd have no room to give them the love they both deserved—and that he wouldn't abide.

He owed the beautiful woman behind him for giving him hope for the future. For protecting their baby.

Christopher lifted Megs onto his bike. She hugged him and wiped at his wet cheeks before allowing him to mount up. Val leaned against the handlebars of the hearse, hands covering his face. Digger, Stretch, and Mortician surrounded Bailey. Her devastation cut through Johnnie. He could never, ever offer her enough apologies for what his grandfather had taken from her. From *all* of them.

As more brothers headed to their Harleys, Johnnie offered a few words of his own to the ones Christopher had spoken minutes ago.

Rest easy, Kaleb Paul. Always riding.

Blinking back tears, Johnnie waited for the rest of the brothers to mount up so they could rev their engines in unison for one, final display.

Chapter 2

Leaning against the bathroom counter, Kendall rubbed her temples, her head pounding with the noise from the main room, quieted only for brief intervals as the brothers recounted stories about K-P. They'd returned to the club several hours ago and Kendall just wanted all the sadness and grief over with. She wanted to crawl into a hole until it all went away.

The door opened and Megan Caldwell stumbled in, not pausing to speak to Kendall, just rushing to one of the stalls. A moment later, Kendall heard her retching. She rolled her eyes, disgusted at the sounds of the girl's vomiting and annoyed that she just couldn't seem to escape her. Every time Kendall turned around Megan seemed to be there.

The stall door opened and Megan walked out, her face flushed and her blue eyes watery. "This baby is making me so sick," she said by way of greeting.

Not as sick as Kendall was of *her*. Gritting her teeth, Kendall frowned though Megan didn't notice. Or didn't care. She'd already turned on the faucet, leaned down and rinsed her mouth out before splashing her face. She grabbed a few paper towels from the dispenser and patted her face.

"Now, I'm hungry," she went on, turning to Kendall as if she wanted a response. "Are you?"

"No."

Megan glanced at the gaudy pink walls with black scroll and the huge mirror like she searched for something. Not a topic of conversation, Kendall hoped. She could go all PC on Kendall and mention the weather, but Kendall *still* wouldn't care.

Heaving in a breath, Megan gave her a tentative smile. Kendall wanted to chew a few nails and spit them out. Megan just irritated the hell out of her. Not only because of Johnnie. Or the fact that she had Outlaw twisted around her little finger. Nor did she irritate her only because all the other guys fell all over themselves to make her happy. No, Megan irritated Kendall just...*because.*

"I'm going to find Bunny. Would you like to come with me?"

Kendall leaned against the wall, slouching so she wouldn't feel like a lumberjack compared to the other girl. "No."

Megan's brilliant smile faltered. Her beauty didn't. "Umkay. Are you all right? I'm so tired. I can't wait until Christopher is ready to go to our room."

"Go without him if you're so tired."

Anger flashed in Megan's eyes and she stiffened before plastering a phony smile on her face. "I want to be around in case he needs me. This has been a really hard day for him."

"Johnnie hasn't had it any easier," Kendall snapped.

"None of the guys have," Megan returned calmly, not backing away. She'd changed out of her black jeans and shirt, and now wore a fitted dove gray dress with her stupid Property of Christopher "Outlaw" Caldwell cut over it. "I wish Zoann was here for Val—"

"Another club whore," Kendall sneered, folding her arms and glaring at Megan.

Megan stiffened, her surface cordiality slipping away. "No. Zoann is my sister-in-law. Johnnie's cousin," she added with a lift of her brow as if to mock Kendall about the extent of her knowledge of Johnnie.

"I know her."

Maybe, she shouldn't have referred to the woman as a whore, but Megan Caldwell brought out the worst in Kendall. Besides, Zoann huffed and puffed around Val, but, when she didn't think anyone was looking, she stared at him like he was the only man in the world. Zoann's behavior over a man who had no intention of committing to her, reminded Kendall of the whores who'd frequented the Torpedoes' MC.

For a moment, she believed she knew more about Zoann than the blonde until the girl cocked her head to the side and studied Kendall. Then, she nodded. "I'm glad Johnnie has someone to confide in. He deserves to be happy and you seem to make him really happy."

Did she make him happy? She wanted to believe she did and hoped he felt the same warmth in the center of his chest when he looked at her that she felt when she looked at him. Their closeness at night soothed all her fears and needs. If only she knew how to make him love her. He kept insisting he didn't fall in love at first sight, but they'd been together long enough now where he should've realized his feelings for her.

Kendall shouldn't have had to hear how happy she made him from a girl she'd rather ignore.

"Well, I guess I better find Christopher and my son—"

"I guess you'd better," Kendall echoed.

With a little huff, Megan traipsed off. Kendall turned back to the mirror the moment she found herself alone again to study her face, roaming to her large cleavage. The door opened again.

Instead of Megan or any other woman, Johnnie stepped in and leaned against the door. He'd been running his fingers through his hair a lot, so the blond strands lay all over his head. The sadness in his eyes made her heart twist and she stepped closer to him before gliding her fingers along his jawline. The stubble that had grown since he'd shaved this morning scraped against her fingertips. She wrapped her arms around his waist and buried her nose against his neck, inhaling his scent. Smoke. Alcohol. The faintest hint of aftershave. Musk. And him. *Johnnie.*

She planted kisses against his throat and up to his mouth. He groaned and pulled her closer, taking control of the kiss and dipping his tongue into her mouth. Heat pooled low in her belly, her pussy slickening in need.

"I'm so glad you're here with me, gorgeous," he whispered, thumbing her nipples and thrusting his erection against her.

Kendall melted at his words and smiled, pulling back to stare into his eyes, burning with a silver intensity that seemed to reach into her soul. With so much on his plate, she wouldn't tell him again that she loved him right now. Besides, she wanted to know how deep his feelings went for her. She couldn't face his rejection.

"Come out with me?" he asked quietly. "I'm about to tell a hilarious story about K-P. Well, it's more about *us* but K-P walked in at the end and—" He rubbed the back of his neck and he shrugged before forcing a smile onto his lips. "I'd like you to be out there."

Unable to deny him as much as she wanted to ask they return to their room, Kendall nodded.

His grin sparkled and he grabbed her hand. Moving away from the door, he opened it, then guided her out. He went to the center of the floor and whistled to call attention to himself.

"You'd never know just by looking at our ugly mugs

how two little guys have woven their way into our hearts," he began when the room had fallen silent. "I'm going to be a father, too, thanks to my old lady." He nodded to Kendall and she blinked, heat rising to her cheeks, not expecting Johnnie to make such an announcement.

Claps and catcalls reached Kendall, Johnnie's loudest of all. She didn't know how to feel about having so much attention fixated on her and wished Johnnie would've discussed his intentions with her, so she could've been better prepared.

Sliding into the seat she'd had earlier, she ignored the stares directed at her, balling her hands into fists to keep from screaming at everyone to focus elsewhere. Like on Johnnie, finally launching into the story he'd mentioned to her in the bathroom.

Losing herself in the cadence of his voice, Kendall blocked out everyone else and concentrated on the anecdote.

"I'm telling you, Outlaw," Val insisted, "Meggie spoiling Little Man. You gotta make her stop with the bottle shit."

Christopher scowled. "Megan know what the fuck she doin'."

Johnnie leaned back and folded his arms, releasing the smoke after he dragged on his cigarette. "I agree with Outlaw, Val. There's no crime for a mother to use her own judgment and go against recommendations."

"John Boy right," Mortician commented, unclipping his phone which indicated a text message. He looked at the screen, then rubbed his face, his expression a combination of resignation and aggravation.

"What pussy textin' you and makin' you so jerked off?"

Outlaw pulled his nine from his cut, laying it on the table before lighting a cigarette.

Johnnie studied the weapon, almost unable to imagine Megs picking it up and firing it to save Christopher's life. But she had and they knew she had their backs when worse came to worse.

"Just some young bitch I'm trying to fucking ignore," Mortician snapped, bringing Johnnie back to the conversation.

"Don't." Christopher sucked on his cigarette and laughed, something he did a lot of lately because he felt worthy in someone's eyes. Namely, Megs's. "I can use a fuckin' extra 5Gs. Call the bitch. Fuck her. Marry her, then deliver my fuckin' money, you smug motherfucker."

Digger sniggered. "Outlaw not ever letting you live our bet down, Mort."

"I'm not even answering this bitch, so I'm sure the fuck not fucking her. EVER. I stand behind my bet and my belief young pussy fuck with a man's head and make motherfuckers stupid."

Christopher shrugged. "I'll take stupid any fuckin' day if it mean I got Megan, so go suck your own dick and then shove those words up your fuckin' ass, assfuck."

"Who is it, anyway?" Val gulped from his bottle of beer.

Frowning, Mortician looked away.

Christopher placed his cigarette in his special ashtray, the one Megan had given him for his 34th birthday and engraved with the grim reaper and his initials. He picked up his gun and removed the clip. "You one fucked motherfucker, Mortician," he said, thrusting his chin toward the cabinet in the corner and indicating Val retrieve the supplies needed to clean his nine.

Mortician cursed when another round of sounds

indicated a new message. *"What you mean, Outlaw?"*

"I mean I think them messages from fuckin' Bailey. And your dick been in a snit ever since you saw her and it ain't gonna let up 'til you make her yours and then you really fucked."

Everyone remained silent since Christopher spoke from experience.

"Might as well put your dick outta its painful misery and get it in Bailey cuz you fightin' a losin' battle, motherfucker."

"Fuck off, Outlaw," Mortician grumbled.

Christopher shrugged, not offended because it was only them. Outside of the presence of the officers, if anyone spoke to Outlaw like that, their teeth would be in pieces on the floor. "I'm gonna throw you the biggest fuckin' bachelor party around, Mort. We gonna roast the fuck outta your ass like celebrities do and you gonna present all us motherfuckers with our 5Gs durin' the celebration."

Not responding, Mortician leaned back and glared at them, balling his fists when another message came through.

"Fuck off and let's get back to discussin' formula and shit for Ryan and Little Man."

"My kid don't drink no formala," Val growled. "Never did. After Zoann finished with her tit milk, she got him drinking out of cups and shit."

Christopher rubbed the oiled cloth around the chamber. "Little Man drink outta cups, too. But Megan say he rest better when he suck on his bottle. Ain't fuckin' arguin' with her."

"Zoann a nurse," Val argued. "And she say—"

"Don't give a fuck what my sister say. Anyway, she the bitch who gave Megan the recommendation on what formula to use."

Raising his eyebrows, Val rubbed his chin. "Really? Which one? I was reading about formulas online when she first stopped her tit milk and Ryan was so fucking miserable. I felt for the kid. Tits are addictive and I can only imagine how it must be when you can get milk from them."

"Best fuckin' thing in the world," Christopher announced, not looking up from his task.

He missed the way Johnnie, Val, Mortician, and Digger glanced at each other. All the better for them. They'd be missing their dicks. Johnnie's feelings for Megs might've been the worst kept secret on the fucking planet, but the other three hid their lust for her quite well. When Christopher announced bullshit like tasting milk from Megs's tits...well, they were only fucking human.

"What formula Little Man drink?" Val asked after clearing his throat.

"Not the one Zoann told her. Gave CJ the flamin' shits," Christopher remarked before they dived into a conversation about the best formula and taking notes on good diaper changing techniques, which they all had experience with because of Little Man.

The door swung open and K-P strolled in, frowning at the sudden silence. "What's up?" he asked slowly.

Christopher snatched his gun up, only half finished with the cleaning, and slid the clip back into place, not answering.

Johnnie knuckled his nose, his nostrils flaring while Mortician and Digger grew quite interested in Mort's phone. Val downed the rest of his beer.

"I miss something important?" K-P persisted.

Not at all, Johnnie thought with humiliation. Just a bunch of bad ass bikers talking baby formula and diaper changing.

"Nope," Christopher said with a straight face. "We was just discussin' whether or not Ryan or CJ had the biggest *dick. My boy win hands down. He got enough dick to lend some out and still don't miss nothin'."*

And that was how Christopher saved them from being the butts of jokes for the rest of their lives.

Kendall frowned as Johnnie finished relating the watered down version of the story he'd told her last night. While he'd been spinning his tale, Kendall's mind had been filled with the *real* conversation and it included Megan, whom he hadn't mentioned *once* just now.

Outlaw stood in the audience, after all.

Combing her fingers through her hair, Kendall admitted Johnnie told her about Megan's breasts because she'd demanded he tell her the full story when he'd abruptly stopped. He hadn't wanted to. In retrospect, she wished he hadn't been so forthcoming. It made the resentment toward Megan she'd worked hard to overcome flare back to life. After seeing his arm going around Megan at church today, Kendall's jealousy and insecurities ate at her.

She sighed as, one by one, the brothers offered up more tales about K-P, before toasting the man's life. Well before she escaped into the bathroom, the same scene had been going on for hours and it wore Kendall down. She didn't want to be amongst all these people, sharing Johnnie, watching tough bikers wrestle with their grief and touch upon their own mortality.

Megan slid back into the seat she'd occupied, off and on, all evening. A while ago, Mortician had escorted Bailey from the table and Kendall hoped Johnnie would do the same soon. A tall woman with brown hair and big boobs took the seat Bailey had been sitting in. She had a plate piled with all types of delicious looking food.

Kendall's mouth watered and she swallowed, starving…

"You should eat," Megan began, as if she'd read Kendall's mind. "I haven't seen you eat a thing today and that isn't good for you or the baby."

Bristling, Kendall glared at Megan, then smiled at the

other woman. "I'm Kendall Miller. You are?"

"Bunny," she responded around a mouthful of food. She pointed to a big biker, wearing a skull cap and having pierced lip, ears, and nose. "I'm his old lady."

"Kendall—"

"I don't feel like eating, Megan," she interrupted.

Bunny frowned at Kendall and scooped more food into her mouth. "Meggie's right. You're preggers like she is. You and the kid need nourishment."

She knew they needed nourishment. Food also helped keep the nausea at bay, not that it plagued her much. But...*food*. Without eating, she'd gain weight because of the baby. Anxiety churned in her stomach and the memories of being hurt and humiliated because of her body made the idea of food repulsive.

"Have you ever been pregnant, Bunny?" Kendall wanted no doubt about who she spoke to.

Bunny grabbed Megan's glass of water and drank the rest of the contents.

"Do you know how thirsty I am?" Megan complained with laughter.

"That shit's hot," Bunny muttered, sticking her tongue out and fanning.

"Well—"

"What did you eat?" Kendall asked before Megan could make some other comment.

"Chili." Bunny glanced at Megan. "Did you keep anything down, babe?"

Megan sighed and shook her head, staring at Kendall. "Not any real food. Just the crackers Christopher brought to me."

"You're scaring the shit out of me, Meggie," Bunny admitted and belched. Chuckling, she covered her mouth.

"Excuse me." After another belch and patting her chest again, she continued. "I don't know if I'll ever get knocked up. I can't imagine throwing up all damn day."

"I threw up for a couple days," Kendall explained, although no one had asked her. They'd sat at her table, so she wouldn't allow them to talk over her. "It didn't last long at all."

"I hate you, Kendall!" Megan squealed and, although her laughter surrounded them, Kendall believed she spoke the truth. "I just want *one* meal to stay down."

"You should've thought of that before you let Outlaw make you pregnant again. Your son isn't even a year old yet. You should've thought about birth control."

Megan got to her feet, her annoying giggling fading away. Fury iced her narrowing blue eyes. "Kendall, you—"

"Kendall, Megs, Bunny," Johnnie greeted, walking behind Kendall and squeezing her shoulders. He bent and kissed her lips. "These fine ladies keeping you company, gorgeous?"

Megan rolled her eyes and sniffed. "Your girlfriend needs to eat, Johnnie," she snarled and marched away.

"I'm sorry, Kendall." Johnnie sighed, staring in Megan's direction. She weaved her way through the crush of people toward her husband who held their son. "I'm going to talk to Christopher about her."

Someone needed to speak to him about Megan. She had no right sticking her nose in Kendall's business. "Thank you," she said, folding her arms and waiting for Johnnie to say they were returning to their room.

Instead, he grabbed a beer from a woman wearing a cut, proclaiming her as property of the Death Dwellers, before turning to Bunny.

"I'm sorry about Megs's behavior, sweetheart."

Bunny sidled an unreadable look to Kendall. "Don't worry about it, John Boy. It isn't as bad as you think."

"No, it's worse." Harsh laughter erupted from him. "But

we are all at fault for her attitude, especially her husband."

Digger, Val, and Stretch surrounded the table, offering greetings to Kendall and Bunny.

Johnnie's silver-gray gaze lingered on Kendall's face before dropping to her cleavage, the half-smile tipping his lips and his overwhelming presence unnerving her.

"Bunny, you ate, babe?" Val called after a few minutes of idle chitchat amongst the men.

She snorted. "Yes. I'm stuffed, too, so don't offer a thing else to me."

"Damn, girl, the man was just checking." Digger drank from a bottle of Everclear. "Don't go all Psycho Bunny on him."

"Haha," Bunny responded. "You're fucking hilarious, Digger."

"These fuckheads givin' you shit, Bunny?" Outlaw asked, joining them, his hands free of his son. Megan lagged just behind him, only noticeable with the movement of her blonde hair.

"Nothing more than usual." Bunny smirked at them. "Is there a hot biker magazine you dudes can pose for?"

Kendall stiffened at their laughter and Johnnie's wink. "If there is, find it for us, honey," he said. "We'll give you a cut."

Megan peeped around Outlaw, a little hand fisted in her hair. "Stop it, Bunny. You're giving them big heads…"

They guffawed at her words.

"We already got big fuckin' heads, baby," Outlaw snickered, wrapping his arm around her waist and pulling her against his side. His hand settled on her baby bump and he kissed the top of her head. Megan flushed and he laughed harder, hugging her tighter. Both Megan and Little Man squealed. "Lucky for us, our nuts just as big."

"I walked right into that one," Megan groaned.

"Yeah, you did, baby. Couldn't fuckin' resist."

"Whatever."

"Yo', Red, you got the classiest motherfucker," Digger said, winking at her. "Maybe, we should start hanging around you to learn a few things."

Scratching his chin, Val eyed Kendall. "Zoann might like me a little more refined."

Outlaw chuckled. "Not enough teachin' for that, assfuck."

Kendall preened beneath the attention. "If you're all *really* nice to me, I might come up with something."

Megan rocked back on her heels. "This should be interesting."

Discomfort settled between everyone at the girl's hard-to-miss sarcasm.

"We need Red," Digger persisted, elbowing Val. "You too fucking young to know shit like that, Meggie girl."

Outlaw frowned and Megan stiffened.

Johnnie smiled at her, tightening his hold on her and brushing her lips with his own. "If I'm real nice to Kendall, I might convince her to cook for us."

Eyeing her, Outlaw tipped his bottle back. "You cook?"

"Yes. A few things like stew."

"The best stew in the world," Johnnie admitted and warmth spread through her at the sincerity in his tone.

"Might be worth a try," Outlaw said with a shrug.

Megan glared at him. "And it might not be."

Outlaw lifted a brow, but didn't say anything more.

Yawning, Kendall squirmed away from Johnnie and got to her feet. "I'm tired. I'm ready to go to the room."

"That's where we headed to." Outlaw kept a hold on Megan and pulled Little Man into his arms. The little boy looked tired and, the moment he left Megan's arms, he screwed his little face up to cry. "Okay, boy. We gettin' in the room soon. Megan been up since early, so I'm takin' her to bed."

Val took the bottle from Digger and drank, then belched. "You know, Prez," Val slurred. "It might be innocent as fuck, but why the fuck you have to make everything sound like you talking about fucking Meggie?"

Drawing his brows together, Outlaw frowned. Megan jabbed him in the stomach. "Have a sense of humor. He's joking."

"He also fucked up," Digger added, holding up the Everclear. "Mr. Ganja man done drank like fuck and been popping pills like a motherfucker."

"Fuck me," Outlaw growled. "Valentine, come fuckin' with me. I gotta talk to you. Megan, baby, I'll be in the room in fifteen minutes."

"Okay, I need to check in with the ladies to make sure they have everything under control."

"No the fuck you don't. You need to get the fuck in bed and rest. Kendall can fuckin' do it."

Megan glared at her husband. "She can't," she snarled. "It's my job."

Before anyone responded, Megan had stalked off toward the kitchen.

Bunny stood. "Er, I think I'll see if she needs anything."

"Do that and thanks for lookin' after my boy while we went to the funeral."

"No problem," the woman said and hurried off.

Settling his hand on Val's shoulder, Outlaw guided the man away. When Digger walked off, it left only Kendall and Johnnie. "I'll be in the room in a bit, Kendall."

Disappointment surged through her at his response.

"I want to stay out here a little while longer. I'd like you to stay with me, but I know you've been up for hours, too."

"Y-you aren't coming?"

"Not right now." He rubbed his head. "I just need…I don't feel like being in there right now."

She nodded. "Fine."

"JOHN BOY!" someone yelled from the other side of the room. "YOU GOTTA FUCKING HEAR THIS ABOUT K-P."

Giving her a distracted kiss, he walked in the direction of the man's voice resounding over the noise, not once looking back.

Chapter 3

Kendall sat in the middle of Johnnie's bed, locked in his room and away from the celebration of K-P's life still going strong outside and in the main room. She glanced at the clock. After two in the morning. She'd been alone since eight. Not once had anyone come in and checked on her. Not even Johnnie.

Especially not Johnnie, she thought with a pang of loneliness and regret. He'd asked her for a chance to make things work between them while he'd been in the hospital, but kept a certain distance between them, running colder toward her than hotter.

Fear of what she'd find if she ventured out kept her rooted in the room. A couple hours ago, some unknown woman had delivered a plate of food to Kendall. She'd thanked her, then sat it on Johnnie's desk, wishing he had a scale so she could weigh herself.

Her stomach had been growling and she'd been feeling lightheaded. She'd resisted digging into the food as long as possible, but hunger pangs had won over her fear of weight-gain. As she'd scarfed her food, shame had gone through her. Her body image concerned her so much that she hadn't eaten even for the sake of Baby Biker. Days ago, she'd resolved to feed herself and worry about the rest later.

However, the moment she'd gotten through with her food, the temptation to run to the bathroom and retch had been so overwhelming she'd gripped the footboard to remain in place.

She didn't know she still possessed the amount of willpower it took her *not* to throw up after all the food she'd consumed. But she had won her battle.

Afterwards, she'd almost gone back out to the party, then changed her mind. She'd been subjected to so much at the Torpedoes' MC when she'd been dating Spoon. Infidelity topped the list of things she'd been better off not seeing.

Another type of fear stayed her. The fear of sexual assault. Her skin still prickled at the hurt and humiliation Spoon had caused her six weeks ago.

She'd spiraled from sanity and independence, with a law career to his drugged-up prisoner with the hopes of her little sister's return. Today was only the twelfth…no, *thirteenth*…midnight had come and gone…day of not having Percodan and Stoli forced into her.

Her fantasy Johnnie, who'd unknowingly kept her sane throughout her captivity, treated her better than the *real* Johnnie. To survive and cling to reality, she'd built him up in her mind to be the most attentive, understanding, and caring man in the world.

He wasn't any of that. Not to the extent she'd made herself believe, anyway. He was distracted, wrapped up in his club, and distant most of the time.

A knock sounded on the door and Kendall stared at the warped wood. Johnnie wouldn't knock to enter his own room. So many men were on premises, most of them members, so they were free to roam wherever they pleased.

They were bikers. Some of them had to have Spoon's characteristics.

Her pulse spiking, she scooted up until her back hit the headboard.

"Red?" Mortician called.

Annoyance curling into her, Kendall sagged in relief and hurried out of bed. Stalking to the door, she yanked it open. "What?"

He puffed on his cigarette, turned his head and released the smoke before smiling at her. "I woke you up?" he asked. From the twinkle in his eyes, he knew he hadn't.

She glared at him, not appreciating his amusement at her expense. "What do you think?"

Another puff and release before he laughed. "That you sitting your ass in here wondering what the fuck John Boy out there doing."

Hot embarrassment rushed through her at his accurate observation. "I am not," she flared through gritted teeth. "I don't care."

"Okay," he murmured with a shrug. "Then I'm not telling you what he's doing."

Kendall bit the inside of her cheek, resolved to pretend Johnnie's absence didn't concern her or hurt her.

"I'm coming to tell you bye, girl."

Her irritation, along with thoughts of proving her indifference, fled, replaced by rising panic. Mortician didn't treat her as if she had the plague. He advised her and looked after her, and had even gone grocery shopping for her when she'd been at Johnnie's house. Before it, along with Outlaw's two houses, had been blown to bits and pieces.

"Where are you going? Are you coming back?"

"Vegas. And, fuck yeah, I'm coming back, Red. Val

sending me on a run to get me away from here and clear my head." He sucked on the stump his cigarette had become, then squeezed the tip between his fingers to kill the flame. "It's hard to believe K-P gone. I just need to get the fuck away. Stop hating on Lowman since John Boy killed the sick fuck and I can't kill him all over again for taking"—He cleared his throat and shoved the butt in his pocket. "Taking K-P," he finished.

"I'll have no one to talk to." Fear of being ostracized made Kendall's voice tremble. Without Mortician, she only had Johnnie, which didn't leave much, considering his attitude toward her. "If you leave," she clarified, noticing his confusion.

"You got John Boy."

Did she? It frustrated her that some of her most in-depth conversations at the club had been courtesy of the handsome man in front of her and not Johnnie, the father of her baby and her...*what*?

Boyfriend? Old Man? Man?

In her head, Spoon had been her boyfriend, when, in actuality, she'd been nothing more than his property. She never wanted to be anyone's property again. She was fighting to reclaim her identity and her dignity, unable to imagine exposing herself and opening herself to physical and mental abuse. So she hid behind Mortician's kindness and the crumbs Johnnie threw to her.

"You got Meggie, too," Mortician continued into the silence.

Scowling, Kendall raised her brows. "*Meggie?*" she echoed.

"Yeah, you got her, Red. She's going to the funeral home with you, right?"

"Yes. She made it clear that's expected of her as the president's—"

Mortician's laugh interrupted her. "Meggie first bitch around here. You with John Boy make you second bitch."

She didn't want to be *second*. Nor should she have to be. That she was didn't surprise her, however. "Nothing new there," Kendall sighed, bitterness rolling through her. "I've never been first at anything."

"You not getting what I'm saying, Red. Don't make you second *best*. It just make you second-in-command over the bitches."

To her, that solidified her second best theory. She'd have to defer to a girl who lived her life as Outlaw's property. Meggie had one baby and was already pregnant with another one. Outlaw kept her at his side, had her watched outside of his presence, handed her whatever she wanted and objectified her as his sex toy. How did that qualify Megan Caldwell to be first and make Kendall second? Because he'd put a ring on it and Johnnie hadn't put one on Kendall's finger?

Kendall was everything Megan wasn't—educated, mature, and career-oriented. Yes, Kendall had gotten off track, but she'd find herself again and get to where she should be. She had experience and options that Megan didn't. And, yet, *she* still ranked second.

"You and Meggie have to settle shit." Mortician had allowed her to lose herself in her thoughts, but now he seemed determined to force that girl on her. "Think about how the president's and the vice president's wives act."

What an unexpected analogy. "Of this country?"

Mortician nodded. "That's what the fuck you two like here. Me, personally, I'm hoping you two can be friends. If you can't, that's cool, too. In front of everybody else, though, you and Meggie need to act like BFFs. Don't want no bitch anarchy and, if the first and second bitch can't get along, none of them bitches will."

Kendall hadn't thought of it that way. Well, she hadn't

thought of it *any way*. Megan enjoyed an established and exalted place in the club. She, on the other hand, remained because Spoon still slithered out there, waiting for her to resurface. Johnnie had enough decency in him to keep her safe and, maybe, he convinced himself they were in a relationship to be able to protect her.

"Well, I'm out, Red. Behave yourself, girl."

He started to turn away but curiosity got the best of her and she placed a hand on his shoulder, stopping him.

"Ma'am? You have something you want to know?"

Yes, but she wouldn't give the rat the satisfaction, so, instead of asking about Johnnie, she said, "how do I befriend Megan?"

He laughed at her. Again. "You something else, Red. I swear. All right, baby. I'll play your game when we both know you about to piss in your pajamas you want to know what's going on with Johnnie so bad." He reached into his cut for another cigarette and cursed when he found the pack empty. "Meggie a young bitch. As in she won't be twenty 'til October or November. She been through a lot, Kendall. Ask her one day. She ended up being her momma's caregiver instead of the other way around. She *can* have a real mature attitude, but, Outlaw, fuck, *all* of us, spoil the shit out of her. She finally having the world revolve around *her* and, all of a sudden, you come in."

Kendall cringed with guilt, a bit of fairness surfacing. Not wrapped up in her own problems, she could be impartial and realize she'd been in a state the day Megan and Outlaw returned from their honeymoon. She'd taken it out on Megan and thrown it in the girl's face that, not only had Outlaw seen her naked, but Kendall had grinded her body all over him. "I don't u-understand," she hedged.

"Don't play fucking dumb because you fucking *do* understand," Mortician chastised.

"Maybe."

Mortician scowled at her. "Meggie love the fuck out of

Outlaw. She *killed* a motherfucker to save his life."

Kendall's hands flew to her mouth and she gasped, unable to imagine the perfect, blonde beauty having such a stain on her soul.

"Don't ever repeat that shit, Red. Meggie don't know *she* killed the assfuck. She think Outlaw did it and we intend to keep it that way."

She wanted to feel something other than resentment and jealousy toward Megan Caldwell, but she'd had Johnnie's heart first and she suspected Megan remained the reason he couldn't commit to Kendall. "I understand," she confessed with bitterness. "She's the untouchable Megan Caldwell, the princess everyone puts on a pedestal and fawn over."

Silent, Mortician studied her and Kendall waited for her chastisement. Every one of them, down to a man, admonished her for criticizing Megan.

"Put on your grown woman drawers and check your bullshit, Kendall," he snapped, his punitive tone shriveling her insides. He'd never been harsh with her, even when he thought her the enemy. "We have a fucking storm brewing with Meggie dealing with your presence. We all fucking see it, but Outlaw gonna draw the line and get her straight. You, though." He pointed to her but closed his mouth.

She might've been a glutton for punishment, but she wanted to hear him say she skirted the fringes of their lives, not important at all. "Me what?" she challenged.

Mortician pulled in a breath, annoyance creasing his brow. "Fuck, man. You a girl like she is. An older chick. You should try to understand her point of view."

"She should try to understand mine."

"Should she, Red?" Weariness laced his words. "You came at her like the enemy, so, to her, you are the enemy. So let's get this big fucking elephant the fuck out of the way. The way John Boy felt about her."

Kendall snorted. "*Felt?*" She begged to differ.

"Yes," Mortician responded with certainty and without hesitation. "Felt. Let me play devil's advocate and say he *still* feel something for Meggie. Is that Meggie fucking fault John Boy being such a stubborn dickhead?"

"In a way it is. He asked her for a walk a few days ago, and she went with him. If she didn't want to encourage him, she would've turned him down."

"Messy shit like that make me understand why you want to keep your ass locked in this bedroom. If Outlaw heard that—and didn't already know—he would've been madder than a motherfucker at Meggie *and* at John Boy."

As if she cared. Maybe, if they were angry with Johnnie, she'd have more of him to herself.

"She probably only told him because she walked out with him in full view of everybody."

"No, Kendall," Mortician growled. "Meggie told Outlaw because she tell him *everything*. Outlaw need that to be able to trust, but she need to trust him, too, so don't come fucking with them. Things just getting good for us again."

Tears rushed to Kendall's eyes and the same feeling of abandonment she'd had since her father's death bombarded her again. "I just want Johnnie. I'm having his baby. I just want…acceptance."

Mortician's features softened and he nodded. "I feel you, girl. Tell that to John Boy. He's gonna hear you."

She swiped at her cheeks and glanced at her toes.

"Peep this, Red. I know it's fucked with whatever going on in John Boy head where Meggie concerned. But you want a motherfucker who so fucking fickle he fall in love the minute somebody else catch his attention?"

"Of course not, but—"

"But it's a fine line," he finished. "True, that." He huffed in a breath. "Where the fuck your girl radar at, huh? Bitches walk in and out of our fucking lives all the time and we fucking forget them by the time they close their fucking legs. But, John Boy, *remembered* you. He fucking *kidnapped* you when he could've kept you here. He might be one, confused motherfucker, but him and Outlaw not related for fucking nothing. Real, true love? They reject like motherfuckers. Outlaw did some shit to Meggie, including leaving her for three fucking weeks. He didn't believe he was fucking worthy. John Boy? Clinging to a feeling not fucking deep in the first fucking place because he afraid of real emotion."

She wouldn't argue with Mortician. Not when he was going on a road trip. She still remember expecting her daddy's return when he'd walked out the door. He hadn't come back, though. He'd been killed...

On impulse, Kendall threw her arms around Mortician. "Be safe and hurry back," she whispered.

Kissing her cheek, he returned her hug. "Don't intended to go nowhere no time soon, Red." He backed away and released an unhappy bark of laughter. "Guess K-P thought the same fucking thing, huh?"

After three in the morning, Johnnie walked into his room, wondering if Kendall had fallen asleep, half hoping she had. Lipstick stuck to his cheeks, neck, and lips, and the cloying scents of different perfumes clung to his clothes and his hands. Mostly, from pushing women away. Not that Kendall would believe that. What woman would?

Kendall's mistrust went deeper than most women's, though.

Johnnie reminded himself she'd stuck by him during his recovery. She swore she loved him. Part of the reason he proceeded with such caution. He didn't want to blurt any statements, then realize, later, he'd spoken prematurely.

The lamp light flickered on and he groaned at his shitty luck. She eyed his body, a hint of red creeping up her neck when she noted…what? He didn't fucking know. Every girl who'd tried to fucking touch him tonight paled in comparison to Kendall.

"Hey."

Instead of answering, she bent her head and stared at her hands. She'd gotten a semblance of her old self back in the week she'd been with him. On the other hand, she hadn't regained all of her feistiness, and Johnnie raged for her. When he got his fucking hands on Spoon…

"I'm tired, Johnnie," she said in a quiet, miserable voice.

So was he. Bone-tired and brain-weary. They'd mourned K-P, given him a proper send-off, placed his photo with the other Free Bird members. Now, life had to go back to normal because they had no room for any in-depth emotions.

The beauty on his bed deserved to have the world at her feet. She had issues, yes, but she needed to feel like the sun rose and set in her. She deserved that.

He wanted to give her no less.

His wound was itching and the bandage prevented him from scratching the way he'd liked. For instance, scraping something across his skin to take the annoying sting away.

Stripping off his clothes and removing his bandage, he headed for the shower, not languishing because he wanted to climb into bed and hold Kendall in his arms, the way they'd slept for the past three days.

After drying himself, he walked into his bedroom again and headed for his desk where he kept his clean supply of bandages and medical tape.

Usually Kendall helped to redress his bandages, but, he supposed he couldn't expect it from her tonight. Once he'd completed the task of seeing to his healing wound, he turned off the light and climbed into bed.

"Is this how it's going to be, Johnnie?" she asked in a small, hoarse voice.

"I don't know, Kendall," he admitted on a sigh, "since I don't know how *this* is."

She shifted in the bed and, even in the darkness, her gaze burned into him. "You out there, fucking other girls—"

"I didn't fuck other girls," he interrupted. "Other girls wouldn't keep their fucking hands or lips to themselves. I spent most of the goddamn night pushing them the fuck away."

"I don't believe you."

"That's not my fucking fault. I have no fucking reason to lie to you."

"Why'd you stay out there so long?"

Johnnie frowned, not wanting to argue with her at three o'clock in the morning. Not after the long day he'd had.

"Why'd you come to the room so early?" he countered in a level voice, his brain recoiling at her sulkiness.

"No one wanted me—"

"Stop it, Kendall. I refuse to listen to your self-pity."

She scrambled in bed and, a moment later, had the nightstand lamp on on her side. "You're callous and unfeeling. I've opened up to you. But it's always Mortician who's giving me pep talks. Not you."

Johnnie gritted his teeth against the surging jealousy towards Mortician finding it necessary to seek Kendall out. Like it or not, though, it irked the shit out of him, the least of which had to do with Mort seeing Kendall undressed.

Motherfucker was running two for two, viewing both Megs *and* Kendall without clothes on. Well, Kendall had had panties and a bra on, some consolation.

"Mortician wanted to tell you he was leaving," Johnnie remarked, the truth.

He hadn't thought anything of it at the time, but, *apparently* Mort did more with Kendall than just tell her goodbye. As soon as he returned, he'd tell Mort to keep his fucking mouth shut and to stay the fuck out of Kendall's face. She had *Johnnie*'s Baby Biker inside of her. He'd do well to remember that fact.

He tugged Kendall into his arms, caressing her back to remove the tension from her body.

He nipped her ear, inhaling her scent, blood filling his cock. He hadn't touched her in five days. Two of those days he'd been in the hospital, the next he'd been recovering from *being* in the hospital, and the last two he'd been helping to arrange K-P's funeral and making nice with Father Wilkins, since Christopher couldn't stand the self-righteous little twerp.

Johnnie skimmed his lips over Kendall's neck, her soft sigh firing his blood. He fucking adored that sound, adored *this* Kendall. The woman who opened herself to him and fought her demons. "Do you want some dick, gorgeous?"

She giggled, her face flushing. "Do you want to give me some?" she asked with a smirk, pushing aside whatever stood between them.

Already naked, he wasted no time baring Kendall. Rocking back onto his heels, he swept his gaze over her body, his mouth watering at the shadow of hair fuzzing her pussy.

He stretched out, shouldering her long legs apart and burying his face against her cunt. She moaned, a shudder already racking her body. He opened her slick lips, thumbed her clit, then allowed his tongue to join in the fun with a slow, leisurely lick.

She yanked at his hair. "Johnnie."

Laddering his tongue up her slit and then back down again in a fast motion, lapping at her juices and reveling in the taste and smell of her. She whimpered and jerked against his lips. He suckled her clit, her gasp his reward. Later, he'd tongue her for hours. Right now, he wanted inside of her. Trailing kisses up her flushed skin, he guided his cock to her hot entrance and buried himself inside of her.

The heat of her body engulfed him and he grunted in pleasure, moving inside her with slow, deep strokes, growling when she canted her hips to meet his thrusts.

She tongued the rim of his ear and he trembled at her branding touch, her pussy walls throbbing around him and curling his toes. She gasped and moaned, writhing beneath him and arching up, her orgasm drawing his cum from him. He filled her up, his come intensified by her little pulses around him.

Chapter 4

By the time Kendall awoke the next morning, Johnnie had already departed, leaving no note as to his whereabouts or what time he intended to return. When she walked into the main room, it surprised her to find Megan cleaning the tables. Bulging garbage bags sat in a line near the door and Kendall wondered if Megan intended to drag them out.

Didn't all golden girls who doubled as a wife, played at motherhood, and moonlighted as a killer, put on their capes and lift heavy crap?

Megan glanced over her shoulder, her gaze edged with irritation and falling on Kendall. She plopped the dishrag into the pan of water and wiped her hands on her apron. She lifted the container. Before moving a step, an older man with a head of silver hair and a neat mustache materialized from the area with the pool tables, and barreled toward her.

"Shouldn't lift that, Meggie," he rebuked. "Not in your condition."

Megan snorted and rolled her eyes. "I'm pregnant, Arrow, not helpless."

Arrow glanced at Kendall and lifted a brow. "Kendall, right?"

"That's almost exactly the way K-P greeted me the first time we met," Megan said softly.

"Babe, no crying. Kaleb adored you, so he wouldn't want you sad over him with you having another baby."

Megan cocked her head to the side. "You're his brother. Aren't you sad?"

"Fuck, yeah. But who said you have to do what the fuck I'm doing?"

Instead of taking offense—or even being afraid—Megan shrugged, her sorrow hard to miss. She removed her apron and sighed. "Bunny's looking after CJ, so if you need anything, ask her." She shifted from foot to foot and shoved hair behind her ear. "My mom might…" Her voice trailed off and she frowned. "She's just grieving for K-P."

Arrow grasped Megan's shoulder. "Babe, stop worrying. Outlaw's my Prez, incentive enough not to fuck up. I have another one. Remember? K-P looking after you from wherever he at. *I'm* looking after you down here."

Her nose reddening, Megan swallowed but nodded.

Arrow headed toward the bar with a sigh, then paused. "Have you seen Bailey anywhere?"

"No," Megan responded weakly, her skin turning a sickly shade of green. She clapped her hands over her mouth and ran toward the bathroom.

Kendall huffed in frustration. While she understood Megan's condition, she needed to get to the funeral home and make it through this day. Resentment towards Johnnie surfaced, deepening her aggravation with Megan. He should never have left her to deal with this on her own.

Puffing a cigarette Kendall hadn't paid attention to Arrow lighting, he nodded to her. "You saw my niece?"

"Not since yesterday at the grave."

"Fuck," Arrow growled, worry creasing his brow. He snapped his cellphone from his belt clip and dialed a number. "Call me," he ordered a few seconds later, his lips thinning. "I'm giving you an hour then I'm riding out and hunting fucking Torps."

"She doesn't live on premises," Kendall offered the moment Arrow hung up, wanting to ease his mind. He'd just lost his brother so he didn't need to stress over his niece.

He glared at her. "You think I don't fucking know that?"

Licking her lips, Kendall reminded herself of all of Johnnie's reassurances. She could speak her mind and no one would hurt her. She was safe, but, sometimes, her head couldn't reason that out and catapulted her back to Spoon's harshness and her captivity.

The bathroom door opened and Megan reappeared, a little less peaked. The sound of chimes filled the air and she snatched her cell phone from her pocket. A frown creased her brow and her eyes widened before she glanced at Arrow and read the message again. Groaning, she shoved the phone back into her pocket.

"What is it?" Kendall asked out of curiosity.

"Nothing." Uneasy, Megan peeped at Arrow again and gave Kendall a minute shake of her head before plastering a too bright smile on her face. "Um, Arrow…" She twirled her hair and lowered her lashes. "Er, Bailey is…she went to see her mom and said not to worry."

Lying bitch. Kendall saw the lie in her features and heard it in the girl's voice. Arrow pinned her with a weary stare and nodded, boiling Kendall's blood on the grieving man's behalf. "Arrow just left a message for her," she pointed out. "Why would she text *you* instead of responding to him?"

Megan shrugged, her stance and darting eyes not ringing true. "I don't know but she did. Now, are you ready?"

Ready to finalize funeral plans for her little sister? No. Never. She had no choice, though, so she stiffened her shoulders and nodded.

Five minutes later, Kendall sat in the passenger seat of Megan's brand new Mini Cooper.

Megan paused at the gate and addressed Stretch,

unperturbed by the three bikers serving as her babysitters. "We're going to the funeral home."

"Yes, ma'am." He smiled and opened the gate, stopping her to impart one, final order. "Make sure you stay within sight of Shady, Cowboy and Slipper at all times."

"I will. Bye, Stretch." Meggie waved at him and sped onto the street, oblivious at the wrongness of having to give her itinerary before being released from the premises with big, brutal looking men following her, too.

"Thank you for bringing me," Kendall offered, envying the perfect lines of Megan's face.

She halted at a stop sign and looked both ways before zooming forward, a Harley on each side of them now and one tailing them. "No problem."

"If you ever need me to watch over Little Man, I'd love to."

"Thank you. I'll keep that in mind."

The chimes sounded again. Another text message for Megan, who chewed her lower lip.

"Is it *Bailey* again?"

Megan braked the car at a stop light. "What? Bailey?"

"Yes. Remember? Arrow's niece," Kendall reminded her in a brisk tone and folded her arms.

As the light turned green, Megan nodded. The bikes rumbled behind them. "Of course. Um…I-I can't discuss this with you. I'm sorry."

Kendall huffed in frustration and glared out the window at her soft dismissal, gritting her teeth at the sight of one of Megan's guards. Johnnie should've brought her instead of the high-and-mighty Megan Caldwell. The night Johnnie had gotten shot and Megan's and Outlaw's house had gotten blown to hell, Kendall had made an overture of friendship and Megan accepted. Either Kendall suffered with delusions or the moment had come about because of the situation.

She *refused* to approach Megan one more time. If they'd ever build a friendship, *Megan* would have to make the next move.

Twenty-five minutes later, Kendall followed the funeral director into his office with Megan trailing behind her.

"Let me extend my condolences to you, Ms. Miller," the wiry man began. The sideburns travelling down the side of his face made him a throwback to another era. "I understand what a difficult time this must be for you."

"Thank you, Mr. Gillson," Kendall responded politely. His jaded tone rang with falseness and she suspected the phrases fell from his mouth by rote. He probably could recite them in his sleep.

Kendall bit the inside of her cheek to prevent her laughter from bursting free at Megan's eye-rolling, refusing to give the girl satisfaction.

He snapped his red suspenders. "I understand you'd like to make arrangements. May I just inform you Mr. Donovan has already made most of them? The only thing left to do is the viewing of the body."

"I can view her for you if you'd like," Megan offered, the sympathy in her eyes grating on Kendall's nerves. She wasn't interested in ordinary conversation, but the moment a crisis arose, she stepped up.

"No, thank you." Disbelief sharpened the words. Who cared? Not Kendall. Not when she felt certain Megan's offer anything more than a tactic to sustain her status as perfect in Johnnie's eyes. "I can do it."

"Suit yourself." Megan retorted.

"Mrs. Caldwell, we can discuss the opening of your mother-in-law's grave to inter the body while Ms. Miller views Caroline."

"I-I thought she was being buried in my father's grave," Megan responded with a frown, shocking Kendall.

Not knowing where her mother was buried, Kendall hadn't thought of a gravesite and she certainly hadn't expected Megan to play any role in obtaining one for her. She wanted Caroline laid to rest. If not, she would've told Megan she didn't need to provide either because Kendall would find a cemetery herself.

"The grave's sealed after Mr. Andrews's burial," Mr. Gillson explained.

Megan nodded. "Okay," she said in a small voice. "K-P was my daddy's friend. It's somehow fitting they're buried together."

Dislike surged through Kendall at Megan's ploy for sympathy. *Her* sister had just died. If anyone deserved compassion, it was Kendall.

"Together, Mrs. Caldwell?" Mr. Gillson questioned with a knowing smile.

Megan squirmed in her seat, her jacket opening to reveal her small baby bump, giving her an even more vulnerable and delicate impression. "Aren't they?"

Mr. Gillson shook his head and slid a folder to her, glee lighting his eyes "I'm afraid not, my dear. The grave was empty until Mr. Andrews was placed inside of it."

For a moment, Megan's mouth fell open as she looked over the documents, then something clicked in her brain and she gasped, color leeching from her face.

The little man leaned back. "Your husband might use *threats* to get his way, but good folk like me have a way of letting the truth be known." He slid a box of Kleenex toward Megan, a smirk on his face.

Instead of taking the tissues, Megan stood. "Excuse me."

Mr. Gillson held up another set of documents and transferred his satisfied gaze to Kendall. "I'm sure Ms. Miller would appreciate your signature on these papers.

You do recall she's just lost her sister. Insensitivity doesn't become you, my dear."

"R-right," she stammered, throwing Kendall a distracted gaze. "I know this must be hard for you, Kendall, and I'm sorry."

More public display of kindness, the falseness of it proven by her preoccupation. Mr. Gillson slid the papers across the desk to Megan, the pen on top rocking with the motion.

"Sign."

Her hand shaking, she picked up the pen and glanced at the other paper, pausing before she signed. "A-are you s-sure m-my f-father isn't in the grave?"

"With all due respect, Megan, I'd appreciate it if you'd handle the mix-up of your father's gravesite another time," Kendall put in with as much equanimity as possible. She'd attempted friendship earlier and Megan had rejected her, only pretending concern in front of the funeral director.

Kendall needed support to get through Caroline's viewing. She didn't need to have a scheming, little, attention-seeker around.

Tears slipped down Megan's pale cheeks and she sniffled, but, instead of engaging in a war of words, she signed the necessary papers, straightened up and headed for the door. "I'll wait for you in the car, Kendall." She hurried out, leaving the door gaping open in the wake of her departure.

Kendall bent over her little sister and sobbed against the stillness of Caroline's chest. No breath. No air. Nothing. Just a beautiful corpse resembling a mannequin. They'd made her up. That was good. Caroline liked makeup. She liked cheerleading. And she liked mashed potatoes and gravy. Not that anyone but Kendall cared.

Johnnie hadn't even thought her important enough to accompany her here and she needed him right now. More than she thought she would.

"Caro," she murmured, lifting herself from her sister's lifeless body and touching her hair. Soon, she'd never be able to touch her again. "Why'd you do this?"

She covered her face and cried into her hands, her heart splintering apart.

"I was going to get you back!" she wailed in a rush. "You should've trusted me. I was doing everything I knew how."

"She knows." Megan stepped beside her and placed a hand on her back. "You're being too hard on yourself."

"What do you know?" Kendall snarled, overcome with grief and bitterness, her head hurting and her eyes blurry. The scent of floral arrangements hung in the air, made her sick to her stomach. "You don't know me or Caroline to know if I'm being too hard on myself or not. Just go away."

Megan glanced away, her nose red, her face wet with tears. But Kendall knew she wasn't crying for her and Caroline. No, she was crying over some stupid grave site mix up.

"I'm sorry for your loss, Kendall. I truly am."

"Are you?" She indicated Caroline. "My sister had her whole life ahead of her and she's gone now! She was like you. Perfect. Everyone loved her." She hunched her shoulders. "Now, look at her. I have to bury my flawless baby sister."

Megan cocked her head to the side, her eyes still filled with hurt. "Maybe, one day, you'll recognize your own beauty, so you can grieve properly for her."

Kendall rounded on Megan. "Fuck you," she snarled.

"You're shedding tears of guilt, Kendall," Megan said evenly, not backing down. "You were jealous of your little sister and now she's dead and you can't *ever* make up for your enviousness of her."

"Envious of *Caroline?*" The truth of Megan's words hit Kendall in the center of her chest and her resentment increased. "I loved her. My mother killed herself instead of staying with me and then Spoon held me prisoner for five weeks." She still couldn't understand why. Grief, he'd said. She might open her mouth to the wrong person and, instead of killing her, he'd bring her somewhere until he found a use for her. "It hasn't been a full two weeks since I've been out and undrugged, thinking and feeling again."

Instead of responding, Megan stood silent, listening, not offering anger or comfort. But Kendall wanted a response. She wanted to know she mattered, too, that her words affected someone enough they'd show emotion. At this point, it didn't matter what emotion, either.

"Any other psychoanalysis of me, *Megs?*"

"You need to get over your jealousy of me," she replied without flinching or rising to the bait. "You have nothing to be jealous of."

Kendall cackled, sounding like a hysterical witch. "You're right. I'm every bit as good as *you*."

A growl escaped her at Megan's steady gaze.

"Those were your words, Kendall. Remember them when you're wallowing in your self-pity."

Johnnie leaned back in one of the club's pickups, arms behind his head, his Glock laying peacefully in his lap. The sun played hide-and-seek with the clouds, brightening the greenery surrounding the dilapidated, isolated house. Weeds and grass grew on the deserted plots of land on each side of the property. The house he was parked in front of—across the street from his target—looked empty. All the better for them. Not that it would've stopped them one way or the other. Staking out a fuckhead in a busy neighborhood would've taken more planning.

Christopher sat in the passenger seat, cradling a Bushmaster. Every now and then he lifted it and aimed it at the home of the enforcer of the Torpedoes, focusing for an accurate aim through the scope.

The man knew they were out there. The visibility and stakeout was meant as a warning because they'd allowed the fuckhead to go unmolested. He'd come out on the porch and pissed his pants when Christopher raised his rifle and shot the shit out of the fucker's car. Message clear: *We can fuck you up if we choose.*

They'd been parked in their spot since early morning and didn't intend to leave until late tonight, which meant Johnnie couldn't be at Kendall's side when she needed it. Of course, she needed to understand the importance of the club. There'd be many days like this one and she'd have to adjust. He sighed.

"Shut the fuck up, pussy," Christopher growled.

Johnnie tensed and glared at the man. His cousin and his half-brother. "What the fuck are you talking about?"

"You, John Boy. Sighin' like a fuckin' pussy. You can't be two fuckin' places. With *her* and with *me.*"

"If I had the choice, she wins every time," he said dryly.

"Lucky for you you *don't* have a motherfuckin' choice."

Johnnie scowled at Christopher, then rubbed his jaw, glancing in the rearview mirror to make sure they weren't ambushed from behind. Digger and Val covered opposite ends of the street. Some of the other brothers hadn't left town yet after K-P's funeral and had been dispatched to various hangouts of the Torpedoes, searching for fucking Spoon.

Motherfucker must have found a dish to run the fuck away with. No matter. Johnnie *would* find him.

They intended to annihilate them and they had a special fuck-you planned for their miserable fucking clubhouse.

"When's the fuckin' weddin'?" Christopher dug into his cut and pulled out a cigarette, passed it to Johnnie, then lit another one and smoked, waiting for Johnnie's answer.

"I'm not—"

"Don't fuckin' lie to me or yourself, assfuck. You *liked* that bitch the moment her and her tits swung into the clubhouse."

Johnnie thumped Christopher's shoulder. "Keep Kendall's tits out your fuckin' mouth."

Christopher hooted with laughter. "I don't want no part of that bitch in my fuckin' mouth, so you ain't got fuck all to worry about."

"You know what the fuck I mean."

"Nope. Sure the fuck don't seein' as how you had your fuckin' fingers up my *wife's* pussy. Me mentioning Kendall's tits don't fuckin' compare."

Point for Christopher *and* his fucking Bushmaster. Johnnie wouldn't, *would not*, touch the subject with that rifle so close to Christopher. Nor would he bring up Megs's naked photo that Logan had attached on a clothesline for Johnnie to see.

"Let's fuckin' see. Megan wrapped her little hands around your big, ugly dick. You stuck your fingers in her pussy and Kendall grinded her cunt all over me. Let's say we fuckin' even and call it a motherfuckin' day."

"Where the fuck did you escape from, Christopher?"

Christopher smirked at him, his smile falling away when the Torpedo's enforcer sauntered into the open, his own weapon strapped to his side. He raised his middle finger at them before grabbing his dick—covered with clothes—and taunting them. The enforcer stomped back inside and closed the door. So much for his fucking fear.

"The same fuckin' asylum you escaped from." Christopher raised the rifle and aimed it toward the house, squinting to peer through the scope. "Fuckin' Logan Land, brother."

Brother. For him and Christopher that word held a different meaning. They were blood brothers, sharing the same brutal father. Not since Johnnie told Christopher of their connection in the hospital had they discussed it.

"I thought you'd hate me."

Christopher stilled, then cleared his throat and lowered the weapon. He didn't ask Johnnie what he was talking about because he knew. Christopher *always* knew. That was one reason their grandfather had hated him so much. Partly because, in Christopher, he saw each of his weaknesses and failures. But, mostly, because Christopher was fucking smart. Atrocious speech aside, the man had a head on his shoulders.

He sighed. "John Peter, you…after I thought about it, I was pissed for a minute. But, fuck, motherfucker, you told my ass when you was fuckin' laid up from a motherfuckin' gunshot. I was happy your fuckin' ass was alive, so, yeah, I was over the fuckin' moon to hear we was blood brothers." He turned toward the window and stared out, shaking his head. "I thought about takin' my boy and packin' me and Megan the fuck up and leavin' this motherfucker behind. Every-fuckin-thing I'd ever feared…" He let out bitter laughter. "I felt like I hadn't been good e-fuckin-nuff to know you and me was brothers, so, yeah, I felt some hate for you, Mort and Val."

Johnnie had no response to that. It was obvious Christopher didn't hate him now. Otherwise, they wouldn't be here together. Either Christopher would've walked away from the club like he'd confessed he thought about, he would've forced Johnnie, Val, and Mort out, or he would've found a way to dissolve the club. Any of those three scenarios were fucked. "What changed your...?" His voice trailed off at Christopher's disgusted glare.

"Who the fuck you think, assfuck?" he snapped.

Megan. Not having to say her name, Johnnie nodded as the enforcer's front door opened again and he returned to the porch. In the distance, gunfire erupted.

Christopher flicked his cigarette out the window. "These motherfuckers." He sighed, lifted his rifle and fired without flinching and without missing. Blood and gore rained onto the porch, splattering the door, the single lawn chair, and window. The Torp enforcer landed in a heap, his face blown away. "Motherfucker ain't liked fuckin' company, I guess."

Johnnie noted Val in his rearview mirror as Digger approached from the front end.

"How many?" Christopher asked, when they slid into the back seat.

"I popped one," Val muttered around a yawn.

"I got one motherfucker and a half," Digger announced.

"What the fuck is a half of a motherfucker?" Christopher asked with a scowl.

"An undead one," Digger grumbled. "I wish fuckin' Mort was here."

"Don't worry. No meat shack duties, brother," Christopher swore. "We pickin' up the two dead fucks and leavin' them where the Torps can see them and get the fuckin' message." He nodded to the dead man on the porch. "This motherfucker goin' in that fuckin' house and is gonna get blown to smitha-fuckin-reens with it." He bent and picked up the case for his rifle, revealing explosives.

"What the fuck, asshole?" Johnnie managed. "You lit up a fucking cigarette and had *explosives* in here?"

"You still here, motherfucker. Apparently, I didn't blow you the fuck up, so *shut* the fuck up."

Another thought occurred to Johnnie. "You came with the intentions of this, didn't you?"

"Get your head out Kendall's pussy, John Boy," Christopher warned, "and think. I ain't a givin-a-warnin-type of motherfucker. Cat-and-mouse bullshit ain't for me. This motherfucker saw us out here and he was gonna call his fuckin' brothers. I hoped to snuff out motherfuckin' Spoon, since fuckhead was his younger brother. Shit never that fuckin' easy, though."

Opening the door, Christopher grabbed his case with the explosives in them. Before slamming it shut, he leaned in. "I'm gonna be a minute. Go collect those other dead fucks. John Boy?"

Instead of answering, Johnnie lifted a brow.

"I'm gonna let Spoon be yours on behalf of fuckin' Kendall. Your woman. Your vengeance. The rest of these motherfuckers? They all fuckin' responsible for fuckin' up me and Megan's house." Christopher's eyes gleamed with murderous fury. "They fuckin' *mine*. My woman. My vengeance."

He closed the door, backed away and signaled Johnnie to drive away.

Chapter 5

Megan screeched through the gates of the clubhouse, the tires on her Mini Cooper spinning to an abrupt halt. She didn't speak to Kendall as she jumped out, just as she hadn't spoken to Kendall the entire drive back to the clubhouse. Megan's attitude infuriated Kendall a little more and made her determined to get Johnnie away from the blonde's influence.

The morning hadn't been easy for so many different reasons. All Kendall wanted was revenge. Logan was already gone but Spoon—as responsible for Caroline's death as Logan—still lived. Spoon had taken her little sister and brought her to Logan.

Kendall might not have been strong enough to physically beat Spoon but she could outwit him. She'd been in his office at the clubhouse as his girlfriend and as a junior attorney from the law offices of Romain, Stone, and Stanley. He kept a portable file box with a USB jump drive locked inside on his desk. He'd once told Brooks those were records only Spoon and a select few had access to. At the time, Kendall had believed the records Spoon referred to were the MC's files. Now, she wondered if it had to do with the trafficking he'd been engaged in with Logan Donovan.

Somehow, some way, she'd get that file. Once she had

it, she'd figure out what to do with it.

Getting out of the small car with new purpose, Kendall scowled at Stretch, Slipper, Shady and Cowboy swarming around Megan.

"Leave me alone," she hollered. "Where's Christopher? I need to talk to him about something."

Probably about that stupid grave mix-up when no one with the exception of Outlaw would give a fuck. Kendall glowered at the back of Megan's head. Maybe, she was being a little unfair to the girl, but when Kendall believed Johnnie had finally set aside his feelings for Megan, Kendall had reasoned better. She'd felt secure in herself, felt worthy to be loved. Now, the more he healed, the more his distraction returned. Because of it—because of all she'd lost—she *despised* Megan.

"What's going on out here?" Arrow's voice cut through Megan's demands that Stretch and the others move. He stepped forward and Kendall felt a twinge of something. Grief, she decided, although she hadn't known K-P very long. Still, his brother resembled him. The silver beard, the set of his jaw, the no bullshit attitude. He lifted a brow at Outlaw's wife. "Meggie, babe, what's wrong?"

"I need to talk to Christopher."

Taking his time, he lit a cigarette and studied her. "He's not here," he reminded her calmly, releasing the smoke and ruffling his fingers through his hair. "He's taking care of club business, babe. You seem damn upset but I suspect you didn't call him because you know where he's at." Another puff and another release of smoke.

Kendall hated to admit how sexy she found Arrow's Sam Elliot vibe, right down to the sound of his voice. He held out a hand to Megan.

"Let's talk. I'm not Christopher and I'm not K-P, but I

have a good damn ear. When Outlaw get back later tonight, talk to him then. He'll have time. Right now, you'll distract him, babe. You know that."

Sniffling, Megan nodded.

Puff. Release. Finger wiggling. "Come on. I'm all ears."

Megan placed her hand in Arrow's and he squeezed. "Good girl." He smiled, releasing her hand long enough to open the door and allow her to duck into the clubhouse before following behind her.

Only then did Stretch and the other three focus on Kendall.

Anger surged through her and she stormed to the driver's side of the Mini Cooper. "I need to get away," she snapped and slammed the door once she'd slipped behind the driver's wheel, her mood worsening when she had to slide the seat back as far as it could go to accommodate her long legs.

She could always demand her Mazda since she knew Johnnie hadn't gotten rid of it yet. It was somewhere on the premises. He'd told her they were going to trade it in for another car and she'd agreed. Even though it was *her* car, she doubted anyone would bring it to her, so she'd have to deal with the Mini Cooper.

"Kendall," Stretch blurted, his face losing color, his concern turning to frustration. "Johnnie...I can't let you leave."

"Tough shit," she snarled, on the verge of losing it big-time. She didn't feel particularly strong but she needed away. She needed to blot out the images of Caroline in her casket and the misery of feeling like she had no one in the world. "Open the gate or—"

"Or what?" he returned, glaring at her. "I'm following fucking orders. I can't let you leave. Take that shit up with John Boy."

"I will," she fumed, refusing to get out and admit defeat, her bravado threatening to desert her. Then her mother's face popped into Kendall's head before morphing into the moment Marie pulled the trigger and painted Kendall with blood and brain and bone. She gripped the steering wheel to hold her trembles at bay. Unable to handle anything and having no one who understood her or wanted to understand her, she steeled her resolve. "I'm going to tell Johnnie how unhappy you've made me. How mean you're being to me. Go ahead. Hold me here when I want to leave and see what he does to you because of that."

Disgust slipped into Stretch's blue eyes and he clenched his jaw. "As long as you tell him you forced me to open this goddamn gate, leave. I don't give a rat's fuck. It's your fucking life." He jogged to the panel and pressed a few buttons, then waved her forward.

Kendall paused as she pulled the car onto the street, her heart banging as the gate clanged closed, a dividing line between her and the security of the club. She glanced at her rearview mirror and found Stretch still at the gate, ready to reopen it for her. Her nostrils flared, a trapped feeling almost choking her. Alone and outside the gate, she felt like a wild animal escaping the confines of a cage. Searching for safety and shelter but not knowing how to find it.

For almost everyone else, lockdown had ended, but Outlaw had decided Megan had to remain on the premises and Johnnie had followed his lead and demanded the same with her. Val tried that chauvinistic bullshit with Zoann and she'd told him to go fuck himself. It had surprised Kendall when even Megan tried to reason with Zoann. They'd all failed and Zoann had left the day of Johnnie's release from the hospital.

But Zoann had somewhere to go. Kendall didn't—

Her condo came to mind. Her mother's house. While Kendall had leased her place, Marie had owned the house.

Kendall shivered. The last time she'd been there, Marie had killed herself. Kendall had no idea what had become of the residence or her own, although she suspected Spoon had done something with both. According to the dashboard clock, one o'clock in the afternoon approached. If she remembered correctly, Spoon would be at his Meth lab today. He wouldn't be at his MC or anywhere near her condo or Marie's house. The club members who weren't with him would be out doing pickups and deliveries or at the clubhouse taking care of business. A business that included selling girls.

How could she have been with Spoon for so many months without knowing he trafficked people?

A knock on the window pulled her out of her speculations and she jumped. Stretch's handsome face peered through the window at her. Pressing the button on the door, she allowed the window to slide down.

"Come back in, Kendall," he coaxed. "I'm sorry for snapping at you, but Johnnie really don't want you leaving right now."

"He isn't here."

"He's with Outlaw," he said with a sigh. "They just want those assholes caught before you and Meggie can go here and there."

"Meggie might be happy to jump when Outlaw barks it at her, but I'm not as inclined to be Johnnie's puppet."

Stretch crouched down, the wind blowing through his thick, brown hair. "Then don't be. He wouldn't want you to be," he amended. "Just…he wants you safe. We all do."

"If he wanted me safe, he'd be here to look after me himself," she pointed out, her anger growing at Stretch's persistence. They were *all* tenacious. If Mortician wasn't telling her to ease up on Megan, then one of them was demanding she follow Johnnie's rules. "Now, move. I have to get going."

Irritation returned to Stretch's eyes and he stood. "Okay.

I tried, Kendall. One last piece of advice. This is Meggie's car and she loves it. Don't fuck it up or Outlaw is going to deal with you himself."

Belligerence roiled into her at the words, the absolute worst thing he could've said to her. Flipping him the finger, Kendall pressed the accelerator to the floor and sped away.

Forty-five minutes later, she pulled to a stop in front of her old building. She didn't have her car, so she didn't have the parking tag to get into the private garage used for residents only. She stared at the pink stucco and red bricks on the building. Some units had big windows and white shutters. Others, like hers, had small balconies. Her plants must've died by now, the thought depressing her a little more.

Tears clogged her throat and she forced herself forward. She had about another hour before Spoon and the other Torps would be roaming about again, so she needed to get a move on. Once she investigated her apartment, maybe, she'd be able to talk to management. Have her locks changed and—

And what? And move back to her own place. Get away from the MC—and Megan Caldwell. She represented so much heartache to Kendall. In Megan, Kendall saw every mean girl she'd ever had to face in high school and every sorority girl she'd come across in college. She was an attention-whore just like the rest of them and spoke whatever came to her head because she had the world at her feet. A husband to take care of her *every* problem.

Rubbing her forehead, she reached the residential entrance and punched in her access code. She lived on the second floor, so she decided to take the stairs. Hungrier by the minute, she'd soon need to eat—Baby Biker did too—so this pre-food exercise would do her good. When she opened the door that led to hallway, she stopped short.

"Hi, Kendall."

"Erm, hi, Fred," she murmured, forcing a smile at the security guard. He'd scared the shit out of her. "What are you doing here? Has something happened?"

He gave her a toothy grin and adjusted his eyeglasses. "Saw you on the monitor," he admitted. "We been seeing Mr. Spoon here on the regular and he said you had gone to Europe." Fred bent his head and shifted his massive weight. "I'm really sorry about Marie."

Kendall's nostrils flared, heat rushing through her at her rising grief.

"Caroline decided to stay there?"

No. Caroline was dead, something she couldn't tell the kind man in front of her, so she nodded, unable to speak.

He placed his fingers on her arm and squeezed. "I'm sorry. I didn't mean to bring up..." His voice trailed off and he scrubbed his face, backing away. "I'm sorry."

Kendall nodded. "I'm just...I'm tired." She started forward, edging past him.

"Yes, ma'am." He turned toward the elevator and jabbed the down button. "Let me know if you need anything. Blankets. Pillows. Whatever."

"I'll stop by the office later or tomorrow," she promised with a frown, wondering what he meant but too overwrought to continue any in-depth conversation. "Meanwhile, can you...I don't feel like seeing Spoon tonight."

He straightened. "I'll take care of it, ma'am. Don't you worry."

"Thanks," she threw over her shoulder, her mind already turning toward the safety of her apartment. She wondered if Johnnie would even miss her when he realized she'd left.

Maybe, walking away from the club would be the only way to force Johnnie away from it, too.

Reaching her door, she ignored the dried floral wreath—a new addition—and unlocked it, then stepped into her apartment. She gasped. Afternoon sunlight filtered through the glass balcony door, shimmering against the white tile. And nothing else. Not one piece of furnishing remained. Not a curtain. Her CD player and all her opera music…gone. Her art books and Sisley replicas…nowhere to be seen.

She stumbled to her bedroom and pushed open the partially closed door. She froze, her heart sink to her feet. A nude, dark haired woman lay sprawled on the bed, her soft snores filling the small space.

Kendall remembered this woman—one of Spoon's favorite whores who stayed on her back and brought in a lot of money. She was also a mean, spiteful bitch and hated Kendall.

Her closet door gaped open and Kendall glimpsed some of her clothes, the sight jerking her out of her shock. Reni turned to her side and Kendall backed up, the door knob poking her side. Reni's phone started ringing and the woman groaned.

Frantic, Kendall looked around, her nerves making it hard to think. Her gaze fell on the camera hanging in the corner, directed toward the doorway. One of the locations within the surveillance range. In between the camera and Kendall's spot stood the bed.

Reni sat up, her eyes widening when she saw Kendall. "Spoon, baby?"

Kendall jumped back and spun on her shaky legs.

"Yes, she's here. What--?"

Not sticking around to hear more, Kendall ran out of the

door and headed for the staircase, praying Reni wasn't carrying her gun. Of all the scenarios, she'd never expected Reni. Why hadn't Fred told her?

Bursting into the stairwell, Kendall's breath escaped in short pants. By the time she reached the first floor, she had to pause to draw in air. Her lack of oxygen and food made her light-headed. Instead of going towards the residential entrance, Kendall tripped toward the atrium located near the security station and the leasing office. That greenery and the noisy fountain first drew Kendall to the place.

"Kendall?" Fred called, his brow creased in concern. He caught her arms, the wall of monitors visible through the glass and steel walls of his office. "Are you okay?"

No. "Yes," she said, her heart rate calming down. "Spoon…his girlfriend is in my condo."

Sympathy joined Fred's concern and he scratched his head. "Miss Reni up there?"

She didn't care that he'd known Spoon was using her house for another woman. She didn't even care if Fred was aware of what Reni did for a living and on behalf of Spoon.

A tall, rangy man sauntered onto the monitors, heading toward the private access gate. Gripping Fred's hands, Kendall choked. "Spoon," she whispered, on the verge of a panic attack. "Get me to my car. Please. Don't let him see me."

"You need some department boys here?" he asked, referring to Portland PD. "I can—"

"No." A sob escaped her. "I need to get to my car. I need for him not to see me."

Uncertainty in his kind eyes, Fred nodded. "C'mon, then. I'll get you to your car all safe and sound."

As good as his word, Fred got her to the Mini Cooper exactly as he promised. Not wasting any time with goodbyes, the moment Kendall slid in and started the ignition, she sped away.

Only when she'd gotten on the road did she realize that,

for once, something had gone in her favor. She'd had Megan's car, so even if Spoon had tried to follow her, he would've been searching for a Mazda and not a Mini Cooper.

Chapter 6

The moment Kendall turned onto the dead end street and drove to the end to Johnnie's clubhouse, she sagged in relief, never so glad to see an MC. Stretch opened the gate but didn't acknowledge her other than to point to a spot where she needed to park Megan's car.

Johnnie's Harley was parked near the entrance, next to Outlaw's and a few others she didn't recognize. The bikes were big, beautiful machines, hell on wheels, perfect matches for the men who rode them.

Before she reached the door, it flew open and Val walked out, a bottle in his hand. His red-rimmed eyes gave his dilated pupils a wild edge. He seemed surprised to see her.

"Where the fuck you coming from, babe?" he asked, his words confirming he hadn't expected to run into her. "I thought you were somewhere inside. John Boy know you traipsing about."

"Where is he?" she asked, surprised at the normalcy in her voice. But she'd had over an hour to get herself together, thanks to the evening traffic.

"At the ruins of Prez's house. That's where I'm headed to." He let the door close and drank from the bottle of gin. "You need him?"

Yes. Terribly. She needed him to hold her and tell her she'd get her life back. That Spoon wouldn't dog her steps for the rest of her days. She shook her head. "I just…it was hard at the funeral home. I needed to get away from here," she admitted. "I wish Spoon was out of the way."

Val smiled in understanding, surprising Kendall. He always looked so gruff and his tear drop tat scared the shit out of her. "Don't let the motherfucker fuck with your head, babe. As long as you with us, he can't do you fuck all. Okay? Johnnie is like a mad dog after Spoon." He drank from the bottle again, deeper. "I almost feel sorry for the assfuck. Know what I mean? Just stay within the safety of the compound, babe. Spoon try to contact you, let John Boy know, but remember he'd need to get through us to get to you."

The road captain glanced over her shoulder and Kendall turned her head to see Johnnie and the others walking on the trail, heading to where she and Val stood. A breeze ruffled Johnnie's hair, the late afternoon sun kissing his light blond hair.

The enormity of her stupidity at her earlier actions hit her and she pressed a hand against her belly. She'd risked both herself and Johnnie's Baby Biker. Johnnie would get Spoon, so she had nothing to worry about. She certainly didn't need any of them pointing out the foolishness of visiting her condo, so she'd keep her mouth shut.

Megan's car was already removed from the parking lot, taken to wherever it was kept until Outlaw gave her a driving pass. The moment the group of men reached her, Outlaw barreled toward her.

"Come with me," he commanded, brushing past her and heading inside.

Not indicating he knew what Outlaw wanted, Johnnie

nodded, leaving Kendall no choice but to follow. Stepping into the clubhouse, she found it still crowded with brothers and their old ladies, who'd come in for K-P's funeral, from out-of-town chapters of the Death Dwellers. Kendall heaved her shoulders, ignoring the cursory glances directed at her.

"Christopher," Megan called, just as they rounded the corner, going toward the offices instead of the bedrooms. Little Man had one thumb in his mouth and one hand fisted in her hair. "What's going on?"

Outlaw halted without warning and turned to his wife. "Talk to you in a minute. I gotta talk to Kendall right now."

A frown creased her brow, Megan's blue gaze travelling between Kendall and her husband. "I haven't seen you all day and I need to talk to you—"

"And ten fuckin' more minutes ain't gonna fuckin' hurt, baby. I got shit I'm doin' and I need Kendall's fuckin' help."

A sense of satisfaction and vindication settled into Kendall. After Meggie's bitchiness today, she received no more than she deserved.

Meggie stared at Outlaw, a combination of anger and hurt lighting her tear-filled eyes. "Fine," she snarled, throwing an evil glare to Kendall before turning on her heel and rushing away.

"Fuck!" Outlaw barked, thrusting his hands through his hair. "Megan, baby, get the fuck back here."

In response, a door slammed.

"Fuck me." Outlaw swept Kendall with a cold glance, spun around and strode to his office. He unlocked it, flipped on the overhead light, and waited until she entered before closing the door again.

He tossed his keys onto his desk and dropped into his chair. "Get Brooks Reddin' here," he ordered without preamble.

He hadn't offered her a seat or an exchange of

pleasantries, which Kendall appreciated. In his current mood, the fear coursing through her brought memories of Spoon's assault rushing back.

"You fuckin' hear me?"

Stepping back and gazing the distance to the door, she remained silent.

Outlaw glared at her and got to his feet. She flinched, trembles assailing her. Instead of grabbing her as she believed he would, he threw open the door. "Johnnie," he yelled, although Kendall couldn't imagine how Johnnie would hear with the racket going on in the main room.

She balled her fists, attempting to calm herself, surprised when Johnnie stepped in a minute later.

"What the fuck did you say to her?" he bit out, scowling at Outlaw and drawing Kendall into his arms.

"Just what the fuck I told you I was goin' to fuckin' say to her, motherfucker," Outlaw growled with impatience.

"Shhh, it's okay," Johnnie crooned, threading his fingers through her hair. She leaned into him, surrounded by his warmth and clutching him.

"He was so an-angry," she got out, the stress of the day converging upon her. "I...Spoon...I'm sorry," she ended, not sure what she wanted to say.

"Ignore him." Johnnie pushed her out of his arms and framed her face, thumbing away her tears. "He's a grumpy motherfucker."

"If you through puttin' her at ease, then I let her answer my fuckin' question."

Stepping in front of her, Johnnie tensed. "Give her a moment, Christopher," he said tightly. "Let her feel safe."

"I don't have fuckin' time for her to feel fuckin' safe. I gotta talk to Megan."

"Kendall could use some of the patience you show to

Megs. Just for now."

Kendall peeped around Johnnie. Outlaw's fierce expression made her swallow. He transferred it from Johnnie to her.

"Listen up, Kendall. You a fuckin' woman. As a general fuckin' rule, we don't fuckin' hurt girls. As fuckin' long as you don't fuck with Megan, you safe. I will never fuckin' hurt you. Scream and fuckin' holler at you if you piss me the fuck off. That's fuckin' it. I ain't got fuckin' time to hold your fuckin' hand. You got twenty-four fuckin' hours to get Brooks here."

"Why?" Kendall mumbled from behind Johnnie.

"His law firm represent your ex old man. I want information."

"He can't volunteer anything to you," she pointed out. "There's such a thing as attorney-client privilege."

"Don't give a fuck," Outlaw snapped without remorse. "Get him the fuck here or fuckin' else."

"I'll see—"

The slamming door cut off her words and she wilted in relief that the force of nature known as Outlaw Caldwell had left. She sagged onto the sofa, situated against the wall and right behind her.

Johnnie remained standing but now faced her. "Are you okay?"

Her heart pounded, nearly banging out of her chest and her pulse thumped through her, but, for the most part, Kendall hadn't been harmed.

Sitting next to her, Johnnie pulled her into his arms again.

"He doesn't like me," she concluded.

Leaning back, Johnnie tipped her chin up. "Christopher doesn't feel one way or the other about you, gorgeous."

"How do you know? The evidence suggests otherwise."

Johnnie lifted a brow, a half-smile curving his mouth. "Is that so, Attorney Miller?"

"Yes," she said around a laugh. Her first legal references in a long while buoyed her.

"Maybe, talking to Brooks is a good thing."

Kendall glanced away, disagreeing with that statement, too. She didn't have a clue what she'd say because she didn't know what story Spoon had given to her former mentor and employer about her resignation.

She'd worked so hard to get her degree. When her father had been killed and Marie sued the trucking company—and lost—Kendall had taken an interest in the legal system. She'd never veered from her desire to become an attorney and now it had been taken away from her. Like her father had been. And her mother. And her little sister.

Everyone and everything that mattered, she'd lost. She pressed her hand against her belly, the realization dawning Baby Biker would be her only blood relative in her life. Her daddy had a sister and a brother, but Kendall hadn't seen them in years.

Johnnie stood and Kendall glanced at him, the heated look in his eyes tightening her belly. But she wanted more than sex between them. She wanted friendship and trust. Stability.

"Wh-where were you today?"

Astonishment flickered into his eyes, but he recovered quickly enough and shrugged. "Handling situations with Christopher."

"What does that mean?"

"Taking care of club business. Nothing to concern yourself with." He reached for her hand and pulled her to her feet. "Let's go to the room and spend some time together."

"Why can't we stay in here?"

Johnnie scowled at her. "This is Christopher's fucking

office. Not mine."

"Let's go to yours."

"I don't have one here."

That wasn't fair. He held an important position, too. "Shouldn't you?"

"No, I shouldn't." His expression closed and the walls banged into place, shutting her out.

She searched for another topic, a question gnawing at her popping into her head. "When are we moving?"

"Moving?" he echoed. His shock indicated he hadn't thought of getting another house.

"Yes." She folded her arms, determined to stand her ground with him. He had to know she had a brain. He treated her brain*less* because she acted stupid. But not thinking for herself dissatisfied her now and she wanted to stop cowering in fear. Maybe, she'd never be able to face down a witness on the stand or argue with a fellow attorney or plead a case to a judge. In her private sphere, though, she wanted respect. "I can't imagine we're going to live here the rest of our lives. And Megan Caldwell might be happy allowing her son to be raised by bikers, but I want *my* Baby Biker to say something other than *fuck* as its first word."

It still horrified Kendall thinking about Johnnie telling Little Man to say *moo* and the child had said *foo*. Why? Because Digger and the others were teaching him the word *fuck*.

"What are you expecting from me?" The sudden coolness in his tone matched the storm gray in his eyes. In moments, he'd gone from reasonable to unfriendly. "I hope like hell it isn't changing me. Coming between my brothers and I. Forcing me to choose between you and the baby or the club."

Her heart banged against her chest and her insides quaked, shrinking into oblivion. Why wouldn't they? She'd always lived in the shadows. "I don't think your putting me and the baby first is too much to ask."

"Putting you first requires what?"

"Making me feel like I'm important," she flared, proud of how eloquent she presented her argument. She felt vital and alive, ready to stand up to him and demand what she needed. "I don't want to be your afterthought."

"You're here, aren't you? You're not a fucking afterthought."

"One day, you're sweet and…and hot and, the next, you're distant and cold." Not one *day*. More like from one *hour* to the next. Yesterday, at K-P's funeral, he'd made her feel wanted and needed, then he'd deserted her for hours. "What do you expect from *me*?"

"I don't fucking know," he admitted. "I'm taking this day-by-day and hour-by-hour."

"You couldn't even come with me this morning," she cried. "When I needed you the most."

He scowled at her. "*I* didn't need to be there. You had Megs there and there's no one I'd trust to take better care of you."

"Your *Megs* is a snotty little bitch," she spat. "She barely spoke to me."

"Did you try to talk to her? Megs wouldn't—"

She didn't want to hear what Megs *wouldn't* do. "Yes, she would," she interrupted. "Because she did. Instead of telling me what *I* should do, maybe, someone should tell her what *she* should do. Starting with manners."

Johnnie scrubbed a hand over his face, incredulity straining his expression, a muscle ticking at his jaw. "Talk to me," he encouraged with unexpected patience and more kindness than she'd anticipated. "You've been through a lot. You told me and that's affecting you. Us. Your relationships with people who are very important to me. Your judgment."

Kendall sucked in a breath, a smorgasbord of emotions slamming into her. Anger because he insisted on referring to Megan as someone important to him and hurt that he found her so...*broken*. As broken as she felt. She wished to reclaim the pieces of her soul that had been scattered about over the past weeks. She just didn't know how or where to start. Her life felt like ashes in the wind, fragmented, floating more out of reach with each passing day.

If she were to ever reclaim the essence of herself, she needed Johnnie's continued understanding. She needed time. And she needed away from this stupid club and fucking Megan Caldwell. She needed *Johnnie* away from this shitty MC and his perfect little bitch, whom he'd loved first.

"Kendall?" Her name fell from his mouth, a plea. For her to talk and be what he wanted her to be. Someone she wasn't. "How can I help you? I want to—"

She licked her lips at the perfect opening. "You can help me by not defending Megan," she argued, unable to keep the anger out of her voice.

"You've pegged her wrong..."

His voice trailed off at her glare and he sighed.

"You can help me by turning in your patch," she continued, voicing her ultimate goal. He had to know that he could no longer have her and *this*. "I've lived the MC life, somewhat, with Spoon, and look how it had turned out for me?" With Spoon, she'd had her own apartment and he'd had his house and, yet, even then, the clubhouse could be a bit much.

Johnnie no longer had a house and lived on the premises full time. House or not, he'd always have to divide his time between her and the club.

Clearing his throat, Johnnie gave her a crooked smile, oozing sex appeal and charm. "You met me in this club, gorgeous," he pointed out with care. "This club is who I am. The essence of me."

"It isn't," she insisted. "You're brilliant. You could be the head of a Fortune 500 company. The president of a bank. *Anything* but this."

Shock entered her eyes and she pressed a hand against her belly, a silent reminder of their baby. Eventually, she'd demand he make a choice. Because she had to. *For* their baby. For her own sanity.

His attention dropped to her stomach and her breath caught at the possession in his gaze. She had to get through to him and make him understand, once and for all, what she needed to be happy. If he wanted to be a part of their baby's life, he'd listen.

"I'm not Spoon," he said quietly, his expression fierce and his mouth tight. "My brothers aren't like—"

She lifted a brow, daring him to speak the blatant lie. "You're out every day," she pointed out slowly. "You've brushed off your injury and for what? To retaliate. To—"

"You can ask a lot of me," he interrupted with returning irritation, "but patching out isn't one of those things. You want me, then you take me for who and what I am. A member of this club. We fear no one and respect everyone. Do we live by our own rules? Yes, Kendall. But I'll never hurt you. I'll never disparage you. I'll never cheat on you. I'll protect you with my life. The one thing—the *only* thing—" He scowled at her and rubbed the back of his neck. "Spoon hurt you," he repeated.

Folding her arms and raising her chin, she frowned at him. "I'm not willing to discuss what Spoon did to me again."

"Why not? When we need to. We discussed it one time. The night I was shot. The night I told you about me and Christopher. You can't hold this in," he pressed. "I can't...talk to me."

Rephrasing his words and not confiding everything to her frustrated her. "I. Don't. Want. To. Live. Here."

"You have an apartment?"

Not believing she'd convinced Johnnie so easily, Kendall's eyes widened at the question. "Not anymore."

"Let me guess. Fucking Spoon took care of it."

Unwilling to explain her visit to her condo to Johnnie, Kendall shrugged, not knowing what had become of her mother's house and no longer caring. After finding Reni installed at her place, in her *bed*, Kendall didn't feel brave enough to drive to Marie's old residence and investigate what had become of her mother's possessions.

"We're closing in on Spoon, Kendall," Johnnie said into the tense silence.

At the mention of Spoon, she glanced away. She'd seen him on the camera today. Reni had been in her apartment, so Spoon lurked nearby. If she told Johnnie what she'd done, he'd be furious. He'd never understand her motives. Since he hadn't taken her there yet, what had he expected her to do?

"If you don't want to live here, fine. I'll get you an apartment."

"You will?"

"Yes."

"We'll move soon, then?"

"No, gorgeous. I said I'd get *you* an apartment. I'm staying here. As for *our* Baby Biker being around my brothers, there's no question in my mind on how that's going down. I'm a fucking biker, so your words not only insulted my fucking club and my brothers, they insulted *me*."

"Just because you're a biker, doesn't mean Baby Biker will be," she retorted with a sniff, unwilling to show how much his possessiveness towards their baby pleased her.

"I know, Kendall," he snapped. "But I'm not going to keep my child away from the club or its cousin. *Cousins*," he amended. "If you don't want to go to our room, I'm having a beer."

Without waiting for her response, he left Kendall alone again.

Feeling like the biggest jerk alive, Johnnie sat at the bar, nursing a beer and ignoring the loud crowd, the attempts at conversation, and the curious stares at his bad mood. *John Boy* didn't get into fucked-up moods. He always laughed, smiled, and joked, so everyone wondered what the fuck was going on, wondered where the fuck *their* John Boy had gotten himself off to.

No one dared ask him, but their expressions said it all.

That John Boy had been an illusion, created to ignore the pain of his past and the weight of his secrets. The one constant in his life, however, had been his love of the MC, and his dedication to it.

He told himself he could handle anything with Kendall. Except having to choose between her and the club. He'd try to do better and not make her feel on the fringes of his life, but, he made this up as he went along. What the fuck was he *supposed* to do? He treated Kendall as *that* moment dictated. Was it right to handle her and their relationship in such a manner? He didn't fucking know.

He'd never shared his life with anyone, not even Iona when they'd been together. He thought he had, but they'd never lived together and she'd demanded he give up the most important part of his life. He'd built his entire identity around the Death Dwellers. Yes, he'd graduated from college and become the "CEO" of a medical laboratory, but he lived and breathed the club. As much as Christopher did.

Fuck, he didn't know if he wanted to share his life now, especially after their conversation tonight.

He drew in a deep sigh and gulped down the rest of his beer, then slid the bottle to the other side, an indication he wanted another one. Fuck, no one manned the bar. With Mortician on the road and K-P...fuck, the bar was their territory. More Mortician's than K-P's but if one wasn't there, the other one was.

"Is there anything I can do?" a voice asked from beside him.

Johnnie couldn't help but laugh at Kendall's question. Every time she uttered those words, it came when she'd done more than enough already.

He raised his empty bottle and pointed behind the bar, unable to hide his annoyance. "Get me a beer."

She chewed on her lower lip and, irritated or not, Johnnie wished she'd taken him up on his offer to go to their room. He wanted to taste her mouth, feel her body shuddering around him.

"I've never served in a bar before."

"I didn't ask you to serve in a bar. I told you to get *me* a beer."

"Yo, John Boy! Where the fuck somebody at," a brother from an out-of-town chapter called. "I need another bottle."

Hesitating a moment longer, Kendall wrapped her arms around her waist and then went around to the bar. Handing him the beer proved simple compared to the orders of mixed drinks and bottles of alcohol swamping her within moments.

He'd remain here and keep watch her over and Baby Biker, but he couldn't help feeling pride at her initiative. Considering her past, her gutsy actions seemed a huge stride in the right direction.

Chapter 7

Kendall gripped each side of the sink, her legs trembling at the sensation shooting through her each time Johnnie tongued her clit. Her breasts jiggled, her body heat warming the porcelain sink they rested in. His arms wrapped around her thighs kept her upright. His nips and licks drew moan after moan from her. She never wanted him to stop, but his relentless pussy eating sent her over the edge and she screamed, her nipples tight and aching, her womb clenching.

Pulling his mouth away and settling his hands around her waist, he rose to his feet and spun her around, lifting her into his arms and burying his cock inside her still throbbing pussy. She wrapped her arms around his neck and threw her head back, shivering at the feel of his lips kissing the column of her throat. He pumped in and out of her, his big cock filling her, stretching her, and possessing her. She clenched her pussy muscles, squeezing his dick, her enjoyment spiking at his harsh groan.

She dug her nails into his biceps and laid her head on his shoulder, falling apart once more. "Johnnie," she breathed.

He stilled inside of her. Tightening his hold on her, he headed for the bedroom. She clenched her pussy around his cock and moaned. With each step, he moved inside of her.

When they reached the bed, he guided them down together, careful to keep his weight off her.

His mouth met hers, his tongue slipping past her lips, filling her with her own taste and his taste, too. Heat swept through her at his mastery of her mouth. He put everything into his kiss—lips, teeth, tongue.

"We're just getting started, Kendall," he swore in a sex-roughened voice, his blond hair tousled, his hot skin singeing her.

Kendall sighed at his tender regard, unable to stop her smile or the goose bumps rising on her each time he trailed his fingers over her belly and pubic bone.

She shivered and he grinned, repeating his caresses.

"Reprobate," she murmured on a gasp.

He nuzzled her breasts, licking one nipple and then the other, before drawing it into his mouth and sucking. Kendall threaded her fingers through his hair, the silky texture stimulating her already overworked senses, leaving her unable to do anything but chant his name.

A moment later, he rolled onto her, thrusting into her in one, long stroke, sending her soaring, flying, gasping, the intensity of her release a new experience.

Opening her eyes, she found him staring at her, unbelievable awe in his expression. "You're so fucking gorgeous, Kendall," he murmured, still hard and thick inside of her.

She tilted her pelvis, encouraging him to move, not ready to hear platitudes when she didn't know what to believe herself.

He brushed his nose against hers. "You want me to keep my dick in your pussy, don't you?"

"Yes."

He swiveled into her, then pulled out in slow torture. "Do me a favor, gorgeous?" he growled against her ear, biting her lobe.

"A-anything," she managed

"Suck my dick."

He slid up her body until he hovered over her, his cock glistening with her juices, rising from his nest of curls and touching her lips. Snatching her out of her lovemaking with Johnnie and catapulting her back into Spoon's assault.

"Stupid, stupid bitch," Spoon snarled, surging forward and shoving his dick into her mouth. "Should I let you fucking live? Huh, Kendall?"

Reminding herself to draw air through her nose, she pounded on his ass and back. Nothing succeeded in stopping Spoon from cutting off her oxygen when she hadn't yet caught her breath from his strangulation.

Lack of oxygen burned her lungs and the coffee and biscuit she'd had churned within her belly. If she didn't catch her breath, everything she'd consumed would come up and choke her, too.

"Death by dick choke, you fucking slut." He rotated and she gagged, a sob managing to break free. "You couldn't fucking do what the fuck I asked of you. You're too fucking stupid." He eased his cock from the back of her throat, allowing her a moment of air. "Just when I managed to get in good with the Dwellers' after I delivered fresh meat to them…" He slammed his cock down her throat again and Kendall shuddered, tears slipping from her eyes. "You fucked up," he snarled.

She could breathe now, though, and scream. She'd come too far, made too many strides to allow herself to be smothered. He tapped his dick against her lips, the signal to open her mouth.

Hollering at the top of her lungs, she thrashed against him, having the leverage and purchase to hit and punch and *scream* so someone could hear her and rescue her. Hands grabbed her flailing arms and she screamed louder, fought harder.

"Kendall!" Johnnie called, shaking her.

A pounding started on the door and she stilled, curling into a ball at Johnnie's shock and fury.

"John Boy, open this fuckin' door," Outlaw snarled.

"Fuck." Johnnie jackknifed off her and jumped to his feet with admirable agility. Kendall scrambled to her side of the bed and wrapped the comforter around her nude body.

"Kendall had a nightmare, Christopher," Johnnie said harshly once he'd cracked the door open and peeped out.

"Fuck me," Christopher snapped. "*Her* nightmare woke up both *my* son and mother-in-law. I can handle my boy, but Dinah only want Megan."

And Outlaw clearly didn't like the pressure Dinah placed on Megan, Kendall thought with returning clarity. His precious wife didn't even have time for her own mother.

Kendall would give anything to have Marie still alive and needing her, doting on her, the way Dinah seemed to with Megan.

"I'm sorry. Kendall didn't mean to wake you and Megan or Dinah and Little Man."

"She didn't wake *us* up, assfuck. We was already awake and fuckin'."

"Goodnight, motherfucker," Johnnie growled, slamming the door in Outlaw's face. A moment later, he flicked the bedside lamp on and studied her from where he stood at the edge of the bed.

"What was that all about?"

Kendall squirmed in the cocoon of the comforter, glancing at his now-softened cock and wincing. He'd pleasured her over and over, but he hadn't come yet. She tightened her hold on the comforter. "I'll suck you off if you want me to."

Instead of moving, he said, "Spoon, right?"

She wouldn't pretend ignorance of his meaning. She'd already told Johnnie about Spoon's sexual assault. Unable to look at Johnnie, she lowered her lashes. "Yes."

Movement. Drawers opening and closing. More movement. A lighter flickering. The scent of burning tobacco.

"Look at me, Kendall."

Humiliation ran deep inside Kendall. From Spoon's actions and her response to him. She hadn't fought him. She'd been caught off-guard and couldn't rally a defense. Spoon had been swift and vicious and violent.

She also felt humiliated over tonight. She'd been present and in the moment until Johnnie asked her to pleasure him in a way he very much enjoyed.

"Kendall?"

Raising her gaze, she bit her lip. Johnnie leaned against his desk, pajama bottoms riding low on his hips, his cock outlined against the thin material, the stitches still visible from the wound he'd received.

The Johnnie Effect.

The man reminded her of a lion, sleek, golden power and coiled strength in every inch of him.

Not knowing what to say, she shrugged.

"What he did to you and what I asked of you…" He rubbed the back of his neck. "You've got to know I wouldn't force you to do anything you didn't want to. I stood in a position similar to Spoon's, I take it."

Kendall swallowed. "You could say that." Not only that but she'd come so close to being caught by Spoon today and she couldn't imagine what he would've done to her.

He lifted a brow. "If we weren't in similar positions, then—"

"He…I've had lovers before. Sugar Daddies," she

blurted, raising her hands in supplication, asking for his understanding. "I-I didn't know how else to p-pay for college. I…loans…um—"

Johnnie scowled at her, puffed on his cigarette. "What the fuck does any of your former lovers have to do with fucking Spoon?"

"I'm…I want you to understand…I-I'm not a whore."

"And?"

She lifted her chin, her shame and hurt running as deep as her humiliation and confusion. "I'm educated. I'm an attorney. I'm better than what Spoon did to me."

Grabbing an ashtray, Johnnie tamped out his cigarette. He set the ashtray aside and folded his arms. "Let me get this straight. You're saying if you were a—" he wiggled his fingers in air-quotation marks—"'whore', Spoon would've had more of a right to force his dick into your mouth?"

Tears rushed to Kendall's eyes and she shook her head, unable to answer. She didn't have one.

"How many men have you fucked in your lifetime?"

Kendall snapped her eyes in his direction, neither seeing nor hearing derision. Still, she hesitated to answer. "How many women have you fucked?"

His eyes twinkled and he smirked at her. "Too fucking many to count *or* remember, gorgeous."

"That's something to be proud of?" she snapped, a wave of sick jealousy hitting her hard.

"Tsk, tsk, Kendall," he chastised with annoying amusement, a touch of wickedness in his teasing grin. "Green isn't a very pretty shade on you."

"Green?" she gasped in outrage, incapable of ignoring the simmering heat in Johnnie's eyes. "As in jealousy?"

He laughed, the sound carefree and boyish. He ruffled his hair and Kendall balled her hands to keep from burying them in the blond silk. "Yes. The putrid green shade at that."

Having no response because he'd pegged her right, she

sniffed.

"Now, answer my question. How many men?" he pressed once his laughter died down.

Kendall looked away from him to regain the composure Johnnie's charm always stole. In silence, she surfed through her sexually active years, beginning with one of her high school teachers when she was sixteen in an exchange for a good grade. After that she'd gone from one older man to the next, attaching herself to men who offered her financial aid, an ego boost, or kindness. When she received all three from one man, she'd float like she hit the jackpot.

"About ten or twelve." Not including him and Spoon.

"You do realize some women would consider *you* a whore?"

She'd never thought one way or the other about how women might view her. They judged her for everything else, however, so she supposed it shouldn't surprise her they'd judge her sex life.

"Do you?"

"No, I don't. Even if I did, I still wouldn't believe you deserve whatever Spoon inflicted upon you. You're rather a harsh judge, sweetheart."

Kendall slanted a glance at the clock. The hands slid closer to four AM. Once she'd served Johnnie his beer, she'd had never-ending orders for drinks. In the end, she'd found it invigorating and enjoyed the interaction. Johnnie had remained in his seat at the bar, declining an invitation to play pool with Digger to keep watch over her. Although he wanted to engage in the game, it thrilled her he thought her more important.

The crowd began to thin out a little after two, so Johnnie had closed shop and ushered her to their room. She'd gone for a shower, happy when he'd joined her, and even happier when he'd began eating her pussy once they were out.

The entire day, from viewing Caroline's body to suffering Megan's presence to her screaming her head off, led to this moment. With Johnnie accusing her of judging other women harshly simply because…because…she didn't know why.

Irritated, she stared at the ceiling. "First, Megan, and, now, you."

Johnnie tensed, any mention of Megan immediately hitting a nerve, which irked Kendall all the more. "What are you talking about?"

"Megan!" she cried. "Accusing me of being jealous of my little sister *and* her."

A range of emotions flashed across Johnnie's face, then he finally croaked, "Megs said that?"

Kendall nodded, still angry every time she thought of the words. "As I viewed Caro's body, she hit me with the brilliant observation."

He scratched his chin. "That doesn't sound like—"

"Of course not. Because Megan can do no wrong," she spat, lashing out in jealousy of Megan and Caroline. Her transparency made her feel foolish and even more inferior. Caroline had been a child under her, and Megan was only three or four years older than her sister. No way in hell should she even feel the need to compare herself to those girls.

But three, thirty, or three hundred, most people craved acceptance and approval from their parents. In her case, she'd had only a mother. Even before Caroline's birth when Kendall was fourteen, Marie had kept a part of herself away from Kendall.

Despite the age difference, Kendall *had* been jealous of Caroline and remained envious of Megan. She just couldn't believe the girl's audacity in mentioning it.

So what if Outlaw had seen Kendall naked? And so

what if she'd gyrated her body on him and given him an erection? In the end, he hadn't slept with Kendall because of his loyalty to *her*.

Everyone bragged about Outlaw and Meggie being open and aboveboard with one another. If so, Megan should've thanked Kendall for telling her about the incident at the bachelor party. But she'd gotten pissy about it, confronted her husband.

Now, her grudge made Kendall's life miserable.

Johnnie heaved in a breath. "I'm tired, Kendall. We need to get a few hours rest before another long day starts." He made his way to the bed, turned off the light, then climbed in. "I'll talk to Megs."

She didn't want Johnnie anywhere *near* his Megs.

"I think she's going through bad morning sickness. She's taking care of her mother. Dealing with her house being burned down. Give her a chance, Kendall. She's dealing with a lot right now."

"And I'm not?"

He sighed. "I didn't mean to sound as if I'm taking her side, sweetheart. I'm sorry if it came across that way. I know you're going through a lot."

"I'm pregnant, too."

"With occasional bouts of morning sickness," Johnnie said gently. "Megs has it every day. She has to be miserable." He pulled Kendall into his arms and kissed the top of her head. "Sleep, sweetheart."

His erection rose against her thigh and she waited for him to finish what they'd begun. Instead, his breathing evened out in sleep, leaving Kendall to wonder what he intended to do about his own release.

Chapter 8

Church overflowed today with members from across the country in attendance. Most of them were riding out right after, so Christopher had called the meeting to take votes on the course of action with the Torpedoes and inform the brothers on what had already been done.

Christopher's politicking surprised Johnnie. Decisions had already been made, some—such as Christopher drawing the Torps to their enforcer's house—without *anyone's* input. However, Christopher never did anything without a reason, so Johnnie decided to sit back and listen, forget all the shit running through his head about Kendall and her reaction to his request for a dick suck.

Motherfucking Spoon needed to be choked himself with a cock.

His anger simmered at a mild degree, so Johnnie decided to shut his thoughts the fuck down before it boiled over and turn his attention back to the matter at hand.

After the facts were presented—K-P's death, the fire bombings of Johnnie's and Christopher's houses, and Johnnie's and Stretch's shootings, Christopher opened the floor.

Arrow stood, a former president in a Midwest chapter, who'd gone nomad a few years ago. He and K-P had had a strained relationship, which had led to Arrow's decisions.

"Word on the street is a Torp didn't kill my brother," he began, staring at Christopher in challenge, not flinching at the coldness creeping into Christopher's eyes. "I heard Logan Donovan rose from the grave and caused all types of damage. Including K-P's death."

"Same here," another brother called.

Val shifted in his seat and Digger stood, heading to the bar. Johnnie remained still, ignoring the unease sliding through him.

"I heard it, too," a third brother added. "Matter of fact, I went roaming last night, looking for any motherfucker wearing Torp colors. Ran across one of their bitches and she said we in bed with the Torps. While protecting Logan Donovan at a house he occupied, someone murdered one of their brothers."

"Who's this Logan Donovan?" a younger member from their Manitoba chapter asked.

Christopher lit a cigarette and then dragged on it before addressing the crowd. "Logan Donovan was me and Johnnie's grandfather. The fuckhead who founded the club." He pinned the young brother with a hard stare. "And your worse fuckin' nightmare." He smoked again, calm and steady. "This why I called the fuckin' meetin'. Address any fuckin' concerns you got and warn you about the war startin' between the Dwellers and the Torpedoes."

Arrow glowered at him and stepped forward. Digger abandoned his place behind the bar and weaved through the crowd to stand beside Christopher. As sergeant-at-arms, he was the last line of defense between *anyone* and the president. He cracked his knuckles, shifted to show his weapon.

Christopher threw his cigarette on the floor and sauntered to Arrow, stopping inches from him. "Arrow, I know you pissed over K-P."

Tension filled the room and Johnnie nodded to Stretch

and Val for them to take position next to Digger. Johnnie signaled Bowlie, in charge of rallying the members of their chapter.

"I am, too. I been knowin' that motherfucker since I was fuckin' ten, so sit the fuck down with your bull-fuckin-shit attitude, motherfucker," he growled. "As for Logan, yeah, his dead ass turned up *undead*." He glanced over his shoulder to Johnnie, ignoring the curses and growls. "Brought a whole buncha fuckin' revelations with him, too. The fact, for instance, me and John Boy blood brothers."

Of all the things...Johnnie wasn't ashamed of his relationship to Christopher. Not in the least. But, after their conversation the other day, Johnnie believed it wouldn't be brought up again.

Dead silence after Christopher's announcement.

"And, yeah, Logan killed K-P, Arrow. The motherfucker also beat the fuck outta my wife's Ma and put *my son* in a fuckin' trashcan to smother him. That motherfucker, Spoon, been eatin' out of Logan's ass to get the fuck in with us. In case none of you know what the fuck all this mean, it mean I'm more fuckin' pissed than all you motherfuckers could ever fuckin be, so get your fuckin' facts straight before you confront me."

Arrow didn't appear mollified. "And the Torps?"

"You fuckin' slow, Arrow?" Christopher snarled. "Yeah, motherfucker. Spoon and Logan worked together. We still tryin' to sort out every-fuckin-thing them two fuckheads did. But the Torps blew up me and John Boy's houses in Long Beach. And the fuckin' Torps blew up my fuckin' wife dream house. And the fuckin' Torps fuckin' *shot* John Boy and Stretch." He stepped back and glared at all of them. "In case you hung-fuckin-over or just fuckin' fucked in the fuckin' head, that mean the Torps our fuckin' enemy because Logan was our fuckin' enemy. But this shit ain't goin' fuckin' unanswered. We gettin' each of them fuckheads, down to a fuckin' man. We see them in their colors, we fuck them before they fuck us. They see us, same fuckin' thing. I wanna know who's fuckin' in and who against it."

"And Logan?" Arrow persisted.

"Dead for real, this time."

"He was supposed to be dead before," an old-timer with a long, gray beard and a skull cap barked. "How we know for sure this time?"

"Because I ain't motherfuckin' Boss." Christopher balled his fists at his sides. "I ain't gonna hide shit from you and I ain't gonna fuckin' lie to you."

"Not anymore." Arrow glared at Christopher before transferring the angry look to Johnnie. "You obviously knew Logan wasn't dead. Somebody sent him money every month."

Jesus. Wherever Arrow got the information from, they knew their shit. If he kept fucking talking, he'd blurt Johnnie had been the one hiding Logan and then what? Brothers were already getting pissed, the older ones familiar with Logan clueing in the younger ones who were not.

"You believe every bullshit you hear?" Christopher said with rising fury.

Fury in Christopher was *never* good. His rage usually led to someone's death. The only one who should've been armed right now was Digger, since no weapons were allowed during church.

But, Johnnie knew his cou—He swallowed. His cousin, yes, but his *brother*. Johnnie knew Christopher, his brother. His 9mm was strapped to him. Christopher rarely went anywhere without his beloved nine.

Waving to Stretch, Christopher returned to the middle of the floor. No one said anything as Stretch disappeared down the hall, returning a few minutes later carrying a stack of papers.

"Hand 'em out."

While Stretch began handing a small stack of stapled sheets to each brother, Christopher spoke again. "K-P was our treasurer. Local and national. Stretch handin' out his last report, along with the reports from the past year. No fuckin' where on these motherfuckers is there *any* payment to Logan."

Christopher knew there wouldn't be. Not because Johnnie had told him but because Johnnie had gone through great measures to hide those payments and no one had ever discovered them. No one would've known without Logan's reappearance.

"I ain't got fuck all to hide. You wanna check my personal fuckin' records? John Boy's? Any of us on the board?"

Shuffles and mumbles, low talking.

"Arrow?" Christopher called.

Arrow flushed.

"We went through a lot of fuckin' shit these past three years," Christopher continued. "This chapter, your mother chapter, especially. Lotta fuckin' turnovers. But we survived it. If we wanna keep survivin', we gotta trust each other." He shifted, lit another cigarette, puffed from it. "Otherwise, what the fuck good are we as a club? We might as well shut the shit down."

"What?" Johnnie bit out. Everything he'd done and gone through to keep the club together in Christopher's absence and he thought to dismantle it? "Is that what you want, Outlaw?"

"Fuck no, John Boy," Christopher answered without hesitation, "but we either fuckin' *brothers* or we fuckin' go the fuck our separate ways. Ain't no fuckin' use havin' a club where no motherfucker trust the other."

"We could always vote you out, too, Outlaw," a voice

from the back called, lost in the standing room only crowd.

"You could," Christopher agreed. "That's up to you, motherfuckers. Another turnover just gonna leave the Dwellers vulnerable. Motherfuckers on the outside gonna think we can't handle our shit."

"You sick fuck," Arrow growled, sitting down and snapping his mouth shut.

No one said anything else, slowly directing their gazes to Christopher, who turned a satisfied smirk to Johnnie. In-club bullshit bypassed.

Shaking his head, Johnnie smiled and nodded.

"Okay, now that you motherfuckers settled that, can we just get to the fuckin' vote? We usin' energy gripin' at each other when we could be out fuckin' up some Torps."

Kendall hadn't wanted to come to the offices of Romain, Redding, and Stanley after eight in the morning, but she'd awakened late due to the little sleep she'd gotten. Actually, Johnnie had gotten her up because church was scheduled and all women needed to be off the premises.

He'd insisted she take Christopher's supped up pickup. It had tinted windows, a huge engine, spikes on the wheels, and winged skeletons on each side. Added to the truck's spectacular showing, Johnnie had a man following her. He called him Fat and said his partner, Skinny, guarded Megan, Dinah, and Little Man.

Still, she hadn't left until after nine and it had taken a little over half an hour to arrive at the offices. The receptionists, legal aides, and secretaries had already gotten to work. Now, they passed the defense department, what Brooks called the Double D and Kendall referred to as the

Pentagon, to gawk at her.

No one asked her anything, which she preferred. Amy, the receptionist in the front office, had widened her eyes when Kendall asked for Brooks, then directed her back to the area with the defense attorneys. Brooks's specialty. One time, it had been Kendall's, too.

She'd been waiting for hours and would've left if Outlaw hadn't given her twenty-four hours to get Brooks to come to the club.

"Kendall?" Brooks's voice cut into her thoughts and Kendall snapped her head up.

She looked up at her mentor—former mentor—not surprised at his pin neat appearance and designer suit. Assurance and authority radiated from him.

"What are you doing here?"

She listened for a welcoming note, but couldn't discern one. Her heart banging in her chest, Kendall got to her feet. "I'm here to see you."

"After telling me you got employment elsewhere with…what…? A few hours' notice?"

"I-I didn't tell you anything," she stammered.

His lips tightened. "I assure you you did," he snapped.

"It wasn't me. I-I mean it w-was…probably." She frowned and drew in a deep breath. She had no memories of the first few days after arriving at the house Spoon had taken her to. Quite possibly, they'd made her call Brooks and tender her resignation. "I don't know," she whispered, desperation creeping into her voice.

Brooks contemplated her before grabbing her elbow and ushering her toward his office. "Hold my calls," he barked over his shoulder. He unlocked the door and pulled Kendall inside, then slammed it shut. "Now, talk to me, Kendall. Tell me what's going on."

Taking a moment to compose herself and shrinking beneath the intensity of Brooks's glare, Kendall gripped her purse and stumbled to the sofa. The familiarity of her surroundings comforted her, although she didn't think she'd feel the same way if she'd gone into her old office.

"Kendall?"

She could do this. Brooks had every right to be angry with her. He believed she'd acted irresponsibly after he'd stood by her and given her a chance to work here.

She heaved in a breath, studied the four abstract paintings. Brooks loved to test everyone's logic, find the known in the unknown. He could discover a family of unicorns, soaring eagles, disgruntled children in the abstract art he collected when it drove Kendall crazy. She saw a bunch of paint spattered onto a canvas that dripped everywhere.

Brooks leaned against his rosewood desk inlaid with ivory, and folded his arms. Crossing his ankles, he curved a finger over his mouth, resting the other hand in the crook of his arm.

Kendall squirmed beneath his deep study.

"Talk to me," he repeated, moderating his tone.

"I didn't call…" Her voice trailed off and she glanced over his shoulder to the Downtown Portland skyline. She raised her hands in supplication, unable to hold back her misery. Before she stopped herself, it all spilled from her—Caroline's abduction, Spoon's demand for her to seduce Outlaw, Spoon's assault, Marie's suicide, her own captivity. And everything else—her biker and her Baby Biker. Logan Donovan. Caroline's hanging.

And, finally, Outlaw's demand for Brooks to visit the clubhouse.

She hadn't *meant* to go into such detail, but didn't know a right or wrong approach. Too late, she realized she hadn't been ready to leave the safety of the club. She was ill-prepared to enjoy the fresh air again or find a physician for the baby. Her near-miss with Spoon and Reni chipped away the little peace she'd managed to steal. She wasn't ready for sunshine or laughter or happiness.

She only felt anger or bitterness or self-pity. Everyone refused to understand how broken she felt, that she'd spent almost her entire life fighting demons, dealing with weight and height and acceptance. Just when she'd gotten to a place in her life where she'd felt useful—her career— Spoon snatched it from her.

Maybe, that's why she made Megan Caldwell the target of her anger and bitterness; Mortician as her guru; Johnnie as the object of her desire. They made her *feel*. And she wanted to feel. Because she wanted to *live* and not just exist.

Brooks sat next to her and pulled her into his arms, laying her head on his shoulder. "I've called Charlotte," he said gruffly, referring to his wife. "You aren't alone, anymore, Kendall. We're here for your." He stroked her hair with all the tenderness of a father with one of his daughters. "The three of us will figure out what to do, but don't mention my involvement with the Torps to her. Once she leaves, we'll discuss exactly what Outlaw wants. Perhaps, it's time I got law enforcement involved and—"

"No, Brooks, please," she cried, jerking away from him and grabbing his hands, her concern for Johnnie ending up in jail overriding everything else. "You can't. Outlaw…Johnnie—"

"Don't concern yourself over my safety, my dear. I knew exactly what I was doing when I got involved with Spoon, so I'll go to the police with the full knowledge I'm putting my life in danger."

She flushed, embarrassed she hadn't thought of harm befalling Brooks. She snatched her hands away and dropped them into her lap. "Wh-why did you…I-I mean get involved with the Torpedoes?"

If *he* hadn't, then *she* wouldn't be in the current

situation. That included meeting Johnnie and getting pregnant.

He shrugged, adjusted his tie. "Risky investments led to financial losses for the company. Our losses led to deep debt. The money the Torpedoes offered…we couldn't pass it up. It was the quickest way to recover and save our law firm." Sighing, he stood and paced to the window. "I've regretted it more than once," he admitted over his shoulder. "We all have. What's done is done. We've learned from our mistakes, so we pick up the pieces and move on."

"Brooks?"

He turned and lifted a brow in response.

"Would you consider *not* going to the police, especially on Johnnie and his club?"

"You really care for this person, don't you?"

She nodded and pressed her hand against her belly.

Brooks's lips thinned in disapproval. "I'm risking my life if I go there and don't say what they want to hear. You do understand that?"

"I don't think—"

"Don't be naïve, Kendall," he scoffed, stalking to his desk and dropping into the custom made leather chair. "I'm on the enemy's team."

"Are you?" she whispered, bewildered. "Didn't you hear what Spoon did to Caroline and me?"

"Every word." Elbows on desk, gold and diamond cufflinks gleaming, he studied her. "I'll go to the meeting and listen to what they have to say *only* if you're in attendance with me. I'm going to assume you have some influence over your baby's father since you're willingly asking me to endanger my life."

Her next thought panicked her. "If you don't go, Outlaw will still kill you."

"Not if he's behind bars."

"He'll make bail."

Brooks scowled at her. "Fine, Kendall. Just pray I say the right things to walk out of the clubhouse in the same condition I'll arrive. *Alive*."

Chapter 9

A few hours later, in the boardroom at the clubhouse, nausea kicked up in Kendall's belly after she, along with Johnnie, Outlaw, Digger, Val and Brooks finished viewing the photos of all the young, naked girls Logan had pinned up on a clothesline in Megan's kitchen.

She was grateful *her* and Caroline's photos had not been laid out, suspecting they were in the manila envelope laying on the table in front of Outlaw.

Brooks sat silent. Earlier today, after Charlotte had arrived and Brooks explained Kendall's ordeal, they'd been more than a little outraged on her behalf and even hinted at giving her another shot in the law firm when she felt ready. If she ever would.

When Kendall had walked into the club and found it much less crowded than it had been the past couple days, Outlaw had taken one look at Brooks and nodded to her. "Good job, Kendall."

Now, twenty minutes later, Brooks gathered the ugly photos and stacked them facedown. "What do you want with me?"

"You either fuckin' in with us or you in with Spoon.

What I want is fuckin' allegiance. I want Spoon and his fuckheads' hideouts. Any we might've fuckin' missed."

Brooks rubbed his chin but Kendall cleared her throat. "I tried to explain to Outlaw attorney-client privilege."

Johnnie frowned at her; Digger shook his head as if he told her to shut up; Val sighed; and Outlaw ignored her, keeping a steady gaze on Brooks. Stretch bit down on his lip, not speaking. Kendall wondered how the quiet and reserved man fit in with *these* brutes.

"Do I have a choice?" Brooks questioned after a moment.

Outlaw placed a gun on the table and Kendall gasped, her hands flying to her mouth.

"What the fuck you think, Reddin'?" Outlaw asked with a cold smile.

One, quick knock on the door before it swung open and Megan stepped inside, halting when she noticed Kendall.

"What's she doing in here, Christopher?" she screeched. "You've never allowed me in."

Christopher scowled at her and got to his feet. "You ain't a fuckin' attorney, Megan."

Kendall straightened her shoulders. She kept her lids lowered, though. She didn't need anyone recognizing her gloating.

"What's going on?" Megan continued, not getting the hint she wasn't welcomed.

"You know fuckin' better then to question me about club business, baby," he said gruffly, moderating his irritation. He beckoned her over, bent and kissed her when she reached him. "Where the fuck you been all day?"

"Out."

"Out? Just out? Ditchin' the fucking guards I have for you and shit. Since when we start keepin' our whereabouts a secret?"

Megan shrugged. "I needed to think."

Outlaw thrust his hands through his hair. "Cut the

bullshit. Okay, baby? I'll be in the room in a little while so we can fuckin' talk about whatever the fuck you needed to think on and why the fuck you got away from them motherfuckers who supposed to be watchin' you."

Her mouth tipped up in a sad smile. "You're busy, so don't worry about me. I-I'm fine. Getting Spoon is more important." She nodded to the manila envelope. "Besides, I've decided I have to work through this on my own."

"You been actin' fuckin' strange for fuckin' days. Wanna fuckin' tell me about that?"

Her jaw clenched. "No."

"Megan, we need to get this meeting finished," Johnnie said with barely restrained impatience. "Brooks has a family to get home to, so, I'm with Christopher."

"Shut up, John Boy," Christopher warned. "You want me to punch the fuck outta you again?"

Megan backed away. "I'm tired, so I'm…good night."

"Get fuckin' back here, Megan."

She didn't respond, just walked away, and closed the door quietly behind her.

"Will she ever fuckin' listen to me?"

"No," Val, Digger, and Johnnie chorused.

"She fuckin' right, though," he said after a moment, then pointed to Kendall.

"Get the fuck out."

"Just a moment, Caldwell," Brooks said at the same time Johnnie growled, "Are you fucking kidding me?"

"Shouldna fuckin' let her in here in the first fuckin' place. She fuckin' you which mean she a fuckin' old lady which mean she on the wrong fuckin' side of the fuckin' door."

Instead of rising to her defense again, both Johnnie and Brooks stayed silent. Not welcomed anymore, Kendall gathered her things and rushed out.

Once again, Johnnie had let her know her importance in his life.

Fog and mist blanketed the ground, the scent of damp earth, motor oil, exhaust fumes, and cigarette smoke filling the air just outside the clubhouse. Drawing in a breath, Johnnie pulled out his own cigarette and lit it, walking toward the trail that led to the ruins of Christopher's and Megan's house.

He paused halfway there and leaned against a tree, debating on going to Kendall and attempting to seduce her. He was in an odd mood tonight, though, and didn't want to frighten her, although he wanted her so fucking bad just then he could almost taste her.

She had the best tasting pussy on earth and the feel of it...sheer fucking heaven.

Groaning, Johnnie adjusted his dick, then puffed on his cigarette before releasing the smoke and glancing at the night sky peeking through the canopy of trees. Stars glittered against a canvas of darkness, nature's nocturnal painting too beautiful for Johnnie to feel so lost.

Two weeks ago, his life had been so simple. Two weeks ago, he'd believed his grandfather still resided in Columbia. He'd expected the fact that he and Christopher were brothers to never become so known. Two weeks ago, Megan had still been on her honeymoon with Christopher and Johnnie thought he'd never find a woman like her or a woman he wanted as much as he wanted her.

He'd been happy to live, to ride, and to fuck. His grandfather had still been out of sight and Kendall had been nothing but a fond memory.

How quickly life changed. Fourteen, short days made a

world of difference. In that span of time, Johnnie had gone from worshipping Logan Donovan to despising him enough to have killed him. Kendall was no longer a fond memory but a vital part of his life. She was so fucking damaged, in ways completely different than he, himself, was.

He wanted to be the man she needed him to be and, yet, he was *him*. *Him* might not be enough for *her*. His world consisted of bikes, alcohol, weed, sex, and money. From the little he observed of Kendall, she'd want more. She listened to fucking *opera* music, for fuck's sake.

The thought of that fucking noise blaring from a speaker popped his fucking eardrums.

Before Megan arrived, Johnnie dealt with women who lived life as hard and as fast as he did. Even though he'd lived in Long Beach and ran the lab—portrayed the businessman to perfection—he stayed away from "good girls" once his last relationship ended. Before *that* relationship, good girls had frightened him. They wanted what he didn't know how to give. Commitment. Attention. Time.

Good girls needed good men and he wasn't that by any means.

Kendall needed that. She deserved it. But the club would always come between them. Like tonight. He'd seen the look on her face when she'd left the board room and he hadn't demanded Christopher allow her to remain. Johnnie's silence in the matter had hurt her.

If Christopher hadn't pointed out that Johnnie's relationship with Kendall put her in the same category as Megan, then, yes, he would've defended Kendall and demanded Christopher allow her to stay at the meeting. Of course, Johnnie would've lost. Megan's hurt feelings stacked the deck against any and every argument he could've put up. But he would've pointed out to Christopher that Megan was acting like a spoiled brat, picked up whatever teeth Christopher knocked out of his head for talking against Megan, and, then, ushered Kendall the fuck out.

However, Kendall *was* Johnnie's old lady and he wanted her accepted as such. With Megan in bitch mode, if the other women also felt Kendall received preferential treatment—especially above Megan—they'd shun Kendall.

Something Johnnie wouldn't allow. She was *his*. For now or long-term didn't matter. She was having his baby.

But he feared committing to her. No, he'd already dedicated himself to her. In his head. Saying the words to her frightened him.

Other than keeping his dick in his pants and out of other women, he didn't know what it meant to be in a committed relationship. Did he put her first in every aspect of their life together?

Johnnie rubbed the back of his neck, wishing he'd brought a bottle and a blunt with him. Maybe, Herb or Al would give up the answers he needed.

As a fucking man, of course, his woman and his child came first. Did putting Kendall first mean walking away from the club as she'd requested? Was he a selfish motherfucker for *not* wanting to leave his brothers and his club?

A small scream interrupted his internal debate.

"J-Johnnie?"

Straightening, Johnnie scowled at the last person in the world he wanted to see in his present mood. "Megan, what the fuck are you doing out here?"

A glint of the diamonds on her ring and movement of her golden hair. "Going to visit my house."

He grabbed her elbow and steered her toward the light, cursing when she yanked herself away and tried to scoot around him. He clamped his hand on her shoulder, shoving aside the memory of seeing her with nothing but red heels in Logan's perverted photograph. What the fuck did motherfuckers say about being careful what fuckheads wished for? He'd hungered to see her naked and, now, the image seared his brain.

"Does Christopher know you're out here?" The fog prevented him from clearly seeing her face, so he pulled her almost against him. She felt so...*delicate*. Nothing at all the way his gorgeous Kendall felt in his arms—strong and lush.

"If he hadn't rode out not long after your precious meeting ended, he'd know."

He released her shoulder and dug into his cut for another cigarette. "Don't fucking move," he growled.

"Piss off," she snapped.

Holding his cigarette between his two fingers, he glared at her. "I'm so fucking sick of your bullshit, Megan. You're making Kendall miserable. You're making me miserable. You're making *everyone* miserable."

She shoved him. Actually. Fucking. Shoved. Him. Hard enough that he almost fell on his ass because she caught him by surprise. She could be the most maddening little thing in the world.

"Kendall is making *me* miserable," she yelled. "I've tried being nice to her and she keeps rejecting my overtures."

"Bullshit." Even before Kendall mentioned Megan's behavior, he'd glimpsed it himself. "Is it too much to ask you to treat Kendall like you treat me? Can't you remember who I am? Our friendship? Be nice to her for me?"

"Can't you remember who *I* am?" she spat back. "Your friend. You *know* me. How can you believe *her* over *me*?"

Tension rose in Johnnie at her question, filled with hurt

and anger. He didn't want to recognize this jealous, spiteful side of Megan. He wouldn't have believed it if Kendall wasn't so distraught over it. He'd defended Megan to Kendall and it only upset Kendall more. At the time, he'd been attempting to smooth things over, but, now, Megan roamed outside at ten o'clock at night just because she was pouting. Johnnie suspected Christopher's absence didn't help her mood, either.

He ignored the tears glistening in her eyes. "Grow the fuck up, Megan. Stop acting like a goddamn teenager and act like Christopher's wife and the mother of his children—"

"Yo', John Boy," Val's voice interrupted his tirade. He stepped into their circle of light, disapproval tightening his lips and anger fanning in his eyes. "Meggie, what are you doing out here?"

She sniffled. "I-I was going to my house."

"You don't have a house, babe," Val reminded her and narrowed his eyes at Johnnie as if it was *his* fault she was throwing a temper tantrum.

"Everything...all of my father's photos...they were all there...I just want..." A sob escaped her. "I know...Daddy...today at the funeral home...Christopher...*where is he?*"

"Jesus, Megan," Johnnie said, determined to hold onto his temper, irritated as fuck. Somewhere, in the back of his mind, he knew he was being harsher than necessary with Megan, but Kendall needed her. Kendall needed him. Kendall needed everyone and Megan's histrionics would distract attention from the focus Kendall should have at this difficult time. "Christopher is out trying to make shit safe. That's where he's at. Big Joe is the last motherfucker I want to hear about right now," he snarled before he could stop himself.

Megan squeaked and Val growled. Johnnie didn't give a fuck. Joseph Foy was as rotten as Logan Donovan. While

Megan wanted photos of her "daddy", Kendall's little sister
needed burying, a victim of Logan and by extension, Big
Joe. Logan and Boss had started their dirty fucking
business.

"He peddled—"

"Meggie, go inside," Val interrupted. "Outlaw should be
riding in any minute. He won't like it much if he sees you
out here."

"Okay," she said quietly, then turned a cool look to
Johnnie. "Don't ever talk to me again. Keep your apologies
because they aren't worth the oxygen you expel to say
them, you jerk." Swiping away her tears, she turned on her
heel and ran back to the clubhouse.

"Get the fuck away from me, Val," Johnnie growled, not
in the mood to hear anything he had to say.

"You better pray like a motherfucker Meggie don't
repeat this conversation to Christopher, assfuck."

"It wouldn't surprise me," he snorted. "She tells him
every fucking thing."

"Then I'm not even gonna cry at your fucking
grounding, motherfucker. Outlaw not going to leave
enough of you to have a funeral over. What the fuck's the
matter with you treating Meggie like that?"

"Can't anyone see the way she's treating Kendall?"

"That's girl shit, John Boy. They will work it out. But
keep fucking with Meggie and you won't be alive to see
them kiss and make up."

"Megan's pouting—"

"Meggie's pregnant—"

"So's my old lady."

Val glanced at him from head to toe, then he shook his
head and gave a humorless laugh. "My respect for you
going down about fifty degrees, fuckhead. Your bitch

bugging over Meggie, so you deciding to take it out on Meggie, who's innocent, by the way. She not responsible because you have a jealous chick and she's not responsible because you wanted your dick in her."

"Shut the fuck up—"

"Get it together, Johnnie," Val warned as the rumble of motorcycle pipes grew closer and closer. "You're wrong treating Meggie like this to make Kendall happy."

He wasn't treating Megan any kind of way just to keep Kendall happy. He treated her as her behavior warranted. And, fuck, maybe, he was angry with her, too, for being so important to Christopher that no one could set her straight. She was also indirectly responsible for some of the recent bullshit going on. Because she'd had Christopher's son. That one event had caused a ripple effect. Megan giving birth to CJ triggered Cee Cee's return, which instigated their grandfather's arrival. In the end, everything combined and led to Kendall's assault and her sister's suicide.

"What the fuck you doin' out here?"

Christopher's voice startled Johnnie back to the present.

"I'm not allowed out here?" he asked, lifting his brow, just then realizing he hadn't lit his cigarette. He scowled at the red roses in Christopher's hand.

Christopher cocked his head to the side. "You got somethin' to say about these motherfuckers, motherfucker?" he growled, holding up the bouquet.

Smirking at Johnnie, Val folded his arms, his amusement fanning Johnnie's temper.

"I need you to talk to Megan," he bit out.

"About?" Christopher challenged, shoving the roses into Val's arms and stepping forward. His leather-gloved hand rested on his side, hovering over his gun.

"Er, Outlaw," Val inserted quickly, "Meggie been crying. She wants some photos of Big Joe."

Christopher didn't move and neither did Johnnie. If he went for his own gun, Christopher would take that as a threat and shoot Johnnie before he unholstered his weapon.

Christopher didn't take his cold green gaze from Johnnie and didn't drop his hand from his side. "Megan ain't been feelin' good and I ain't been here for her the way I should."

"Every time we're facing a crisis, are we going to have to put up with her pouting?" Johnnie snapped.

"Come fuckin' again?"

"I need you to talk to her," Johnnie repeated coldly. "She's being a bitch to Kendall."

Johnnie gritted his teeth at the cocking of the gun.

"Call Megan a bitch again, motherfucker, so I can use your fuckin' teeth for target fuckin' practice."

"Christopher?"

Johnnie swallowed at the sound of Megan's voice.

"Jesus H. Christ, thank you, Meggie," Val mumbled.

"Go inside," Christopher ordered.

Silence.

"Draw your Glock," Christopher snarled. "Talk out of hand to Megan and I'll beat your fuckin' ass to a motherfuckin' pulp. Call her a bitch and I'm puttin' a fuckin' bullet in your head."

"Christopher!"

"Get the fuck in-fuckin-side, Megan."

"No." Megan stepped into view, not flinching when Christopher turned his angry gaze to her. She put her hand on his forearm and pushed it down. She glanced up and sighed. "Not a full moon. You don't want to kill your brother, Christopher."

"You ain't fuckin' heard this motherfucker talkin' about you—"

"I h-heard," she responded, her voice cracking. She cleared her throat. "It's...he's protecting Kendall."

"Not at your fuckin' expense."

Megan shrugged. "It doesn't matter." She turned a small smile to Johnnie, although it didn't reach her eyes. "Tell him, Johnnie. You wouldn't allow anything he said about Kendall to have it come between you. Right?"

Would he? Did he become everything Kendall needed? Or had he been all she needed when they first met? Was that what it meant to be committed to a woman?

The confusion he'd felt earlier returned, draining away most of his irritation and anger. He spared Megan a glance and shook his head. "Right," he agreed with a tight smile.

What about what *he* needed?

Megan tugged at Christopher's arm and licked her lips, her cheeks flushing. "Come to bed, Christopher."

He shoved his gun away, but anger wafted from him. Johnnie wondered if Christopher delayed retaliation in Megan presence. She grabbed his hand and put it on her belly. "Talk to your son. He's keeping me so sick. Tell him to stop."

Tenderness gentled Christopher's look, although tension stiffened his shoulders. She stood on her tiptoes and urged Christopher's head down, slanting her mouth over his then allowing him to take the lead.

"I wanna fuck you hard and fast, Megan," Christopher whispered roughly. Despite the low tone, Johnnie heard anyway.

Meggie nipped Christopher's chin. "Promise?"

"Fuck me, Megan."

She smiled at him. Christopher frowned. Maybe, he realized the difference in her attitude, too. Even her smile seemed forced. Unfortunately, Johnnie had witnessed Meggie kissing Christopher before. This kiss compared to the other one he'd seen lacked something. Out of everything else he had to deal with, if Christopher would handle Megan for Johnnie, and make her treat Kendall with understanding, then they could focus on other things.

"We tell each other everything, right, Christopher?" she

asked quietly.

"You know we do, baby." He bent and kissed her again. "Why?"

She watched Christopher, before looking at Val and Johnnie. Her shoulders slumped but she nodded. "I'm a big girl, Christopher. You and Big Joe..." Her voice trailed off and Christopher stared at her.

This was the second or third time she'd mentioned her father tonight. Other than wanting attention, Johnnie couldn't imagine why Big Joe dominated her thoughts all of a sudden.

"What about me and Boss, Megan?"

"You killed him." A tear slipped down her cheek but she caressed Christopher's jaw. "Would you really want to hurt Johnnie? Especially over *words*?" Although she didn't face Johnnie again, she addressed him. "Same for you, Johnnie."

"Fuck, Megan. Fuck, fuck, fuck."

Her point taken, her words stayed with Johnnie as he made his way through the main room, declining invitations for drinks and turning down May's offer for a quick fuck. Opening his bedroom door, he found Kendall on the bed, his iPad in hand, her ginger hair spread across her pillow.

"Hey." He shoved his hands into his pockets, trying to get the lay of the land. Was she angry, sad, or tired? All three? He was almost afraid to ask. Any conversation between them would lead to an argument and he was so fucking sick of it. Sometimes, he believed she misconstrued everything on purpose, just to have a way to vent and get out all the bullshit eating away her happiness.

"Do you know human trafficking is the fastest growing criminal enterprise in the country?"

"No." He sat on the edge of the bed, trying not to stare at the mounds of her breasts.

"You do now. I just told you."

"Yes."

"Numbers reach into the hundreds of thousands, Johnnie," she said quietly. "Men. Women. Children. Adults. Undocumented people. Documented ones. It doesn't matter. They're forced into labor and into the sex trade and—"

Stretching out beside her, Johnnie took the iPad from her hands and laid it on the night stand next to him. "Kendall, gorgeous, don't torture yourself like this."

"Caroline needs justice."

"Caroline will have her justice and so will you," he swore. Yes, when Johnnie got his hands on Spoon, he'd make that motherfucker beg then take pleasure in killing him slowly.

"What about the others? They need justice, too."

"What others?" he asked slowly. "The other victims of Spoon and my grandfather?"

"Yes. Them. The ones we don't know about. The—"

"That's impossible." Johnnie drew her closer and tightened his hold on her, sniffing her fresh scent and nuzzling her neck.

"It isn't," she insisted, her breath hitching. "What did Brooks say? I'll bet he wanted to do something."

"I can't discuss club business with you," he whispered against her ear, shoving the covers further down her body and raising her tee-shirt to bare the smooth skin on her midriff.

"You can do something. You have the power to make anyone you can find who's involved in this pay."

He nipped her ear and slid his hand in her pajama bottoms. He fingered her clit and rolled onto her, the scent of her arousal going straight to his dick. Rolling onto her, he inserted a finger into her hot pussy and slanted his mouth over hers, absorbing her soft moan. She rolled against his hand, driving him wild. He couldn't wait to get inside of her.

Leaning back on his haunches, he bared her pussy and hurried to undress himself. He kissed around her navel and from one side of her pubic bone to the other before widening her legs and nosing her slit. Her pregnancy gave her a richer, earthier scent and taste. Opening her pussy lips, he glided his tongue in one long lick along her seam. She lifted her lips and groaned, her fingers sliding through his hair.

"That feels so good," she breathed.

From the day he'd met her, Kendall loved to have her pussy eaten. It made him happy to oblige her, pussy eating connoisseur that he was. Alternating between sucking her clit and licking around and over it, he increased the pace when her hips began to move faster.

"Johnnie!" she screamed, jerking against his lips, her juices dripping down his chin.

He lifted himself above her, resting his weight on his elbows and guiding his cock to her entrance. He sank into her and shivered, the grip of her cunt around his dick pure bliss. Starting a slow, in-and-out rhythm, he closed his eyes, her taste filling his mouth and her scent surrounding him.

He'd never wanted a woman as badly as he wanted Kendall. He just needed to get it right, find a happy balance, make her understand how much he needed and wanted her. He buried his face in the crook her neck, licked the heated skin behind her ear, grunting in pleasure.

Knowing he wouldn't last much longer, he thumbed her clit. When her orgasm washed over her, she gasped, digging her nails into his back.

One, final time, Johnnie thrust into her then exploded inside of her, trembling through his release, then collapsing on top of her. A moment later, she squirmed beneath him.

Only then did Johnnie realize that she hadn't once moved while he'd been inside of her. She'd just laid there, taking him as if she'd had no other choice.

His satisfaction evaporating, he rolled onto his back. "Kendall?"

"Yes?" she responded, hoarse, her just-fucked voice the sexiest sound in the world.

"Did you want me?"

"It doesn't matter," she retorted in a clipped voice. "You had me, didn't you?"

He stared at the ceiling, not knowing what to say to her. "If you didn't want me, you should've pushed me away. I wouldn't have forced you."

"Would you have fucked another woman?"

What a way to look at this situation. If she didn't feel he'd force her, she believed he'd cheat on her if she didn't capitulate. Patience, he reminded himself. She needed patience. Instead of going into a long debate, he answered with a simple, "No."

"You ate my pussy, so I owed you."

Johnnie glared at her and sat up. "Is that how you fucking feel?" he growled, then cursed, not wanting to lose his temper with her.

"I needed to discuss a very important matter and the only thing you wanted was a fuck."

"Kendall—" Drawing in a breath and gritting his teeth, Johnnie grabbed his jeans. More curses fell from his mouth. He *should* be able to show her all sides of himself, and not tip-fucking-toe around her sensibilities. "I heard every word you said. I intend to do my part and rid the world of Spoon and whoever else in the Torpedoes who are involved in this sick fucking shit. What more do you want me to say?"

"Nothing. I don't expect you to say anything. Just as you didn't say anything when Outlaw put me out because his spoiled brat wife threw a fit."

"I couldn't say anything," he explained, striving for patience and understanding when he wanted to kick the fuck out of something. "He's right. You didn't belong in there. You're my old lady. I want you to fit in around here."

"Why?" she said bitterly. "It doesn't matter what I do, I'll never fit in. I'm an attorney. They aren't."

Johnnie sighed. "Bailey's in school. She wants to be a psychologist or something. With the exception of Christopher, all of the club officers are college graduates. Some of the old ladies are, too."

"I don't fit in here."

"You'll never fit in as long as you look at the situation as you do."

Curling up, she turned her back to him. "I didn't expect you to agree with me, since you never do."

"You've been through a helluva lot, but you need to fucking open your eyes. None of us are responsible for what happened to you or your sister. We want to help you—"

"No one will help me as long as Megan forbids it."

"Kendall, for all that's fucking holy, can you not bring Megan up for one fucking conversation between us? You sound fucking obsessed with her. She isn't that fucking important to our relationship."

"She's important to *everyone's* relationship. Because Outlaw makes it so."

"And that's not about to fucking change."

Silence and then a change of subject.

"I'll fuck you whenever you need relief," she offered.

"You have my dick hard as stone with your generous fucking offer," he sneered, fed up with her bullshit for the night. After the arguments with Megan, Val, and Christopher, he wanted a respite. He thought he'd find it here with her. *Wrong!* Now, he needed to fucking rest for the goddamn hundredth round with her tomorrow. "If you don't want my dick in you, keep your fucking legs closed when I try to get in you. Simple as that. I don't need sympathy pussy."

"This conversation is over with," she decreed before lifting herself up and flicking off the lamp on her side of the bed, blanketing the room in darkness.

Weary, Johnnie climbed onto his side of the bed, feeling as if the weight of the world rested on his shoulders.

Chapter 10

A delicate, warm body curled against Mortician and he mumbled, not wanting to move or open his fucking eyes. His head pounded like a motherfucker and not even the silky hair tickling his nose or the bare ass pressed against his dick enticed him.

It took a fucking lot to fuck him up. K-P's death shook him to his depths and he wanted to shove everything aside. He'd been grateful when Val pulled him aside and told him he needed him to make a run.

Mortician had agreed. If he stayed in Hortensia, thoughts of K-P would pull him under all over again and he didn't need to deal with that fucking shit. He *wouldn't* deal with it. By the time he got back to the club, he'd have his head on straight again, not feel so torn up over K-P.

Not feel so lost over Bailey leaving—

Sccccccrrrrrreeeeeeccccccchhhhh!

Aww, man.

Memories from last night seeped into his brain and he growled.

No fucking way—

"Will you Lucas Banks take thee Bailey Andrews—"

No. Fucking. WAY.

He cracked an eye open, gripped a slender hip. He jerked to a sitting position, then fell right the fuck back, his hangover bitch slapping him. "Bailey!" he snarled, shaking her. He still hadn't seen her because if he moved too much he'd blow chunks all over her.

It might not be Bailey. He hoped like fuck it wasn't.

It couldn't be Bailey. He'd...he'd left her, hadn't he? Just gotten on his bike, hugging the Columbia, appreciating beautiful fucking scenery and letting the wind blow through his hair and against his skin. *Alive.*

Alive. When K-P was dead.

All the way to Vegas, he'd held onto the feeling, appreciating his surroundings more than he had in years. In Oregon, he'd relished the serene coastline, feeling the salty breeze of the Pacific before entering Northern Cali, where he'd ridden through the Avenue of Giants. The first time he'd seen a real redwood tree he'd been on a run with Prez, John Boy, Val, Boss and K-P, and Mortician had been in awe that something so fucking tall and ancient could be so majestic. Seeing was believing and he'd wanted to show Bailey...

"I Bailey Andrews take you Lucas Banks—"

FUCK. NO.

Fuck him up the dick with a spiked pitchfork. If he'd married her—

"Bailey, wake up. Did a little Elvis motherfucker marry us?"

The warm body stirred, pushing her ass against his hard dick. Now how the fuck would this shit work? Should he fuck her and risk hurling? Or ignore his hard-on and risk blue fucking balls?

Even though his entire being rebelled at the idea he'd married Bailey—that he held Bailey in his arms—logic told him the truth. He *smelled* her. Her hair. Her skin. Her pussy.

Her eyelashes fluttered against his arm and she sighed, the sound so sad his heart hurt. "Lucas," she whispered.

Mortician gritted his teeth against how she affected him. "Are we married?"

Silence. A heave of her shoulders. And, then, a small nod.

"Get up," he ordered, removing his arms from under her head and making a minute move away from her. "We getting an annulment."

"We've already consummated the marriage."

Of all fucking days for him to have gotten piss-fucked drunk, it was last night, leaving him without the ability to rage and scream. Then, again, if he *hadn't* gotten piss-fucked drunk, they wouldn't be in this fucking position.

"Did I cover my dick?"

"No."

Of course fucking not.

"Did I come in your pussy?"

"Amongst other places," she muttered.

Other fucking places didn't concern him. As a matter of fact, *other* places sounded like music to his fucking ears right about now. Ass. Mouth. Belly. Thigh. Cheek. Fuck, *eye*. Just not the pussy. Coming *in* pussies led to babies coming *out* of them.

"How many times I came in you?"

"Um—"

"Not the other places either. The pussy is my main concern."

She cleared her throat and he cracked his eye open again. Still dizzy like a motherfucker. He squeezed his lids shut. "Bailey?"

"Tw-twice."

"Tell me you got on the fuckin' pill in the two weeks

since we first fucked."

He'd bet she hadn't. The day he'd taken Bailey's virginity, Logan had killed K-P. Birth control would've been the last fucking thing on Bailey's mind.

"Why the fuck you accepted my invitation to ride with me?"

Another sigh from her and more gritting *his* teeth. He felt like a blind fucking mouse, unable to see Bailey's expression, so fucking hung over he couldn't bear to open his eyes.

"Why'd you invite me?"

He heard her hurt and grief and misery, but, fuck *he* hurt and grieved, too. "I just wanted to spend fucking time with you, girl." They'd spent time together, too, and he'd kept his hands, dick, and mouth to himself for the entire three days it had taken to get here. Out of consideration for her, he'd stopped every evening. If she hadn't been with him, he would've made piss stops, then continued on. "Let you know I'm here if you need me."

"You could've told me without asking me to come on the run with you." Tears laced her words and Mortician felt like the dirtiest dog alive. "I'd already told you goodbye."

"You would've been gone by the time I fuckin' got back. You jetting. Remember?"

"D-does it matter?"

Yes. "Fuck, Bailey," he bit out. "Why the fuck…did I propose to you or did you fucking sweat my dick and drag me to the altar?"

She sucked in a breath and a big sob broke free. Mortician balled his fists at his sides to keep from reaching for her. He ignored her tears for as long as he could, the same way he'd tried to ignore her solitary walk next to the motorcycle hearse carrying her dad's body.

The movement on the bed turned his stomach and vomit bubbled up, expanding his cheeks. He tried to swallow it, but the nasty shit kept filling his mouth, a disgusting fucking tsunami, determined to break free.

It leaked from his nose.

Fuck. No.

No fucking choice but to open his mouth and let it all out. Alcohol he'd fucking drank twenty years ago heaved from him, spattering his chest, his dick, his thigh. *Everywhere.*

Fuck, how women fucking put up with morning sickness, he'd never understand. If *he* was a girl, he'd sew his pussy the fuck up instead of bringing up demon vomit every day. And Meggie suffered with it again.

Kendall was fucking pregnant, too. What the fuck went wrong with their dicks? Shooting fucking industrial strength sperm or something? Bailey *better* not be pregnant. He groaned again, his head fucking hurting worse.

Who the fuck was he kidding? He hadn't been lucky *then* and he doubted he'd be lucky *now*.

A cool cloth brushed his brow and he jumped. It slid over his face, her scent close enough to him to remove the smell of stale alcohol, sour food, and bile stinking to high fucking heaven. He might be a lucky motherfucker to have that shit out of him.

"I can help you to the bathroom," she offered in her soft, sweet voice.

Mortician popped open an eye again. His head still hurt but blowing the chunks helped his nausea.

"I have to piss *and* you wouldn't help me one fucking bit. I'm twice your fucking size—" And then some—"I'll squish you like a fucking bug when I fall."

"You might not fall, Lucas."

"Trust me. I *will* fall flat the fuck on my ass."

"Then how are we going to clean—"

"You're not," he barked, sounding like a cruel dickhead. "Welcome to the real fucking world, Bailey. K-P didn't want you with me for a fucking reason. He knew all about fucking Sharper Banks. *Reverend* Sharper Banks, my father," he clarified.

"Your father's a minister?" she squeaked.

"And my stepmother's a whore, so don't fuckin' feel sorry for me."

Blessed silence passed for long moments and Mortician wondered what Bailey made of his statement.

"Okay, Lucas. We can file an annulment. Afterwards, please drop me off at the bus station. I'll be out of your life by the end of the day."

Mortician should've felt relief, instead of feeling as if her words had ripped his heart right out of his chest.

Chapter 11

Mr. Gillson closed the lid on Caroline's casket and Kendall clutched Johnnie's arm, unable to stop her tears, wanting to see her little sister once more. All the things she should've said to her in life bubbled up. Too late. She was gone.

The good died young so they wouldn't be corrupted by the bad and the bad lived to overcome their sins. Or so someone said.

What a crock of shit. Most bad seeds *never* overcame their sins. Case in point—Logan Donovan. He'd been evil right to the very end and, yet, he'd lived seventy-five years. Caroline had been good and only had sixteen years.

Kendall regretted all the time she *hadn't* spent with Caroline. She saw her two or three times a month. Took her to the mall or a movie, or dinner, on a spa date. Perfunctory outings she felt obligated to do as Caroline's big sister.

Mr. Gillson and his assistant began rolling the casket away and Kendall reached out to touch it, her heart breaking. A sob escaped her and she felt dizzy and nauseated with her grief and guilt.

"I'm so sorry, Caro. So, so sorry," she cried.

Arms wrapped around her and pulled her into a warm embrace.

"Kendall, sweetheart," Johnnie murmured, hugging her tight and holding her against his body. He caressed her back and whispered soft words to her.

Hysteria flirted at the edge of her brain. "I need to tell her how much I love her. I don't think I ever did."

"She knows," he reassured her.

Kendall doubted it. She'd treated Caroline as Marie had treated Kendall. Standoffish. As if there were always something more important than her. Kendall knew why. She knew it then and she knew it now.

Worse, if Caroline was still alive and Spoon hadn't taken her, Kendall wouldn't have treated her sister any differently. There would've been no reason to recognize her worth as a family member—a human being—and Kendall would've continued on stewing in resentment. Of a child. Her sister.

She wailed at the realization and trembled. She'd never make up the lost time she could've spent with Caroline. Somewhere, deep down, Kendall believed she had time to overcome her negativity towards her. Caroline was *sixteen*, so time should've been on their side. But no. Time never stopped.

Like Mother Nature, Father Time showed no mercy and took no prisoners. Life happened. Seasons changed. Time moved…forward. Always, always forward.

"Kendall, dear, should you go to the grave?" Charlotte Redding, Brooks's wife, clucked with concern and cleared her throat. "Maybe, you should take her back to…wherever, Mr. Donovan. She *is* in a family way."

Johnnie stiffened against Kendall's cheek at the disapproval in Charlotte's voice. "She's right, sweetheart. You're getting too worked up to go to the cemetery."

She didn't want to go but she had to go. Caroline

deserved better than only a handful of strangers. Heaving in a breath that ended on another sob, Kendall straightened and swiped away her tears. But more fell. "I'll go. I have to go."

Mr. Gillson frowned back at her, hovering near the entryway with the casket. Father Wilkins, halfway down the aisle, glanced over his shoulder at her. She didn't know who'd gotten the church or the priest. Probably, Johnnie, she thought dully. She'd have to thank him. Caroline's body deserved to be blessed.

Kendall's gaze fell on Meggie's. Tears glistened in her blue eyes and the sympathy in her features…Kendall didn't want to think about it. She didn't want to recognize the girl's sadness and exhaustion. Or her paleness.

She wasn't there because she *wanted* to be there. She attended as Outlaw's old lady, meaning she had no choice in the matter. She certainly hadn't known Caroline for her to cry over her. Who cried for a stranger?

Seeing her gaze on Meggie, Outlaw tightened his hold on the girl, his look mocking Kendall. Even, now, in Kendall's grief, he'd side with his wife over her.

Digger and Val stood in the pew behind Outlaw and Meggie. It surprised her to see Arrow sharing a pew with Stretch, Brooks and Charlotte. Derby, president of a support club, and his old lady, Gypsy, were there as well as Bunny and her Dweller boyfriend. A Black guy with a President patch sat next to a pretty Black lady. Other Dwellers—Bowlie, Slipper, Cowboy, and Shady—were there, too.

Most of these people, Kendall didn't know. But they'd come for her and Caroline. Because Johnnie had asked them to.

The thought strengthening her, she straightened her

spine and took her place behind Father Wilkins, not having to look to see if Johnnie followed her.

She just knew he did, his presence strong and sure behind her.

Johnnie kept a close eye on Kendall as the motorcycles accelerated their engines and formed a single-columned convoy with Arrow leading. The hearse and the single limousine in which Johnnie and Kendall rode in divided the formation at the middle mark. Val rode in front of the hearse, Christopher and Digger flanked each side, and Stretch fronted the bikers behind the two vehicles.

When they'd arrived at the church, it had been drizzling. Now, the sun broke through the clouds.

He hated Kendall's distress, and wanted to reach out and comfort her. But he didn't know what to say or do. He didn't want to do anything to further damage her and, yet, he almost wished Kendall opened up to him the way Megan told Christopher everything.

Fuck. Megan again. This time, his thoughts of her were different, though.

Johnnie didn't think he was comparing the two women. He just wanted a way to help Kendall and he couldn't help her if she wouldn't open up to him. He understood her distrust. After all she'd been through, she had every right. Trust issues wouldn't allow her to just readily open up. He even got her bitterness. At times, though, it overwhelmed him.

Four days ago, she'd been pissed because he hadn't come to her defense when Christopher ordered her to leave after Megan's tantrum and offered him her pussy whenever he needed a fuck. Since that night, she'd become even more distant toward him.

He scrubbed a hand over his face.

He couldn't say one fucking word about Megan. If he wanted to walk away from the bar for a minute to talk to any of his brothers, she panicked. He had to stay within her sight at all times.

Trauma and fear instigated most of the demand, but, some of it, was control and manipulation.

"Th-thank you, Johnnie." She twirled the buttons on her black dress, one of the outfits she'd purchased yesterday when they went shopping.

Her voice slivered through the wall he'd began to erect between them. "For?"

She indicated outside. "This. The church. You're giving Caroline a wonderful send off. You got some of the brothers to stay for the services and invited your friends from the local clubs. You—"

Fuck. Sighing, he squeezed the bridge of his nose. His admission would breach his No Bullshit Zone. He should fucking lie to her to have some peace. No. If he had to lie to her to have a relationship with her, he should just walk the fuck away. "It wasn't me, Kendall."

Her nostrils flared, reddening her nose a little more. "Wh-what?"

"It was Megan."

"Mr. Gillson said you'd already planned everything," she chirped through tight lips, raising her chin. "You don't have to pretend she did this for me to forgive her for insulting me."

Johnnie turned toward the window. The breeze fluttered Megan's and Christopher's jackets. The two of them looked great together and made one another so happy. He might never have the same thing. "I'm not pretending anything, Kendall. I didn't do this. Megan tries to make things right for everyone. She talked to me and Christopher and suggested we get some of the brothers to stay for Carolyn's funeral."

"Of course, if she suggested it, it had to be done." She sniffed. "You didn't tell me she'd spoken to you. Where was I?"

"Sweetheart, you have nothing to concern yourself with Megan. She's my sister-in-law and my president's wife."

"Old lady," Kendall corrected.

Johnnie scowled at her. "Be a fucking fool and call her Christopher's old lady in front of him. I fucking dare you."

Kendall's lips trembled and she pinned him with an accusatory stare. "Will you ever put me first? You can't even admit when I'm right, preferring to curse and yell at me than to side with me."

"If you were right, I'd tell you," Johnnie snapped, then regretted it when she started to cry. But, fuck, this was hard.

He needed a fucking drink *and* a fuck. Damn it to motherfucking hell. What the fuck should he do now?

Press Kendall for pussy? Jerk the fuck off? *What*?

Whether he liked it or not, the *only* real relationship he had to go by was Christopher's and Megan's and he felt like a fucking dickwad for it. The history between the three of them and the dynamics of their relationship made it a betrayal to Kendall.

The one thing Christopher did was place Megan ahead of everything and everyone. On the other hand, she knew the importance of the club to him and willingly—the exception being a few days ago—stepped into the background.

Maybe, he'd try to make Kendall feel as if she were the most important thing in the world to him without feeling smothered and obligated. Because, damn it, he *did* care about her. He'd give his life to protect her, give his arm to put a smile on her lovely face.

He clung to the memories of their first night together. Although he didn't like to dwell on the fact that half his fucking brothers had seen her naked, she'd come to *his* bed. Drew him in the moment she'd sat up, heavy-lidded with sleep. He'd wanted her to stay that night, but she'd insisted on leaving because he wouldn't kiss her.

"I saw you with her at K-P's funeral."

What the fuck? "With who?"

Her glare swept her sadness away and his head began to throb. He knew they would argue again.

"Megan," she snarled. "You left me in that pew to help her mother. The minute Megan walked up you pulled her into your arms."

"Are you fucking kidding me?" he managed, dumbfounded. That day had been filled with so many emotions, he barely remembered most of what he'd done. But he remembered that more because of Dinah's fuckeduppedness than anything else. "I did what the fuck Christopher told me to do."

"He goes into fits when anyone looks at her. I know he wouldn't tell you to hug her."

"I wasn't fucking hugging her. Christopher refused to let go of Dinah because the woman wanted Megan. He told me where to situate his wife and to keep a grip on Dinah. I held her fucking collar the entire way down that aisle."

"If you say so."

The car glided to a stop; they'd reached the cemetery. Kendall sat across from him, a dull glower marring her face. A few moments later, he got out and held his hand out to her, smiling at her as he assisted her out.

Instead of returning his smile, she glanced beyond his shoulder and Johnnie turned. Megan stared in the direction of the tallest spot in the cemetery, the rise of green where her father's monument stood.

Frowning, Christopher regarded Megan's profile and the tears sliding down her cheeks. He scratched the side of his head. "We can visit Boss after the ceremony."

She went still, slowly shaking her head. "No."

Without another word, she rushed away and Christopher trailed behind her.

"C'mon on, gorgeous. Let's get you through this ceremony, so you can go back to the club and rest."

Megan was losing weight. Sitting at the bar with Kendall behind it and Christopher, Megan, Val, Digger and Arrow occupying the seats, Johnnie made the observation. She sat on the stool while Christopher loomed next to her, speaking to her in low tones. Little Man and Dinah were asleep, the two baby monitors on the bar in front of her confirming that.

He hoped Kendall thanked Megan for everything she'd done on Caroline's behalf. So far, though, nothing.

"Kendall?" Val held up a bottle of beer. He reeked of Mary Jane, his blood shot eyes and dilated pupils cause for concern. "Set me up with a bottle of Stoli."

She turned and glanced at the alcohol situated within the recessed cabinet below the monitors. Her hips swelled in the jeans she wore, her ass tempting Johnnie to carry her off, caveman-style, to their room.

"Yo', Kendall babe, motherfucker drank all the Stoli," Christopher called. "You gotta get some from the storage room."

"I'll get it," Megan offered, popping to her feet and heading behind the bar.

Before she took two steps, Christopher looped his arm around her waist and dragged her back to her seat. "The fuck you will. 'Til Mort get back, the bar Kendall's territory. You fuckin' sit."

Throwing Christopher a putrid glower, Megan opened her mouth to speak.

"No fuckin' arguments, Megan."

"Don't worry, Outlaw," Kendall responded. Her smile tentative, she gave Megan an inscrutable look. "She can assist me with this. I need to get you and Johnnie another drink anyway."

Arrow raised an empty bottle of brandy. "Me and Digger need another one, too. Let Meggie get Val's Stoli while our girl fix the drinks. Otherwise, Meggie'll have to do up our drinks. Kendall has this down pat, though."

"What's she doing but opening bottles and handing them to you?" Megan retorted, her blue eyes snapping with anger and accusation.

Sighing into the silence, Christopher leaned down and kissed her, then stepped back to allow her room to move. "Get the fuckin' Stoli before I change my fuckin' mind, baby."

"Meggie girl, don't be like that," Digger called, flicking ashes from the cigar Arrow handed to him a little while ago.

After arriving from the funeral home and sharing a brief repast that the women had prepared, Johnnie had hustled Kendall to their room so she'd rest.

He didn't dwell on any type of emotions overlong, but, just from K-P's funeral, he understood the grief and exhaustion Kendall was feeling. He wanted to give her a chance to regroup.

An hour ago, she'd walked into the main room and joined the rest of them, wearing jeans and a white t-shirt. Her hair in a ponytail revealed the delicate skin on her graceful neck.

"Valentine," Christopher blared in the wake of Megan's departure.

"Yo?"

Kendall rested her arms on the bar, breaking into Johnnie's attention directed to Christopher and Val.

"Is he named after St. Valentine?" she asked, low.

He thumbed her lower lip, leaning forward to nip her earlobe.

"Not here," she chastised, giggling.

Pink stained her cheeks and Johnnie grinned, caressing her suddenly too-warm skin.

"It's just us," he protested, stealing another kiss from her.

Megan glided back into the room, Stoli in one hand and Patron in the other. She smiled and sat one bottle in front of Val before handing the other one to Christopher.

Christopher smirked at them, amusement glinting in his eyes. "You know I been drinkin' brews, right, baby?"

Her lashes lowered and she licked her lips. "Just in case you wanted tequila, I thought I'd bring you a bottle."

Laughing, he shook his head and went to her, pulling her into his arms and cradling her head against his chest. "I'll fuckin' take that."

"Jealous much?" Kendall whispered under her breath.

Instead of responding to the tightness in Kendall's voice—what the fuck could he say?—Johnnie kissed her again before answering her question about Val. "Valentine is his real road name."

She drew her brows together, her confusion clear. Irritated that Megan managed to discombobulate Kendall—*all* of them—he swallowed. Kendall was smiling and calm. She was flirting with him and appeared happy the guys were laughing with her. He wanted to see *this* Kendall more and resented Megan's intrusion.

Although Kendall had mixed-up what she'd witnessed at

K-P's funeral, she continually attempted to befriend Megan.

Johnnie didn't have the fucking patience for the petty bullshit.

Kendall gripped his arm and squeezed his bicep ever so slightly as if she believed he wouldn't detect her attempt to feel him up. "How'd he get that name?" she asked with innocence, although mischief flitted into her eyes.

Val belched and scratched his neck. Though his wound was healed, it still bothered him. Every time Johnnie saw Val touch his scar, the spot where the bullet entered Johnnie's chest itched.

"How'd who get what name?" Val asked, belching again and pulling out his cigarettes.

"How'd you get your road name?" Distancing herself from the smoke, Kendall folded her arms and rested against the counter situated near the kitchen door and holding one of two landlines on premises. "Valentine is interesting."

Val puffed his chest out. "I'm such a romantic motherfucker, that's why."

"You mean you a mushy, annoyin' motherfucker over bitches," Christopher piped in. "Shoulda saved my motherfuckin' brain and just called you fuckin' Candy."

Arrow slammed his hand on the bar. "No, Love Letter would've worked better."

"Motherfucking Rose, too," Johnnie inserted, guffawing.

"Fuck all you assfucks," Val growled, red-faced.

"I never knew that's why you were called Val." Resting her elbows on the bar, Megan leaned forward, then glanced back at Christopher. "You never told me that."

"You never fuckin' asked, baby."

She leveled a stare at Val. "You never told me, either."

Val squirmed on his seat, his gaze roaming from Christopher to Johnnie and then between Megan and Kendall. "Meggie, babe…Outlaw fucking right. You never asked."

A low growl from Christopher's throat made Val backtrack.

"I-I mean I-I never volunteered it, babe. Didn't think you'd be interested."

"I'm always interested in you all."

"You're doing just fine, babe," Arrow assured her, puffing at his cigar smoke. "We know you're here whenever you need us, so don't worry about what you don't know. Too much other shit to concern yourself with."

Arrow's answer appeased Kendall and Johnnie wanted to send a few girls to fuck the man's brains out as thanks.

"What's going on?"

Fuck. Of all the fucking voices he expected to hear tonight. Sabrina. He'd fucked her a month ago. The next morning, after she'd used her vacuum like mouth on his dick, his grandfather had visited and his world had fallen apart.

She tapped him on the shoulder. "Hey, Johnnie."

Christopher pointed his bottle of tequila in his direction. "You lucky I'm in a good fuckin' mood."

Of course, Christopher would recognize why Johnnie had fucked Sabrina. She was young—about twenty-two—blue-eyed and golden haired.

Yes, *then*, he'd fucked her because of her resemblance to Megan. However, he'd also had her because she was tall with big tits. Like Kendall.

Megan, who was blushing and throwing him the evil eye and groaning. She knew, too.

For the first time in fucking years—if ever—the heat of embarrassment swept into Johnnie's cheeks.

"Can I have a strawberry wine cooler?" Sabrina asked Kendall and giggled, then pointed to him. "Johnnie'll pay for it."

Kendall's brows snapped together and every stride they'd made tonight in their relationship disintegrated. Bad enough she had to face Megan every day *and* put up with her bratty bitchiness, but, now, one of the girls he'd fucked had to show up.

"Kendall, that's Sabrina," Digger stated, blowing smoke rings from that fucking cigar as if Kendall wasn't about to get bonkers. "Sabrina, Kendall. Johnnie's old lady."

Disappointment drooped Sabrina's features and her shoulders sagged.

"Hi Sabrina," Megan called.

Closing his eyes, Johnnie cursed. He didn't need anything else to ruin the tentative peace with Kendall.

"H-hi."

"MEGGIE!" Dinah screech's trumpeted over the monitor in her room.

Sabrina backed away, fear rounding her eyes. Not that Johnnie blamed her. Dinah sounded like a madwoman.

Kendall remained focused on Sabrina, in another skin tight jumpsuit, this one white, the material so thin her nipples and pussy were not only outlined but visible. "How do you know Johnnie?"

"Let's talk, Sabrina," Megan ordered, clutching the two monitors in her hand. The more Dinah screeched, the more fatigued she appeared. "I asked you a long time ago to stop coming here. Christopher and I are together. I know Johnnie's nice enough to purchase your drinks..." She scowled and her voice trailed off. Dinah screamed again. "Come with me, please, so I can explain this to you for the last time."

Gripping Sabrina's wrists, Megan tugged her toward the hallway, the whore too stupefied to do anything but go along.

Tipping his bottle back, Christopher shook his head. "Fuckin' Megan."

"Yeah, you one lucky motherfucker, bro." Val downed half the Stoli, looking straight ahead. "Not many chicks would do shit like that when they dealing with dickheads."

Maybe, Johnnie deserved Val's shot. Megan didn't have to do what she did. On the other hand, she owed it to Kendall for her behavior.

"Tell me the fuck about it, Valentine." Christopher threw him a tight smile. "Let's go take a walk while Megan get whiny Dinah settled and Sabrina straight."

Although Kendall hadn't said whether she'd bought Megan's story or not, at Christopher's request, her body tensed. "Take a walk where?"

"On the fuckin' moon, babe," Christopher retorted with a snort.

"Shut the fuck up, Christopher," Johnnie snapped, then turned to Kendall. "Outside."

"Can I come with you?"

Come with him? "I'll be right outside, gorgeous. No more of Christopher's women will show up, asking me to purchase drinks for them."

Christopher looked as if he'd jump on him and pound Johnnie to death. As he should, too. Later, he'd tell Kendall the truth about Sabrina—if she really believed Megan's lie. Now, though, he didn't want any explanations upsetting his shit.

"John Boy, you hangin' with us a minute or what?"

Johnnie regarded the plea in Kendall's eyes, her panic. "You're amongst friends. I'll have one cigarette."

"They've been smoking all evening around me. You can, too."

"Yo', Red, that a lil' dig?" Digger questioned.

She shook her head. "I'm pregnant. I shouldn't be around smoke."

"Then get your fuckin' ass from behind the motherfuckin' bar, Kendall," Christopher snapped. "Megan havin' my baby, in case you forgot. We try not to fuckin' smoke too much around her, but we modified the fuck outta our behavior for my girl. Only so fuckin' much we can give the fuck up or change. If Megan have to accept our smokin', *your* fuckin' ass do, too."

Johnnie got to his feet, fed up with how Christopher spoke to Kendall. "Let's talk, brother."

"Ain't a motherfuckin' thing to talk about, *brother.* Check your bitch. Ain't a fuckin' reason why shit always end up an argument in fuckin' regards to her. But it do. *Every. Motherfuckin'. Time.* You wanna pacify her? Fine with my ass. Be one pacifyin' motherfucker. I don't give a fuck. But Kendall ain't fuckin' comin' in here and disruptin' shit." He glared at Kendall and tears rushed to her eyes. "I'm doin' what the fuck I can to make havin' you around this motherfucker easy on my wife. Under-fuckin-stand? But I know Megan, Kendall. The way she fuckin' actin'? I think you know the fuckin' reason. I think you pushin' her buttons some fuckin' kind of way and makin' *her* look like a motherfucker. If that's the case—" He transferred his glare to Johnnie. "Rein Kendall the fuck in, John Boy. We can have Team Megan and Team Kendall. I give you fair fuckin' warnin', Team Megan gonna fuckin' win every-fuckin-time."

He finished just as Sabrina came hurrying out and he beckoned her over.

"Y-yes?"

"Don't set fuckin' foot in this motherfucker again. Now, get the fuck outta my face."

"Jesus, Christopher!" Johnnie exploded, watching as Sabrina stumbled back.

"Club Ass, John Boy," he said coldly. "What the fuck you expect?"

"I expect to have club pussy left for us single motherfuckers to stick our dicks in," Digger said with a scowl.

Christopher laughed. "Overdramatic motherfucker."

"Yeah, dude." Despite the tension, Johnnie chuckled. "More pussy than you assholes know what the fuck to do with hang around the club."

"Let's step the fuck outside." At the door, Christopher halted and turned back to Johnnie while Val and Digger walked outside. Cool air blasted into the warm room. "You comin'?"

Johnnie wanted to go. The conversation outside, away from Kendall and Megan, with weed and alcohol passed between them, would be just what he needed—club talk, X-rated and uncensored discussions about girls, harassing Christopher about his feelings for Megan.

Kendall didn't want him to go, though, and she'd buried her sister today. Sighing, he shook his head. "No."

Christopher nodded, no censure in his face, just understanding. "Okay, John Boy. Have a good night, Kendall."

At Kendall's relieved smile, he decided the sacrifice had been worth it.

Chapter 12

Two days later, Kendall sat in the room, waiting to run an errand with Johnnie. Her heart and head wasn't into going anywhere right now. She wanted to be inside, out of the cool breeze and sunshine, thinking about…everything.

Instead of getting closer, she and Johnnie were drifting further and further apart. Their evening together in the bar had been ruined by Megan and Sabrina. Kendall had been having so much fun, until Outlaw had decided to appease his wife's hurt feelings.

More like jealousy. Kendall saw the way Megan stared at Johnnie. She had Outlaw, but she *still* expected Johnnie to drop everything for her. Just like he had at K-P's funeral.

It had been six days since Johnnie had approached her for sex. That night, she'd said everything all wrong, but he'd come into the room and found her on the website reading up on a very tough topic. She'd wanted to talk to him and he'd wanted sex. While he'd been inside of her, everything that she'd read ran across her mind. All her thoughts focused on Spoon…and Logan Donovan.

Johnnie's grandfather. She didn't believe she held their

relation against him. He'd killed the man, after all. But…God…she hadn't been able to respond to Johnnie's lovemaking and he hadn't realized it until the end because he'd been so lost in pleasure. The words had spiraled out of control once he'd asked her if she'd wanted him.

Did he want her? Did he love her yet? Or was she so unworthy…so damaged and broken…that he'd never love her?

At the moment, it didn't matter. She needed to get up and start living again. She'd survived. Baby Biker had survived. Life went on. Sooner or later, Johnnie, who lived at warped speed with the rest of the bikers, would tire of pacifying her. No one knew she kept an internal count of when Spoon had nearly ruined her. Almost seven weeks now. And she'd just been amongst the lucid and free for about four weeks.

Since she didn't intend to make her home at the MC, she knew she needed to find her backbone and move forward. She needed to put one foot in front of the other and take one step at a time towards her future.

Her mother and sister were gone.

They'd left her behind. To live. Whether or not her mother wanted her happiness was debatable, but Kendall didn't wish to be stuck in her life without reaching for rainbows and grabbing her sunlight.

In captivity, *Johnnie* had been her rainbows and sunshine. Even then, in her drugged up state, she'd looked to something to keep her sane. She'd fought to live.

Caroline's gorgeous face popped into her head and Kendall shuddered, tears rushing to her eyes. She'd fought for Caroline. Not herself. Pretty screwed, when Kendall thought about it.

She swiped at an escaping tear. Now, she had Baby Biker to fight for. She wanted Johnnie, too, but he wanted his club. He placed everything before her. Another thought occurred to Kendall. She needed to fight for herself. She'd be no kind of mother to her child—no kind of woman to Johnnie if they worked through this—if she didn't get her head on straight. She needed to live for them. Step out into the light for them. She'd see to herself later. But Spoon, the asshole, had put both Caroline and Baby Biker in jeopardy.

Her phone started to ring and Kendall's heart dropped. Not just a random tone pealing through the space.

Spoon.

Fear slithered through her and trembles racked her body.

God, why was she shaking? Spoon wasn't anywhere near her. He was on the telephone, unable to get to her to hurt her. She drew in a deep breath, remembered her sister's body. Remembered the baby inside of her and her terror when she'd been at her condo.

The ringing stopped, then started again. Anger surged through Kendall and it felt a helluva lot better than the God awful terror.

She snatched her phone from inside her purse, which sat right next to her, and jabbed the button to answer. "What do you want?" she snarled, sucking back renewed tears. Pent-up resentment and impotent anger steamed inside of her. "Say what you have to say and then don't call me again."

"Who the fuck you think you talking to, you stupid cunt?" Spoon snapped in response.

His anger felt as if it could snatch her through the phone and strangle her. Her breath came in short pants and she barely remembered he wasn't near her.

"Wh-what...I—"

"Shut up, Godzilla, and fucking listen."

Mortification surged through Kendall and all the fear and panic she'd fought so hard to overcome began to build within her again.

"You in with those motherfuckers, Kendall," he barked. "If you don't do as I say, when I get even with each one of those fuckers, I'm going to make you fucking suffer before I kill your two-timing ass."

"I-I-I'm not afraid of you anymore, Spoon," Kendall managed, cringing when he hooted with laughter. Her voice shook as much as her body, so he knew her words held no meaning. To her it did, though. To her, they served as a reminder that she *had* to do this. She had to stand up for herself…stand up to Spoon. At least, over the telephone.

"You're not afraid of me, baby?" Shivers raced through her at his ice-cold tone and nasty snicker.

She shook her head, the fact that he couldn't see her almost not registering, thrust back to that day in her office, out in the open, vulnerable and exposed. Spots danced behind her eyes.

"You'd better be very afraid of me. I don't waste my fucking breath saying shit I don't mean. Those pricks think they got the better of me by taking out some of my boys. I still have an ace in the hand, cunt, and some loyal members to get *you* and them."

She couldn't ever leave the MC. Never. She didn't want to fall prey to him again. "I-I have to g-go," she stammered.

"You hang up that fucking phone and I'm taking aim at Johnnie. He's in the parking area right outside the club as we speak."

No. He couldn't be out there. If any of them saw Spoon, he'd be too dead to make this call. He had to be messing with her head.

"Here's what I want you to do."

"How do I know you won't hurt me?" she whispered, desperation creeping into her.

"You don't. But you can bet on it if you don't do what the fuck I say."

Her head shook in denial, but she knew she'd do it. If she went to Johnnie right now…people would get hurt. *He* might get hurt.

"Are you fucking listening to me?"

"Yes," she pushed out. "Wh-what is it you want me to do?"

"I want their books."

Even as horrified as Kendall felt in that moment, disbelief removed some of her panic. He couldn't be asking her to steal their financial information. She swallowed. "Their what?"

"Their records, you fucking idiot. Are you sure you're a fucking attorney? You're one clueless fucking bitch."

"Not clueless enough for you not to ask me to do this," she flared before she stopped her words.

"I have so many fucking crimes against you that I'm going to personally see that you pay for. DON'T ADD TO YOUR FUCKING BEATING. You hear me?"

Loud and clear. Words flew right out of her head and she gripped the phone tighter. In that moment, Spoon had an unseen gag on her, blocking her retorts.

"I'm going to fuck up their profits from any and everything they do. And you, Johnnie's fucking slut, are going to help me fucking do it."

After that pronouncement, he went silent, then he laughed again. "Speak, pet."

Speak? Yes, he wanted her to speak. He wanted her to agree to betray Johnnie. "I-I-I—"

"Eye-yiyiyiyiyi, what? Other than you sounding like a fucking moron. Send me to the fucking dollar store where you bought your law degree from, huh, Kendall?"

Her brain pulled her back *there* with Spoon and during her captivity. She didn't remember much of being held at that house, but…but…what? She didn't know. She couldn't know. Spoon would hurt her again.

"Fucking talk to me, Kendall. When can you bring me the books?"

The free fall Spoon's words sent her in lulled for a moment, leaving Kendall hanging in a precarious stupor. Somehow, when he asked her to deliver the books, she slammed back to earth. Words formed and logic reentered her head.

"I-I c-can't. Th-they're in Outlaw's o-o-off-fice. Be-besides if I do that, they'll kill me." And Johnnie would hate her.

"If you don't do it, *I'll* kill you."

She had to think this through and be reasonable. For Spoon to kill her, he'd have to get to her. According to him, he observed them, in view of the compound but hidden from Johnnie and the others.

"Wh-when do you want it?"

"Three days, Kendall. Or I'm moving in."

This couldn't be happening. Spoon wouldn't push her back into that nightmare again. He wouldn't risk himself by going against *Outlaw* of all people. Johnnie was more reasonable. Maybe, because he had less to lose. He didn't have a son or a wife like his president. But *anything* that threatened him or the club, Outlaw took as a threat to Megan. He'd do mean, scary things first, then ask questions later. Spoon wouldn't do this. "You're bluffing." She wanted to spit the words but it took all her willpower to push them from her mouth. "I don't believe you."

"I don't give a fuck. You'll find out in three days, won't you, idiot?"

"H-how can I reach you?"

"When I call you in three fucking days?" he said in conversational tones, but ended on a blare. "YOU'LL FUCKING REACH ME."

"H-how will you...how will I get them to you?"

"Let me worry about that. Just do what the fuck I say, cum hole."

The dial tone rose in her ear like a siren screaming a warning. Her scalp started to itch and Kendall raked her nails through her hair in a frantic effort to squelch it.

She wrapped her arms around her waist, rocking back and forth. Johnnie needed to know this. No, he didn't. She didn't trust Spoon not to use her to lure Johnnie out in the open.

He was already in the open and vulnerable to Spoon. As long as he didn't know about Spoon's phone call, he wouldn't act on it. He'd be safe. Besides, she wasn't Megan Caldwell, who ran and opened her big mouth for *everything*. She'd stay silent and keep Johnnie safe.

She'd die if harm came to him.

Her phone lay harmlessly on the bed, but she stared at it like it was a viper waiting to strike. She snatched it up and shoved it into her purse. It had to stay out of sight. Johnnie might scroll through it and see Spoon's number. He'd ask questions and, then, where would she be?

The door flew open and Johnnie sauntered in, his blond hair a little askew, excitement brimming in his silver-gray eyes. "I know, gorgeous," he greeted, raising his hands. "I'm late again. But I'll make it up to you. I promise."

His apologetic tone interrupted her dangerous thoughts and her heart wrapped around his soothing words. He smelled of cigarette smoke and outdoors. Safety. Instead of waiting for her response, he walked to his desk and gathered his keys and wallet.

"Ready, sweetheart?"

Ironic all the endearments he used didn't affect her as soul-deep as all the jabs Spoon gave her. But every word Spoon spat at her touched upon one of her insecurities or fears. Anyone could offer frivolous blandishments. Any woman, *every* woman, was 'sweetheart' to Johnnie.

But where it counted, like right now, and noticing all wasn't right with her mattered most.

"Kendall?" Some of his enthusiasm slipped away and he lifted a brow, studying her intently, noticing *something* now that actually focused on her. "Are you okay?"

She nodded, not knowing what to say. She never knew what to say. In her entire life, she'd never had anyone to go to whom she could request help from. Even the lover who'd gotten her help for her eating disorder had offered. Kendall couldn't remember exactly what had triggered the need to hold everything inside.

Her mother had emotionally and mentally checked out from Kendall when Kendall's dad had been killed. From the age of ten, she'd been lonely and alone. Perhaps, she'd been shy or self-conscious of her height and weight. Even then, she'd been tall for her age and chubby at the time. She...God, the taunts and bullying...no, she couldn't think of that again. Couldn't relive it.

Arms enveloped her and she leaned into Johnnie, resting her head beneath his chin.

"Talk to me. What's the matter?"

She arranged her scrambled thoughts. "I'm...where are w-we going?" she asked instead.

Johnnie disentangled from her and studied her closely. Not seeing anything. *Never* seeing anything. He placed a soft kiss on her lips. "Shopping for a new ride."

"A...a...oh!" They were leaving so he could buy a car? The compound had several vehicles available. With Spoon's threats, they shouldn't venture out so far or anywhere. "Erm—"

"Curb your excitement, love," Johnnie teased with a rueful chuckle. "I've seen more enthusiasm in road kill."

Unable to resist his banter and the sparkle in his eyes, Kendall rolled her eyes and giggled. "Very funny." She could do this. Maybe, she could find her backbone. If Megan could *kill* for her man, Kendall could certainly protect Johnnie in the way she saw fit. She wasn't an idiot. In spite of all the whirlies in her head, instinct reared up and told her Spoon had prepared a trap for her to walk headlong into.

Well, she wouldn't do it. She *would*, however, tell Johnnie about the phone call when she deemed the time right.

"What do you think, Kendall?"

Johnnie glanced at the shiny new Navigator, the chrome wheels and black paint gleaming in the sun. He'd loved his ride and those motherfuckers had shot it up, something else he intended to take out of Spoon's ass when Johnnie got his hands on him. This new one...*fuck*...a fucking beaut. And while he could stare at it for hours and decide upon the proper penalty to fit various infractions against his new Navigator, he needed to keep his head about him around Kendall. Otherwise, the first thing he'd do when he drove his SUV off the lot would be parking somewhere and fucking her brains out.

The breeze hitting her face brought color to her cheeks and her wealth of red hair blanketed her shoulders and back. Her height...her curves...she was like no woman he'd ever met. Her exceptional looks made her stand out wherever she happened to be and her long legs...Pausing, he dropped his sunglasses into place and adjusted his dick. He didn't want to throw her back to a bad place if she happened to see his lustful leer.

As soon as he had Spoon's nuts decorating his rearview mirror, Johnnie would find a way to help her through everything. Just like grief, recovery from trauma had no timetable. Everyone reacted differently and no one would rush her if they valued their well-being.

"Do you like it?" he asked because she hadn't answered the original question.

She shrugged. "It's pretty." Not much different from his old one, except it was a later model.

"Pretty?" he growled, affronted. "Look at her. She's a beauty. But I want your opinion."

"If I don't like it, you won't buy it?" she asked with skepticism.

He laughed. "Of course I'll still buy it, gorgeous."

"Then why ask me?"

Some of his exuberance slid away and he sighed. So much for sweet, gentle Kendall. He didn't want her cowering in fear and she had to get the anger and bitterness out of her. He was the only person she could vent to. But, fuck, he wished she wouldn't argue or find fault over everything. Just because she stayed so unhappy didn't mean she had to ruin his joy.

He drew in a breath and flinched. If only Kendall could find just a part of her old self. "I wanted to know what you think of it."

Kendall rolled her eyes and snorted. "It's a car, Johnnie," she huffed. "What should I think about it?"

Johnnie scraped his hands through his hair and turned away from her. At the passenger side, he opened the door, on edge over Kendall's odd behavior. She jerked and jumped at every little sound, reminiscent of the frightened woman she'd been when he'd kidnapped her.

"Tell me if you like it, sweetheart."

"I haven't thought one way or the other about it. I have more important things on my mind."

He was ready to get a nut off over the vehicle and she said it wasn't important? He scowled at her. "You overthink everything. If you'd just *live* for one damn day, you'd be happier."

"I am living," she flared. "I'm living while Caroline is dead. I'm living while Spoon is hunting for me. I'm living while you insist on putting your stupid club before me."

Johnnie stiffened and removed his shades, all the better to glare at her. He didn't want this to spiral into round fucking two hundred fifty in their daily arguments. Not now. He wanted to get the fuck in his car and drive the fuck off the lot. He wanted Kendall to smile. The Death Dwellers meant everything to him. To insult one of them meant insulting all of them. "Don't call my club stupid, Kendall. It's *me*. If you think my club's stupid, then you think I'm stupid."

"You're about to plunk down how much for this vehicle?" She threw him an accusatory stare. "Children are starving. Families are living on the streets."

"What the fuck does that have to do with anything?" he snarled, starting towards her then stopping, knowing what a setback she'd have with an angry approach from him. Every fucking move he made needed a forethought around her. "Whether I buy this motherfucker or not, children will still starve and families will remain homeless, so what the fuck's your point?"

"It hasn't been a good month since my release from Spoon—"

"Enough, Kendall. I empathize with everything you've endured." A fucking refrain he was getting sick to fucking death of. He understood, but, *Jesus*…"Baby, you've got to stop *counting*. All it does is pull you back. Look to the future. Once Spoon is dealt with and you feel safe enough, go back to work. If you have to count, go forward. Count the days until you return to work. Give birth to Baby Biker."

"You don't understand—"

He approached her and gathered her in his arms. "I do and you're brave and smart and strong. My dream come true. You lost something with what Spoon put you through."

She pushed against him. "My sister and my mother," she yelled, tears rushing to her eyes.

No one better not *ever* accuse him of being an impatient, heartless motherfucker. Her tears tore him the fuck up. He didn't give in to his frustration at her quagmire and fuck something up, though.

"Shhh," he comforted, tightening his hold on her, even though she stood in his arms ramrod straight and angry. "Besides them. You lost you, sweetheart. I don't expect you to just act as if nothing's happened. But, damn it, Kendall." He pulled away from her and paced. "Everything's a competition or grounds for an argument with you."

"I didn't want to come out here with you. If I'm making you so miserable, remember you forced me to come with you."

Johnnie nodded. "I stand by that decision, too. You're rotting away in that goddamn room. Hiding from life. I refuse to allow that to happen."

"It isn't your choice," she spat, her brown eyes darkening.

Johnnie squeezed the bridge of his nose. "You're right, gorgeous." So much for basking in his new ride.

As fucking if.

By the time they completed the transaction for Johnnie's new Navigator, dusk bruised the sky in purplish blue. His stomach growled and he realized he hadn't seen Kendall eat anything today. He must be mistaken. She *had* to eat being pregnant. After urging her to start off in her car while he waited for his second set of keys, she left. He'd brought her car with him with the intentions of trading it in since Kendall would be getting her own new car soon, but the asshole hadn't wanted to offer what Johnnie wanted for it, so back with them it went.

Headlights bounced against his Navigator, reflecting in the paint like shimmering liquid. Fuck, his heart skipped a beat and he fell in love all over again. While he mourned his old ride, the new one…

The salesman handing him the keys and shaking his hand interrupted Johnnie's thoughts. He didn't waste time in getting on the road. Although she only had about a five minute head start, he wanted to catch up to her as soon as possible.

She needed to get a grip.

As she sped away from the dealership in her Mazda, Kendall knew how she handled situations spiraled more out of control with each passing day, but her stress level had gone through the roof. Spoon circled, while Johnnie walked out in the open. It seemed so unfair that he had her on lockdown but he jeopardized his own life, coming and going as he pleased.

Kendall shouldn't have made such a big deal over his purchase. It was *his* money. Or…*whoever's*.

She shoved the unpleasant thought away, pressed her foot on the accelerator. She needed to focus on an apology to Johnnie, so she pulled into the parking lot of a McDonald's and rubbed her temple.

She'd been a first class bitch to him, when Johnnie deserved to have the joy she'd seen in his eyes when he'd been showing her his new Navigator.

Over the past few weeks, Johnnie had lost a lot, too. The man he'd believed his grandfather to be. The man himself.

K-P. His house. Meanwhile, he'd had to accept the fact that he would be a father and deal with Kendall.

He deserved a new Navigator. Kendall knew how he'd loved his old one. He'd told her as she'd redressed his bandages a day after his release from the hospital.

The small blood droplets had concerned her and she'd told him.

"I'm fine," he'd insisted gruffly.

His sadness touched something deep in Kendall, this new, exposed side of him opening her heart to him a little more. He'd gazed off into space and Kendall had ruffled her hands through his hair, loving the texture. Loving him.

"Talk to me," she'd whispered. "You've been here for me. Let me do the same for you."

He'd stared at her, his gaze shuttered, and she would've given anything to know his real feelings for her.

"You're grieving for your grandfather?"

She'd taken a wild guess based on the knowledge that even when you hated someone, you could love them, too.

A huff of laughter. "The man he was."

A muscle had jumped in his jaw and Kendall caressed the spot with her fingertips, wanting to soothe him.

"The man I thought he was," he amended and cursed. "Not that either, Kendall," he said quietly. "That day I found out that Christopher was my brother, my trust died. I fucking hated him and I pushed it all aside. Now, I remember the man from my childhood. The one thing I always held against him was his treatment of Christopher."

He pulled her into his arms and stroked her back absently.

"If I would've found out about his death while he was still in exile, I would've mourned him. I would've had that right."

"You still have that right."

He shook his head. "I killed him. He was unarmed, but I had no choice. He'd stepped out of hell to spend time on earth. Yes, I grieve for him, but I'm so fucking angry. He fucking needed to die years ago. I'd love to know what the fuck Big Joe had been thinking. Why he allowed him to live. I didn't do it soon enough, though. K-P's gone. My house. My Navigator."

Sure she'd misheard, Kendall raised her head from the crook of his arm to stare at him. "Your Navigator?"

A smile broke through the other emotions. "Sexy Sally. I loved her. She was the only one I'd park my Harley for."

"Sexy Sally?" She giggled. "Navigator Sally doesn't have the same ring as *Mustang Sally*."

Johnnie chuckled and pulled her back into his arms. "That song was the last thing on my mind when I named her."

"You're a *biker*," she teased. "What makes you choose an SUV over a hog?"

"In Sally I saw the fruit of my accomplishments if I chose…" His voice had trailed off. "I bought her with the salary I earned as the CEO of the club's medical lab. It's a legitimate business, Kendall. Yes, it's to launder money through, but the money earned there is legal."

"How was that important?"

"It showed me I had options. I could succeed on either side of the law. I realized I chose to be *John Boy*. I hadn't become him to defy Logan or to please Christopher. I live this fuckin' lifestyle because I love the fuck out of it."

A horn honked and Kendall jumped and remembered her location, giving the two cars on each side of her a cursory glance. Any minute Johnnie should be driving by. He'd only needed to wait for keys.

What—

A knock on her window. Kendall turned her head and a scream caught in her throat. Goon. One of her wardens from her captivity. Grabbing her purse, she lunged for the passenger door, rearing back when Guard appeared on that side.

Goon banged on the window. "Open the fucking door."

Glancing over her shoulder, she saw a truck blocking her exit. A car on each side of her Mazda squeezed her in.

The barrel of a gun tapped against the passenger side. Guard had it aimed right at her. She didn't need to look to know Goon had his gun trained on her, too.

"Open the fucking door."

She shook her head and whimpered, crying out at the vibration against her side. When it buzzed again, it got through to her a call came through. Shoving her hand into her purse, she pulled her phone out and saw that Johnnie was calling.

"Kendall, where the fuck are you?" Johnnie growled into her ear.

She wanted to live to hear that sound again. "I'm at Mickey D's," she answered, hoping he detected the fear in her voice. Because she was so very afraid.

"What—"

"I'm counting to three, then I'm blowing your fucking head off."

She'd never escape if she was missing her head. "I needed to use the little girl's room. I-I'll see you at the compound. Bye."

Her fingers trembling, she dropped the phone away from her ear, but didn't disconnect the call. Unlocking the door and gripping the phone, Goon yanked her out.

"Get in the back. Not a fucking word, hear me, slut?"

The muffler on the truck roared and Kendall realized someone moved it away from her bumper.

Guard shoved her into the back seat, then scooted in behind her. Goon slid into the passenger seat and, a moment later, sped away. The two men started arguing over who'd fuck her first, before Spoon arrived, and

Kendall bit back a sob.

All Johnnie's precautions didn't matter. Spoon still found her.

Or, maybe, she'd found him when she'd gone to her condo.

Hopefully, hearing her, Johnnie would realize she was in trouble.

Because, maybe, *just maybe*, if she would've opened her mouth about Spoon's earlier call, she wouldn't be in her current predicament.

By the time Johnnie reached the first stoplight, he saw no sign of Kendall. The speed he'd seen her driving compared to *his* speed shouldn't have allowed her to completely disappear. Not liking his gut feeling, he picked up his cellphone and dialed her number.

After five rings, she answered.

"Kendall, where the fuck are you?"

A pause then a response. "I'm at Mickey D's."

McDonalds? He'd just passed the fast food place.

"What—"

"I needed to use the little girl's room. I-I'll see you at the compound. Bye."

"Ken—"

The call dropped. Or, more to the point, she'd hung up. Muffled words came through the earpiece and alarm bells resounded in his head. Speeding to the U-turn he needed, he redirected his route as his cellphone began ringing.

"I'm on my way—"

"Wh-what do you want from me?"

Her voice seemed fucking far away from the phone.

"Where are you br-bringing me?"

Her panic hit home. The alarm surging into him shocked him, but didn't mitigate his fury. The two combined reached into his soul, a combustible mixture that pulled the worst of him up.

Johnnie and fear didn't associate on a regular basis, but Kendall lived with it every day. Now, she'd gotten into trouble again, but still found a way to call him back. Good girl.

Just as the thought crossed his mind, another one popped up. She'd pay dearly if the almost-obituary subject discovered her subterfuge.

While he didn't appreciate his distress, knowing some motherfucker terrorized his Kendall...*Fuck.* All Johnnie needed was a clue. One clue and he'd have Kendall in his arms again.

"Wh-where's Spoon? Where are you bringing me?"

Mumbling, but the the clear fucking response he needed. Johnnie gripped his steering wheel tighter, sick to his stomach and blind with rage.

He slammed on the brakes and drew in deep breaths, refocusing on his surroundings, growling at the horn honking behind him.

If the motherfucker tailing him had slammed into the back of his new Navigator...

Didn't fuckhead know Johnnie's woman was in trouble? No, of course not.

The honking worked on his ass and he slammed his palm down on his own horn. Diddly Doefuck swerved around him and accelerated past.

"Who lives on Fortification Avenue?"

Buzzard fucking meat, that's who. He had what he needed. A location.

"Shut up, bitch," a gruff male voice ordered. "We're bringing you there and waiting for Spoon. To pass the time, we'll take turns getting to know what your pussy feels like."

A small blessing he was so well acquainted with the city, Johnnie knew Fortification was an avenue had been cut in two, one side having upscale apartments and the other houses dotted here and there. His guess? They headed to a house.

"No!" she yelled.

Flesh met flesh and Johnnie winced, anxious to reach her, wishing he'd spot her in her vehicle or whoever's.

Another hit and his rage burned, threatening to erupt inside of him. Those motherfuckers had touched her and he'd show them no mercy.

He'd go in, kill Spoon and his minions, and get Kendall to safety. Ice picks and pipes would become quite fucking intimate with dicks and asses.

He laughed at the idea, hearing *that* Johnnie's maniacal sound. The Johnnie who was the killer...

Turning onto Senate Road, he drew in a deep breath, remaining within the speed limits. The tree-lined street had wide open spaces and not many houses. A vehicle could be seen a mile away. Like the one just ahead, reaching Fortification and disappearing onto the avenue.

He slowed to ten miles an hour, counted, then followed the route of the other car. Not wanting to give himself away, Johnnie stopped far enough away to not draw attention. Cursing, he parked behind a compact sized car. It would've been fucking a-okay if there'd been a van or another SUV. Not a car comfortable enough just to hold a fucking gnome.

Removing his knife from his boot and his .38 from his cut, he got out and ran down the street, stopping when he reached the house he believed Kendall in. A moment later, Kendall's scream settled his uncertainty about her location.

The sound spurred him to the front door, where he knocked. Such a nice little house, the kind that Zoann or one of her sisters might like.

No answer and another scream made him pound on the door. He could've kicked the door down, but he wanted the motherfuckers to look death in the eye.

"Get the fuck away from that fucking door," a voice yelled.

Not giving a verbal response, Johnnie slammed his fist against the door again, his dagger blade tapping against the wood and cutting into his palm.

"You're going to get your turn, Farmer! Now stop that fucking knocking."

Farmer?

Losing patience, Johnnie kicked the door.

"I'm gonna crush your fucking balls," the Torpedo brother growled as he swung the door open. "What the fuck—"

Johnnie's dagger to his throat stopped his words and the man fell to the floor, gurgling blood and writhing.

He hadn't had his new ride for two fucking hours yet and already he'd get blood in it. Johnnie kicked the dying man and grimaced at the blood he'd sprayed on him—and thus would dirty his new Navigator.

"Yo—" Worm Snack number two started.

Raising his gun, Johnnie fired his gun twice, obliterating Worm Snack's face and deciding to let asshole number one suffer and bleed out. Pity he didn't have time to enjoy the show. Bending, he yanked his knife out of the man's neck, another warm gush of blood spraying his hand. Wiping the blood from his dagger on the asshole's cut, Johnnie got to his feet and went to Kendall, easily discoverable by her sobs.

Naked and tied to a day bed, she shook, tears falling onto her bruised cheeks. Her breasts were reddened and the terror in her eyes told Johnnie he needed to get her away.

"Kendall," he murmured, hurrying to her and cutting the ropes from her wrists and ankles.

She blinked once, twice. Again.

He pulled her into a sitting position and drew her into his arms. "It's me, baby. Johnnie."

It took her a moment, but then she sagged against him and threw her arms around his neck. "Y-you c-came f-for m-me," she sobbed.

"Shhh," he soothed, gliding his fingers through her hair. "Of course I came for you, sweetheart."

"I-I tried to b-be brave. I didn't t-tell you a-about Spoon's c-call, but—"

"Explain later. I have three bullets left and my knife. I know at least two more assholes are on the way." Including Spoon. He fucking wished Mort or Val was with him, then the fucking problem would be solved. "We need to leave."

He refused to risk her safety, so he'd get to Spoon another day.

"Th-they blocked m-my car to keep me fr-from going f-forward. Then th-they g-got into my car and—"

Without a word, Johnnie snatched the comforter from the small bed and wrapped her in it, drowning her babbling out before scooping her into his arms and hurrying forward. "Close your eyes, sweetheart," he ordered as they came to the gore he'd created. "Fucking asshole," he snarled at the sight of the huge pool of blood standing between him and the doorway.

Slushing through it, he made it outside and went to Kendall's car. After opening the door, he placed her in the passenger seat, then went to the driver's side. Keys were still in the ignition. "Thanks, fuckers."

Kendall drew in a sobbing breath. Johnnie clenched his jaw to keep from lying in wait anyway, started the car and circled the moon-shaped driveway. He pulled in front of the compact car. He turned it off and halted, the headlights of another car momentarily blinding him.

"Who…who's th-that?"

The car slowed down and pulled alongside Kendall's car, blocking him.

He debated reversing the car. No. He couldn't. They'd be fired upon before he moved an inch.

"Get down!"

When she didn't respond or move, Johnnie shoved her down. "Stay there," he hissed. Opening the driver's side at the same time, two fucking Torpedoes exited the car. A shot exploded through the night, glass flying everywhere. If Johnnie hadn't ducked, he'd be missing his brain.

Yanking his gun and his knife out just as another shot sounded, Johnnie lifted up quickly, using just enough time to locate one assfuck and aim. The report of the other gun drowned out his.

"Farmer," someone screamed.

Not Spoon, though.

"Farmer," the voice sobbed.

He didn't have time to wait for the man's next move. He'd worked with these motherfuckers before and knew they packed fucking assault weapons. He had one chance and it would be him or assfuck. If he won, then it would be a fucking awesome night in the neighborhood. If he lost, then Kendall and Baby Biker were doomed, too.

The clip snapped into place and Johnnie raised up again, the thought of anything happening to his woman or his baby fucking with his head. The first shot hit assfuck's shoulder and gave away his location. He needed to fucking start carrying his Glock.

Bullets sprayed the back of the car, getting closer as the assfuck walked and fired. Johnnie crabbed his way to the front fender, stood and fired, hitting assfuck's head just as he'd turned to shoot up the front of Kendall's car. Bullets rained into the air as fucker fell, then the night went silent.

Not stopping to think or explore, Johnnie hurried to the passenger side with the shattered window and pulled the door open. Kendall lay right where he'd pushed her, glass covering her hair and back.

In the distance, sirens wailed. Of course, the fucking war zone would attract attention and a concerned citizen would want the cops. He hoped like fuck Kendall hadn't been shot, but he'd have to discover that later, too. He opened the glove compartment and removed the registration. License plates would be a motherfucking problem and would be traced back to Kendall but he'd fucking deal with it. Spying her purse on the backseat, he got it and her cellphone, placed the strap on his shoulder, then lifted her into his arms.

She was warm, vital, alive—and terrified.

In moments, he reached his Navigator with Kendall strapped in the passenger side. She appeared unwounded physically, except for a few cuts from the glass and the hits to her face.

Luck was his to be had tonight. He drove alongside another car and reached the stoplight at Senate Road, just as the cops turned on the opposite side, heading towards the last street along this stretch, where four dead bodies awaited them.

Chapter 13

Shell-shocked, Kendall stumbled behind Johnnie and into the club. If he hadn't had such a tight grip on her hand, she would've fallen, but he stood next to her, her strength in her time of need. During part of the ride home, he hadn't asked her anything nor had he blamed her. Every now and then, he offered a soothing word or inquired about her injuries.

When they'd gotten a good distance from Fortification, Johnnie had pulled the Navigator to the side to check her injuries and wipe some of the blood away from him. He'd picked glass out of her hair and skimmed his fingers over her back in a caress so gentle Kendall wanted to cry. Ghastly visions of her gruesome death had caused her to shake.

After placing the glass in the cup holder, he'd leaned over the console and wrapped his arms around her and she'd held him fiercely, clinging to him, never wanting to let him go. For long moments, they'd remained in each other's embrace and Kendall realized how worried Johnnie had been about her safety when he'd nosed her hair.

"God, I could've fucking lost you, Kendall," he whispered.

In slow degrees, his muscles had relaxed beneath her caresses. He'd tipped her chin up and tasted her mouth in a sweet, gentle kiss that made her cry all over again. A desperate need had wafted from him and Kendall knew he needed to make love to her. She, herself, felt a pang of passion. No, more than a pang, more like a rising tide threatening to consume her, but she'd pulled away and he'd closed his eyes, his lashes fanning his cheeks, his breathing hot and heavy.

"I'm sorry, gorgeous. I know you can't have me right now."

He'd pulled away from her then started out toward the clubhouse.

Now, Outlaw paused in setting a glass of clear liquid—water or 7Up—on the table next to Megan's head, where it rested on her forearms. It was a light crowd tonight. Digger leaned against the bar, whispering to a girl with bone-straight hair.

After pulling Megan to her feet and holding the glass to her lips, Outlaw kissed her forehead, then nodded toward the hallway where the fascinating Grim Reaper mural glared at everyone. Once Megan had left, Outlaw signaled to Digger and sauntered toward them, his tanned skin and bulging muscles exposed because he wore no shirt beneath his cut. He glanced at her. "What the fuck happened, John Boy?"

"The Torps," Johnnie rasped, anger still dripping over his words. "Motherfucking Spoon."

"She o…you okay, Kendall?"

Kendall wondered why Outlaw had gone from asking Johnnie about her well-being to asking her directly. She nodded.

He smiled. "I'm glad. Wouldn't want John Boy goin' off the deep fuckin' end if something happened to you."

Heat rushed to Kendall's cheeks at Outlaw's teasing tone and Johnnie's wink. Digger joined them and handed Outlaw a bottle of tequila, his favorite drink. He held it up to her. "You might want a little? It'll calm you, so you can calm him." He used the bottle to point to Johnnie.

"I'm the calmest motherfucker around," Johnnie said with a tight smile, snatching Outlaw's bottle and opening it. He took a deep swig. "I fucking needed that." He placed an arm around Kendall's shoulders. "As for her, asshole, she can't have alcohol. In case you've forgotten she's fucking carrying my Baby Biker."

Outlaw swept his gaze over her and shrugged. "Baby Biker, huh?"

"That's so fucking poetic," Digger added, chortling with laughter. "We need you around, Red. We don't have cutesy shit like that in our lives."

Johnnie and Outlaw shared a look, then sniggered. "You right, motherfucker," Outlaw agreed, his laughter transforming his features from beautiful to breathtaking.

Comparing them through the sweep of her lashes, Kendall noted Johnnie's similarities to Outlaw. They both had full lips and gorgeous eyes with thick lashes ringing them. Their coloring differed, but their aquiline noses and god-like builds matched, even though Outlaw stood a tad taller.

Outlaw, Johnnie, and Digger laughed, but Kendall hadn't heard their conversation, zoning out to make her parallels.

"I'm glad you and Baby Biker okay," Outlaw said with a smirk.

"C'mon, John Boy, let me get plates for you two. In between chucking her guts, Meggie managed to cook."

"Let me help Kendall to our—"

"No," she interrupted, flattening her palm against his chest. She wanted to talk to Outlaw for a moment without Megan—his extra appendage—growing from his side. "You must be hungry. I'll wait here."

Johnnie glanced at Outlaw and the man sighed. "Hurry the fuck up," he ordered, grabbing Kendall's elbow and leading her to a nearby table.

The moment Johnnie disappeared, Outlaw swigged from his bottle and stared at her.

Kendall knew she looked a wreck between the bruises and the tears and the emotions. She squirmed in her seat.

"The baby okay with the bullshit you went through tonight, babe?"

"Yes," she responded, lowering her lashes. The way he'd yelled at her the other night was a distant memory. "S-so you've forgiven me?"

He stretched his long legs in front of him and folded his arms. "For?"

"The bachelor party."

"Lemme get this fuckin' straight." He lost the nonchalant pose and leaned forward. "You just got fucked up by the Torps and you askin' me about your pussy grindin' on my dick?"

She frowned at his words, flushing in embarrassment. He was being so nice to her, so she'd thought to take advantage of his good mood and clear the air between them. This man meant a lot to Johnnie and she didn't want any bad blood between she and him. "I wasn't asking about that, per se."

"Lemme tell you this, *per se*," he growled. "Drop this fuckin' bullshit, Kendall. I ain't wanted your fuckin' ass then and I especially ain't interested in you now—"

She gasped. "I wasn't coming on to you."

"Don't give a good fuck neither way." He glared at her and snatched his bottle.

"I'm in love Johnnie and I just want us to get along. You were being so nice," she admitted, her lower lip trembling.

"You fuckin' hurt, Kendall. What the fuck you expected me to fuckin' do?"

"I-I don't know," she admitted, bewildered. "I-I just—"

"Get along with Megan and you get along with me," he said flatly. "I don't know how many different motherfuckers gotta tell you that fuckin' fact before you get it the fuck through your motherfuckin' head."

Johnnie walked out of the kitchen and relief settled into Kendall. He balanced two covered plates in one hand and held a bottle of alcohol in the other. He glanced in her direction and his smile faded. Within moments, he reached her side to glower at Outlaw.

"What the fuck did you say to her, motherfucker?"

Remorseless, Outlaw got to his feet. "Ask your bitch. Now fuck the fuck off cuz I gotta see about my girl."

"Christopher—"

As if he had bad hearing, Outlaw gave no indication he heard. He just sauntered away without looking back.

"It takes a bit to get used to Christopher," Johnnie said with a sheepish smile.

"It's okay. I just apologized to him and he-he thought I was hitting on him."

"Let's get to our room." Not responding to her explanation, he led the way and waited until Kendall had unlocked the door before closing it behind them to speak again. "Drop that goddamn bachelor party, Kendall."

He sat the plates down, slipped out of his shoes, his eyes blazing. "If you stop bringing it the fuck up, everyone will eventually forget about it. My fucking preference, by the way. You're mine and I hate the thought that these motherfuckers know all the beauty beneath your clothes."

She'd once had a professor who'd divided the class into defense attorneys and prosecutors, giving each side one week to build a case against the other side. She'd been on the prosecution side and they'd lost. Ridiculous how many holes and inconsistencies their case had now that she thought on it. Her group had gotten the chance at a retrial, although they'd been split into the two opposing sides.

She'd been on the winning team. She'd been able to go back and study the notes, determine what they'd done wrong and rewrite their case. That's what she wanted to do here. Find a gigantic eraser and wipe the slate clean. Start over. Rewrite all her shameful behavior. Her stupidity. "They've never felt me," she whispered finally, wanting to make amends and erase all the ugliness from her life

Johnnie had taken off his shirt and sat on the bed, beginning to eat the meal Megan had cooked. She wished Johnnie ate something she'd prepared.

"I don't know what I would've done if I'd arrived too late."

Kendall didn't know if Johnnie spoke to her or not. Eating shrimp stew, he stared at his stereo system, a bleak look in his eyes.

"You didn't. You saved me."

He glanced at her, his gaze shuttering and nodded, but she saw him withdrawing from her before her very eyes.

Exhausted, Kendall turned toward the bathroom without another word, wishing, most of all, she could rewrite this evening.

"Johnnie?"

Ignoring Kendall, Johnnie continued reviewing the accounts from their legitimate businesses and recording revenue and expenses. As usual, he focused his sole attention on the books. Their biggest source of legal income—the medical lab—was thriving. Two separate factors helped: doctors drew shit out and sent patients for one test at a time, while they *observed* because patients trusted their doctor's advice and followed along. Whatever.

Their laboratory profited from it. Their biggest source of illegal revenue came from their gun-running and their steadiest from the hydrogrows. Line by line, Johnnie maneuvered the numbers, funneled money from their criminal enterprises to their lawful ones and diverted to their Panamanian accounts. They'd begun to pull back from their Swiss accounts thanks to the Feds tightening regulations to increase income to the IRS.

Big Joe had cultivated European relationships and had visited every year to keep shit going. A fucking pain in the ass pacifying motherfuckers to keep their shit protected. The passage of FATCA in 2010 fucked things a little more. All laws were made to find loopholes and get around, but it sure made shit fucking harder.

Johnnie usually took care of the books for the medical lab only. K-P oversaw the rest. Or he had—

"*JOHNNIE!*"

He clenched his jaw, sliding his pencil to the next line, hoping she got the message to leave him alone.

"Johnn—"

Not happening. "What the fuck do you want?"

Her near-death still fucked with his head and mocked every insistence he needed time to develop deeper feelings for her. He scowled at her, ignoring how gorgeous she looked sitting on the edge of his bed, her hair falling around her shoulders and down her back. She needed more clothes. Though seeing her in his t-shirt and pajama bottoms filled him with a sense of possession and pride, she was a woman and women liked pretty, frilly things. Not to mention, the few outfits she had were wearing out because of overuse.

Realizing she hadn't answered, annoyance surged through him. "What the fuck's your problem?"

Folding her arms, she raised her chin, the tears in her eyes beating Johnnie's conscious.

"*You!* You're my problem."

As if she had to tell him. But he wanted to know if his

idea of the problem and hers matched. "How's that?"

Her chin wobbled and her nose reddened. "Since the incident with Spoon's goons you've ignored me."

Yep, right on target with his. But, fuck, how could he explain to Kendall how he felt? Four days ago, he'd been like a little excited boy over his new Navigator. In the span of five minutes, one phone call turned his joy upside down. He could've lost Kendall. Every time he looked at the faded bruises on her cheeks and the healing cuts caused by the shattering glass, his stomach turned.

Every time he remembered he'd had to leave before he could pull Spoon's intestines out through his nostrils, rage filled him. And, every time, he listened to her sobs—in the middle of the night when she thought he slept—helplessness overtook him.

He wanted to apologize for being so goddamn careless with her safety. Then, he'd have to remember she could've been raped and murdered. If she hadn't been smart enough to call him and leave her phone line open—

Christopher had long ago had a tracking device installed in Megan's phone and on her car. Johnnie and the boys had ragged on him for being fucking overprotective and even more fucking obsessed. Now, though, Johnnie understood and he believed Christopher's need to know Megan's every move was a good plan to follow.

"Look, gorgeous, in a couple hours, you'll have me for the rest of the evening. I promise." She was with him, safe, so he needed to minimize his assholery. "I'm a little preoccupied right now." He nodded to the laptop Christopher kept under lock and key. The fake one sat on top of the file cabinet in his office. "I'm not ignoring you on purpose."

Kendall bowed her head, her sadness raw and real. Her

flame-colored hair draped one shoulder, streaming down to her tits. She wore no make-up and, though it allowed a clearer view of her pain, it also made her look vulnerable. "What else is new? And you are ignoring me on purpose."

Johnnie sighed with regret and guilt and pushed away from his desk. "All right, Kendall. You're right," he admitted. He glanced at his watch. "I'm taking a fifteen minute break. Then I have to get the books finished and talk to Christopher. Deal?"

Twisting strands of hair around her finger, Kendall weighed his offer, then nodded. "Deal."

He sat beside her on the bed and put his arm across her shoulders, pulling her against him and kissing the top of her head. Her breasts pressed into him and her scent filled his nostrils. He wanted her so bad, but fuck if he knew how to approach her. She seemed perfectly satisfied with the current state of their relationship—sexless.

Releasing her before he threw her back and ravished her, Johnnie leaned forward and placed his elbows on his knees. "So what do you have to say?"

"I haven't been to an OB yet," she began quietly. "I don't have much of anything to wear and I'm already looking like a stuffed pig in the couple outfits I do have."

Johnnie calculated in his head how many weeks she should be and frowned. Although he understood why she hadn't seen a doctor yet, he wanted their baby healthy. Certainly, Kendall did as well, but she had so much to handle—so much she feared—that the need for a first prenatal visit eluded her. He squeezed the bridge of his nose, hating how much he had to limit his responses as much as he had to ignore his physical needs because of Kendall's fragile state. Fragility exacerbated by the events of four days ago.

He glanced at her and smiled. Her brown eyes held no sparkle, only uncertainty. "You don't look like a stuffed pig." He meant those words. Her skewered perception of her body served as further proof that she still needed a lot of patience and understanding. As a matter of fact..."You barely eat, sweetheart, which isn't good since you're eating for two."

She dropped her gaze, her nostrils flaring. "I'm trying to keep my weight gain to fifteen or twenty pounds. It'll be easier to lose it that way. I've already gained four pounds," she whispered, her brow creasing.

"How many pounds do you weigh?"

Biting down on her lower lip, she wrung her hands together. "You aren't supposed to ask a woman her age or her weight."

He chuckled at her. "And you're not supposed to discuss religion or politics in mixed company. All of it is bullshit. You are who you are and if others can't handle it, then fuck them."

She licked her lips and Johnnie groaned, his dick hardening. What he wouldn't do to have her pretty mouth sucking him off. "I'm ashamed to admit how much I weigh."

Discreetly adjusting his cock, Johnnie shrugged. "May I take a guess then?"

Wide, fearful eyes met his but she gave him a reluctant nod and he grinned, unable to deny the pleasure he felt at the amount of trust she placed in him to allow him to guestimate her weight.

Grabbing her hand, he kissed each finger and gave her a tender smile. "Stand up," he ordered, though he remained seated.

She didn't question him. She just followed the command.

He took in her shoulders, back, and narrow waistline, ending at the gorgeous globes of her ass. All he needed to do was slide the pajama bottoms down to bare those delicious cheeks. She shifted her weight and Johnnie refocused on his perusal. That beautiful ass flared into round hips and endless legs. Placing his hands on her hips and turning her, her tears should've surprised him. They didn't.

He cleared his throat, but didn't comment. Nothing he could say, anyway. The best way to help her was showing her he accepted her 'as is'. Studying the front of her body would be much harder on his resolve. Ignoring her luscious tits served as the biggest challenge. They were fucking perfect, a fucking wet dream bouncing to life.

Sliding his hands beneath her top, he traced her waistline and flicked his thumb over her soft skin, pressing a kiss beside her navel. She tensed and he laid his forehead against the pillow of her breasts, his heart pounding and his dick hurting.

For the briefest moment, he thought about finding relief with some Club Ass, but he'd promised Kendall they'd make their relationship work. Infidelity couldn't be in the equation. He'd gone ten days without sex—a long time for him—and he could go longer. As long as she needed. He kissed her belly again and released her hips, raising his head. He reached up and thumbed her tears away.

He'd gone down this path about weight with her. Now, he had to see it through. If he offered an inane compliment such as *you're gorgeous no matter what size you are,* she'd die a little more inside. If he guessed too far below her weight, she'd feel self-conscious. If he blurted a number too high, she'd believe herself fat.

And if he told her, he enjoyed *all* types of women…well, fuck, he didn't know what. Spoon's assault had stunted her feelings and reactions.

Drawing in a deep breath, he met her gaze. "Well, gorgeous, my educated guess is somewhere between one hundred thirty and one hundred fifty." Chicken shit way out, but he worked with the tools he had.

Silence.

He scrubbed his hand over his face, mentally adding expressionless to her silence.

"I-I'm one h-hundred thirty-nine p-pounds."

"You're six feet, Kendall," he pointed out as calmly as he could.

"I was once one hundred sixty pounds," she sniffled.

"You're six fucking feet," he repeated again, incredulous. "You *should* be a hundred fifty, a hundred sixty pounds."

She covered her face with her hands and shook her head. "I was huge! No one liked me. No one wanted to be with me."

Johnnie stood and pulled her into his embrace. "Kendall, love, sometimes to have friends you have to show yourself friendly."

"I did! In school, boys my age laughed at me and called me all kinds of names. They went for the blonde girls. The delicate girls."

Like Megan. Fuck. Now he got why Kendall disliked Megan so much. It might've been subconscious on Kendall's part, but she took out on Megan what she'd experienced in her youth.

"I had to sleep with older men. They were the only ones who wanted me. My first lover was one of my teachers and we did it in his classroom so I could bring up my grade."

"That's in the past," he reminded her, harsher than necessary. The idea of some old fuck using a vulnerable girl pissed Johnnie off. He restrained himself from demanding a name to add to his *You're Fucked* list. The Torpedoes took top priority on his latest list, anyway. "Don't dwell on that, sweetheart."

She had too much other shit from the present she dwelled on. He didn't need her dredging shit up from the past to make her even more miserable.

"When was the last time you ate?" he whispered, kissing her temple and her forehead. He moved to her hairline and she shivered.

"I had toast and juice this morning," she responded, breathless, not immune to him.

Her reaction pleased him.

"You need to eat." So did he but it had fuck-all to do with food. His dick jumped and he knew she felt it because she squirmed against him. Her movement made him grit his teeth. "Baby Biker has to eat, too." So did Daddy Biker. Her body melted against his and he groaned. Not considering his next words, he placed his hands on each side of her neck, the feel of her hair like silk against his fingers. If he didn't fuck her soon, his dick just might explode. Moderating his words from X-rated to boring, he said, "I want you, Kendall."

She heaved in a breath as if he'd just proposed they listen to a fucking law lecture. "Okay," she mumbled.

Her defeated tone served as a bucket of ice thrown over his body. He wanted her to want him, too, not open her legs to him because she felt obligated. He swallowed and stepped away from her, regretting his words as high color slid into her face and uncertainty darkened her eyes.

He gave her a half-smile and looked at his watch. "Rain check, sweetheart. Fifteen minutes went by five minutes ago." Turning, he walked to his desk and shut the lid on the laptop, already sleeping from lack of use. He gathered the bank statements he'd downloaded and printed and headed to the door. "I can have food sent to you or you can come out to the main room." Which she hadn't ventured into in four fucking days, so he already knew her answer.

"Wh-where do you want me to be?"

That answer shocked the fuck out of him and halted

him. He turned. She looked so alone. So vulnerable. Every stride she'd made and every fear she'd overcome in the past several weeks had been wiped away the other night.

"Wherever you're most comfortable. I won't be in there with you because I do need to discuss our accounts with Christopher, but no one will hurt you."

Kendall wanted to stop Johnnie and invite him to bed, but she couldn't do it. Not after their discussion about her weight. And not after the other night, which brought back the horror of Spoon's assault. But she had no one but herself to blame. She shouldn't have underestimated Spoon. Because he'd called her on the phone, she'd believed she had the upper hand. Instead, he'd gotten high, which, in turn, led to his fury at what he considered her blatant disrespect, so he'd sent his boys after her. And they'd caught her. Her only consolation: she hadn't gotten Johnnie, Outlaw, or any of the others involved by relaying that Spoon watched them. He'd also followed her and Johnnie. She didn't want to think what would've happened if, for any reason, she'd ended up returning to the compound with Johnnie in his new Navigator at first.

They would've been killed.

She sank onto the bed and hugged her waist.

All she wanted to do was hold Johnnie and never let him out of her sight. If she took him in her arms, though, and allowed him to make love to her, she doubted she'd be able to respond. She believed she'd just lay beneath him, unable to separate her terror of being with Spoon and her desire to be with Johnnie. Her inability to have sex with him concerned her. She'd be devastated if he took his needs to another woman.

Maybe, she shouldn't have spoken when he'd told her he wanted her. Maybe, she should've given him a little smile and let him have his way with her. This was *Johnnie*. He'd had her several times since her assault. He'd know what he could and couldn't do with her. He'd—

A knock interrupted her thoughts and she raised her head. "Come in," she called morosely.

Bunny stepped in, carrying a tray with three sodas. Megan trailed behind her and irritation replaced everything else. Megan. Pale, exhausted—and still gorgeous. Every blonde beauty those boys had spurned Kendall for. Nineteen years old. Probably one hundred pounds soaking wet and hovering about five feet or five feet one. Worshipped by everyone.

And currently marching to Kendall with a Styrofoam plate filled with food. She held it out to her and smiled. "Johnnie said you needed to eat."

"And what Johnnie wants from you, Johnnie gets," she snapped, grabbing the plate from Megan, who bristled.

"Kendall, I don't know—"

"Babe," Bunny interrupted, taking Megan's hand and guiding her to the chair Johnnie had spent half the day in. "Sit." She sat a can of 7Up in front of Megan and popped it open. "You have to check on your mom in a little while, so rest while you can."

Sipping from the can, Megan threw Kendall an evil glare.

Bunny laughed nervously. "Kendall, there's a fork already on your plate. If you don't mind, me and Meggie wanted to hang out with you for a few."

"A few what?" Kendall responded sulkily, picking up the fork and stabbing a potato wedge before shoving it into her mouth.

Megan snorted. "A few days."

Bitch.

"Um, we've been wanting to check on you for a couple days." Bunny paused and glanced at Megan, but the girl had a blank look on her face and her blue eyes gave nothing away. "We've been so worried about you."

An uncomfortable silence fell into the room and Kendall concentrated on her food.

"Kendall," Megan began coolly, "I want to know if you need anything. Even if you just need someone who'll listen, I'm here." She drew in a deep breath. "I really am. We haven't gotten off to the best start, but I understand what you're going through and—"

"Understand?" Kendall interrupted, affronted that girl would even *think* to compare Kendall's horrible experiences to hers. Whatever she'd gone through didn't come close to Kendall's. Every time she saw Megan Caldwell, each of Kendall's insecurities waylaid her. "I doubt that."

Tears glinted in Megan's eyes and she cleared her throat. "Maybe, you should ask me," she said softly. "You might be surprised."

She had no intentions of asking Megan *anything*. Instead of answering, she tasted the corn. She'd allow herself four of the ten potato wedges and two forkfuls of sweet corn. She absolutely wouldn't touch the cherry pie but she would take a bite of the roast.

As she followed her plan, ways of making up her lack of sex drive to Johnnie bounced in her head. She couldn't decide on anything until something Bunny said caught her attention. Regretting not being able to eat everything, Kendall sat her plate aside.

"A barbeque would be great," she put in.

Bunny and Megan looked at each other, then both of them turned to her.

Bunny grinned. "Yeah, Meggie thinks the guys need a break from all the intensity."

Kendall shifted on the bed and scooted higher, leaning against the headboard. "Are you sure you can handle that? I mean you haven't been feeling good."

"I'm fine," Megan mumbled, shifting her gaze away. She sounded hurt and sad, but Kendall refused to entertain the drama queen. "I just think—"

"You've been running yourself to the ground with your mom," Kendall continued, taking a wild guess. She didn't know what Megan had been doing. "Handling a big barbeque might not be so wise. Right, Bunny?"

Bunny frowned but gave a reluctant nod. "Yeah, babe. Um, Kendall's right."

Megan stiffened. "You and Gypsy and the others will help me and—"

"I doubt Outlaw will like you straining yourself."

Tossing her hair over her shoulder, Bunny lifted a brow at Kendall. She knew Bunny sat on the fence about Kendall's genuine concern for Megan.

Perhaps, her motives lacked sincerity, but, Kendall wanted Johnnie and the other brothers to see she had what it took to look after everyone and arrange events. Be the go-to old lady, so to speak. Until she convinced him to leave the club, she wanted Johnnie happy with her ability to lead.

"Okay," Megan agreed. "We can plan the barbeque together."

Together? "Erm, I didn't mean us doing it together. I'd like to take the entire burden off your shoulders and do it myself."

"Babe," Bunny started, "um, I mean…um…have you ever planned something like this?"

No. "Who hasn't?" She sniffed. Kendall knew how to cook some things, but she certainly didn't know how to barbeque. How hard could it be?

"Meggie…" Bunny began, her brow furrowed. "Babe. Why don't you let Kendall do this one? I-I mean, your days are a hit and miss, right? Sometimes you don't throw up and other days you can't stop. I mean—"

Megan's shoulders drooped and her hurt deepened. "Fine. I'll do one of the meats."

Bunny smiled brightly. "Yeah, babe, with you helping us, we do up a mean brisket."

"Okay, then," she mumbled, getting to her feet and picking up her can. "I need to see about Momma, so, if you'll excuse me."

As she passed by Bunny, the woman grabbed Megan and hugged her. "It's going to be okay. I promise."

Kendall rolled her eyes. When would these people ever learn that *they* were the cause of Megan being such a snotty little bitch? As for the brisket, Kendall would shut her out of that, too. If none of the others wanted to show Megan that everyone suffered disappointments, Kendall would.

After all, she shouldn't be the only one to be so disillusioned with life.

Chapter 14

Mid April brought in clear, sunny skies, mild temperatures, and blooming flowers. The trees in the wooded area behind the clubhouse thickened with green leaves.

The body count rose. Torpedoes—6. Dwellers—0. But Johnnie didn't expect their luck to continue, which had everyone on edge. Spoon left his brothers out in the open, prime targets for them. On the other hand, his underground activities must include plans for a big retaliation.

This evening, they were barbequing. Tables, containing brisket, ribs, sausage and hot dogs, were set up on the north side of the property. Coolers overflowing with beer stood in front of the tables. The women laughed and talked amongst themselves.

Johnnie glanced in the direction of the fence, where a blanket holding one woman in particular lay. Megan. Boycotting the picnic because Kendall had suggested and arranged it. She had Dinah and Little Man with her, one as much a child as the other.

Since K-P's death, Dinah had lost all touch with reality and Johnnie knew the constant care Megan gave to her mother wore on her. He also knew nothing would interfere with Christopher's determination to make the Torpedoes pay for what they'd done. Christopher wanted their heads, more to avenge Megan's house than anything else. So, for the time being, he allowed Megan to exhaust herself with Dinah and gave her a pass on her bitchiness.

Johnnie wanted to shake her for her inexcusable and abominable behavior toward Kendall. On the other hand, he valued his life too much to either say anything to her *or* put his hands on her, so he followed Christopher's lead and let her attitude pass.

Little Man squirmed on her lap and irritation surged on her face, the wind ruffling her golden hair and the baby's black curls. He whined and Christopher materialized from wherever.

"Hey, boy." He bent and plucked Little Man from Megan's arms. "Stop givin' your Ma a rough time."

"He's teething, Christopher," Meggie said quietly.

"Okay, baby. Just rest with Dinah. I'll take him for a little while."

Megan glowered in Kendall's direction and pressed a hand to her belly. Did all pregnant chicks do that? "If you don't mind, I'll take him and Momma inside."

Christopher sighed and handed his son over. "Okay, Megan.

"Johnnie!" Kendall called, drawing his attention away from Megan's perplexing behavior.

Without delay, Johnnie reached Kendall's side and obediently tasted the brisket she held out to him. His nostrils flared at the charred exterior and tough, bloody interior. Forcing the food down, he smiled. "Who cooked?"

Amusement lit Bunny's eyes and she pointed to Kendall. A tall, busty girl, Bunny had been dating one of the regular brothers for almost four and a half months. She was one of Megan's friends trying to make Kendall comfortable.

"It's delicious, isn't it, John Boy?" she asked, giggling.

Chuckling at Bunny's mischief, Johnnie winked at her. "The best I've ever tasted."

Instead of laughing, Kendall bristled. "I put a lot of work into this meal," she said tightly. "Instead of making fun of me, you should consider this is my first time and I was trying to do something special."

Bunny's amusement died and uncertainty rose up. "Hey, babe, I didn't mean any harm."

Two weeks had passed since Caroline's funeral. That coupled with Kendall's most recent attack made her willing to leave their room only in the evenings to tend the bar. With the out-of-town members gone and with the Torps situation, not much went on at the clubhouse. Kendall wasn't needed behind the bar, but they all agreed it might help her to feel more accepted.

The more they tried to make Kendall feel welcomed, the more pissed Megan became.

Kendall glanced between him and Bunny, frowning. She bent slightly, to make herself not as tall. She'd never said it but Johnnie noticed whenever Bunny or one of the other old ladies were around, she did it. The tallest woman there, her height bothered no one but *her*.

"I have to use the bathroom," she said stiffly and walked off.

Bunny's eyebrows drew together and she tugged at the ponytail she'd fashioned in her hair and swept to one side.

An embarrassed laugh escaped his rising anger. "They're setting a bad example, aren't they?"

"Who?"

"Kendall and Megan. Who else?"

Bunny tugged harder and scrunched her nose. "I-I'm not picking sides or anything and…and Meggie probably *could* be a little more understanding." She paused and glanced around, visibly relieved when she saw Christopher talking to Val.

"No shit. She could be much more understanding. Kendall's been through a lot and we all rallied around Megan when she needed us," he fumed.

"Yes," Bunny agreed, drawing the word out and lowering her lashes. She licked her lips, opened her mouth, then thought better of it. "Maybe...maybe, you need to look at the situation a little closer." Not adding anything more, she turned and headed for her old man.

Sounds of retching and a screaming baby reached Kendall before she opened the door with the sign *Chicks* on it. Except for Dinah Nicholls, who sat at one of the tables staring into space, the clubhouse was deserted.

Kendall hovered in the doorway, a part of her wanting to reach out to Megan and, at least, hold her little boy while she threw her guts up, but she couldn't do it. Especially not now when the barbeque designed to showcase her worthiness was such a miserable failure.

She backed away and stared at the door. Maybe, she should've accepted Megan's offer to cook the brisket, but, just as she intended, she'd shut her out, convincing Bunny and the others Meggie needed rest. While *they* declined Megan's offers out of concern for Megan, to Megan, it seemed as if they were spurning her.

Now, because of it, Kendall's barbeque was a disaster. Tension hung in the air like a poisonous cloud. Instead of having fun, everyone danced around...Megan.

It frightened Kendall to think what might happen if Johnnie discovered her role in Megan's behavior. He kept his distance from the girl because he knew Kendall needed his show of loyalty. He stayed at Kendall's side in the evenings and called everyone over to introduce her, if they didn't already know her.

He bent over backwards to make her feel happy. When she wondered if she had happiness in her. She didn't know how to be happy and doubted she ever had.

The door opened and Kendall jumped back. She'd been staring at the door like a dork, not moving one way or the other.

"Ma ma ma ma ma," Little Man chanted around screams, yanking at Megan's hair with one hand.

The entry door opened and Meggie gazed in that direction, a touch of happiness lighting her eyes.

"Meggie girl." Mortician smiled.

She sagged in relief. "You're back," she said, then glanced around. "Where's Bailey?"

Mortician scooped Little Man out of her arms and nodded toward the door. "Out there." Little Man grabbed Mort's dreads, stuffing his little fist in his mouth. "Yeah, boy, teeth hurt like a motherfucker when they coming in."

"Mortician!"

"Aww, Meggie, girl, I'm telling the truth." He gave her an under eyed look. "You didn't open your mouth, did you?"

Megan rolled her eyes. "You know better than that."

"Go to bed," he said gruffly. "I'm gonna talk to Prez."

"No, don't. I…please…I don't want to hurt him. I'll…I'll work through it. I…Mr. Gillson just shocked me and I knew what Christopher…how he…my daddy—"

Instead of allowing Mortician to continue and coddle Megan over a grave mix up and feeling left out, Kendall stepped forward and hugged the man, encompassing the baby as well.

"What's up, Red?" he asked, hugging her back and kissing her cheek.

"E-excuse me." Megan squeezed past them and went to

her mother. She whispered something to her, then headed for the exit.

"Meggie!" Dinah screamed the moment she lost sight of her daughter.

"Yo', Dinah," Mortician called, sauntering over to the woman and placing his hand on her shoulder. She jumped. "She coming right back. She getting Bailey for me. Remember? K-P's daughter?"

Dinah trembled, then screamed, encouraging Little Man's hollering.

Kendall decided Outlaw had radar where his wife was concerned. He barreled through the kitchen door—since that way led to the barbeque—and paused to grin at Mortician.

Outlaw slapped his hands with Mortician's. "Bout time you got back, motherfucker."

"You missed me, Prez?"

Outlaw set his tequila bottle down. "Fuck yeah." He lifted Dinah into his arms and tightened his hold when she started struggling. "Get the fuck to work. Bring me a fuckin' fizzy special." He nodded to Little Man who struggled as much as his grandmother. "Don't fuckin' drop my boy. Where Megan?"

"Outside," Mortician responded.

Pausing, Outlaw lifted a brow. "For?"

Mortician shifted Little Man and scowled. "To get fucking Bailey."

Outlaw stared, speechless and shocked. "Kendall, get your man, Digger and Val in here," he ordered after a moment, hooting with laughter. "Time to pay up, motherfucker."

Not saying anything else, he carried Dinah away, cursing roundly at another ear-splitting scream.

"Fuck." Clutching Little Man, Mortician stomped behind the bar. "C'mon, now, boy, give Uncle Mort a break."

By the time Kendall went through the kitchen and rounded up Johnnie and the others, Little Man's whining continued, Bailey and Megan sat at a table and Outlaw was walking back into the room, carrying a Styrofoam cup.

Kendall intercepted Johnnie as he headed to their table and put her arms around his waist, leaning into him to kiss him. Her body responded to the small contact. She wanted him so badly.

Val reached Bailey and kissed her cheek. "How are you doing?"

"Idiot," Megan chirped, glaring at him.

He chortled with laughter. "Maybe, Meggie, but I'm a fucking idiot about to be 5Gs richer."

"What are they talking about, Johnnie?" Kendall asked, wondering why Mortician hadn't shared the 411 on Bailey with her.

"A fucked up bet, sweetheart." He stepped away from her and smirked at Val. "You're not the only one, fuckhead. I'm part of the fucking bet, too."

"What bet?" Kendall tried again.

"I'll tell you about it in our room, gorgeous," he promised in a distracted manner, caught up in the insults flinging back and forth between them.

Megan stood, pulling Bailey up with her. "C'mon. Let's leave them to trade insults."

"Okay," Bailey agreed, starting behind Megan.

"Hey!" Outlaw yelled. "Ain't you fuckin' forgettin' somebody, baby?"

A frown creasing her brow, Megan turned. "Who?"

He pointed the bottle in Kendall's direction. "Her."

Instead of inviting her back, Megan shook her head. "She has her barbeque to preside over, Christopher," she hissed and rushed away.

An hour later, Johnnie glanced over his shoulder in the direction of the pool tables, where Val, Digger, Christopher and Stretch flanked Mortician. Kendall stood behind the bar, though, and she didn't want him out of her reach.

Despite how badly he wanted to shoot the shit with the guys, Kendall feeling safe took precedence.

He felt bad on her behalf. Her first event—a bust. He gulped down his beer, knowing the problem. Megan. Although he didn't know what Bunny meant, he didn't appreciate Megan's latest infraction.

Kendall leaned on the bar, directly in front of him, aiming for a kiss, which he was happy to give to her. Maybe, later, he'd try to make love to her. He didn't want to set her off, but he needed to be inside of her. Jerking off only went so fucking far. He caressed her cheek.

"I want you," he whispered, wishing she understood just how much.

Her eyes lit up and a flush stained her cheeks. "I want you, too."

"John Boy!" Christopher called. "Get the fuck over here. I want to talk to you, then leave you the fuck alone to get to my gorgeous fuckin' girl."

Mortician whispered and they laughed, even Christopher.

"You fuckin' right, motherfucker," he said with a smirk.

Glancing between Kendall and the guys, Johnnie felt left out. He knew they were being lewd and crude, and he wanted to join in. Kendall needed him, but, fuck, if he didn't want to spend some time with the boys.

"Johnnie, come the fuck over here," Val demanded,

laughing like a lunatic.

Irritation flashed in Kendall's eyes but she covered it with a wink at Johnnie. "I call dibs on him."

"Don't be like that, Red," Mortician complained.

"Just a few minutes, Kendall." Johnnie planted another kiss on her lips. Getting to his feet, he hurried to the pool area.

"Johnnie, Johnnie, ever so tall, who's the fairest one of all?"

Kendall's words took Johnnie aback. She had issues to work through, yes, but her need for attention got fucking exhausting. More than that, her need to compete with Megan. Although the very thought was blasphemous because of Megan's huffy attitude lately, Johnnie suspected Christopher calling his wife gorgeous set Kendall's insecurities off. Again.

"My fuckin' wife," Christopher answered into the sudden silence.

Kendall's face fell and anger and frustration stole away his anticipation of talking amongst his brothers.

"Shut the fuck up, Christopher," he growled and paused his advance toward the pool tables.

"Don't worry," Kendall responded with a forced smile. "He's her husband. He had to say that."

Mortician tipped back his bottle of vodka, then snorted. "Yo', Red, you don't learn, do you?"

Balling his fists, Johnnie glared at him, remembering he needed to take Mortician aside and warn him to keep the fuck away from Johnnie's woman. "What the fuck's that supposed to mean, asshole?"

"Just what the fuck I said, John Boy," Mortician snapped, his body tensing up. He glowered between Johnnie and Kendall. "Red need to stop fucking competing with Meggie. Life'll be much fucking easier around this motherfucker."

"Ain't no competition between no bitch and Megan."

Nothing new, but the finality of Christopher's statement grated.

"Megan fuckin' first always, hands-fuckin-down."

"No need to start an argument," Kendall inserted, chuckling. "Just because you feel that way, Outlaw, doesn't mean *they* do." She beamed a smile in Johnnie's direction, the uncertainty in her brown eyes hitting Johnnie in the center of his chest. "Johnnie thinks *I'm* first and *I'm* the most beautiful one. You, too, right, Mortician?"

For a moment, everyone went silent and Johnnie wondered if they'd let her comment pass. On the other hand, Kendall was as out of touch with reality as Dinah Nicholls—only at the opposite end of the spectrum.

She fought through her emotions in her own way, reaching a turning point and graduating from fear of her own shadow to anger at her plight. That anger came across as bitterness and a rejection of almost everyone's kindness.

Dinah had just given up. Checked out of talking, thinking, damn near *living.* Unlike Kendall. Filled with self-doubt and uncertainty, she needed constant attention and reassurance.

"Kendall—" Johnnie began.

"Wait, John Boy, I gotta answer Red." Mortician stepped next to him and gave Kendall a level look. "I told you you gorgeous, Kendall. So's Meggie, though. And, Bailey," he added on a swallow. "Zoann beautiful, too. That don't make you any less gorgeous, but, no I *don't* think you the most gorgeous."

"What's going on out here?" Megan called from the doorway. She stepped amidst their circle and looked from one to the other, throwing Kendall a dirty look. "Another party I'm not invited to participate in."

"I'm fuckin' sick of this bullshit, Megan," Christopher

snarled, jerking her away from Mortician. "From this bitch and from you cuz you fuckin' better than this. Fuckin' ruinin' what coulda been a decent fuckin' barbeque if you woulda just gave us one of your pretty smiles. All this competition bullshit endin'. *NOW*, Megan. You fuckin' first in my eyes. I thought you, amongst any-fuckin-body would fuckin' reach out to Kendall. Just when I'm fuckin' distracted with Club Business, you been actin' like a spoiled little bitch, poutin' cuz Kendall gettin' some attention."

Anger flared in Megan's blue eyes. "I have not!"

Mortician winced. "Prez—"

Christopher scowled at Mortician and the man snapped his mouth shut.

"The fuck you haven't been actin' fuckin' spoiled, Megan," Christopher continued, looming over a foot taller than Megan, but she still looked ready to clock him. "I'm tellin' you this fuckin' bullshit comin' to a stop here and now. Ain't no bitch replacin' you, but that don't fuckin' mean there ain't no room for other bitches in our fuckin' circle."

"Christopher—"

"Don't fuckin' Christopher me."

"Shut up," she snarled. "You don't know what you're talking about, so shut up." To emphasize her point, she shoved him.

Well, she tried to. One thing about her, Megan had a fucking temper.

"The fuck I don't know, baby. I got two fuckin' eyes. I see how the fuck you been actin'. I'm orderin' you to cut it the fuck out. To-fuckin-night."

Megan blinked. "Ordering me?" she asked in a strangled voice before narrowing her eyes.

"Aww, fuck, Prez, why you always got to stick your dick up your ass with Meggie?" Mortician asked.

Megan jerked Christopher's bottle out of his hands and

splashed the contents on him. "You big jerk!" she cried, slapping his hands when he yanked the bottle away.

He wiped his wet face on his arm. "Calm the fuck down, Megan. You pregnant, remember? This simple shit. Behave. Welcome Kendall. Act like you have a fuckin' brain and everythin' gonna be fine again."

Megan stiffened, hurt and furious. "Why can Kendall work behind the bar and I can't?" she blurted.

Christopher rolled his eyes "You ain't workin' behind a fuckin' bar," he spat, kicking the chair in anger. "Motherfuckers adore you just cuz you *you*."

Did Megan cower? Of course not. She picked up the closest bottle and lobbed it at Christopher.

Kendall's eyes rounded and she went white as a sheet. Johnnie wondered if he should remove her or let her see this play out. Would it help her to understand she could go batshit, over-the-top wild, and no one, *no one* would hurt her?

"Mortician hugged Kendall. He's never hugged me!"

Christopher yanked her toward Mort and shoved her into the man's arms. "Hug my wife, motherfucker, so she can be happy."

Mortician rocked back on his feet, not touching Megan just looking at the top of her head suspiciously before glancing at Christopher. "You not...you not breaking my fucking fingers if I touch her, are you, Prez?"

Megan jumped back and jabbed Mort's shoulder. "Johnnie doesn't break your fingers for touching Kendall."

"You not Kendall," Val called. Instead of more anger, Megan's chin wobbled and Val winced.

Clearing his throat, Mortician pulled Megan into his arms in a loose hug, gingerly touching her back, then stepping away. "There. I fucking hugged you."

More silence. They were waiting on Megan. Johnnie searched his mind, veering between annoyance at her, admiration for her backbone, and concern over her misery. He wanted to scream her ear off, but it wouldn't help her. And not because Christopher would murder him. No, *something* had triggered this extreme reaction to Kendall. He could only think of one thing.

"Megan, what's the real problem? Are you jealous that I'm with Kendall?"

The promise of murder from Christopher and a combination of emotions from Kendall met the question. But it needed to be asked. They needed peace between Megan and Kendall.

"Jealous of you and Kendall?" she asked, after a moment, the amusement in her eyes showing glimpses of *Megs*.

"You wish," she said around laughter.

Understanding slid into Christopher's eyes and he smirked. "You jealous cuz this bitch showed me her pussy?"

Megan stiffened and Kendall turned red.

"That's it, ain't it, baby?"

She opened her mouth, threw Kendall the evil eye, then snapped it shut again. "I'm going to bed," she said in a choked voice, turning on her heel and tripping toward the hallway.

"Megan—"

"Now not the time, Prez," Mortician said with a bit of uncharacteristic desperation.

"At least you all see the way she really treats me," Kendall interrupted in a shrill voice. "Crying over some stupid grave mix up with her dad when we were supposed—"

"FUCK, Red." Mortician slammed the bottle onto the bar and thrusted his hands through his dreads.

"What the fuck you say?" Christopher managed, turning

ashen, ignoring Mortician's reaction.

"Oh fuck," he grumbled.

"Megs!" Johnnie called, realizing he hadn't called her by his special name in days.

Val got to her and dragged her back to Christopher who stood frozen.

"That's why she does this," Kendall started.

"Not now, Red," Digger warned, discomfort crossing his face.

Johnnie barely heard Kendall. An inkling of the real reason for Megan's attitude hit him and he glanced at Christopher, who looked condemned to death and a little helpless. Someone had told Megan how Christopher had disposed of Big Joe? The very thought made him sick and he wasn't even her husband. Joseph Foy might have been a perverted motherfucker—something Megan was accepting—but he was still her father. Boss had shown her the best of himself.

"Her father has been dead for over a year," Kendall screeched.

Johnnie winced at Megan's flinch and the water filling her eyes. She'd been huffing a bit before she'd accompanied Kendall to the funeral home, but, since then, she'd become almost impossible. This really had nothing to do with Kendall.

"My sister killed herself—"

Feeling as if he were caught in the middle, Johnnie appealed to Kendall. He stared at her, willed her to understand he wasn't siding with Megan or trying to disrespect *her*. "Kendall, I need to talk to you about—"

"What she talkin' about, baby?" Christopher interrupted, unaware of Johnnie's position in this situation.

Megan stared at Christopher, her anger clear but her hurt

achingly evident. Johnnie felt shitty at his treatment towards her. They'd been friends. But he didn't handle emotional ties well. Especially with women. He'd shown Kendall his loyalty the only way he knew how. By sitting with her while she tended the bar and turning on Megan. His actions revealed to Megan how much Kendall meant to him. In doing so, though, he'd hurt her—Megan. And this had nothing to do with loving her. Because he no longer did. It had to do with fairness.

Christopher took a step toward his wife. "Megan?"

"Mr. Gillson," she croaked, after a moment, tears slipping down her cheeks. "My father's grave. He told me, Christopher."

Mortician heaved in a breath, a pained expression on his face, and nodded to Johnnie. Val looked horrified and Digger just bowed his head.

"Told you what, Megan?" Christopher asked carefully, although he knew what she alluded to. They all knew.

She exhaled a sob and bit her lip, blinking furiously. "That it's empty."

Those three words hung in the air, all the ramifications behind them suspended.

Christopher closed his eyes, took a step toward her and stopped. "That little motherfucker told you that?"

Color swept into her cheeks and she glared at Christopher, her angry gaze touching each of them, as brutal as physical blows. "He showed me the papers," she shouted.

"Calm down, Meggie," Val ordered. "You having a baby."

Sucking in a breath, she glowered at Val and regarded each of them again. Shame pulsed through Johnnie and he barely met her eyes when she looked at him. "You all knew but I had to find out from a stranger."

They stayed silent, but Kendall spoke.

"Is it such a big deal?" she asked without a bit of

sympathy, missing the import of Megan's discovery.

"Shut up, Kendall," Megan got out.

The dam had broken, the ugliness finally exposed, and she intended to let it all out.

"You don't know anything about this, so stay out of it. You made your position clear at the funeral home. And when you told me I couldn't do anything at the barbeque."

Kendall and Megan would drive all of them fucking crazy. As sympathetic as he was to Megan's revelation, he wouldn't allow her to further distress Kendall. "Yeah, Megan, she made her position clear because you told her she was jealous of you and her little sister…" His voice trailed off as the rest of her words sank in. "What did you say about the barbeque?"

Hurt crept into Megan's eyes, but she focused on Kendall. "And you wonder why I don't like you."

Kendall licked her lips and tensed, glancing at Johnnie.

Christopher reached for Megan and she went into his arms, sagging against him and sobbing her heart out. But she didn't turn him away and she didn't shut him out.

What could Johnnie do to have such an open relationship with Kendall? *Choose her and leave the club.*

The answer floated into his head and Johnnie tensed, unable to entertain that thought, *unwilling* to do so. It was much easier to focus on the drama enfolding before him. At Megan's quieting.

Christopher swiped her tears away, grabbing the napkins Mortician handed him and pressing them to her nose before guiding her to a seat and crouching in front of her.

Johnnie stayed at the bar, watching as the rest of them flanked her.

"You…you got rid of him, didn't you?" she asked in a trembling voice. "In the m-meat shack."

"Yeah."

"Why didn't you tell me?"

"Fuck me, Megan, what the fuck I was gonna say? Ain't it bad enough I fuckin' *killed* him?"

"Wh-what?" Kendall managed, but no one responded to her.

Megan sniffled. "Why'd you get the grave? For me or for you? Or for both of us?"

Christopher stood and shrugged, pacing in front of Megan. "You mostly. You loved the fuck outta Big Joe and you needed a place to grieve for him."

She fell silent, blinking back her tears. She looked toward Mortician who nodded. She sighed and grabbed Christopher's hand, laying her cheek against it.

"I've gone to his grave a lot these past weeks," she began softly, kissing his palm, "took in his obelisk, the words *a man amongst men.* You do...you do such *stupid* things, Christopher, and you make me so mad." She dropped his hand, sniffled and shuddered. "But...but I know you did what you thought necessary." She swept them all with a glance. "All of you."

Mortician patted her shoulder and withdrew his hand when Christopher gave him a warning glare. "Why you didn't say something when Gillson first told you, girl?"

She rubbed her head, exhaustion ringing her eyes. "After Johnnie accused me of running to Christopher with everything? Besides, I've tried to deal on my own."

Digger rolled his eyes. "Meggie, girl, since when you listen to any of us brain dead motherfuckers? You don't even listen to Outlaw."

"The biggest brain dead motherfucker around," Val added.

"Fuck you, assfucks." Some of Christopher's tension eased from his shoulders. "Digger right, though, baby. Not only that, you tried to fuck me up with that fuckin' bottle."

She shrugged.

"This why we all fucking love you, girl," Mortician chortled. "You not afraid. You tried to knock your husband the fuck out with no apologies because his fucking ass deserved it for kicking that chair. Fuck, if I had to go to the front lines, I would take you any fucking day."

"Shut the fuck up, Mort. You knew, didn't you?"

"Yeah, Prez," Mortician said slowly, stepping back. "I called Meggie to talk to her about...something—"

"Fuck off, motherfucker," Val called with a smirk. "You called Meggie to talk about Bailey. I call her all the time to talk about Zoann and get baby tips..." A red hue crept up his neck. "Never-fucking-mind."

"The point is all you fucks call my wife for woman advice." He looked down at Megan again. "Why you told Mort and not me?"

No answer.

He nodded to Johnnie. "It was because of what this motherfucker said, huh, baby?"

A reluctant nod to Christopher, then she admitted. "Partly. You're dealing with the Torpedoes and, after a while, I didn't know how to bring it up. I didn't want to hurt you and...and...I-I didn't know what to do, Christopher."

"First fuckin' thing? N*ever* listen to what no other motherfucker gotta say bout what the fuck you tell me. I ain't keepin' shit from you, so you ain't keepin' shit from me. That's what makes us so fuckin' good together, yeah? We fuckin' friends." He leaned and whispered something in her ear and Megan blushed to the roots of her hair. "Am I fuckin' right, though?"

"Yes, Christopher," she said, a little breathless and embarrassed.

"We was all on fuckin' edge that night, but you ain't act

no different than usual. Just the way I fuckin' *expect* you to act. Gettin' shit out in the open. Keepin' it fuckin' real." He nuzzled her neck and nosed her hair. "Actin' like a wild, wicked little bitch and makin' me love the fuck outta you even more." He grabbed her by the neck and pulled her in for his kiss. "I been tense like a motherfucker, baby, and all that's goin' on. I don't know what I woulda been doin' if you kept your pussy from me."

"God, Christopher," Johnnie complained when Megan pulled away and frowned at him. "You have no fucking couth."

"Yeah, Prez, maybe, you wanna take Meggie to your room?" Mortician suggested.

Digger snickered. "You about to forget we here and get her naked in front of us."

Christopher growled and started for Digger, but Megan grabbed his wrist while Mortician slapped the side of Digger's head.

"Fuck off, bitch ass. I ain't gonna get my ass kicked because you making Prez remember old fuckin' shit."

Little Man started wailing and Megan tensed.

"Stay there, Meggie." Val headed for the hallway. "I got him."

"I need to check on Momma," she mumbled, not stopping Val from disappearing to get Little Man.

"No the fuck you don't. You been losin' weight."

"I've been having morning sickness," she countered, resting her head on the hand propped up on her elbow.

"You didn't fuckin' have it so much on our honeymoon. It got real bad after all that bull-fuckin-shit went down here. A lot of it got to do with fuckin' *Dinah*," he snarled.

"Stress doesn't give you morning sickness. Babies do," Megan protested. "Anyway, Momma can't be alone, Christopher."

"Keep it up, Megan, and she ain't gonna be alone ever fuckin' again. I'm gonna put her somewhere to get her some fuckin' help."

Leaning back, Megan closed her eyes and shrugged. "Might be best. She keeps talking about Thomas and K-P and…and Daddy. Every time I see her, she makes me promise I'll never leave her over and over again."

"You givin' her a lot more than she fuckin' deserve, baby," Christopher growled, taking the glass of water from Mortician who'd gone and gotten for Megan. "She left you on your fuckin' own when your step fuckhead fuckin' molested you. I still can't forgive that bitch for that. Thomas stabbed you, almost fuckin' killed you, and she kept fuckin' yappin' about where the fuck I buried him."

"She's my mother."

"Yeah, well, when she could've been your mother she was failin' you fuckin' left and right. Ain't forgot that bitch druggin' my boy either. I'm givin' you fair fuckin' warnin', Megan…"

Arrow walked in, interrupting Christopher, who narrowed his eyes at the man, not in challenge but in contemplation.

"I got a job for you."

"What?"

"Go down the hall and around the corner. Last door on the left. My mother-in-law in there. Megan need some rest. Go sit with her."

"I'm not a fuckin' bitch sitter, Outlaw."

"It's okay, Christopher." Megan staggered to her feet. "I'll go."

Arrow glowered at Christopher, but, like the rest of them, couldn't say no to Megan.

"Sit, Meggie," he said gruffly. "Outlaw's right. You need to rest."

Nodding to the rest of them, Arrow disappeared down

the hall.

Christopher smiled in relief, then pulled Megan to her feet. "You forgive me, baby?"

She thumbed his lips, her adoration clear. "Always, Christopher."

"You and Kendall gonna try to fuckin' get along?"

Whatever Kendall had heard in the past few minutes, the hostility and resentment always lurking in her eyes whenever she saw Megan had slipped from her gaze. Now, Kendall looked *guilty*. And she was guilty of how unfair she'd acted. They both were.

"I guess," Megan mumbled without enthusiasm.

Christopher laughed. "Do it for Johnnie."

Her gaze flew to Christopher's, as startled as Johnnie felt. She gazed at Johnnie, then back to Christopher, and nodded. "Okay."

"As for you workin' behind the bar, ain't fuckin' happenin'. You direct the chicks whenever we have a function and you take care of every fuckin' body like always. That's all, baby." He glared at Kendall. "I want some pussy, so I ain't gonna fuckin' get into Kendall tellin' *you* you can't fuckin' help at a fuckin' function *here*. I'm gonna let John Boy handle that."

From Christopher's look, Johnnie knew he expected him to confront Kendall.

"Don't know how Kendall ended up behind the bar, Megan," Christopher went on, "and I don't give a fuck. That's not somethin' you ever fuckin' doin'."

"Okay," she agreed, yawning and rubbing her eyes.

Christopher scooped her up into his arms and she leaned against him, trusting him to take care of her. With Megan in his arms, Christopher didn't focus on anything else, not even goodnight to them.

"She's so little," Kendall blurted with wistful envy and the heart of the problem clicked into place in Johnnie's head.

Undoubtedly, Megan had been jealous of all the attention Kendall received—amongst other things—but Kendall had fed the flames of the jealousy.

Chapter 15

Kendall didn't feel like talking. She didn't feel like touching. She didn't feel like doing *anything.* If she wanted to be honest with herself, it shamed her how she'd misjudged that girl. Because of Johnnie. And based on her…on her *looks…*she couldn't finish the thought. She'd acted with the same biased, bad behavior she'd always pinned on others toward *her.* Now, though, she didn't know how to ask forgiveness, so she pushed it aside like she did everything else. Hopefully, Johnnie wouldn't press her for a discussion about the confrontation between Megan and Outlaw and he wouldn't take her up on her earlier offer for lovemaking.

As they walked into their room and turned on the lights, Kendall removed her shoes and headed for the bed, crawling in and curling up. Facing *away* from Johnnie.

He sighed. "We need to talk."

"No." Easy enough.

She knew what he wanted to talk about. More specifically, *who.* She wanted to continue with her charade and remain distant from Megan. Megan had been hurt and abused but befriending her would force Kendall to face her insecurities. She'd have to admit that she needed help to go forward with her life. That the more she tried, the more mired she became. She'd have to face the fact that she didn't know how to cook a lot of different things because she'd hated food. Food had been the enemy to her. Her only consolation was she didn't know *anything* about barbeque since she, her mother and little sister, hadn't grilled food. She'd have to face how scared she was of never getting her shit together and how paranoid she was about losing Johnnie. He was with her because of their baby, so she wanted to keep him close and have him to herself to make him love her.

She couldn't tell any of that to him. He'd know how fucked up she was.

"I'm sleepy," she said into the silence. "Baby Biker and I need rest."

"Kendall, sweetheart," he crooned, stretching out behind her and pulling her into his arms. He kissed the back of her head. "I want to help you. Let me. Talk to me."

"No," she almost snarled and he stiffened. "I have nothing to say to you about your *Megs.*"

Sudden tension brimmed from him, whirling into the air and wrapping around her.

"Christopher has gotten Megan straight." His tight voice contrasted with the understanding tone a moment ago.

"More like *she* got *him* straight," she snorted.

He released her, moving off the bed. Away from her. She curled up tighter.

"Jesus, Kendall, get off your high fucking horses. You had all of us against Megan. For what? Because you're too goddamned blind to see you're amongst friends. You've managed to vilify Megan when even *she* reached out to you. Stop comparing yourself to her. You. Are. Not. HER."

She wilted against the pillow, tears falling from her eyes. Anger surged through her and she wanted to fight and throw things and call him a stupid fucker. Or storm out. Or…or…something. But defeat stole everything else.

"If you want her so bad, fight for her," she told him, without heat. "But you know Outlaw would kill you, so you'll settle for me."

"I don't fucking believe you. Settle? For you?" She flinched at his ugly laugh. "I don't have to settle for anyone, Kendall. Least of all you. You want to know why I'm with you?"

"Because I'm pregnant for you. Because I'm in trouble. Poor, pitiful Kendall."

"If you feel that way, then you're the one who's settling. Why the fuck do you want to be with someone you feel puts you second?"

"You don't put me second," she flared. "You put me dead last. Behind Megs and Christopher and your club. Your brothers. Your obligations. If you can fit me in, then you think of me."

"Do you honestly fucking believe I'd sit at that fucking bar, not speaking to almost *anyone*, for anyone else? I can barely take a fucking piss without you making me feel like I've deserted you and thrown you to the wolves."

"You would've done it for Megs."

"Fuck Megs!" he roared and something smashed against the wall. "I'm so fucking sick of hearing about fucking Megan, I don't know what the fuck to do with myself. Let's try to put this into fucking perspective once and for fucking all. Then I expect you to get the fuck over it and move the fuck on."

Kendall glanced over her shoulder.

"Did I fucking love her? Yes," he gritted, pacing. "Do I still love her? No. I clung to my time with her just because I'm such a stubborn motherfucker. I didn't *want* to let her go. I fucked up with you, Kendall. I *know* that, and I'm sorry. But, believe me, I wouldn't babysit any one. Yet, I'm doing it for you. There's no girl I would've bought fucking clothes for. Or let live in my fucking room with me."

"All that's trivial, Johnnie. Where it counts? You *don't*

do. Moving away from the club. Defending me no matter what. When Outlaw told me to leave the meeting, you gave a perfunctory objection on my behalf then stayed silent. When Mortician said I wasn't the prettiest, you didn't say *you* thought I was."

"What the fuck? Are you out of your fucking mind?"

She stood up, sick at heart. He didn't understand her at all and never would. "No. I'm very much in the present." Her tone was as shaky as her insides. "This isn't working between us. You're mean and callous, expecting me to be someone I'm not. You can't even tell me you love me. You can't promise me you'll eventually leave the club—"

He choked, his eyes widening, his skin going pasty white before flushing red. "You're right," he snarled, a vein throbbing in his forehead. "I *am* expecting you to be someone you're not. A *fighter.* Shame on fucking me for wanting the woman I met. The one who'd preferred walking away from me if I didn't kiss her."

"My entire *life* has changed since then."

"Yes, it has and I wish I could make it all better. Take all your pain away. But it happened, so we deal with it. We work through it. You can't divert attention from one discussion and bring up another or refuse to address the issue at hand." He clasped his hands in front of his face and contemplated her. "Do you want me to say I love you? I can't. Circumstances threw us together…what…?…*thirty six fucking days ago?*"

His nostrils flared and she didn't know how to stop the direction of the conversation. She hadn't meant for this to happen. She just wanted his complete and utter loyalty.

He rubbed his neck. "I'm…Later, today, Kendall, I'll start looking for an apartment for you and have you out of the club as soon as possible. You won't have to worry about Spoon. I'll have guards for you." He turned and headed for the door, but paused. "I...Kendall..." He heaved in a breath. "Do you want to know if I imagine spending the rest of my life with you? Yes. Can I fall in love with you? Yes." He opened his mouth to say something else, then shrugged. "I'm truly sorry it turned out like this, gorgeous. Have a good night."

Without giving her a chance to change her mind or defend herself, he left her, not bothering to look back as he closed the door.

Chapter 16

Two days later, Johnnie stood outside the clubhouse with Christopher and the rest of the officers, along with regular rank-and-file brothers, enjoying the clear, breezy day and decompressing from the bullshit.

Well, the club bullshit. Girls? A different fucking story.

Some of the wannabes and hangers-on were performing tricks on their bikes, attempting to impress club members.

Owning a Harley was a requirement for membership. Hand standing didn't factor into consideration since the Death Dwellers was *not* a fucking stunt club. Earlier, before this, he'd accompanied Christopher, Val, and Mortician to target practice.

Johnnie exalted in the knowledge that none of them threw a knife with his skill and precision. He had a perfect, sure aim and hit his target every goddamn time. It was a tossup between him, Val and Mortician on who was the better shot. Christopher forfeited a place because he aimed for the head. End of story. At close range or far away, the man didn't bullshit. If he pulled his nine—or any gun—with the intentions of pulling the trigger, someone's head was getting fucked up. No warning shots in the leg or arm or knee.

The door opened and Arrow walked out, a cigar hanging

from his mouth. He held the door open and, a moment later, Megan and Bailey ducked past him. Christopher did a double-take, but his wife turned her heart-stopping smile on him and he scowled at her, tipping back his bottle of beer and thumping Mortician's shoulder.

Pretending disinterest, Mortician's jaw clenched and he reached into his cut, pulling out a cigarette. Since the noise of the mufflers prevented conversation, Megan pulled Bailey in the direction of the pathway. Christopher's hand flexed near his nine, the attention Megan garnered from the other brothers not sitting well with him. She and Bailey were dressed almost identical—in high tops, jeans, and long-sleeved Tee shirts, with the only differences being Megan's very noticeable baby bump and her billowing golden hair. Bailey had *pig tails* of all fucking things, and Johnnie wouldn't even consider how gorgeous and innocent the style made her look. He wanted to laugh like a maniac at Mortician's poorly hidden jealousy.

Val nodded to Johnnie, then thrust his chin toward Mortician, high-fiving with Digger.

Wondering at Kendall's whereabouts, Johnnie looked over his shoulder at the door. Arrow had allowed it to close but he stood just in front of it, blowing smoke rings, unconcerned he might have contributed to a mutiny by letting those two out if Christopher or Mort lost their shit.

A moment later, the noise died down and shouts and cheers went up, although Johnnie had lost the last few minutes of the performances. Arrow roamed next to him, his cigar clutched between two fingers and poised mid-air.

"Where's Kendall?" Johnnie asked before he thought better. As promised, he'd backed away from her, although he hadn't brought himself to look for an apartment for her yet.

"With Dinah and Little Man."

That was news, although not much. "Any particular reason why?"

Arrow puffed on his cigar and shrugged. "Meggie asked her to come outside with her and Bailey when I agreed to let them out for fresh air. She refused." He smiled and his eyes crinkled, detecting Johnnie's displeasure. "Why don't you go in and check on her?"

Because he was still irritated with her and he felt like a mean bastard.

"Meggie got her an appointment with her OB."

"Did she?"

"Uh-huh. They're working on warming up to one another, but we need to give them 'A' for effort."

Yes. Some old ladies *never* got along, always competing with one another. Johnnie had seen it several times and never thought his club would have such a problem. But life was fucking strange.

"Hey, fuckhead," Christopher yelled, drawing Johnnie's attention. Christopher wasn't barking at him, though. He was talking to a younger man who'd gone to Megan and Bailey.

Mortician shifted and pretended he didn't give a fuck they were laughing at the stranger's conversation. Even if they patched things up, Johnnie swore he'd never get so out-of-his head jealous over Kendall he'd stalk towards a man—like Christopher—with the intent to murder—again, like *Christopher*—just for talking to her.

"Boy's got it bad for her," Arrow commented in a lazy drawl as a yelp pitched through the air.

Johnnie frowned at Christopher, who'd punched Dumb Doefuck and was now dragging Megan back toward the clubhouse. "Megan likes to provoke him."

"Don't think so. He's had her inside for two solid days, resting. She's going stir crazy."

"So you fucking decided to let her and Bailey out, right,

Arrow?" Mortician words confirmed Johnnie's suspicions that he wasn't as immune to Bailey as he wanted to pretend.

Arrow lifted a brow at Mortician, who scowled.

"Fuck off," he growled, although the man hadn't said a thing.

Stretch was staring at the prone man as if he wanted to rush to him, but knew he couldn't.

"Prez," Mortician called sourly when Christopher approached them. He gripped Megan's hand while she glared daggers at his back. "Why you fucking left Bailey?"

"Ain't my fuckin' woman," Christopher snapped.

"She ain't mine either," Mortician retorted.

"Then shouldn't be a fuckin' problem, assfuck."

"Would you let me go, Christopher?" Megan asked with a sniff.

"When I get you inside and back the fuck in bed. I put you on fuckin' bed rest. Remember, Megan?"

"You're right here. What can happen?"

Before he responded, the door opened and Kendall peeped out. She remained still for a moment and Johnnie smiled at her, a silent encouragement for her to join them. Panic entered her eyes and she ducked back inside.

Kendall stood in the center of the main room, drawing in deep drafts of air. She'd laid Little Man down for his nap, made sure Dinah remained asleep, and then decided to take Meggie up on her offer to go outside, never expecting so many new faces.

The small bit of confidence she'd managed to gain by serving behind the bar had withered a little more after Johnnie's desertion. He'd just given up on her...on them. She'd heard all the commotion this morning and found

Bailey with Little Man while Meggie showered. She'd intended to leave when the little blonde walked out. Instead, Meggie hadn't blinked an eye, greeting her with a cordiality bordering on friendly. She looked much better than she had for the past few days. Kendall supposed she followed her husband's dictates.

By the time Meggie summoned Arrow and begged him to walk outside with her, she'd even gotten Kendall an appointment with her obstetrician, a woman whom Meggie swore by. Bailey had intended to sit with Little Man and Dinah, so Kendall could join Meggie, but Kendall didn't feel up to it.

Then, her charges had fallen asleep and Kendall found herself bored and hungry. She'd forced herself to eat, trying to calculate the calories in her head, but knowing she had to feed Baby Biker. Afterwards, she'd decided to join Meggie and Bailey, a part of her still not believing they'd accept her so easily.

Sunlight glimmered into the room as the door opened, dimness descending with its closing.

"Kendall?"

Her arms tightened around her waist at the concern in Meggie's voice. "I'm fine."

"You should go back out there," she offered. "Johnnie isn't quite as unreasonable as my husband."

"You accept his unreasonableness," Kendall retorted, still not able to pull herself out of that place where she accepted—or believed—continued overtures of kindness.

"And he accepts mine," Meggie replied with a trace of amusement. "It's a give and take situation."

Shut up, Kendall. They'd made peace and she wanted to cement that into a friendship. She just didn't know how. It was easier to push everyone away rather than leave herself vulnerable to ridicule and hurt.

"You're nineteen. What do you know about relationships?"

"More than you do. My husband's in *my* bed. Your man is sleeping wherever."

Kendall gasped and turned around, but Meggie didn't flinch. Instead, she stepped forward.

"I'm rested. I still have the godforsaken morning sickness that makes me want to *kill* Christopher. But I'm feeling better, all in all."

And? "Your point?" she asked with a haughty sniff, furious. Meggie knew where Johnnie slept. She wanted to know, too, although she couldn't bear to hear he shared another woman's bed.

"You're hurting," she said simply, softly. Without judgment. "Johnnie has been sleeping in an empty room down the other hallway. Alone."

"Do you think that matters to me?"

"Yes," she responded without hesitating. She tossed her hair over her shoulders. "You're jealous of me and I'm jealous of you. We're even, so let's work through it and get along."

"Jealous of me? You?" Kendall blurted, so surprised she forgot her derision. "What do you have to be jealous of me over?"

"You have a career. You're established and can bring something of value to your relationship. Your own money. Your own car."

"You can have those things, too," Kendall said slowly.

Meggie cocked her head to the side and smiled. "Would it confuse you if I told you I don't…I'm happy being Christopher's wife and the mother of his children? Being the facilitator of the women here?"

"Facilitator of women?" Kendall chuckled. "I've never heard that term."

"I made it up," she informed her with a giggle.

"In answer to your question, it does confuse me. How can you be jealous of me if you're happy with who you are?"

Something Kendall had never been.

"It's the idea of it, wondering what it would be like to have the ability to bring justice to-to all those girls Logan and Spoon—"

"You know about them? But Outlaw said—"

"Call him Christopher. Let his boys call him Outlaw."

Kendall's heart pounded at the olive branch Meggie extended. She bit down on her lip to keep from lashing out in disbelief.

"And I *didn't* know. But he told me the other night after the confrontation about my daddy."

"Did he really kill—"

Meggie lowered her lashes and nodded. "Yes."

"How can you be with him?"

"I love him, Kendall." She walked closer and sat in a seat, inviting Kendall to do the same. "And, God forgive me for saying this, but my father was no better than Logan." She rubbed her temples and her eyes watered. "I loved the man that he was, though. I sought him out for protection. My stepfather molested me, raped my mother, and beat us both all the time."

Kendall gasped, not wanting to hear Meggie's story from the girl's own mouth. The only girl who'd confided in Kendall had been her little sister. Most of the time, Kendall either dismissed Caroline's words as childish or didn't know how to respond.

"I wanted Daddy's help for me and Momma and I ran away from my house, a month before my eighteenth birthday. I met Christopher *on* my birthday when a club member brought me here after I stole five dollars from him to buy myself…" Her voice trailed off.

"To buy yourself?" Kendall asked in a choked voice, in spite of herself. "Five dollars wouldn't buy much."

Meggie shrugged. "It doesn't matter. It got me here. Without that happening, I never would've met Christopher or had my son."

"Then you're where you belong, Megan. You wouldn't be here if…"

Meggie lifted a brow, a wordless agreement of Kendall's words, a silent encouragement for Kendall to *heed* them.

"If what?" she prodded.

Kendall swallowed. "You didn't belong here."

"Neither you or I have the answer to life's greatest mysteries. I can't tell you why your mother and sister killed themselves. I can't explain why my stepfather hated me enough to almost stab me to death or why he got off on hurting my mother. We really only have power over what *we* do, but we hand over our control to others when we give into our pain and fear." She frowned and bowed her head. "That's what my daddy always said, anyway. And, yet, he did it, didn't he? He gave in to drugs and the inclination to exploit little girls. Or, maybe, he meant them, yes?"

"Yes," she croaked.

Meggie looked at her through the sweep of her lashes. "May I offer you some advice?"

As if she hadn't been offering her advice for the past half hour. "Yes."

"Johnnie's Christopher's brother," she began, lowering her lashes and missing Kendall's returning glower, "so he's stubborn and it isn't easy for him to accept love."

Sure she'd misheard, Kendall blinked, since Megan's revelations didn't differ from what Mortician had already told her.

"Neither of them enjoyed healthy relationships growing up. What Johnnie accepted as love from Logan was more like a sick obsession. It takes…you have be able to put up with a lot. But it's worth it because *they're* worth it."

"You really do love Out...Christopher, don't you?" she asked, admiring and envying at once.

A shudder went through Meggie and she closed her eyes, but nodded. "He's my entire life. I love him with my heart and my soul. I don't know what I'll do if anything ever happens to him."

Kendall didn't want to think of that, either, because then she'd have to think of something happening to Johnnie. "That's your advice?"

"No. My advice to you is to make Johnnie *fight* for you. He needs a good shaking up to realize what you mean to him."

"Yes, of course," Kendall admitted with sarcasm, "because you know *everything* there is to know about Johnnie."

"I never said I do," she said evenly.

"Johnnie and I have been in each other's presence on a regular basis for several weeks," Kendall said heatedly. "He isn't the type of man to fall in love so quickly. I'm a grown woman. I don't have to resort to games to get him."

Meggie winced, but the opening of the door prevented her from responding.

"Stay the fuck in here, Bailey," Mortician growled, jerking her to Meggie's table and sitting her down.

"What? Am I a prisoner now, you humongous ass?" Bailey yelled.

Mortician glanced at Meggie who rolled her eyes and shrugged.

"Talk to her, girl," he ordered.

Meggie frowned. "What do you want me to say?"

"I don't fucking know, Megan," he shouted.

"Let Christopher hear you screaming at Meggie," Bailey

said with a sniff, "then he'd kill you and I'd be free."

"You fucking free now, you annoying little fucking pest."

"You asked me to come back with you!"

"Because I'm a stupid motherfucker, Bailey. But, I fucking *swear* to you I'm leaving your young pussy alone." He crossed himself, then jabbed a finger at his groin. "Get fucking thee behind me. This officially a young pussy free zone. Feel me?"

"Go to hell."

"Tonight," he went on as if Bailey hadn't spoken, "a party going on. The Bobs gonna be here. I'm having my dick sucked by as many of them bitches as possible. Motherfuckers think I'm taking your pussy. Ain't about to pay no fucking twenty Gs."

"You'd do that to me?" Bailey asked in a strangled voice. "Cheat?"

His chest rose and fell in angry pants, but he rubbed a hand over his face, regret flashing in his eyes.

"I'm your wife!"

Kendall started, although Meggie didn't flinch. As a matter of fact, Mortician looked to her as if seeking guidance. She threw him an evil look but kept silent.

He shoved his hands in his pockets. "I told you don't say that shit out loud."

"It's the truth."

"I should've followed my first mind and got the fucking annulment."

"Our marriage was already consummated."

Mortician glared at Bailey and Kendall's heart sank. Where was the kindness and consideration he'd always shown to her? He looked so angry. She couldn't help but wonder if he'd do something to Bailey when he got her alone.

"Blame my fucking dick! I tried to talk the motherfucker out of fucking you. He just wouldn't listen."

Bailey's appalled look wavered when Meggie's shoulder shook with *laughter*. Bewildered, Kendall could only study the unfolding scene, like she'd been studying all of them since she'd met them. By watching them, she was finding herself again.

"This shit not funny, you two," Mortician bellowed, his affronted look making Kendall smile, too. "Go ahead, Red. Join these two cackling witches. I know you think this funny, too."

She did, so she allowed a bit of laughter to escape.

"What asylum did you escape from, Lucas?" Bailey asked, shaking her head. "Who talks to their, um, you know?"

"Don't worry about what I do anymore, Bailey," he ordered. "I mean it, this time. We're through."

Bailey's amusement died and she heaved in a breath, hurt darkening her green-brown eyes.

"I can't fucking take this, Bailey," Mortician went on, his voice softening. "Acting with you like fucking Prez do over Meggie. I'm *not* a jealous motherfucker."

Kendall snorted and Mortician scowled at her.

He pulled at his dreads and gritted his teeth. "By the fucking way, Aunt Flo show up yet?"

"Is that Arrow's wife?" Kendall asked into the sudden silence.

Everyone ignored her and Mortician looked distinctly worried.

Bailey pinned him with an unreadable expression.

"*Motherfucker*," he snarled, "you telling me I knocked you the fuck up?" He hooted with bitter laughter. "I want Prez to get rid of every-fucking-thing in this motherfucker. Whatever the fuck we eat, drink, and smoke. Obviously, there's something in this motherfucker working on our dicks. *No* fucking other reason we have three pregnant bitches on our hands." He stalked to Meggie. "*You* started this, Megan."

"Whatever," she said. "It's not like I have a penis wand I'm waving. I couldn't make *myself* pregnant. Same goes for Kendall and Bailey."

"The minute Prez put his dick in your pussy, he got you pregnant. There's been a fucking baby boom around this motherfucker ever since. *You started it.*"

"Nuh-uh. That would be Zoann. She gave birth to Ryan two months before I had CJ."

"She not here spreading fertility fumes. *You* are."

The door opened bringing in Christopher, Johnnie, and a bunch of the others. Christopher paused.

"You got a fuckin' reason bein' in Megan face?"

Not responding, Mortician turned away.

"What the fuck that was about, baby?"

Megan shrugged. "He was talking to Bailey. I just happened to be at the same table."

Christopher made his way to Megan and pulled her to her feet, kissing her. "I think you fuckin' know what the fuck goin' on with Mort and Bailey." He bent and nipped her ear. "How about I split the five thousand with you?"

"What do you think is going on?" Meggie asked, thumbing his bottom lip.

"I think that motherfucker married her and fuckin' accused you of emittin' fertility fumes."

"You're sooo bad, Christopher. You heard?"

"Just the stupid fuckin' fertility fumes shit. The rest I read on your fuckin' text messages."

"Yes. Mr. Psycho Stalker strikes again," Val offered, taking a seat at the next table over.

"Kiss my motherfuckin' Mr. Psycho fuckin' Stalkin' ass, you motherfuckin' Hallmark card."

Johnnie sat a bottle on the table with Val. "Any of you ladies know how Valentine got his fuckin' road name?"

"Shut the fuck up, John Boy."

"Does it have anything to do with romance?" Kendall asked, caught up in the moment.

Johnnie winked at her. "Mushy, sappy, gaggy fucking romance, gorgeous."

"I'm gonna kick your ass," Val growled.

Johnnie tipped the bottle back, then passed it to the man he traded insults with. "Good fucking luck, assfuck."

"Bailey, girl," Digger called, pulling a chair between the two tables as Christopher guided Meggie back to her seat and took one of his own. "You part of the sisterhood now?"

"I've always been part of the sisterhood," she said quietly. "My dad was a biker."

"And so's your uncle," Arrow added, dropping into a chair behind Bailey. He put his hand on her shoulder and squeezed it. "You holding up real well, princess. K-P would be proud of you."

Bailey swallowed, her nose reddening and tears rushing to her eyes. She nodded.

"Don't worry," Arrow continued. "I'll uphold your virtue. Any motherfucker look at you wrong and I'm castrating first, asking questions later."

Christopher grabbed the bottle from Digger and smirked at Arrow. "Then you best get to sharpenin' your fuckin' knife."

"How so?" No one answered, so Arrow focused on the back of Bailey's head. "Princess?"

"I-I'm having a baby."

"Whose?" he barked.

"It doesn't matter."

"The fuck it doesn't, Bailey," he argued. "K-P's gone, but *I'm* here and I'm not gonna let no motherfucker get away with hurting you."

"I don't want him hurt," she whispered. "I've lost enough."

"You pregnant, huh, Bailey?" Christopher asked, the humor in his green eyes removing the harshness from his male beauty.

My God, where did these men come from? Kendall wondered.

"I'm not touching a bitch alive." Digger shook his head and pointed to Val. "Keep your dick in your pants, brother. Me and you the only fucking ones don't have a bitch pregnant at the moment. Let's keep it that fucking way."

"Your dick started all this baby bullshit," Mortician accused, pointing to Val.

"You just fuckin' called my fuckin' wife a bitch, motherfucker?" Christopher snarled.

"I think he did," Johnnie said blandly. "Sounds like he included Kendall, too."

"Fuck, I'm sorry," Digger snapped. "I don't mean to offend them. Meggie know how the fuck I feel about her."

Christopher glanced over his shoulder. "How the fuck is that?"

"You want my fucking shovel, Digger?" Val called. "You can dig your own fuckin' grave. Save one of us the trouble."

"You're all idiots," Meggie hissed with a sniff as Mortician stalked off and disappeared down the hallway.

"I agree," Arrow said. "So let's get back to Bailey."

"Yo', Bailey," Christopher began, laughing at whatever Johnnie whispered to him. "It's been a rough fuckin' time, babe. Just tell us the truth. We ain't gonna fuckin' worry about collectin' no fuckin' bet."

Meggie choked and shook her head, pinching Christopher's arm.

"We're married," Bailey confessed quietly.

"Booyah!" Digger shouted and pumped his arms. "Cha-fucking-ching."

Christopher and Johnnie got to their feet, bumping fists. Val and Digger hugged each other.

"We got somethin' to take fuckin' care of," Christopher announced, ignoring Meggie's putrid glare.

Bailey swiped at an escaping tear, then turned to Arrow. "I want to leave, Uncle Arrow. Can you get me a plane ticket?"

"I…you and Mortician, isn't it?"

She nodded, grabbing his fists when he went to stand up. "Don't. He only gave me what I asked him to."

A red hue crept up Arrow's neck, Part anger and part embarrassment. "What about the baby?"

"It's his. What about it?"

"You keeping it?"

"Yes."

Arrow nodded. "Let me talk to him—"

"No, please. I just want to get my things and go."

"Fine." He glanced between Kendall and Meggie. "Would you two help her out? I'll go look in on Dinah."

Chapter 17

Christopher led the charge into Mortician's room, finding Mort sitting in his desk chair, glaring out of the window.

"Time to pay the fuck up, motherfucker," Christopher chortled, dragging Mortician to his feet and pulling him to the closet.

"That bitch can't *ever,* ever fucking keep her fucking mouth shut."

"And you can't keep your fuckin' pants zipped, so you fucks belong together," Christopher observed, filled with cheer. "Open that fuckin' safe, Mort, and pay the fuck up."

"I shouldn't be fuckin' penalized just because I fucked her. I believe it was if I got fucking *hooked* on one pussy."

"No, the fuck it wasn't," Christopher countered. "We bet you'd fall in love with a young bitch. Let me refresh your faulty fuckin' memory about how this began. It went fuckin' somethin' like you gettin' on my ass with the words: *'that's what the fuck I'm talkin' bout. Young pussy. I'm stayin' far away from that shit. Next thing you know a man hooked on one pussy forever'.*"

"I said a man get addicted to showing a young bitch how to fuck and get addicted to that shit."

"You one stingy motherfucker, Mort," Val called.

"Yeah, bro," Digger added. "Outlaw bet you a grand. Your dumb ass upped the fucking ante."

"And I don't have to fucking pay," he shouted. "I'm not addicted to Bailey."

"Ain't said shit about you bein' addicted to Bailey," Christopher taunted. "Her pussy? Yeah."

Mortician growled.

"Don't like me talkin' about Bailey's pussy, do you?"

Johnnie thought sure Mortician would attack Christopher. Maybe, put himself out of his fucking misery.

"Yo', bro," Digger began. "You showed Bailey how to use her pussy?"

One thing for Christopher to say it; quite another for anyone else to do so. With Christopher, he had to ignore it. Anyone else, all fucking bets were off. Mortician balled his fist and punched Digger right in the mouth.

Digger bounced back to his feet and lunged for Mortician. Christopher pulled out his nine and fired into the ceiling. The report scared the shit out of Johnnie and he *saw* him do it. The rest of them jumped like frightened pussies.

Shoving his gun back into his cut, Christopher pulled out his cigarettes. "Next time, I'm puttin' a bullet in one of your fuckin' asses. Wonder how that would look? You fuckheads showin' up in the fuckin' ER with half your fuckin' ass cheek blown the fuck off."

"You cold, Outlaw," Digger complained. "I might have to change my fuckin' drawers."

"Excuse me?" Kendall called, her eyes wide, seeming unsure if she should run.

"No one got shot," Johnnie reassured her.

She remained in the doorway and nodded. "Okay," she

mumbled. "I-I thought Mortician m-might want to know B-Bailey asked Arrow to take her to the airport and they just left."

Mortician went still, like his world stopped, and he heaved in a breath. "Thanks, Red," he responded in a bleak voice. He nodded to his closet. "Take your fucking money and get the fuck out."

They all looked to Christopher and he shook his head slightly, puffing on his cigarette. "You fucks leave me with this miserable fuck."

"I don't want to hear anything, Prez."

"Too fuckin' bad cuz I don't fuckin' remember *askin'* you if you wanted to fuckin' hear it."

Johnnie went around Digger and Val, heading to where Kendall stood in the door and waiting for the other two once he reached it.

"I'm going to get ready for the party," Val said quietly.

"Who are the Bobs?" Kendall asked and Johnnie winced, not wanting to give an explanation about those women.

"Where you heard about them?" Digger asked, removing the handkerchief he'd pressed to his lips.

"Mortician," she responded calmly.

"How the fuck he came to tell you about them?" Johnnie bit out.

"He wasn't talking to *me* in particular. He was talking to Bailey and he told her he'd have his…" her voice trailed off and she snapped her mouth shut, blushing.

"Let me guess." Val shook his head. "He wants his dick sucked by the Bobs."

Kendall nodded.

"That motherfucker gone," Digger remarked. "His nose so open behind Bailey you can park a few of our fucking bikes up in it."

"How can you make that assumption from his disgusting words?" Kendall hissed "And who are the Bobs?" She glared at Johnnie, expecting an answer.

"The Bobs are the girls who suck good dick," he explained with a sigh, heat creeping up his neck.

"Yeah, we got a whole fuckin' new set after Meggie got here," Digger added without prompting. "Course, *we* had to help K-P interview those bitches since Meggie wouldn't have liked Outlaw letting those chicks suck his dick."

Johnnie growled, tempted to punch the stupid fuck in his mouth himself.

"You, too?" Kendall asked, her eyes wide, pointing to Johnnie.

"Yes." He couldn't lie about it since big fucking mouth had spilled the fucking beans.

"You're going to the party?" she went on shakily.

He'd fucking intended to. Not to get his dick sucked, but just because he didn't have anything else to fucking do. "Yes, I'm going, Kendall. We'll probably all end up in Christopher's room, though."

"Christopher's going?"

"Fuck, he our Prez," Digger said. "Him and Meggie make it to almost everything."

"Meggie?"

"Well, yeah," Val said. "He get her out of there before the fucking and dick sucking start."

She stiffened and backed away from Johnnie. "I have to check on Dinah."

"Thanks, fuckheads," Johnnie snarled after she hurried away, deciding he'd let her cool off before he went after her and talked to her.

Christopher "Outlaw" Caldwell walked around

Mortician's room, looking at the motherfucker's miserable face. He knew Mort had bullshit from his past that fucked him off but he'd try to talk some fucking sense into the motherfucker before he fucked up completely with fucking Bailey.

"You fuckin' love Bailey, Mortician?"

Mort cut an evil glare at Christopher and it deepened when Christopher smirked at him before turning away and going to his nightstand to open the drawer. *Obviously* Mort's fucking frame of mind prevented him from being a proper fucking host and offer Christopher some fucking herb while he played Dr. Fucking Outlaw. Snatching up the baggie and the cigarette paper, he got their roll together and replaced the shit where he'd found it—along with a few bills. He lit it up and took a few puffs before walking over to the man and handing it to him.

After waiting for another hit for several minutes, Christopher snatched the roll back and scowled at his brother. Motherfucker hogging the herb when *he* hadn't offered it to Christopher in the first fucking place.

"Let me be."

"As fuckin' much as I'd fuckin' like to walk the fuck away and send a fuckin' girl in to suck your dick, I can't fuckin' do it."

"You don't have to do it, Prez." Mort unclenched his fists. "I'm getting four bitches in here. One for my dick. One for my mouth. And one for each fucking hand."

Christopher had experienced similar times and he shook his head in fond memory.

"You know you wish you could join me in a fucking pussy fest," he growled.

"No the fuck I don't, motherfucker."

"Maybe, not now because Meggie pussy still new to you—"

Narrowing his eyes, Christopher stalked to Mortician. "I'm givin' you a fuckin' pass *one fuckin' more time* cuz your dumb fuckin' ass kinda fucked in the fuckin' head right now. Consider this fair fuckin' warning, assfuck. DON'T MENTION MEGAN'S PUSSY."

"I don't think I can spend my fucking life fucking one bitch, Outlaw." He wised the fuck up and didn't mention any part of Megan's body again. "I don't think you can, either."

How to convince a motherfucker who didn't believe in fucking love or the fucking power of it? It made motherfuckers cut little fuckheads' tongues out before shooting the fuck out of them when said fuckhead let shit about empty graves slip.

"I think you fuckin' bluffin'. You a stingy motherfucker and don't wanna pay the fuckin' money. How about this? Keep my fuckin' Gs. Put it toward your fuckin' weddin'." He snickered. "Ex-fuckin-scuse me, motherfucker. You already fuckin' married."

"I notice you didn't say anything about being able to hold up your vows."

"Ain't fuckin' fallin' for your bullshit, Mort. I fuckin' understand. You tryin' to get me to blow you the fuck away, but I ain't puttin' you outta your fuckin' misery." At least, he'd *try* not to. Let him keep up with that bullshit, though. "Besides, *you* think what the fuck you want, I don't give a rat's fuck. As long as my wife know better, I'm fuckin' straight. Ain't a motherfucker in the world I gotta answer to but her."

Mortician came to his feet. "I don't want to answer to no bitch and I don't want to fuck one pussy for the rest of my fucking days and I don't want to look at a dude around a chick and want to fuck him up because I hate the thought of a motherfucker up in her grill."

Christopher let him walk out the fucking rage in him.

"Whatcha say about young pussy?"

He rubbed his jaw. "You know because you told me a little while ago."

"True," Christopher agreed, shrugging. "But you ain't gettin' addicted to it til you fuck it. Then it ain't only young pussy. It becomes a girl, bro. *Your* fuckin' girl. Your fuckin' heart and soul." Replacing the roll with a regular cigarette, he went to the cabinet where Mort kept his alcohol and pulled out an unopened bottle of tequila. Once he'd opened it, he handed it to Mort and they passed it back and forth between them.

"I don't have a motherfucking heart and I sure the fuck don't have a soul."

Maybe, Mortician was the wrong one to talk to. Maybe, it should've been fucking Bailey. Because Christopher identified like a motherfucker with Mortician's feelings. He'd felt the same way about Megan and no motherfucker in the world could've told him different. *She* was the only one who got through to him. Her actions. Her words. Her innocence.

He didn't want any-fucking-thing tainting her sweetness and he was a vile enough motherfucker to protect it by any means possible. *Except* giving her up. Because once she got through to him and made him *believe* in her love, *their* love, not one fucking thing could take her away from him. And woe fucking be it to any motherfucker who fucking tried.

It surprised him how much he wanted the same for the men who were not only his brothers but his *brothers*. His family. His friends.

Mort needed Bailey, a gorgeous fucking chick. Young and innocent. Well, she had been until Mort fucking got to her.

"I gotta go find Megan." He'd back off. No use wasting his fucking breath and his fucking time bitching at a stubborn fuckhead.

Mortician shoved the bottle back at him, halting his departure. "You don't get tired of just feeling Meggie's..." His voice trailed off at Christopher's growl. "Of just Meggie?" he amended.

Christopher swigged from the bottle, then gripped the neck of it and rubbed his nose. "When Megan had my boy, I couldn't fuckin' touch her for six weeks."

"Did you let any chicks around here—"

"You know the fuck I didn't," he interrupted. "You just tryin' to be an ignorant motherfucker tonight. Not bein' able to touch her was hard, Mort. But not as hard as I thought. You know why? Cuz me and Megan friends. You know how much I like fuckin'. Eatin' pussy. Gettin' my dick sucked." He paused in his inventory to drink from the bottle and remember the way Megan learned to suck dick during her recovery. It made him even crazier behind her. Not that Mort needed to know that shit. "But, fuck, Mort, that's not the most important fuckin' thing no more. Knowin' no matter what, Megan got my fuckin' back, takes fuckin' precedence over every-fuckin-thing."

"Damn."

"You and Bailey friends, aintcha?"

Reluctantly, Mort nodded.

"You got her with your kid or she got a baby in her from another motherfucker?"

Mortician's face darkened with anger. "She's pregnant for me."

"And you lettin' her fuckin' go, assfuck? With your baby growin' in her?"

"I'm not ready to give up fucking other bitches," Mortician insisted.

"Fair fuckin' enough. I'm sure Bailey gonna need dick soon, too. Shit work both ways, know what I fuckin' mean?

While you gettin' addicted to a young bitch, that fuckin' young bitch learnin' to love dick." He turned toward the door, surprised at Mort's shock. Obviously, that shit hadn't fucking crossed his mind.

All right. It wouldn't have fucking crossed Christopher's mind, either, if he hadn't fucking experienced it first-fucking-hand. But, hey, something needed to wake Mort the fuck up.

He hoped like fuck the motherfucker heeded his fucking words. If that didn't open his eyes, maybe, this would.

"I'll give you six fuckin' months. I'll make sure them other motherfuckers give you six months, too."

"Six months for what?"

"To work things out with Bailey or walk the fuck away from her. You figure out you *really* don't fuckin' love her and let her fuckin' go, *you* win the fuckin' bet. You decide to get with her, you pay the fuck up, motherfucker."

Chapter 18

Kendall dropped into the recliner next to Dinah's bed and covered her face in her hands, not wanting to think about the Bobs or Johnnie having his dick sucked by those whores. They discussed those women like they discussed the weather, reaffirming Kendall's determination that Johnnie choose her and their baby or the club. But he couldn't have both.

Sooner or later, temptation would become too great for him and he'd let one of those girls touch him. They hadn't made love in days and if he intended to attend their disgusting party…

She heaved in a breath, not wanting to think about Johnnie with anyone else.

"Meggie?"

Kendall dropped her hands from her face and stared in the direction of Dinah. Her blue eyes stared at Kendall.

"Where's Meggie?" she croaked. "I want Meggie!"

Erm…

A wildness entered Dinah's eyes, tears filling them. "She's gone, too? She left me like K-P and Joseph? I don't have anyone."

She'd only sat in here while Dinah had been asleep, only interacted with Dinah when Meggie had been leading her around. Meggie had been so very tired, trying to take care of everyone and everything. Kendall understood a little better why Christopher protected her so fiercely, especially from his mother-in-law.

"Where's Meggie?" she sobbed. "Dead, isn't she?"

"No," Kendall managed. "But she *is* pregnant and she needs to rest. Christopher ordered her to bed. She was running herself into the ground taking care of you."

"I don't care! I'm her mother. She's *supposed* to take care of me. She's all I have left."

Her thin face made her eyes look huge and haunted. She'd been abused, her self-worth beaten out of her, leaving behind a pathetic shell of a woman who barely retained her sanity.

Kendall shivered, seeing herself.

"Do you have to use the rest room?"

Dinah must've been sleeping for hours. Just the thought made Kendall's bladder throb.

"Only if Meggie's here."

Kendall considered her options. "Dinah," she began. "I promise I'll get Meggie for you if you get to the bathroom." She swept her gaze over the woman's frail body, revealed by the covers she'd kicked aside. Food stained her pink nightgown. "And let me help you to get cleaned up."

Tears filled her eyes again and slid down her cheeks. "I don't want to do anything but die," she confessed. "I told her. I told her if she left me I'd kill myself."

Standing and inching closer to the bed, Kendall sat on the edge, thinking about what she needed to say. As an attorney, she needed to come up with a firm but convincing argument. For...for *Meggie*. It no longer mattered why Meggie wanted to be friends—if it was because Christopher expected it of her or just because she...she really *liked* Kendall.

Kendall twisted her hands together. "Is that fair? Telling her that, I mean. You must've worried her sick."

"I didn't. She told on me! She *always* tells her brute of a husband *everything*. I hate that and I hate him, threatening to have me locked away if I didn't drink his nasty drink." She bristled with anger and resentment. "All I do is sleep."

"If you're asleep, you can't hurt yourself."

"No one would miss me."

Kendall scooted closer and reached for her hand. "Meggie would miss you. It would break her heart if anything happened to you."

For a moment, she remained motionless, not responding to Kendall's touch or her words. But, then she wrapped her bony fingers around Kendall's hand and Kendall wanted to weep at the hope bringing some life to Dinah's eyes. "Really?" she sniffled. "She'd miss me?"

"Of course. Just like...just like...I'll bet she misses the way you once were." Kendall bowed her head, thinking of her own mother, shuddering at the thought of all the blood. The images were always there, lurking at the back of her mind. Marie hadn't been the mother Kendall had dreamed of having, but, she missed her and wished she was still alive. Their relationship had been odd and strained and, yet, Kendall couldn't remember a time, after she'd become an adult, when she'd gone to her mother and tried to bridge the chasm between them. She'd just gotten more and more bitter. "Do you remember how you used to be?"

Her jaw clenched. "No."

"I think you do," Kendall chastised. "I think you're afraid, though. Afraid of facing...*life*. Because it's hard and mean and cruel."

"*I* don't have to face it as long as Meggie is here. She

protects me."

Irritation surged through Kendall and she cocked her head to the side. "Who protects her?"

"She doesn't need protection," she said without malice, growing droopy. "She's a fighter. She stood up to Thomas and got away when I couldn't."

"Let's get to the bathroom before you go to sleep again."

Her eyes popped open. "I'm not going to sleep until I see Meggie."

Footsteps pounded into the room and both Kendall and Dinah glanced toward the door. Relief settled deep into Kendall. Arrow. Dinah's face fell.

"Kendall, babe, thank you but I'll take it from here." He puffed on his cigar.

"Make him go away," Dinah pleaded, tightening her grip on Kendall's hand.

"Not happening."

"You aren't K-P," she sobbed. "You can't come in here and be nice. You aren't K-P, so you can't expect to get me like he did."

Arrow barked a laugh. "My dick has better things to do than to fuck a pathetic excuse for a woman like you. K-P wasn't fucking desperate, so you must've acted like you had a shred of fucking pride. I'm here because of your girl. K-P admired Meggie and she deserves every bit of happiness she can get, not a selfish bitch who can't get out of bed to piss on her fucking own."

Dinah tensed and scooted closer to Kendall, who'd gone rigid with fear.

"I'm telling on you," Dinah sniffled. "I'm telling Meggie."

"*Tell* on me," he mocked. "You tell your daughter. *I'll* tell her fucking husband."

Turning her back to them, Dinah wailed and Arrow started toward her, barely giving Kendall a glance except to growl at her, "Get the fuck out."

She didn't want to leave this frail woman with this oversized, mean biker. His massive hands would make quick work of Dinah's scrawny neck, either snapping the bone in it or strangling her. And…and she knew how cruel bikers were sexually. Here, though, they'd said she was safe. She could speak her mind and stand up to them and no one would hurt her. Because she was Johnnie's. Dinah belonged to no one, though, and none of them particularly liked her. Arrow swung the woman up into his arms.

"D-don't hurt her," Kendall pleaded, fear trembling her insides.

He paused and frowned at her. "Get the fuck out. I'm not hurting her and I won't hurt her, but somebody needs to call her on her bullshit. Now, *get out!*"

Fear getting the best of her, Kendall stumbled out. She needed to find Johnnie. He'd know what to do. The noise in the main room daunted her. Before she reached the entryway, she heard heavy breathing and grunts and squinted in the dimness, afraid to focus, knowing she had to, though.

Digger leaned against the wall, eyes closed, pants unzipped, gripping the hair of a nearly naked girl. She went to the bar and found Val behind it. "Where's Johnnie?"

"He went outside a few minutes ago," he said without concern, pouring a row of shots.

"Why?"

Val frowned. "Cuz he's a grown fucking man and wanted to fucking go the fuck outside."

Kendall recoiled back and spun on her heel, looking for a friendly face, only seeing a bunch of women there to pleasure any man who crooked their finger at them and men who stared at her like she belonged in a freak show.

She didn't care what she'd find. Better to have the

evidence of Johnnie's infidelities now rather than later.

A couple minutes later, the evening sky promised a beautiful night. The breeze cooled Kendall's heated skin and she drew in a deep breath, trying to get her bearings. Blindly, she walked to the edge of the property where the pathway through the woods started.

A giggle reached her and then a groan. Overwrought and overworked, she froze.

"Wicked little bitch," Christopher growled.

Another giggle. Were none of these people who they presented themselves to be?

"He's going to come back soon," Meggie coaxed, startling Kendall.

Christopher laughed again. "You little nympho, I ain't fuckin' you out here with all these motherfuckers lurkin'. Besides, like you said, Johnnie comin' back with my boy soon." Leaves rustled. "Wait, baby."

Meggie gasped. A moment later, Kendall saw why. He stepped from behind the tree, his gun raised.

"What the fuck you doin' here, Kendall?" he snapped, shoving his gun back in his pocket.

"You could've shot her, Christopher," Meggie accused, stepping beside him, her lips swollen and her cheeks flushed.

"Then you need to fuckin' educate her. How Not to Get Fucked Up 101." He jerked out a cigarette and lit it, not ashamed of the imprint of his erection straining against his jeans. "How the fuck long you been fuckin' standin' there any-fuckin-way?"

"I-I was looking for Johnnie," Kendall murmured, embarrassed and confounded.

He blew the smoke up and pointed over his shoulder. "That way."

She started away from the two of them.

"Yo', Kendall?"

"Y-yes?"

"Watch over CJ for about an hour. I gotta wicked little bitch who want some dick really fuckin' bad."

"Yeah," Meggie called, poking her tongue out at Christopher, "but don't tell my husband."

Christopher laughed and flicked his cigarette away, scooping her into his arms.

Johnnie paused at his bedroom door and heaved in a deep breath. He'd seen Kendall on the trail when he'd taken Little Man for a walk. She'd hovered back and he hadn't known how to approach her, so he'd focused on the little boy, hoping she'd make a move to join them.

She hadn't.

When he'd discovered Christopher and Megan gone, Kendall had shrugged, her lips tightening. Johnnie returned inside. Not seeing the two of them, he'd figured out fairly quickly the reason for their disappearance.

One thing about Christopher, he usually didn't stray too far over the mark of the time he'd request for Little Man's babysitting duties. Christopher had gotten his son about five minutes ago, walking, in nothing but his jeans, amidst the growing number of bikers and groupies.

Enough was enough, however. The past few days had begun to intrude upon Johnnie's and Kendall's relationship, just as it had the week Logan made his appearance.

Knocking once, Johnnie opened the door and found Kendall sitting at his desk, braiding her damp hair. She'd taken a shower and now wore one of his t-shirts and a pair of his pajama bottoms. Her hands paused at his approach.

"Hey."

"Hi, gorgeous."

Not responding, she finished her hair. It looked as if she wouldn't say anything more. Pushing aside his rising annoyance, he placed his hands on her shoulders, bent and kissed her neck.

He'd come in to talk, but, *fuck*, jerking off wasn't what he wanted. He wouldn't do anything with her but fuck her pussy and, if that's all she ever wanted, he'd have to live with that. His hands roamed to her breasts, her hardened nipples pressing against the material of the t-shirt and tempting the shit out of him. Caressing them, he guided her to her feet and turned her to him, slanting his mouth over hers, his dick hard and hurting.

He inserted his fingers into the pajama bottoms and found her feminine seam, running a finger along the hot slit. She moaned and ground against him, her arms slowly wrapping around his neck, her tongue cautiously meeting his. She sighed into his mouth, then smiled up at him. Taking his hand into her own, she tugged him toward the bed and sat on the edge.

She raised her gaze to his and brought her fingers to his belt, unbuckling it before she opened his fly, Johnnie's cock jumped. He should stop her, but he wasn't that fucking noble, and groaned when she wrapped her lips around his dick, slurping half into her wet, hot mouth.

Johnnie gripped her gorgeous red hair, impatient with the braid, deciding to deal with it after she sucked him off. He pumped in and out of her mouth, stroking her cheek and holding her head in place when cum gushed down her throat.

Scooting back on the bed, she slid out of the pajama bottoms, then pulled off the t-shirt, while Johnnie undressed, too. He climbed onto the bed and rolled onto her, kneeing her thighs open, his dick still hard, and sank into her in one stroke. Gripping her hips, he drove into her, barely remembering she hadn't had an orgasm yet. He jerked out of her and she squeaked. After the heat of her body, the cold air hitting his wet cock sent goose bumps over his skin. He trailed his tongue between the valley of her breasts, down the center of her body to her navel, and, further, to his goal—her clit. He licked her with no finesse, no intent to lose himself in her scent and taste. No, he wanted her to come and she did, yanking his hair, her juices sliding over his tongue and driving him fucking crazy.

Traveling up her body again, he pushed his dick into her, sliding his tongue into her mouth at the same time. God, she tasted sweet.

Their moans and groans combining, Johnnie shuddered inside of her, his ears ringing and his head spinning.

He collapsed next to her, breathing hard, thinking of everything he wanted to say to her. Drawing her into his arms, he kissed the top of her head.

"We have to leave about nine tomorrow morning to get to the doctor's office by ten. Rush hour traffic and all. I'm also a new patient, so I have to fill out the forms."

Johnnie popped his eyes opened. Tomorrow, he'd intended to follow up on a lead regarding Spoon. He hadn't expected Kendall to have her first doctor's appointment since they hadn't discussed it. They hadn't discussed *anything* substantial.

"Let me guess," she began in a brittle tone, "you can't come."

"I didn't expect you to have the fucking appointment, Kendall." He drew in a deep breath to calm his temper. "I didn't come in here to fight."

"You came to fuck. I understand."

"I came to talk," he corrected.

She went silent and then, "About?"

"Us. Baby Biker. What else?"

Lifting herself on an elbow, she turned her big, brown

eyes on him and Johnnie couldn't hold back a tender smile. He loosened her destroyed braid the rest of the way, allowing her hair to spill free and the sweet scent of her shampoo curled around him.

"Have you thought about my request?"

He wrapped a portion of her hair around his hand and frowned, attempting to remember what she'd asked him to consider. "Which was?"

"Leaving the club."

All his pleasure and goodwill drained away and Johnnie dropped her hair. "I'm not leaving my club, Kendall," he gritted.

"Then I don't want you sleeping in here with me," she said after a tense moment.

"Are you fucking kidding me?"

She sat up and pulled the covers with her to cover her beautiful body from his gaze. "I didn't stutter, did I?"

"No, you didn't stutter. Hear me clearly because I'm not stuttering either. I'm *not* leaving my club for you or anyone. That's non-negotiable. Ask anything else of me and I'll try to do it."

She opened her mouth and Johnnie pressed a finger to her lips.

"I promised to find an apartment for you, but I haven't looked yet. Tell me now—do you want to move away from the club?"

"Yes," she answered without hesitation, sinking his heart. "But only if you move with me."

"Okay," he responded, relief replacing the disappointment. As long as he gave Kendall the fucking choice, she'd shut him out, pulling one excuse after the other out of her ass. The knee-jerk decision not to sleep in his room a few days ago had been borne of frustration and fatigue. Now, he was rested. Today, they hadn't worried about revenge. Not that the motherfuckers didn't have it coming to them, but they'd needed the break. He stood from the bed, the scent of sex, of *her*, hardening him again. "I'm taking a shower, then we're getting some sleep." Hopefully, *after* he got more pussy.

"I told you you couldn't sleep in here with me until—"

"Tough shit. You don't want to fuck me? Fine. But I'm sleeping in here and *you're* sleeping in here with me. I'm sick of this bullshit and it fucking stops here and now."

Kendall gasped and Johnnie anticipated some form of retaliation. Instead, she flopped onto her side, jerked the covers over herself and muttered, "asshole."

Although Johnnie sighed—his belligerence fucked the prospect of getting more pussy—he smiled, too. Kendall had actually called him an asshole.

She'd come a long fucking way. He hoped she liked the surprise he had in store for her.

Chapter 19

Kendall followed Johnnie through the stands of trees. The familiar splash of the waterfall heralded his close proximity to the cave and the unsurpassed beauty of the landscape calmed him. He'd found the hidden cave that backed up to the small waterfall by accident. He'd been sitting at the edge of the stream, breathing in the scent of the evergreens and decided to go exploring. He'd followed the path of the stream and entered a clearing, immediately transported into a paradise on earth.

Over the years, he'd visited often, rarely bringing anyone here. Christopher, Mortician, and Val knew about it. K-P had known about it. No one else. Then he'd brought Megan and, now, Kendall, who trekked behind him.

"We've been walking forever," she complained, silent until now. If not for the crunch of twigs and the rustling of leaves, he wouldn't have known she was with him.

"Just a few minutes more, gorgeous," he called, hiding his smile and adjusting the knapsack he'd filled with goodies. He hoped she enjoyed his surprise, wanting it to serve as a turning point in their relationship. He wanted to show her how much she meant to him.

"I'm a city girl. I don't like hiking or whatever we're doing to God knows where."

Finally, they reached a cave. Darkness was descending, the horizon layered in color, changing the fiery red of sunset into the grayness of dusk.

"Do wolves roam out here?"

She stepped closer to him and Johnnie made a soothing noise as he walked deeper into the darkness of the cave.

"Oof," she gasped, barreling into him at his sudden halt.

A moment later, he lit lanterns, illuminating the area before he turned and gauged her reaction to the rose petals and candles and table cloth held in place by the lanterns. In the corner were blankets, surrounded by pillows.

Kendall's mouth dropped open.

"Surprise, sweetheart," he murmured, pleased at her reaction.

She blinked and turned in a circle, looking at everything in silence.

Happy he'd gotten something right with her, Johnnie laughed and crouched down, opening the knapsack. He pulled out paper plates, plastic utensils, four beers, bottled water and a covered container.

"Why'd you do this?" she whispered, her bewilderment clear.

"I wanted to take you on a date," he responded, the bewildered look in her eyes making his heart turn over. "That can't happen until the threat's removed, so this is the next best thing."

The lantern light played off her red hair and beautiful features. Long lashes framed her sad brown eyes. He stood to his full height and closed the short gap between them, settling both hands on each side of her neck and caressing her nape, threading his fingers through her hair. Wanting to hold her and reassure her, he leaned in, drawing her closer. She brushed her lips against his with the lightest, barest touch that sent goose bumps racing along his spine. Her light, tender kisses felt more erotic than deep, open mouthed tongue twirling. In response and overwhelmed she'd initiated the kiss, he gave her another gentle kiss and she shivered. Sensation travelled through his body. She opened her mouth beneath his and his tongue explored, as she pressed her body closer to his, feeling every soft inch of her body. She ground against the length of his erection.

He pulled away and gazed at her, smiling at her swollen lips and dazed expression. "You're so gorgeous, Kendall," he whispered. "You're smart and loyal and ambitious. You're a wonderful woman."

For once, her height or her body didn't shame her, as if it gladdened her that she stood almost eye level with him. Her shoulders straightened and her spine stiffened.

She grabbed his cock, over his jeans, and started massaging. He laid a hand over hers and stopped her. "No. Let's eat first, sweetheart. Talk and enjoy each other's company."

He guided her to the blanket near the tablecloth and helped her down onto the ground, then sat next to her. He opened the container and revealed quartered turkey and lettuce sandwiches. He opened beer for himself and handed her a bottled water.

After months and months of battling his feelings for Megan, he realized what everyone had been trying to tell him. Even Megan herself. Now, looking at Kendall, he wondered how he could've been so blind, so fucking stubborn.

He caressed Kendall as if he'd seen her for the first time in a long time. He pressed his lips on her forehead, trailing her hairline with the eyes of a man with the blinders finally removed.

"Kendall," he whispered, nothing but the night sounds and their breathing surrounding them. "Let's get married."

She blinked, a startled laugh escaping her. "Married?" she echoed in disbelief, licking her lips, lust and heat brightening her eyes. She nibbled his lower lip. "Do you love me?"

He pinched her nipple. "I think...yes," he answered when she tensed.

Jerking away from him, she glared at him. "You don't. You're only marrying me because of Baby Biker."

The night verged on spiraling to fucking shit unless Johnnie found a way to recover the mood from a few moments ago before he'd given that impulsive proposal. Fuck, he'd been caught up in the moment and it had just slipped out. "I'm not marrying you because of the baby," he insisted. "I do...love you."

The realization shocked the shit out of him, although he'd never be able to say that to *her*. She'd take it the wrong way and draw some fucked-up conclusions. The lone reason he'd stumbled over the admission. He'd never thought he'd feel this way about anyone. Circumstances had kept them from spending a lot of time together and, yet, he looked forward to taking her into his arms every night. Or just seeing her gorgeous face. The spark that lit her eyes whenever he returned. Her smile. Sometimes shy. Sometimes uncertain. But all her.

"I love you, Kendall."

She shook her head.

"I want to marry you. You're gorgeous. You're smart. You're strong. Do you know how many people wouldn't have made it through all you survived?" He gave her a light kiss on the lips. "I admire you—"

"I'm not marrying you. You go from wanting to make a

go at a relationship to loving me and wanting to marry me? That's—"

His frustration building, Johnnie shoved his fingers through his hair. "Jesus, Kendall. That was almost six fucking weeks ago. We've spent time together. We've lived together—"

"And what? All of a sudden you've had an epiphany?"

If that's what she wished to call the conclusion he'd reached tonight, then, yes, he'd had a goddamn epiphany. "What the fuck do you want from me?" he bit out. She'd thrown a heartfelt proposal back into his face.

"Sincerity and honesty."

"Fine, Kendall. Since this dinner is fucked, please allow my dishonest, insincere fucking ass to escort you back to the goddamn MC."

She swiped at her tears and Johnnie's anger deflated. He didn't want her to cry. Fuck, pregnancy hormones ran rampant and she needed to adjust to his change of heart. He'd back off for now and broach the topic later when she wasn't so stressed out…when *he* wasn't so fucking stressed out.

Between now and then, he'd convince her of the sincerity of his proposal and make her see how much she meant to him.

Chapter 20

Louis "Stretch" King pulled his bike to a stop in front of a non-descript house that blended in with the middle-class neighborhood. The kind of place he'd want to live in if he ever settled down and had children, with its red bricks, green shutters, and neat flowerbeds.

He shook his head and sighed. At twenty-five, he had more than enough time to figure shit out. For the most part, he was out. His blood family hated him. His MC brothers embraced him, going out of their way to protect him and allow him time with Hanson. Of course, *most* of the brothers *didn't* know, but Outlaw, John Boy, Mortician, Val, and Digger knew and they accepted him for him.

Dismounting his bike, he pulled the sheet of paper from his cut and double-checked the address. He had the right place. His cellphone started ringing and Stretch frowned, recognizing Hanson's ringtone. He'd gotten the idea from Outlaw, who had Meggie on speed dial with *Love In An Elevator* as her tone. Despite everything, Stretch was curious as hell to know why his Prez gave that beautiful girl *that* tone.

Stretch hadn't answered Hanson's first call, so it

stopped and started again. Fuck. He needed to sit the fuck down for a minute. Stretch had a job to do for Prez and he couldn't let Hanson's alluring voice and wicked ideas distract him.

Shit, just the thought of Hanson distracted him and Stretch adjusted his dick. They'd been unable to get enough of one another after Stretch had been wounded the night Outlaw and Meggie's house had been destroyed. Although the shot hadn't been anything worth noting—he'd gotten released the same fucking night—it made both Stretch and Hanson realize the precariousness of life.

The wooden door swung opened and a shirtless man stepped out. Shirtless was fine. Yeah, shirtless was cool but his six pack, wide shoulders, and corded muscles...

Fuck. Stretch backed away, his heart racing and his body tightening.

Hair so dark it looked black until the sunlight beamed on the strands and revealed the brown highlights. He walked closer, his bright blue eyes hard and searching.

A frown marred his perfect features. "Are you Stretch?"

Stretch swallowed, his hands growing clammy. He was who he was but he knew better than to assume *anyone* else had similar proclivities. That was the quickest way to get himself insulted, shunned, or hurt. Killed, even.

"Asshole, you checked in or what?"

"Checked in?" he echoed stupidly.

"Yes," he snapped. "Your fucking body is standing in fucking front of me. Your fucking mind is somewhere else. Checked the fuck out from business," he added on a whisper.

"Right. I-I'm here," he stuttered. He'd better be there. He'd been sent to make the purchase for the explosives Prez needed. Nothing to play with.

"Follow me then."

His phone started ringing again and the other man rounded on him. "Shut it the fuck off," he snarled, snatching the device from him and doing the task himself then slamming it against Stretch's chest.

The moment they reached the interior and the door slammed, Stretch was shoved against the door and patted down. There were recessed shelves in the hallway and the man snatched a metal detector wand from one of them, passing it in front of Stretch, then behind.

"Where's your fucking heat?"

"Saddlebags," Stretch answered.

He stared him in the eye, his look inscrutable, a lock of dark hair falling onto his forehead. "Who am I?"

Okay, the questions were beginning to work on Stretch. "Who are you?" he growled. "You haven't fucking told me."

He flashed a blinding smile, his straight, white teeth as perfect as the rest of him. "I would think Outlaw already told you.'

God. Jesus. Fuck. Outlaw had.

Stretch needed to pull his shit together, but he hadn't been himself since K-P's murder and he missed his gruff ass so much. The others missed him, too, and they'd known him longer than Stretch. They had their shit together, so Stretch had to do the same. He searched his mind and the man's name came to him. "Cash," he muttered. "You're Cash McCall."

He nodded, then laughed. "Didn't Outlaw fucking teach you not to give your hand away?"

"I-I d-don't understand."

"Because you don't have fucking common sense, asshole."

That stung and anger surged into Stretch. "Fuck you, motherfucker. I'm not fucking here to answer your goddamn questions or fucking impress you with my knowledge. I'm fucking here to get what the fuck Outlaw ordered."

Cash stilled, his eyes twinkling. "Impress me, huh?"

Fuck. Stretch had to play this off. He hadn't said anything that would give away his attraction to this beautiful man. On the other hand, the asshole was just the type of brute who'd want to bury him if he discovered how Stretch felt. But he couldn't turn a switch on and off or wire his brain not to develop attractions to this man or that woman. With women, it was cut and dry and Stretch got more pussy than he knew what to do with. Even if he hadn't, he'd make a move and they'd accept or decline. Case closed. He did what genetics bade him and the world expected of him.

With men? Not so easy.

"Follow me, woo woo boy. I need to find out what the fuck Outlaw is giving you to keep your head in the fucking clouds. No wonder you fuck with bombs."

Stretch flipped Cash off and trailed behind him, his amused chuckles annoying the fuck out of him. He fucked with bombs because he liked mixing dangerous shit. He liked testing the fates and winning to see another day.

At the back of the house, they walked through the last door at the end of the short hallway. The climate controlled room was filled with large white bags marked fertilizer, potassium chloride and sawdust. He had tables containing baskets of nails, empty plastic containers, reels of thin wires and the white powder Outlaw sent him for. The unattainable RDX that Stretch itched to get his hands on to create the explosive Outlaw needed.

"You have a regular fucking Bombs R Us."

Cash smirked at him, the pride he felt visible in his features. He folded his arms, drawing Stretch's gaze to his pecs and obliques. Heat crept up Stretch's neck and he glanced away, knowing he sported a red face.

"Woo Woo Boy?" Cash called.

"Fuck off."

"Look at me."

Manning up, Stretch returned his focus to Cash. He'd stepped closer and the aftershave he wore caught up to Stretch's brain and went straight to his dick. This was so fucking wrong. The last visceral reaction he'd had to anyone was the day Meggie had bounced into the kitchen, looking for Outlaw and finding K-P and the Bobs.

He hadn't had some freaky fascination with her like John Boy, but he'd wanted her. Her gorgeous face and killer curves alone gave them wet dreams. But it was her innocence that had them wild for her. Not too many virgins crossed their paths. Now, she'd been in Outlaw's bed for months and Stretch—several of the brothers—fantasized about the dirty things he'd taught her.

Now, they had to contend with Kendall and Bailey. At least, Bailey was gone, but Kendall was still there and if John Boy knew the way some of the brothers lusted after her, a fifth of their membership would be fucked up.

Zoann crossed his mind and a cold sweat slid down his spine. Another gorgeous chick. Another chick the boys discussed fucking into oblivion.

Stretch wanted a partner that made him feel like Hanson and Meggie did. Man or woman, he wanted someone to accept him for who he was. The biker life didn't suit everyone, but, Prez and John Boy had managed to get gorgeous civilian girls to stand at their sides.

Stretch didn't know the status of Zoann's relationship to Val. And Bailey?

Not that they mattered. Well, they did, but Outlaw scared the shit out of Stretch more than any one of the other dudes.

Outlaw…Stretch swallowed. Black hair. Corded

muscles. Big dick.

"Fuck!" he snorted, hating to remind himself he favored certain men and certain women. It just so happened Outlaw and his wife fit the bill. "Fuck times two."

"Woo...Stretch." Cash squinted at him.

Stretch's nostrils flared.

Squeezing his temples and sliding his fingers down his jaw, dark with stubble, Cash sighed. "Let me give you some advice. Better I do it, than Outlaw. You know shit about a motherfucker, don't let him know. That's your ace in the hand. If I were an enemy of the Dwellers, you just let me know you've been fucking checking up on me when you gave me my name."

Stretch backed away, putting distance between himself and Cash. "*Outlaw* told me your name."

"Good try, dumb ass." Cash shook his head and grinned again. "My first name? Yeah, I'm sure. That's all the fuck you need to know. Right? More than likely, he told you I'm *Ghost*." He lifted a brow. "That fucking ring a bell?"

God, it did. That was exactly the name Outlaw had given him. Riley, the club's PI had given Outlaw the report on Ghost—Cash McCall—and he checked out. Former military and loyal nomad in the Death Dwellers.

"Well, Woo Woo?"

Embarrassment heaped on top of his annoyance and Stretch wanted to punch him. Not to mention he hated that fucking name. "Let's make the transaction, asshole, so I can get the fuck gone."

"Soon enough, *Woo Woo*." He headed toward the door, his long legs eating up the space. "Have a drink with me first. I won't keep you too long. Wouldn't want to keep you from turning into some mad scientist motherfucker."

The last thing Stretch wanted was to remain in the company of that insulting asshole, but he wouldn't give him the satisfaction of knowing he'd gotten to him.

In more fucking ways than one.

Chapter 21

April slid into May and, although she and Johnnie slept together and made love, Kendall felt on the fringes of his life after their confrontation in the cave. The detached, offhanded manner he'd first treated her with returned, disturbing her, although he continued to hint at something more. Something long-term and permanent. But he wouldn't listen to her whenever she broached the subject of him leaving the club. Nor had he said he loved her again. He just expected her to adapt to being locked on the property while he disappeared every day, then guarded her every night.

Brooks visited several times. Christopher always invited Johnnie to the board room, but, *at least*, Johnnie respected her enough to decline, watching wistfully as Val, Digger, and Stretch followed behind their leader.

Kendall thought more and more about her conversation with Megan. Her belief that *Kendall* was in the position to do something about the human trafficking Spoon and Logan were involved in. If Johnnie didn't take more than just a sometimey interest in her, Kendall knew she'd have to walk away. Raise Baby Biker without him. She'd prefer being alone rather than having a man who thought of her *sometimes*.

The fact that he continued to refuse to even think about leaving the club pissed her off a little more. Seeing the site for Meggie's new house cleared made Kendall long for something similar. Her own house. Johnnie's utter and undying devotion.

Today, though, she'd had an AHA! Moment. After thinking about Meggie's conversation, she'd resumed researching human trafficking online. Years after passing the country's first anti-trafficking laws, the state still led the way on both sides of the law—amongst the worst offenders while still leading the fight with a dozen additional laws.

As long as swine like Spoon existed, though, the battle would be never-ending. She'd lost her little sister and she wanted to do something. Meggie was right. Kendall *was* in a position to do something. She was an attorney. She could call one of the non-profit organizations and offer her services pro bono. Or she could go to the police and tell everything she knew about Spoon and the Torpedoes.

Admittedly, not much, which might be a problem. Spoon had told her only a small bit and Logan had spoken in riddles to Johnnie, insisting *they*—Kendall, Meggie, Bailey, and Zoann—could bring in money if they were sold off.

And if she went to the cops, she'd put Johnnie and the Death Dwellers in jeopardy.

The stronger she became, however, the more she wanted to do something. For herself and Caroline and *to* Spoon.

Breathing in deeply, Kendall knocked on the door of Meggie's and Christopher's room.

"Come in."

Kendall opened the door, pausing when she saw Meggie curled up on the bed. Her morning sickness came and went now and she had more days where it didn't plague her.

Today didn't seem to be one of those days.

A stack of children's books sat on the bed, near the brick wall. Little Man cuddled close to Meggie, fussing around the baby bottle he drank from.

"Isn't he too old?" she asked in greeting.

"According to who?"

"Baby books. Doctors. Mommie blogs."

"Since *they* aren't paying for his formula, then they have nothing to say about it."

"What about his teeth? Won't his teeth cut crooked?"

"Circumstances stopped me from nursing him. If not, I'd planned to do it until his first birthday." She yawned. "I'm going to wean him from the bottle when he turns one."

Kendall pressed on her sensitive breasts. "Nursing until his first birthday?" The thought made her wince. "Again, what about his teeth? This time, though, I'm thinking of the damage to your nipples."

Meggie laughed and shifted on the bed. "The boys are gone?" she asked, not responding to Kendall's comment.

"Yes." She looked at the end of the bed, tempted to sit but not knowing if she should. Another indication of her stunted growth on female interaction. She'd never had a close girlfriend. At her age, it seemed rather silly to do all the things young women did.

Meggie sat further up and nodded. "Have a seat," she offered.

"Do you think I'm too old?"

"Um, too old for what?" Meggie chewed on her lower lip and a cold sweat broke out on Kendall.

She was feeling stronger, but she still felt...*inadequate*...paired with this girl who seemed so comfortable in any situation.

"To...to—"

"Toooooo?" Meggie urged, giving her an under-eyed look.

Sliding into the space on the edge of the bed, Kendall bowed her head.

"You aren't too old to do anything. You're what twenty-six? Twenty-seven?"

Kendall peeped at Meggie to see if she teased her, but she really thought she was that young.

"It doesn't matter," she said with a dismissive wave. "Age is nothing but a thing…" Her voice trailed off and she giggled, then cleared her throat. "You're never too old to do anything you wish to do."

Little Man rolled on his belly and lifted up on his elbows. He fisted his mother's hair, then stuffed it in his mouth.

"Silly goose!" Meggie chastised, tugging her hair from his mouth. "*No* eating Mommie's hair." She kissed his forehead before guiding him to his back and raspberrying his tummy. His giggles pulled a smile from Kendall. "I love you," she gushed, rubbing her nose against the baby's.

He rolled from her grasp and babbled before inching ever closer to the wall. Meggie retrieved the forgotten bottle from the bed and sat it on the nightstand.

"Are you bored?" Kendall asked, rubbing her belly. She hadn't started to show yet and couldn't wait to see the evidence of her baby growing inside of her.

"Yes. Very. There's not a lot to do right now. Not many visitors allowed in. We aren't allowed out. Arrow is looking after Momma. Christopher is off on Club Business." Hands behind her head, Meggie rolled her eyes. "This sucks."

Kendall licked her lips and wiped her clammy hands on her thighs. "I've taken your advice. I want to get Spoon."

"Good for you, Kendall," Meggie cheered with a bright smile. "He has it coming to him. Whatever you intend to do to him."

"I thought of going to the police, but then I decided not to because of the position it would place everyone here."

Meggie nodded slowly and pulled Little Man back when he lunged for the footboard. He was lively and quick. "I agree. So what are you going to do? Help out Brooks Redding? Tell him what you know."

"That's just it, Meggie," Kendall said quietly. "I don't know a lot. Not how involved they were with the trafficking. Or if just Logan and Spoon participated. Who the girls go to. Or where. Nothing."

"No, no, Christopher Joseph," she screeched, reaching for Little Man who had wiggled between his mother's feet and Kendall's sitting space. Picking him up, she gave him the raspberries again, rewarded with another happy laugh. She swung her feet to the ground, her son in her arms, and settled next to Kendall. "I'm sorry, Kendall. That must be hard to swallow. But Christopher and Johnnie and—"

"We can do something. You and I."

Meggie lifted a brow. "We're on the most wanted list for the Torpedoes as much as our guys."

"That doesn't stop them from taking action. We can figure out something to help out."

"Um, hello? Earth to Kendall. We're both *pregnant*. While the idea of helping out is very appealing, we can't do it at the risk of our unborn babies."

"You were the one who said I'm in a position to help out," she snapped, frustrated at Meggie's attitude. It seemed ingrained in the girl to go the opposite of whatever Kendall suggested.

"Helping out is a lot different than putting ourselves in unnecessary danger."

Kendall tuned Meggie's argument out, desperate to do this, prove to herself and Johnnie—*everyone*—that she could take care of herself and knew how to fight her own battles. She looked at her watch. "It'll be no danger. The hardest part will be getting off the premises."

Meggie rubbed her son's nose again and, for a moment, Kendall thought she wouldn't answer. "I don't have a good feeling about this."

"If I have to, I'll go alone." Although she'd prefer to have company with what she planned, she'd stand firm and go alone if she had to.

"What do you have in mind?"

"You'll come?"

"I'll listen to you and then decide if I'll come."

"There's no more than two brothers on the premises right now. Every day, they go *somewhere* around this time and are gone for three or four hours. I can get up to Spoon's office. He has a locked portable file. It has a USB drive in it. I know because I saw him put it in there a couple times when I accompanied Brooks on business."

"I'm liking this less and less." Meggie frowned at her. "That drive could be a red herring."

Kendall narrowed her eyes and Meggie flushed. "I doubt it," she said through tight lips.

"Think about it," the girl rushed on, not backing down. "Why would he leave a *portable* file out in the open when he knows several people know about the USB? It might be to see who's loyal to him and who isn't."

"Spoon is really cut and dry," Kendall insisted coolly. "He wouldn't waste his time…Oh never mind!" She got to her feet. "I'll do it myself."

Meggie huffed out a breath. "Wait. I'll come. I have a better chance of getting us off premises than you do anyway."

Even though Meggie hadn't offered the words to brag, the truth of them still chafed Kendall, but she ignored her annoyance.

"Let me see if Arrow can watch over my son. If not, I'll

call Bunny. Either way, I'll be ready to leave in ten minutes."

"Stop right here," Kendall instructed, not much later and two blocks from the Torpedoes' clubhouse. Unlike the Dwellers who had a compound on a dead end street that backed onto the woods in Hortensia, the Torps had a wooden structure that spanned almost a city block, close to downtown Portland.

Meggie backed the Mini Cooper into a tight spot between a pickup and an SUV.

"What now?" she asked, her brow scrunched in a frown.

Now, Kendall prove herself to Johnnie, show him that she'd be at his side through thick and thin. She was a strong, independent woman worthy of such a strong and willful man.

"Now, we go to the clubhouse," Kendall responded. "You go to the bar and strike up a conversation while I get upstairs to Spoon's office."

Skepticism glittered in Meggie's eyes and, for a moment, Kendall thought she'd changed her mind about helping her to do this. Instead, she leaned against the headrest and turned to Kendall, a small smile tipping her lips.

"I'm already showing." She splayed her fingers over her baby bump. "Dr. Will said you always show quicker with a second baby. I just figure it's because I'm almost twenty weeks. Further along than I thought when I realized I was pregnant again."

Kendall really didn't want to hear…Her thoughts skidded to a halt. How many times had Meggie reached out to her in some small way and she'd rejected the overture? Now, she'd left the safety of the MC to help her. At the least, Kendall could listen to her talk about her baby. Besides, they had that in common. And Megan had been pregnant before, so Kendall could use her as a go-to resource.

"You'll find out the sex of the baby your next appointment?"

Megan laughed. "I already know. It's another boy, just like I told Val it would be. Christopher doesn't know yet, though. I want all this behind us before I start bombarding him with baby stuff." She cocked her head to the side. "How far along are you?"

"Nearing eleven weeks," Kendall confided, surprised at how contented she felt at being able to discuss her pregnancy with another woman who seemed quite interested. "I can't wait to find out the baby's gender."

"I think we're in the season of boys. Christopher and Johnnie were the only two boys of all of Logan's grandchildren." She frowned and glanced out the window. "I wonder what makes men monsters, Kendall. Men like their grandfather. Spoon." She bowed her head and sighed. "My father." She slanted a glance to Kendall, her smile sad. "Whatever Spoon is doing...I know Christopher is going to get him, but I'm going with you because I don't want you facing this alone. But also because Big Joe...my daddy hurt those little girls. I owe it to them, so let's do this and get back to the MC before Christopher and Johnnie return, so they'll have no reason to worry. They'll be angry when you hand over the drive, but we'll be safe, so they'll get over it. I just hope it's there and it contains what you believe it does."

"Don't worry, Meggie. It will." Although Kendall spoke with certainty, unease slid into her but she had to do this. She opened the passenger side door. "Time to rock and roll."

"Hey, pretty lady, which part of heaven did you fall from?"

Kendall rolled her eyes at the greeting Megan received after she sashayed into the bar and sat on one of the stools. Instead of entering that area when they walked into the door, Kendall went left toward the staircase. She paused on the third step.

Kendall hadn't recognized the bartender's voice, so, hopefully, Spoon hadn't had a chance to show Meggie's photo around.

Kendall chose a time when nearly everyone except a few prospects were on premises, tending the bar. The Torpedoes MC saw bartending as a low-tiered, menial job, so their officers and regular members thought it beneath them. Unlike Mortician who seemed to enjoy the job himself. Not only that, the Dwellers deemed want-to-be members as probates.

Noticing the differences between the two clubs didn't mean she wanted to live her life as Johnnie's...*whatever*. She certainly didn't want to raise Baby Biker in an MC.

Drawing in a deep breath, Kendall tip-toed the rest of the way up the stairs, cursing Spoon for the pervert he was.

Reaching the second floor, Kendall scowled at all the baseball paraphernalia. She noticed a baseball on the file cabinet in the hallway and smiled at the time Spoon had gotten hit in the head—knocked on his ass—with one, receiving a mild concussion.

Apparently, all bad-ass bikers had some type of weakness. With Spoon and his boys, it was baseball—playing, watching, and discussing it. When they weren't up to no good. With Johnnie and his brothers, it was two little boys—Outlaw's and Val's sons.

Surprised at the pleasant thought, Kendall glanced in the VP's office, finding it empty just as she knew it would be. She almost sagged with relief at being correct. Getting that jump drive would be so easy.

Not wanting to waste a moment of time, she hurried to Spoon's office, blinking at the sunshine glaring through the opened blinds. The black plastic file box sat on the desk, in the usual spot, between the wall and the banker's lamp. Her fingers itching with anticipation, Kendall jerked the box to the edge, scowling at the sudden beeps. The sound spurred her to work faster. Popping the top open, she reached in and grabbed the drive, adrenaline pumping through her.

Being proactive exhilarated her. In her hands, she held the means to make a difference, find out who the girls were and get them rescued somehow.

A shadow bounced off the floor and desk, the specter of menace rising in the air. Fear slithered into her and her mouth dried. Kendall didn't want to turn, didn't want to see death looming in front of her.

"Cunt!" Spoon snarled, his voice echoing down the hallway and rising above Meggie's screeching. "Fucking biting me."

"Christopher is going to castrate you," Meggie fumed.

Hands yanked Kendall by the hair just as Spoon grunted and cursed.

"Little bitch, come back here."

Meggie was getting away and that was good. She didn't have to suffer. She'd get back to her husband...tell him about his soon-to-be born son. Kendall had gotten them—

"Oomph," she gasped, knocked against the desk, the drive falling to the floor, her breath whooshing from her lungs. Whoever had grabbed her thunked to the floor while the door slammed and a baseball rolled to a halt next to the head of the man. Meggie had used the baseball Kendall had seen on the file cabinet to knock him out.

Meggie leaned against the door, colorless, tearful, and breathing hard. "Do something, Kendall," she begged.

Spoon banged against the door.

"Why'd you come back for me?"

Meggie's eyes widened. "Because we're family," she snapped, trembling. "Do something."

Kendall shook, seeing the door buckling thanks to Spoon's relentless kicking. He had the key, but he wasn't using it for a reason. He aimed to hurt Meggie. "Get away from the door," she whispered.

With a little sob, Meggie ran to Kendall's side. The man she'd clobbered with the baseball groaned. The door flew open and Kendall reacted, pulling Meggie behind her, knowing no other way to protect her.

"Move," Spoon snarled, his face scratched and bleeding, furious because Meggie had fought him. "I'm going to fucking kill her."

"She's pregnant. Leave her alone. You want anyone, take me."

The other man swayed to his feet and blinked, scowling at Kendall and rubbing his head.

"What the fuck happened to you?" Spoon asked, his gravelly tone reminding her of a demon from a B grade horror movie.

"I was getting her—" He pointed to Kendall— "when something hit me in my head."

Narrowing his eyes, Spoon glanced at the floor, honing in on the baseball and lifting a brow. He howled with laughter. "Bitch knocked you the fuck out with a baseball. You probably have a concussion, asshole."

"We got to get them off-premises," the man said with meaning. "Remember? The meeting."

"Are you fucking stupid? You think I don't remember it? Brothers should start arriving soon." Spoon stepped closer and Kendall backed up, wedging Meggie between her, the desk, and the wall.

Kendall knew he intended to hit her. Before he got the chance, she girded her resolve and barreled into him with all her might, a growl escaping her.

"Run, Meggie," she screamed, landing on the floor along with Spoon.

She'd caught him off guard. Just as he'd done to her that day in her office. Balling her fist, she punched his jaw, knowing she only had a few seconds before the other man pulled her away and killed her. Or subdued her so Spoon could kill her.

A loud thud distracted her from a third hit to Spoon's face. He shoved her away, toppling her to the floor. The other man yanked her to her feet and rapped her hard on the side of her head before wrapping his arms around her to contain her struggles.

Spots danced in front of Kendall's vision, but she renewed her fight when she heard Meggie's scream of pain. A moment later, Spoon dragged her back into view and pulled her to her feet using her hair to maneuver her. Kendall glimpsed two other men in the background, laughing when he punched Meggie and she dropped to the floor.

Bile rose to Kendall's stomach and her belly heaved.

Spoon dragged Meggie back to her feet, He bent and slanted his mouth over Meggie's, yelping and jumping away from her. He massaged his bleeding lip where Meggie had bitten him, his eyes going from anger to fury.

"Meggie, stop," Kendall cried. "Please. God, please."

But she wasn't listening. When he grabbed her hand and forced it to his erection, she squeezed, the defiance and determination in her eyes alarming Kendall.

Spoon screamed in agony until one of the men stepped

forward and assisted in prying Meggie's fingers from his dick. He stared at her, his chest heaving, a couple of tears sliding down his cheeks.

He dropped into a nearby chair...and laughed. "Outlaw got himself a live one." He glared at her. "You wild fucking bitch."

Bouncing to his feet, he stalked toward Meggie, stopping until one of the other men yanked her arms behind her back and held her in place.

Spoon turned to Kendall. "Since you didn't have the pleasure of watching Caroline fuck herself up, I'll be nice enough to allow you to watch Megan Caldwell die." He aimed a blow right in the middle of Meggie's body.

Crying out and crouching over, Spoon's next blow landed on the back of Meggie's head. The man who'd been holding her released her and she crumpled to the ground.

Seeing Meggie's body on the floor snapped something in Kendall, made her want to watch Spoon die if she couldn't kill him herself. She elbowed her captor, stumbling at his abrupt release. Although she wouldn't win, she charged Spoon and swung wildly, kicked blindly, screaming in anger and humiliation, heartache and fear.

She wanted to kill him and make him suffer the way she'd suffered. She wanted to tell Johnnie how much she loved him. She wanted to sit with Meggie and discuss their growing babies.

Instead, someone grabbed her around the waist and looped rope around her wrists, nearly cutting off her circulation.

"Go find a fucking Mini Cooper," Spoon ordered through bloodied lips, not taking his gaze from Kendall and rattling off Meggie's license plate number. "Park it outside and get these two bitches in there." He turned toward the door. "Make sure the meeting doesn't start without me. It won't take me long to finish these two and dump their bodies."

Signaling his men to move Kendall, he turned and lifted Meggie into his arms, leading the way out the door to bring Kendall and Meggie to their deaths.

Chapter 22

"How fucking many do you want in the clubhouse, Christopher?" Johnnie growled, on edge. More than being blown to bits and pieces could go wrong. They were going to firebomb the Torpedoes' MC. If they survived and could be identified, they'd go to jail for a very long time. Not to mention a fucking *bombing* would be headline news.

"That's motherfucker number twenty-five," he said calmly.

The building took up half a block, flanked by a street on the left and green space on the right, including a huge white oak. Thick branches pressed against the windows on the side. At night—through drunken and high eyes—those branches appeared to be able to burst through the windows and snatch fuckheads out of the beds. One motherfucker had simply pulled his dick out of the whore they'd been taking turns with and ran the fuck away.

"Five more, then I go and do it."

Johnnie tightened his hand on the steering wheel, glancing around for Mortician, Digger, Val, and Stretch. They'd each offered to do the actual bombing, but Christopher refused, insisting it was his idea and his vengeance.

"I wonder if Megan okay?" he asked, frowning as one

man hurried from the club. He felt in his pocket for his phone for the fifteenth time since their arrival.

A moment later, the Torp fell face-forward, blood spurting from the area of his head. No sound of gunfire because they all had silencers on their weapons. Mortician ran forward and moved the man before Johnnie counted to ten.

"What's wrong with her?"

"Okay back to fuckhead twenty-five." Christopher pointed to another man entering the club, then sighed. "She worried bout this shit, of course."

"You fucking *told* her, asshole?"

"What the fuck was I supposed to do? Better her be prepared in case my ass blown off, John Boy. She'd be fuckin' hatin' my dead fuckin' ass."

"You fucking fuckhead, she's probably fucking worrying herself into a stupor."

"No the fuck she ain't. She fuckin' stronger than that."

"Just call her, asshole. Let her hear your voice."

Christopher was one stubborn motherfucker because he shook his head. "Nope. Don't even have my fuckin' phone on right now. I turned it the fuck off just like the rest of you turned yours off. Can't have no fuckin' distractions today. Megan'll understand."

Johnnie wouldn't argue. That was between Christopher and Megan. He had enough problems with Kendall. The way he'd handled the entire situation once they returned to their room pissed him off. Yes, fucking sexual frustration had led him to general frustration.

The door opened and Johnnie jerked. While he'd been lost in his concerns over Kendall, Christopher must've reached his magic number. He started the pickup and backed out of the immediate range of the building.

When he faced forward again, he didn't see Christopher and dread pitched through him. Christopher wouldn't have...?

Mortician jumped in the backseat and grabbed Christopher's Bushmaster. "I'm gonna fucking murder Prez if he go get his ass killed." He spoke so fast, his words jumbled together. He grabbed a clip and stuffed it in his pocket. "Kamikaze motherfucker. I can't believe he doing this shit. What the fuck gonna happen to Meggie if something happen to *him*?" He didn't wait for an answer to his rant, just jumped out, and ran, getting halfway before the explosion burst blew glass, concrete, and wood in every direction.

Johnnie couldn't process what his brain told him before he saw a figure on the opposite end climbing out of the second story window.

Christopher reached for a tree limb, a knife between his teeth. The moment he reached the ground, another explosion ripped through the middle of the building and he dove for cover.

Debris rained around them—glass, wood, and dust.

A pickup sped by—Val saluting him as he passed. Fire blazed from the roof, another explosion shaking the ground.

Christopher sprinted across the street, grabbing Mortician's shoulder and dragging him toward the truck. They entered the truck, the noise of car alarms and crackling wood and distant sirens splitting the air around them.

"Go, go, go, motherfucker," Christopher ordered, the third and last explosion bringing the rest of the building down, his eyes bright, blood smeared on his hands and cheeks.

Johnnie sped away, unable to talk, his heart not yet recovered from thinking Christopher had been blown up. "What did you do?" he asked after ten solid minutes of silence.

By now, Christopher had found something to wipe the blood from his face. He paused. "What the fuck you mean, what did I do?"

"Did I fucking stutter?" Johnnie snarled, furious at Christopher's selfishness. How could he have risked his life in such a way? "I thought you had one cylinder, asshole. One would've—"

"Let's see what the fuck I did?" He narrowed his green eyes in concentration and swiped sweat from his brow. "Walked the fuck in and locked the fuckin' door. Didn't want no brother-shootin', house-fuckin-up, little-girl-peddlin' motherfuckers gettin' the fuck away. I went the fuck upstairs and slit the fuckin' throat of the motherfucker who fucked up my wife's house. Placed some explosives there. Looked for the assfuck who shot you. Ain't fuckin' found him. Went the fuck *back* down, placed the big fuckin' explosive and ran like a motherfucker up-fuckin-stairs when I realized the motherfucker explodin' in fifteen fuckin' seconds instead of fifty. Any-fuckin-thing else, John Boy?"

"What the fuck happened to the remote controlled detonation?"

"You askin' me this shit *now?* Shoulda fuckin' asked me earlier. Yesterday. Two days ago—"

"I thought you were going the fuck in there and planting the shit," Johnnie interrupted.

"Me and Stretch decided to do shit different."

What could he say? He didn't know when Christopher had made the plans. Over the past few days, Christopher had invited him to the board room. When Johnnie declined, opting to stay with Kendall, he hadn't insisted.

"How'd you…set this…this took more planning than what we talked about with Brooks."

Christopher pulled out his phone and turned it on, pressing a number. "One, I needed to know I had that motherfucker's full loyalty and cooperation." He put the phone to his ear and continued. "Riley fuckin' checked him out and he passed. I don't pay that motherfucker for nothin'. He a good ass PI. Brooks *told* me who did what because motherfuckin' Spoon told *him*."

"Where was I? You planned all this—"

Frowning, he pressed another button on the phone before dialing again. "Look here, Johnnie, shut the fuck up. I'm tryin' to let you make your bitch feel safe. I wasn't bringin' you in those fuckin' meetins when your mind woulda been on *her*." A mixture of anger and concern dropped into his face as he pulled the phone away from his ear. "I left fuckin' Spoon for you and had Brooks summon other motherfuckers. So take care of your fuckin' woman, get her fuckin' straight, and then worry the fuck about meetins."

"This club means as much to me as it does to you," Johnnie fumed, slapping the dashboard, the stress of the last few hours pushing through. "You make it sound like—"

"Answer this motherfucker, Megan," Christopher ordered and rubbed his eyes, repeating his dialing and resuming the conversation. "I don't make it sound like shit. I'm fuckin' tellin' you the fuck like it is. Kendall need to get her shit together, so *you* can get *your* shit together."

"I resent that—"

"Don't give a fuck," Christopher snapped, slamming the phone into his lap. "I ain't got time to hold your fuckin' hand while you holdin' Kendall's fuckin' hand. With or without you, them motherfuckers had it fuckin' comin'. You know what the fuck it did to me seein' you fuckin' *shot*, motherfucker? *After* Megan's and my house was burnin' before my fuckin' eyes. One is bad e-fuckin-nough," he yelled. He picked his phone up again, but, instead of dialing, he opened an application. "Both was un-fuckin-forgivable. Then, when me and Brooks found out not only fuckin' Logan and Spoon peddled those little girls…I wanted to shove fuckin' pins up their dicks and dynamite up their ass. So fuck the fuck off. You made your fuckin' choice sittin' out there with Kendall."

Johnnie met Mortician's gaze in the rearview mirror. He'd been angry with Christopher for running into the building, but he'd been bugging out over Bailey's departure, so he wouldn't have known all the plans, either. Just that they were hitting the Torps' clubhouse that day.

"Kendall wants me to leave the club."

For a moment, neither Christopher nor Mortician spoke.

Christopher's clenched his jaw. "Do what you gotta do, Johnnie," he said without any of the emotion he'd just shown. "I'm gonna support you no matter what."

"You want to leave?" Mortician asked, subdued. The morning had affected him. No, Bailey had affected him.

"No. But I understand why she's asking, given her experience with Spoon."

No one answered. They wouldn't pressure him one way or the other.

"You want to leave, John Boy, go ahead. Do what you need to to make you and your woman happy," Mortician offered. "But Prez left Spoon for you at your request. *You* got to put him to fuckin' ground."

"What the fuck?"

"Wassup, Prez." Peeping over the middle seat to the raised phone in Christopher's hand, Mortician choked.

"Megan, baby…what…?" Frantic, Christopher dialed the phone again.

"What the fuck's going on?" Johnnie demanded.

"Meggie's car was parked near the Torps' clubhouse, an hour ago," Mortician answered, sliding back into his seat.

"Mort, pull that app up," Christopher ordered, his voice and hands shaking. "See where the fuck her car at now."

They all had the app because Christopher wanted each of them to have the ability to find Megan if he was unavailable.

"Johnnie, call Kendall. See if she answer."

The fear in Christopher's voice twisted Johnnie's gut and he grabbed his phone out of his pocket, realizing his own fingers were shaking as he turned his phone back on and dialed Kendall's number, getting the same result as Christopher. No answer. But he wouldn't panic yet. A couple of times, he'd called Kendall and she didn't answer. He'd had to leave a message.

"Where the fuck Arrow?" Christopher barked into his phone. He'd called the club, a good thing. Kendall might be involved in something with Megan on premises. "He's fuckin' *where?*"

He slammed the phone to the floorboard. He drew in deep drafts of air and hung his head in his hands. "Torps took out Gem. Val called Arrow to help with the cleanup."

"Prez," Mortician spoke, a hint of relief in his voice. He shoved his phone at Christopher. "Meggie car is here now. On Fortification. Got there about twenty-five minutes ago."

"Jesus H. Christ," Johnnie growled, swerving into the next lane and ignoring the angry horn honkers. "Torps place. That's where they'd taken Kendall when they got her."

Christopher nodded, not saying a word, just staring straight ahead.

"Meggie fine, Outlaw," Mortician said quietly.

A muscle ticked in Christopher's jaw and he balled his fists in his hands. "She better be," he responded in a low, vicious tone. "If she ain't, whoever fuckin' responsible is gonna wish they'd been blown the fuck up with the rest of them motherfuckers."

Chapter 23

Matthew "Val" Taylor straightened his white Tee shirt and shrugged into his cut, cursing the slowness of the sinking pickup, along with the body of the Torp Mort had picked off. Things were about to get rough. Not only had the Dwellers set off a bomb, they'd done it out of the jurisdiction of their police payoffs and in broad fucking daylight.

Outlaw had the biggest set of balls of any man Val had ever known. Now, they had to get rid of evidence. Clothes. Bodies. Weapons. Anything and everything that might be traced back to them. They also needed an alibi. They'd each put suggestions on the table, fine-tuning any holes. Only John Boy and Mortician hadn't been in on the planning and Val wondered if they might not be their weakest links in this do or die situation.

John Boy was dick deep in Kendall and Mort…Who the fuck knew? Bailey had gone on the trip with him and Val was pretty fucking certain Mort had put his dick out of its misery and finally gotten it in Bailey. Then, she'd fucking left and Mort was losing his shit, left and fucking right. They'd deal with that soon. At the moment, they had more important things to concentrate on than Bailey's pussy being acquainted with Mort's cock or that fucking bet the assfuck had yet to pay up on.

"I think it's done," Digger said.

Bubbles broke the surface of the river, but the pickup was finally submerged.

Stretch flicked a cigarette butt into the water. "You don't have much time to get to Zoann's."

No, he didn't, but he'd chosen this area because of its close proximity to her house. He'd called her and used all the powers of his seductive skills so she'd agree to let him look after their son. Tough to crack, but he'd worn her down. He'd arrived early this morning, along with another brother who had remained in the pickup until Zoann left. Then, Val waited for a while to make sure she wouldn't return before calling the brother in and leaving him with Ryan. They'd chosen a brother as close to him in build and looks as possible. More people than Zoann needed to see "Val" with Ryan.

She'd called two times already to check on their boy and Val admired her dedication and adoration of his son. She might despise him—or tried her damnedest to—but she loved Ryan.

Bidding Stretch and Digger farewell, Val started toward Zoann's house, hoping none of them ran into any complications. By the time he arrived, he had exactly ten minutes to spare before she arrived home and discovered his underhanded misdeeds. He banged on the door, scowling at the loud music and glancing at his watch.

He wasted two fucking minutes trying to get assfuck to hear. With the clock ticking and frustrated at what he needed to do, he yanked his knife from his boot and slit the screen to unlock it. Yanking it open, he tried the knob to the door and found it unlocked. *We Will Rock You* blasted through the house. He hurried to the source of the noise—Zoann's stereo system—and turned it off. The moment he did, he heard Ryan's whining and his heart dropped to his balls. Following the sound, he came to Zoann's bedroom, where he found his son in the middle of her bed with no sign of the man he'd left in charge.

Ryan's diaper bulged and Val thought about what he'd heard about the condition of Little Man. The moment Ryan saw Val, he held out his arms, his whine turning to cries.

Swearing he'd fuck up Gem Outlaw-style, Val rushed forward and took his son into his arms, murmuring soothing words to him. He wouldn't have enough time to clean Ryan up and change Zoann's bed, so Val decided to see to his son first. He had no clue why Ryan had just remained in the bed, but chose not to question the small favor.

He snatched a clean diaper and the baby wipes from Zoann's nightstand. He'd just removed the sopping wet one when he heard her call his name.

Fuck. At least Ryan's wails had calmed to babbling sniffles.

"In here, Puff," he called, his dick choosing this inopportune time to get hard. But Val always got hard for Zoann. When he'd first met her, years ago, and she'd been enamored of her big brother and her cousin.

"What are you doing in my bedroom, Matthew?" she bit out. "And what happened to my screen door?"

Val scooped Ryan into his arms and turned to her. Her beauty hit him in the gut as it always did. The gleaming strands of her chestnut-colored hair reminded Val of how it felt to glide his hands through the flowing silk. Suspicion brightened her whiskey-colored eyes. "He couldn't sleep, so I brought him in here to feel closer to you."

"And my ripped screen?"

He didn't have a good answer, so he snapped his mouth shut.

One of these days, he had to broach the subject of her rape. Sooner rather than later, too. Outlaw had decided not to bring it up to her, but he had their PI, Riley, investigating who her attacker had been. Outlaw had made it clear he'd allow Val to handle the man—when and if he was found—but he'd gladly do it, too.

Shit had a way of getting fucked up worse before they smoothed out, so Val figured it might be a good idea to warn Zoann of the shit storm brewing. First, they had to get out of this shit storm with the Torpedoes.

She'd moved close to him, the light scent of her perfume and the cinnamon gum she liked to chew hitting him in his gut.

"Fine. Don't tell me. I'm used to your juvenile behavior," she snapped, snatching Ryan from him. "Why isn't he dressed?"

Having no good answer for that, either, Val shrugged, coming across as an irresponsible dickhead.

She glared at him. "Would you get him something to wear out of his nursery?"

His nostrils flared and he swept a glance over her, stopping at the swell of her tits and traveling down, thinking of her pubic bush, but unable to see even an outline since her uniform top hung to right beneath her hip. She flushed, not as unaffected by him as she pretended.

She rocked back on her heels. "Would you watch over him while I take a shower?" she asked, peeping at him through the fringes of her lashes and making his dick hurt.

"Sure thing, Puff." He reclaimed Ryan, rewarded with his smile.

"I-I have leftover chowder if—if you haven't eaten the sandwiches I left in the fridge for you."

Zoann was inviting him to dinner? He had a vague

memory of her mentioning sandwiches this morning, but, he'd been so anxious to get her the fuck away, he'd ignored her. He could only hope Gem had eaten them.

"Yeah, I'm starving."

She smiled, shy. The gesture sped up his heart, more erotic than the most come-hither look and more heartening than a brilliant grin, made him almost dizzy with wanting her. He searched his brain to remember what he'd told her last night. The desperation of the situation made most of his words utter bullshit. Ironic when he hadn't been sincere, he'd gotten through to her.

She hurried toward her private bathroom, her hair fluttering behind her.

"Ma-ma?" Ryan asked, his blue-green eyes wide.

"Your mama is some kind of woman, huh, son?" Val smiled at Ryan's unintelligible response. "Worth every fucking minute, too. A girl needs a little bit of crazy in her to keep motherfuckers on their toes." Ryan raised his chubby arms and Val nodded. "You got it, buddy. I might be leaving here with blue balls, though. Don't think she'll let me fuck her right now…" His voice trailed off and he frowned. *Maybe,* he shouldn't have said that to his son. "Let's get you dressed and we'll see what happens."

Thinking how small Zoann's house was with only the kitchen, eating area, living room, her bedroom and Ryan's, he headed into the hallway—so small two motherfuckers couldn't fit in it—and turned right.

He pushed the door open and staggered back at all the blood. Splattered on the ceiling and walls. Pooling on the floor. Dripping from the rails of Ryan's bed. Jesus Christ.

Val's gaze fell on the body pieces, identifiable as Gem's thanks to the head on the changing table. The breeze from the gaping window fluttered the curtains. That must've been the escape route. Tightening his hold on Ryan, he squinted at the words written in blood on Ryan's light blue walls.

Torps rule.

Val slammed the door shut, considering his limited possibilities. Zoann and Ryan weren't safe here. That was fucking sure. Obviously, the Torps were watching them as closely as they were watching the Torps. Those fuckers were hitting where they were most vulnerable. Their women.

He could only be grateful Meggie and Kendall were safe on the compound.

Relieved at the knowledge, he considered his options again and got the same fucking result—not a fucking clue as to what to do.

If he told Zoann about Gem—no way would he *ever* allow her to see that fucking gruesome bloodbath—he'd have to confess about some of the other shit. And she'd *really* fucking hate him.

Wasn't he fucking hateable at that moment? He'd put Ryan at risk and couldn't imagine—didn't want to fathom—what he would've done if—

He glanced at his son, part him and part Zoann. Shaken to his core, he dialed the club number and explained the situation to Arrow when the man answered, sounding so much like K-P Val forgot for a moment the man was gone.

He went back into Zoann's room and closed that door, too, glad to hear the shower running. Zoann was too fucking nosy and suspicious for Val to even attempt to keep her in the room. The moment she heard the clumping of boot falls she'd want to investigate. For that matter, the moment she saw Ryan undressed, she'd try to take care of the matter herself.

Any way he approached it, he was fucked.

Unless…

He lifted a brow at Ryan, then glanced at the closed

bathroom door. Not wasting any time to contemplate the logic of his idea, Val sat Ryan on the bed and stripped, grabbing his son again and tearing open the tabs on his diaper as he hurried to the bathroom.

Stepping into the humid little box of a room, he paused, appreciating the steamy outline of her body, the clear shower curtain fogged by the hot water she loved. He thought of the blood again and swallowed.

That pieced up body in there could've been...*her*.

Zoann's scream pierced the space and both he and Ryan jumped.

"Get out!" she snarled.

He smiled at her outrage. She was very much alive. As prickly as ever, but alive.

Stepping forward and ignoring Ryan screwing his little face up to cry because he picked up on his mother's distress. Zoann wrapped the shower curtain around her and Val laughed.

"I can still see you pretty cunt, Puff," he told her, lying like fuck.

"*Pig!*" she screeched. "Get out of here. I don't know what you intend to do with our son here..." Her voice trailed off and she jerked in frustration, pulling the lightweight rod down. She yelped when the edge of it hit her head. Rod and curtain hangers bent and dangled over her hands.

"Let go," he told her.

"Get out," she countered, her lips trembling.

A boy through and through, Ryan rose to the occasion and came to Val's rescue. He started to cry and reached for Zoann. She'd never refuse their son. She glared at Val, but released the curtain, allowing Val to untangle her, so she could grab Ryan.

He didn't care the little boy was screaming right now, only that he kept Zoann preoccupied enough to allow Val to climb in behind her and settle his hand on her hips. He pressed his erection against her ass and she stiffened.

The water rained between them, hitting Val's chest and splashing against Zoann's and Ryan's head.

"I want to fuck you," he murmured, bending and biting her neck.

"You're a pig, that's why. You don't care that my son is here."

"You got it fucking right the first time," he growled, squeezing her ass cheeks. "*Our* son."

"Whatever! Just go. There's no way I'm fucking you with him in here with us."

He grabbed the soap from the holder that contained her shampoo, conditioner, and body wash, and began lathering his body. He'd smell like a girl, but who gave a fuck?

She went to get out, but Val stopped her. "Let's get Ryan clean."

"I'll give him a bath later," she argued.

"He's here with us now. And the water isn't bothering him."

Anger lit her eyes to sparkling amber, but she stiffened and nodded.

"Now, hand him to me. I'll hold him while you soap him."

"This isn't right," she complained, following his directions. "I'm breaking every good mom protocol in the book."

"You're one of the best fucking moms I know, Puff," Val muttered, fascinated by the play of her slim fingers spreading the soap on Ryan's arms, legs and torso.

"Let's hold him up to remove the soap," she instructed, not commenting on his compliment.

"What about his dick?"

She jabbed him. "He doesn't have a dick!"

Confusion knit Val's brow and he turned Ryan to look. All this time, he'd sworn his child sported a bat and two balls. Confirming what he already knew, he pointed. "Then what the fuck is that?"

"A penis. He's too young to have a dick."

Oookkkaaayyy. "Whatever the fuck you want to call it, shouldn't you wash it?"

"Not without a washcloth, asshole."

"Oh. Right."

"I hate touching him there even with the cloth. It doesn't…" Her voice trailed off, a haunting look on her face. "You'd never understand what it's like to be defenseless and at the mercy of a sexual deviant."

He stilled, his heart twisting at the pain in her eyes. Adjusting Ryan in a one-arm hold, he rubbed her wet cheeks with his other hand and knew it wasn't only water, but tears. "And you do, Puff?" he croaked.

She trembled and stared at him, her eyes huge. Instead of opening up to him, she shook her head. "I'm cold, Val. I want to get out."

If he calculated correctly, someone should just be arriving about now. Fucking insanity possessed him, thinking they could cover this shit up. He had to get her away from the house, anyway, so he needed to say something. But, fuck, he didn't want to give this up right now. And, he *knew* Zoann. Knew the derision she held for bikers. Although he was now aware of the reasons she'd push him away, once and for all, and, more than likely, limit his visits with Ryan or put a stop to them altogether.

She'd also find some fucking dickhead to marry who wouldn't be right for her. Not like he was.

Sighing, he turned the water off and grabbed a towel from the rack to wrap Ryan in. His heart skipped a beat. The baby thing—similar to what Meggie put Little Man in—sat just inside the door. She paused and glanced at it, lifting a brow in question.

Val cleared his throat, spotting her hair dryer. "I wanted to dry your hair and I thought we could lay him in there."

He expected her to argue, but she nodded. "Okay. That's where I put him sometimes when he wakes up before I'm finished dressing."

As she gave her explanation, Val bent and secured Ryan in the contraption. She stepped around him and pushed something on the side, starting a gentle, side-to-side motion.

"He needs a diaper."

"He's fine. Let me play in your hair for a little while." He led her to the mirror and stopped her, then turned her to face Ryan. "You can keep a watch on him while I do this."

Meekly, she obeyed him. He plugged up the dryer and turned it on high, not wanting to risk any noises reaching Zoann while he collected the comb and brush he needed. Maybe, he wouldn't have to take her away to keep her safe. Maybe, he could spend a few days here with her.

Halfway through, she elbowed him and he lowered the dryer's speed. "Ryan's asleep," she whispered. "For some reason, my hair dryer lulls him."

She glanced over her shoulder at him, stared at his chest, and met his eyes. Her breath hitched and Val groaned, unable to deny his body what it most wanted. *Zoann.*

He slanted his mouth over hers, unapologetic in the possession in his kiss, tasting her need and her surrender. He wouldn't last long enough to eat her pussy. Twisting his hands in her hair, keeping his mouth over hers, he tweaked her hardened nipple, skimmed his hand over her belly and, lower, massaging her pussy bush.

He fingered her clit, swallowing her moan, and inserting two fingers into her. Her cunt was hot and wet, ready for him. Lifting her around the waist, he didn't question her capitulation. He aligned his dick with her slick entrance and thrust into her, not having to urge her to wrap her legs around his waist.

"Val," she murmured softly, nipping his chin. The tears in her eyes surprised him but he shuddered when she clenched her pussy around his dick. He clutched her ass, grunted at her consuming heat, and ravished her mouth. She threw her head back, her hair cascading over his arms, her breasts thrust up.

He licked her nipple before biting gently. Keeping one hand around her waist, he shoved the other between them and thumbed her clit, rewarded when her orgasm broke over her. He pushed into her a final time, cum jetting into her.

When he came back to himself and caught his breath, Zoann had her arms wrapped around him and her head on his shoulder. He kissed the top of her head.

"Puff?"

"There was a bombing," she whispered. "At the Torpedoes MC. It's all over the news. Rival clubs at war. All I could think about was Christopher and Johnnie. And-and you."

Holy fuck.

She squirmed against him and blinked back more tears. "I came in, swearing I'd be angry with you. And I-I was. Especially when I saw my screen. But then…then I started th-thinking about our conversation last night and…and how scared I was when y-you were shot. I'm sorry f-for everything, Val. All the things I made you pay for that wasn't your fault. I don't know…I can't imagine what I would've done…if the Dwellers..." Her voice trailed off and she throbbed around him. She brushed her nipples against his chest and trembled.

He knew how sensitive her fucking tits were and growled at the sensation traveling through him.

"When was the last time you fucked?" he asked, sucking

the skin on her neck.

"The last time we were together."

Almost two fucking years. He stilled at the realization, knowing he wasn't anywhere as pure. He'd just participated in an orgy two days ago...*fuck.*

He started moving inside her again. A sudden, loud crash interrupted his rhythm and startled Ryan awake.

Zoann pushed at his shoulders. "Oh my God, Val! Let me down. Someone's breaking in. I have to get my bat."

He'd discuss the odds of a bat winning against a bullet another time. "See to Ryan. I'll investigate the noise. I'll call when it's all clear."

He didn't wait for a response, hurrying away and stopping long enough to put on his pants. Rushing to Ryan's room, he found Arrow, Bowlie and Slipper, staring at the overturned changing table.

The body parts were gone. Most of the blood wasn't.

"I can't keep her in her room much longer," he growled. "Especially now that you assfucks fucking tipped this over."

Arrow scratched his jaw. "Sorry," he whispered back. "We didn't bring enough supplies for all this fucking blood, Val."

"What was the fucking noise?" he hissed.

"A disagreement."

"A—"

"Matthew," Zoann interrupted, walking into the room and coming to a halt, losing her color when she looked at the blood...the *words.*

She stared, took it all in, and Val knew he was completely and irrevocably fucked.

Heaving in breaths, she turned in a slow circle, her gaze finally falling on Val. She didn't ask for an explanation—

Zoann wouldn't. Not with her history. She'd just assume the worst.

"Who's bl-blood?"

Val stepped forward and she backed away. "Zoann—"

"Who are the Torps? Torps...*Torpedoes.*"

"Listen—"

The accusation and hurt in her eyes cut him to the core and she hiccupped. "You dirty, evil, fucking *biker*," she snarled, bitter tears and hatred welling in her eyes. "Get out. I don't ever want to see you again."

"Clean this up, you two," he ordered, grabbing Zoann's arm and yanking her to her bedroom, ignoring her screeches. Ryan moved restlessly on her bed. He clapped his hand over her mouth and pinned her robed body to his. "Shut up. You're waking up Ryan and I need your full attention right now."

Her tears rained on his hand and he shoved aside his rising guilt. He shouldn't have taken advantage of her vulnerability but he was fucking human and couldn't pass up the chance to get inside of her again, enjoy the gentle Zoann that she rarely showed anyone.

"I'm not asking, Puff. I'm telling you that you have to either let me stay here with you or come to the clubhouse for a few days." She shook her head. "I don't know what the fuck you think went on here—" Probably not half as *bad* as what had *really* gone on. "I don't give a fuck right now. But you have those two choices and I want an answer about what's it going to be." He slid his hand down.

"Fuckhead, murdering bastard," she cried. "I *save* lives and you *take* them and *ruin* them—"

Yeah, yeah, yeah. He knew that. She knew that. For whatever reason, she'd chosen to ignore it this evening and several times before. He covered her mouth again to cut off her insults. "I don't have fucking time for this, babe," he growled against her ear, angry that he'd fucked up again with her. "We're going back to the clubhouse. You're taking a couple days off until we settle this with those assfucks. Nod your fucking head so I know you understand me."

She struggled in his arms and refused to comply, so he dropped his palm and loosened his hold on her. For a moment, she didn't move and neither did he, then she turned and slapped him so hard across his cheek fucking Tweety Birds circled his fucking head. She raised her hand to slap him again, but he caught her wrists.

"You like this fucking house?" he snarled, furious at his stinging cheek.

"Don't worry about what I *like*," she spat. "Concern yourself with what I hate. You!"

He ignored the words, although…fuck, he'd known what would happen. No use in looking back. "If you don't get some shit for you and my son, I'm going to drag you out of here and make the call to have it blown the fuck up. Then you won't have a fucking choice but to come with me at the clubhouse."

"You think? I *always* have a choice, Matthew."

He didn't like the sound of that. She had her four sisters, but Val's greatest fear was another man swooping in and stealing her away.

"You want this fucking house you will *choose* to come with me."

Pushing her away, he turned his back on her impotent anger. He'd pushed her into a corner for the time being because, if she knew nothing else, she knew he didn't make idle fucking threats.

Chapter 24

Pain careened down Kendall's side and straight into her belly, the sound of a song snapping her awake. She couldn't quite place the tune. She only knew she'd heard it before. Abruptly, it stopped then started again. Another sound began and Kendall tried to blink. She knew that sound, too, but she couldn't place it.

One eye swelled and rope cut into her wrists and neck. She sucked in a sob, unsure of her location or Meggie's whereabouts. Only knowing Spoon had gotten to them. They'd been so close to getting out, too. So close to getting that portable file. Then everything had gone to hell and Spoon had gotten them.

"She awakens." Spoon's nasty laugh sent shivers through her, but she remembered Meggie and her baby. Judging from the pain, she wouldn't have her baby for very long.

She drew herself up and shuddered at the pull of the rope, cutting into her throat. "Where's Meggie?"

Spoon lifted a brow, his hollow eyes disturbing her. How had she never noticed before? Had she been so lonely…so overwhelmed by the attention he bestowed upon her in the beginning…she'd ignored his true character?

"Where is she?" she yelled, fury at her stupid decisions and his cruelty rising up in her.

He snickered, then shrugged, leaning forward. "Wouldn't you like to know?"

Tears slid down her cheeks and another pain hit her belly. She gritted her teeth. "Christopher…Outlaw will gut you if you've hurt her."

"I *owe* that motherfucker," he snarled. "But *he's* the least of my fucking concerns right now. I want fucking Johnnie."

New fear clutched at her heart and Kendall slid forward a little, the pain more intense now, warm wetness sliding down her thighs. Spoon lowered his lids and focused between her legs, then nodded.

"The brat you're losing. *Johnnie's fucking brat*. He encroached on my territory. I'm going to feed him his fucking dick."

He stood from the chair he'd been in and stalked toward her. He reached above her. As he crouched down, Kendall noticed the knife glinting in his hand and she shrank back. His cheek caresses sent shivers through her. Licking the tears from her skin, he shoved his fingers inside of her. She attempted to twist away but the ropes tightened.

"Move a little more, Kendall," he whispered against her cheek. "You'll strangle yourself." Removing his hand from her body, he waved his bloody fingers before her and smiled.

Kendall growled, wishing she could get away to kill him because he was killing her baby. The blade glinted in the light at the same time Spoon grabbed handfuls of her hair.

"I'm going to kill you. As I've killed Megan. And as I've had Zoann killed." He slid the knife through her hair, then raised up the cut strands. "There's nothing he'll be able to do to get any of you back." He pulled more of her hair and the rope tightened around her neck. "We're striking today. Brooks is helping. He's called a meeting at the clubhouse with thirty of our members." He cut more of her hair. "The Dwellers are *dead*. Do you hear me? You three bitches won't be alone too long in Hell. I'll send those fuckheads down to join you soon enough." In silence, he hacked the rest of her hair away, then sat back on his haunches to study her.

A phone began to ring. *One and Only* by Adele. Christopher was calling Meggie. Within minutes, her phone started to ring, too. She didn't have a special ringtone for Johnnie, but she guessed it was him. The phones had awakened her, she realized.

Johnnie had been calling her whenever they completed whatever tasks they were involved in for the day. She'd just never appreciated how soon after he finished did he made the call. She'd just assumed he'd done other things first. Like she'd assumed so much these past few weeks. Most of them wrong.

By now both phones had stopped and started again. She didn't know Spoon's game. It would make sense if he picked one of them up to tell Johnnie or Outlaw where she and Megan were.

Spoon lifted her cut hair to his nose and sniffed, his eyes glazing over. "I'm going to jerk off to the feel and scent of your hair."

Movement caught Kendall's attention and she bit the inside of her cheek. Meggie. Blood dripped from the side of her head and her nose. Bruises covered her arms and thighs. And her belly. She'd been crying. She'd been stripped. As pale as a ghost, the blood dripping down her legs smeared her thighs. She held a vase in her trembling hands.

She must've stared too long in Meggie's direction because Spoon looked over his shoulder, roaring to his feet and charging toward the girl.

Frantic knocking began on the door and Spoon paused, scowling between the two of them. Just long enough for Meggie to crack the vase against Spoon's head. He sank to the floor, Kendall's hair fluttering around him, the knife he held clattering to the ground.

Meggie grabbed the knife and stumbled toward Kendall, ignoring the pounding on the door. Spoon groaned, dazed rather than knocked out.

Something thumped against the door and Meggie began slicing through the rope on Kendall's wrists. "They're going to kill us," she whispered.

"No," Kendall swore. "No. You're doing fine. Just get me free, Meggie, and I swear we'll get out of here." But Meggie didn't have a lot of strength with her beating and blood loss.

Suddenly, Meggie wrenched back. Spoon had grabbed her by the hair and snatched her away from Kendall, throwing her aside like a rag doll. She landed with a loud thud just as the door burst open.

"Hands the fuck up," Christopher snarled. A howl of rage erupted from him and Kendall knew he'd spotted his wife.

Gunfire blasted and Spoon screamed, dropping to his knee.

"*Johnnie!*" Christopher boomed. "*Mortician!*"

"Aww, fuck, man," Mortician managed, staring in her direction.

"Did you find—" Johnnie's voice stopped. Staring at her, he didn't notice Christopher kicking Spoon until he begged for mercy.

Mortician sucked in a breath. "Meggie?" he whispered.

Johnnie spared a glance over his shoulder, his eyes widening when Kendall crumpled on the other side of the sofa. He knelt in front of her and hugged her before pulling back and taking inventory of her. Her hacked off hair. Her battered face and body. And their baby…

Withdrawing his knife, he had her free within moments and Kendall sagged against him, sobbing and holding on for dear life, never wanting to let him go.

"Prez! Prez!" Mortician hollered. Nothing. Spoon's pleas and the sound of flesh meeting flesh continued. "Outlaw, see to Meggie. I'll take care of this piece of shit."

Johnnie laid Kendall on the sofa near where Meggie lay, unmoving. He took off his cut and removed the shirt he wore, placing it on Kendall and then putting his cut on again.

"Christopher!" Mortician yelled, getting through to him because the sounds of Spoon getting beaten to death ceased. "I'll take him—"

"No, Mort." Thick with rage and heartache, his voice trembled. "You not doing shit." He took out his gun and aimed it at his head.

"No, Christopher," Johnnie called. "This is too easy. He deserves…he deserves more."

Christopher struggled with the urge to shoot and the desire to see Spoon suffer. But Meggie groaned and he started, the relief on his face combining with the fear and the pure loathing. He holstered his gun and ran to Meggie, lifting her into his arms and nosing her hair. "Christopher," she croaked. "The baby—"

"It's okay, baby. You here and that's all that matter." He drew in a deep breath. "Get that motherfucker to the meat shack, Mort," he rasped. "John Boy, I'm gonna let you do what you gotta do, but I'm gonna start this motherfucker off. He's gonna wish for fuckin' death." He lifted Meggie up and she bit down on her lip.

Kendall wondered why she wouldn't cry out in pain. It was obvious she was hurting terribly.

"One of you call Val. Tell him we'll be around in a

fucking minute." He tightened his hold on her. "I don't ever want you motherfuckers talkin' to me about havin' the trackin' device in Meggie's phone. Call me what the fuck you want, but my fuckin' stalkin' saved both her and Kendall."

Not waiting for a response, he turned and hurried from the room. Mortician stepped forward and lifted Spoon, throwing the man over his shoulders while Johnnie scooped Kendall into his arms, his face grim.

"It's okay, Kendall." He kissed her forehead. "You're okay. You're safe now."

For the first time in her life, Kendall believed that she was. With a nod, she laid her head on his shoulder and sank into unconsciousness.

Johnnie stared at Spoon, sprawled out on the table in the meat shack, tears and snot dripping down his face. Sweat popped off his chilled skin, his balls shriveled with the cold and the pain from Christopher's *turn*. Piss dripped onto the floor.

Mortician lounged in the corner, a cigarette hanging from his mouth, his plastic gloves and rubber apron already on. Five minutes ago, Christopher had stormed out, the ice pick he'd used to poke tiny holes in Spoon's arms and legs protruding from one of the man's knees. His fingernails lay in a bloody heap beside him.

Spoon was right where Johnnie wanted him, but he wrestled with disappointment that he wasn't responsible for getting Spoon to this point of suffering. He swallowed, unable to recall Kendall's softness. Her pretty face. Her feminine voice. *Anything* to keep a small bit of humanity inside of him. And he needed that right now. Desperately. Not for Spoon. No, that motherfucker had a slow, painful death coming. Johnnie intended to bring him to the brink of death before pulling back and allowing him to live.

He was versed in torture and death. Because it was who he was beneath it all. Beneath the smiles and the laughter. Christopher didn't have the patience for dragging out some assfuck's demise. Not like Johnnie. None of them did.

"Yo', John Boy," Mortician called. "See all them tiny holes Prez put in fuckhead? They bleeding. He probably have a little internal bleeding going on, too, with the whup ass Outlaw put down. I don't know what kind of freaky, scary shit you concocting, but whatever the fuck it is, I say get the fuck to it before he bleed out."

"I wouldn't want that to happen." He stepped next to Mort and grabbed a half full bottle of tequila, then returned to Spoon, pouring the alcohol on each wound, the man's screams not appeasing his simmering rage. "I don't want you to wonder at your fucking crimes, bug food. Okay?"

"John Boy, please—" he croaked, choking back a sob.

"Please? Did I hear *please*?" Johnnie laughed, slipping away the cloak of humanity and going to that place...*that place*. "Kendall said please, didn't she?" He yanked the ice pick away, focused on the dripping blood, remembering his lost baby. He jabbed Spoon, not paying attention to where. "What about those little girls you stole, drugged and sold?" This time, he allowed the ice pick to remain, bent and grabbed his blade from his boot.

"Aww, fuck. I knew you had to go all Freddy Bates on me." Mortician scowled at him. "Norman got that bitch in a fucking shower, John Boy. You know? To wash the blood the fuck away."

"And Kruger?" Johnnie dragged his blade along Spoon's forearm before thrusting it into his muscle. "With fucking razors on his hand?"

"Fuck off. Motherfucker didn't have to clean up."

"I swear, Johnnie," Spoon cried. "I fucking *swear* I'll leave. I-I'll leave the fucking country. I swear."

"Shut the fuck up," Johnnie snarled, flicking the alcohol in the fucker's face. "You hurt Kendall." He grabbed Spoon by the throat and squeezed. "How the fuck does that feel, motherfucker?" he breathed, almost unable to release him when he began turning purple. He paced next to the table where Spoon choked and gasped for breath. "It's unfortunate I can't use *my* dick to choke you." He glanced at Mortician, opened his mouth to speak to Spoon again.

"What the fuck you looking at me for?" Mortician snarled. "Don't even think to fucking suggest using *my* dick to choke his ass."

Johnnie flipped Mortician off, then turned back to Spoon, wiping the blade on his pants since he hadn't put on another shirt. They'd gotten Kendall and Megan to the hospital and left. He couldn't sit and worry himself sick over Kendall while Spoon had a chance of slipping away from the injuries Christopher had given to him. He knew Christopher was already on his way back to be at his wife's side.

Johnnie wanted to be at Kendall's side, too. He wanted to hold her and love her and promise she'd never get hurt again. Only, he couldn't promise that. Because as long as she was with him, she *would* be at risk. He had no idea how they'd even gotten into Spoon's hands. As far as he knew, their compound hadn't been breached, which meant her and Megan had left.

And why shouldn't they? Because of this asshole, they'd been virtual prisoners. He'd have to talk to Christopher. Perhaps, then, Megan wouldn't have convinced Kendall to put herself in danger. Perhaps, then, Kendall would still be carrying his baby biker.

Baby Biker was gone. Johnnie hadn't realized how attached he'd grown to it...until now. When he couldn't go to a doctor's appointment with Kendall. Or promise her how truly happy his impending fatherhood made him.

His nostrils flared and he glared at Spoon, plunging the knife into his hand. The asshole had a high tolerance for pain.

"We're not into vigilante justice, motherfucker, but, in this case—" The faces of Caroline and the other nameless, little girls they'd come across. The grown women, too, and they were tragic and sickening and nauseating. But, they were...of age. He swallowed, reminding himself Logan had been involved, too. Logan had gotten Spoon involved and Spoon had gotten his entire club involved.

Mortician's phone rang while Johnnie shoved his bloodied knife into his cut to get a bucket and fill it with water. Returning to Spoon, he threw it on him, hearing his wheezing and seeing his gasping for breath. He must've had a collapsed lung and broken ribs. He wanted him to live a while longer. He had his toenails to see to. His teeth to pull. He had—

"John Boy," Mortician called.

Spoon moaned, his weak gaze pleading for mercy.

"You want compassion, buzzard feed? Ironic considering what an unsympathetic motherfucker you are." He slapped the man's face. "You're a bad motherfucker, huh? Fight me. Stand the fuck up. Face a real fucking man."

"Johnnie."

"You can't, can you? Even before you were one-step away from corpse-hood."

"Fuck, man. JOHNNIE!"

Johnnie snapped his gaze to Mortician, annoyed at the interruption. "What?" he growled.

"Get through here. Kendall asking for you. Me and Val got to get to Zoann's house and bring Spoon. Dead or alive,

300

Prez don't give a fuck."

"Bring Spoon to Zoann—"

"Outlaw gave the order to blow it up. The Torps hit it, too, and we got to make sure we wiped out all those motherfuckers. You know she won't cooperate. I think Val wanted that motherfucker to go boom boom pow and just fucking scared to tell her."

Johnnie narrowed his eyes at Spoon. "I wonder what's best for you. Fucking finish you here then have you blown to bits and pieces?"

"No, no, no! Please, Johnnie. PLEASE."

Mortician lit another cigarette. "I'm giving you ten more minutes. I say if he's dead, he's dead when we get there. Just avenge your woman and your baby. Those little girls."

Johnnie's pulse kicked up at Mortician's green lighting his walk into insanity.

Chapter 25

Christopher stared at Megan, hooked up to various machines, antibiotics and fluids dripping into her from the IV. Their new baby...*gone*. Gone like Kendall's and John Boy's baby.

None of this would've happened if the two of them would've stayed fucking put. Megan was going to drive him to the fucking mad house. When he'd seen her...his heart dropped to his fucking dick just thinking about her so still on that floor.

He'd thought...fuck him...if she would've been...

He squeezed the bridge of his nose.

"Christopher?"

He blinked the moisture from his eyes, wanting to stomp something for being so pussified over her. Coming to his feet, he shoved his hands into his pockets. "Baby." He cleared his throat, gritting his teeth at the break in his voice. "Megan," he said gruffly.

"The baby?" she whispered, her eyes huge, tears already forming because she *knew*. She knew it was gone.

He leaned over and kissed her mouth, thumbing away her tears. "I'm sorry, baby. I'm so fuckin' sorry."

A sob escaped her and she clutched his hand.

"What was you doing there? Huh, Megan?"

"We were looking for a file," she sniffled groggily. "We were trying to get something on Spoon."

Christopher thrust his fingers through her hair, nuzzling her neck, anger bubbling the fuck up. "You got in fuckin' Club Business?" he snapped, reminding himself she was in the hospital recovering from a beating and loss of blood.

"W-we didn't mean to." Her eyes slid closed, then opened again. "I told Kendall she was in the position to do something to help girls like her sister."

He might not have been on the premises a lot recently and it might've *seemed* like he wasn't paying attention to Megan, but he fucking *swore,* he'd bet his fucking dick, Megan had had that conversation with Kendall a few days ago. Kendall wasn't the fucking type of bitch who went the fuck out and did shit immediately. No, she kept her fucking mouth shut, hid shit better brought to fucking light, and *still* fucking hesitated and thought out shit. So how the fuck did that conversation come to fucking play *here?*

"You told her that today?" he asked to be certain. Bitch could always fucking surprise him.

"No," Megan slurred. She drew in a breath, ending on a sob. "I…don't worry…I love you…I'm sorry I lost our baby."

He was sorry, too, but he had Megan, the more important one. *Selfish motherfucker.*

"I'll give you many, many more," he swore, flipping off his conscience.

A little snore escaped her and he stared at her. She was barely lucid, but he wanted fucking answers and there was no motherfucking way he would wait.

He was getting a fucking idea of what the fuck had happened. He shook her gently and her lashes fluttered before her lids raised. She focused on him and, in that unguarded moment, Christopher saw everything he needed to know. Everything he *already* knew. How much she adored him. How much she valued him. If he lived to be a hundred, he'd never stop showing her how mutual her feelings were.

"Christopher—" Her eyes started to close.

"Baby?" He squeezed her shoulder. "You was hurlin' like a motherfucker when I fuckin' left and told me you was stayin' in the room 'til I got fuckin' back. How Kendall got you to change your mind?"

She frowned in concentration. "I had a bad feeling."

"Yeah?"

"Uh huh," she admitted with a nod and a yawn.

"Not fuckin' bad e-fuckin-nuff if you fuckin' went."

Silence. But she rarely volunteered information, so he'd go the usual route.

"Kendall wanted you to help her get what?"

"A-a file. I think. USB."

"A fuckin' computer drive?"

Another nod.

"Fuck me…what the fuck wrong with you, Megan? Spoon might be a stupid motherfucker but he ain't *a stupid motherfucker?*"

She blinked. "Huh?"

"If he had a fuckin' file out in the fuckin' open he was fuckin' testin' motherfuckers," he yelled. "Where the fuck your fuckin' brain?"

Tears rushed to her eyes and she sniffled, starting to cry outright. Her blood pressure began to rise and Christopher thrust his hands through his hair. His own pressure was rising. He balled his hands into fists. He hated his fucking fear and vulnerability, and she'd put herself in that position. Fuck, he should put her over his knee and spank her.

He bent and kissed her cheek. "I'm sorry, baby. I'm not meanin' to be a fuckhead to you."

She smiled. "Yes, you are."

Unable to stop it, a grin broke free. "Fuck me, Megan, you scared the fuck outta me." He pulled in a breath, just realizing his heart still hadn't settled back into place. "Ain't she told you—if you fuckin' forgot or don't fuckin' know—I mean…Kendall…ain't she told you it was a fuckin' phony lead."

Her brows furrowed and she bit her lip, then her eyes widened in comprehension. She swallowed. "I-I'm tired—"

"No the fuck you ain't," he growled, knowing, deep down, that she *was*. But knowing *her* so well he'd seen her grasp of the events. "I wanna know what the fuck happened. Unless…" Narrowing his eyes, he cocked his head from side to side, watching her avoid meeting his gaze.

"What you said to her, baby? Tell me. I swear I'm gonna be fuckin' reasonable. John Boy," he snarled, then coughed to cover his rising anger. "She that motherfucker old lady, baby. So tell me. What'd you say to her?"

"I-I think I told her it was a red herring."

Christopher growled and she snapped her mouth shut, so he coughed again. "Motherfuckin' cold killin' me, baby."

"You're sick?"

He waved away her concern. "Ain't nothin' but a fuckin' thing. So you told her she was a stupid fuckin' bitch—"

She frowned at him.

"Er, Kendall. You fuckin' told Kendall—"

"I don't quite remember," she hedged.

Bullfuckingshit, but he'd let it pass. "After you *might've* fuckin' told, er, Kendall, she asked you to fuckin' go?"

"No." Her head listed to the side. "I volunteered. Otherwise, she'd go on her own and she'd already asked me."

"And you already turned her the fuck down?"

"Yes. But I-I couldn't let her go alone, especially with the bad feeling I had…" her voice trailed off and her chin wobbled. "I-I'm sorry," she said again. "If I would've insisted we stay, I wouldn't have lost our baby."

He wouldn't mention right now that Kendall had also lost *her* baby. "It's okay, Megan," he whispered. "I swear, baby. I know you hurtin' right now, but I'm right fuckin' here for you. Don't think you goin' through this shit alone."

"I know," she responded without hesitating, her eyes drifting closed again.

This time, Christopher let her fall asleep. The doctor said she was looking at two or three days in the hospital. Perfect for Christopher. Megan wouldn't be around to see heads fucking rolling. Kissing her forehead and her lips again, he swiped at the drying tears, his heart hurting for her and their baby. He hadn't put nearly as many holes in fucking Spoon as he should have, but, fuck, he'd wanted to hurry up and get back to Megan. If Johnnie hadn't wanted the motherfucker, he would've just beaten the fucker to death in that fucking house.

The door opened and Christopher glanced over his shoulder, scowling when Zoann marched into the room and headed for him. He anticipated she intended to slap the shit out of him, so he grabbed her hands just as Val walked in. His lips thinned in disapproval at the tight grip Christopher had on Zoann's wrists.

"You bastard," she screamed, struggling to free herself. "You had my house blown up."

"I sure the fuck did," he snarled, wanting to shake her until her teeth rattled for being stupid enough to spit that information out. Thankfully, no nurse or doctor bitches were in the room.

She already knew what happened, so, why the fuck deny it?

"One of the brothers was fuckin' killed and cut the fuck

up in that motherfucker. You fuckin' insistin' on goin' back."

"It was my *house*," she cried. "You had no right to—"

"I had *every* fuckin' right, Bitsy," he growled and they both stilled. He hadn't called her by the name he'd bestowed upon her a lifetime ago in fucking years. He'd never thought to call her by that name again, but, fuck him, after he found out what Logan had done to her, betting Christopher's death or Zoann's virginity.

Dirty, fucking, vile motherfucker.

His grip on her slackened. She pulled her hand back and cuffed him on the side of his head.

"E-fuckin-nuff, Zoann." He gripped her hand again, glaring at Val when he stepped forward.

"Don't call me Bitsy ever again," she sobbed. "You don't have that right. You left me and I needed you. I waited for you, Christopher. I waited for you to help me. You never came." She swiped at her tears.

Christopher flinched. He'd always been so proud of Zoann. She'd been spirited and perky and had dogged the fuck out of him. When she'd turned into the vile bitch she'd become, he'd swept aside any feelings and all the memories of him and his little sister.

"Boss told me," she went on, grabbing his attention. "Boss told me that you were sick of me. You didn't have time—"

"Big Joe was a fuckin' liar," he snarled. "I always had time for you."

"I looked for you. Every time I went there, it was always the same thing. And no one had time for me. Except…except Matthew," she finished on a strangled voice. "It wasn't all the time. He just…he seemed like he cared."

"Christopher cares," Meggie called weakly.

"You're his wife," Zoann snapped back. "You're required to say that."

"Boss was a fuckin' liar and that's the fuckin' truth. I'm sorry I wasn't there for you when you needed me, but you ain't fuckin comin' in here insultin' Megan."

"Why you needed Christopher so bad?" Val asked.

She lowered her lashes. "It doesn't matter," she said after a moment. "It's over. I don't need any of you now, so I'm not staying at your stinking club. *Ever.*"

"Puff—"

"Zoann—"

"Let me talk to her alone," Meggie called, interrupting both of them.

Not a fucking good idea. She was just this side of fucked up with the pain meds and sedatives.

"I don't think so, baby," Christopher began. All the activity prevented her from sinking completely into oblivion. But, then, she wouldn't have a fucking filter and would blurt any-fucking-thing to Zoann.

Zoann threw him a venomous glare. "I want to talk to her."

Of fucking course. Val looked horrified but Christopher shrugged, then indicated they leave. He walked out of the room in time to see Mortician and Johnnie coming down the hallway. Fucking Johnnie still hadn't put on another shirt and Christopher wanted to laugh at the way those nurse bitches ogled him.

And Mort. *That* motherfucker…Christopher was waiting for his balls to explode. As much as he liked to fuck, he hadn't touched one fucking bitch since Bailey's departure. Motherfucker thought no-fucking-body noticed his dick hiatus. As much as he worshipped his fucking cock, it was hard *not* to fucking notice.

The moment they got into range, Christopher intended to blast Johnnie for having a throwed off bitch around

Megan.

He took a good look at him. Devastated. Angry. Christopher's *brother*. They'd been through so much shit together and Johnnie needed to be happy. He needed his own family and a good woman.

Kendall might've made a fucked up decision that'd led to some disastrous fucking goings-on, but, Megan was alive. Besides, Kendall probably wanted a piece of that motherfucking Spoon herself. He wanted to shake the fuck out of her, but, just as he had to give Bitsy a fucking pass, he had to give Kendall one, too. When all was said and done, those girls had been through some fucking horrors, so they needed some fucking understanding.

Christopher would just chain Megan to the fucking bed when he had crazy motherfuckers to deal with.

"So, excuse me," Johnnie finished, breaking into Christopher's thoughts and he realized he'd gotten the tail end of the conversation.

Hanging his head, he stuffed his hands into his pockets and walked toward Kendall's room.

"What the fuck with the hang-fuckin-dog look?"

Mortician rubbed his neck. "John Boy think Kendall never going to be safe as long as she's with him."

"Don't fuckin' tell me," Christopher snapped. "He's breakin' the fuck up with her?"

Val nodded.

Glaring at the two of them, Christopher followed the direction Johnnie had gone.

He would start fucking charging for turning into Dr. Fucking Love.

The though made him smile—

"Christopher!"

Zoann's cry cut into his thoughts and he spun,

everything else shooting from his head.

Focused on his sister. The tears in her eyes. And the uproar going on amongst the nurses rushing to Megan's room.

And rolling a defibrillator in.

Chapter 26

Johnnie placed a kiss on Kendall's forehead, rubbing his hands through her ruined hair, slightly vindicated at Spoon's demise and his role in it. But it didn't bring her little sister back. It didn't bring all the other girls back. Nor did it take away all of Kendall's personal pain. Or put their baby back in her womb.

Nothing could do that. If not for him and his grandfather, she wouldn't have suffered half as much. She was strong and smart, deserving a man who wouldn't have the club as his mistress in their marriage. Because he couldn't...he just *couldn't*...walk away from the Death Dwellers.

Selfishly, he didn't want to walk away from her either. He wanted to marry her, have many, many babies with her. God, he was such an asshole to think this, but she'd been drugged and given alcohol. Who's to say the baby wouldn't have been damaged? He would've loved it anyway it was born, but, maybe, this way was best.

Distant commotion broke into his brain, but Johnnie ignored it, wanting to be at Kendall's bedside.

She looked so peaceful in sleep, even with all her injuries.

Jesus. If Christopher wasn't so paranoid about Megan's safety, Kendall would've gotten killed. Both of them would've gotten killed. He would've been hurt to his core if something had happened to Megan, but if anything had happened to Kendall, he would've been devastated.

He kissed her again and flattened his hand on her belly. Penance for always believing in and protecting Logan? Perhaps. Something to do with the sins of the father falling upon the child.

Kendall's eyelashes fluttered and she stared at him through glazed eyes.

"Kendall, sweetheart," he croaked, caressing her belly.

"Johnnie," she whispered, attempting to lean toward him and over the railing to hug him.

"Keep still," he ordered.

"M-Meggie?"

"Is fine," he reassured her, although he really didn't know. He hadn't asked and no one had given him the status of her condition.

"Baby Biker?"

Baby Biker. He drew in a deep breath to keep from roaring in rage. "Gone, baby."

She covered her mouth with her hands, but the sob still bounced in his head, breaking his heart.

"It's my fault," she cried.

"No. It isn't. Megan—"

"Told me not to go," she whispered in a broken voice.

"What?"

"I didn't listen. She came because she didn't want me to go alone. I wish she would've let me."

Johnnie stroked her hair. "Shhh. It's okay, Kendall."

"It isn't," she insisted, sobbing her heart out. "Baby Biker—"

"Is at peace." He wished he believed that. But he didn't know where anyone went in the next life. Had never really thought about it. Now, though, with their baby lost…gone before it had even had a chance to take its first breath. Now, he wanted to believe different.

His heart twisted and it felt as if it would splinter. Their baby, *his* child...son or daughter, it didn't matter...lost. He fought the urge to cry, the heat surging through him a combination of grief and guilt.

What now? Where did they go and what did they do? In the back of her mind, Johnnie knew she'd always believed he was with her because of Baby Bi...Fuck, no. He couldn't think of the baby that way anymore. It hurt too bad. It was his precious angel now. Kendall's, as well.

He got the bed railing down and gathered her in his arms, allowing her to cry out her pain and frustration, embarrassed at his tears sliding down his cheeks. "Don't worry, sweetheart," he whispered once he controlled his sorrow. "Everything's going to be fine. I promise."

Opening her eyes, Kendall glanced at the chair Johnnie had been in the last time she'd awakened. Empty now. Like her life. Like her belly. She'd lost Baby Biker. Her baby...Johnnie's child.

She covered her face with her hands and a sob escaped her.

"Kendall?"

Christopher's voice startled her and she jerked her head to the other side of the room. He stood near the window, the sunlight framing him, silhouetting his long, muscular body and glinting off his blue-black hair. He walked forward, the dark circles around his eyes and the tightness in his mouth alerting Kendall to his concern. He stopped at the edge of the bed, his green gaze roaming from the top of her head to the foot of the bed where her feet were tucked beneath the covers.

"You okay?"

She licked her lips, wanting to cry all over again at softness of his voice. She wasn't okay. Far from it. She shook her head. "I lost Baby Biker," she sniffled.

"My wife lost ours."

Huh? "What do you mean—"

A chill settled into Christopher's eyes and he gave her a hard stare. "Listen up, Kendall. I didn't take this directly to Johnnie because he'd defend your miserable fuckin' ass. As well he fuckin' should. You wanna fuckin' tell him, that's your fuckin' business. But seein' as how you been such a tight fuckin' lipped bitch about life and death shit, I suspect you keepin' the fuck shut up about whether me and him become mortal fuckin' enemies."

Tears rushed to Kendall's eyes and she turned her head away, not having the strength to order Christopher gone. She couldn't begin to express the sorrow over Meggie's lost baby, but she'd lost hers, too. She was paying the price for her stupidity in the most horrible way imaginable. She hadn't heeded a single word anyone had tried to impart to her.

And for what?

She'd wanted acceptance, had needed to do something to make Johnnie see her worth to him. After so many weeks of hiding, she'd wanted to feel like she had value to *herself.*

Christopher stared at her, not showing her a shred of...*anything.* Kindness. Humanity. Not even like. Palpable hatred clung to him and she trembled. He was a horrible asshole.

"Get your fuckin' shit together. I ain't tellin' your ass, I'm fuckin' orderin' you."

"If I could get myself together, I would," she spat, dropping her gaze.

"You fuckin' can. You just too fuckin' busy bein' a

baby fuckin' Dinah around this motherfucker. Feelin' fuckin' sorry for yourself."

"You don't understand, so please leave and I *am* telling Johnnie."

Christopher shrugged. "Don't give a fuck. I love that motherfucker, but ain't *no*-fuckin-body more important than Megan. Your fuckin' bullshit got my wife hurt. Made her lose our baby. She went into fuckin' shock. You fuckin' hear me? This baby was takin' a lot from her. I almost fuckin' lost her. And, I fuckin' swear to you if she'd...if Megan left me and CJ because of *you,* I woulda fuckin' killed you. So you tell Johnnie what the fuck you want. Or don't fuckin' tell him. I don't give a fuck. Just thank the fuck out of your lucky stars my girl breathin'."

Another sob escaped her and she turned to him, allowing him to see how much his words hurt her. Looking at him, she knew it didn't make a difference. "Leave."

"Shut the fuck up." He thrust his hands through his hair. "What the fuck was you thinkin'? You wanted to go the fuck to steal Spoon's fake shit, that was *your* business. You got Megan into it. *My* business now." Folding his arms, he glared at her and she shrank back at the fury in his eyes.

"She didn't have to go."

Christopher stepped toward her, then paused, barking with laughter. Not nice, though. "You fuckin' guilted her into goin'. Don't play fuckin' stupid. I know the entire fuckin' story."

"Of course you do," she returned with bitterness. "She's your puppet. She has to tell you everything."

Closing his eyes, Christopher drew in deep breaths, a muscle ticking in his jaw. "If I was you, I'd shut the fuck up," he growled after a minute, his look glacial enough to lend ice to the Artic. "I'm a fuckin' minute from blowin' you the fuck away."

The second death threat in less than five minutes soared Kendall's heart rate and pulse. Machines started beeping, but Christopher didn't move. The door opened and a nurse hurried in, Johnnie and Mortician right behind her.

"Aww fuck," Mortician said when Johnnie came to a halt and looked between Christopher and Kendall.

The nurse pressed a couple buttons on the machine and recorded the numbers in the palm of her hand. "I'm going to have to ask you gentlemen to leave. I'll be in to give you a shot to bring your pressure down, Ms. Miller."

None of the three "gentlemen" moved. Johnnie glared at Christopher and Christopher returned it with a murderous one of his own. The nurse started past Mortician and he halted her, bending to her ear and whispering to her before winking.

The woman nodded and giggled. "I'll be back in a moment," she purred.

Mortician's smile widened but the moment the door closed, he turned to them. "Shoot it the fuck out. At least you two already in a fucking hospital."

"Shut the fuck up, Mortician," Christopher demanded, the calmness in his tone more frightening than him screaming.

"What the fuck did you say to her?" Johnnie snarled, his fierceness surprising Kendall and soothing some of her hurt caused by Christopher.

"What the fuck needed to be told to her."

"You have a fuckin problem with her, come to me. Leave Kendall the fuck alone."

"That what the fuck you want, John Boy? Me comin' to you when *she's* the fuckin' bitch responsible for my girl's pain."

Johnnie got right up in Christopher's face. "Megan's a grown fucking woman. Kendall isn't responsible for one fucking thing that happened to your wife, so if you know what the fuck's good for you, you'll leave Kendall the fuck alone."

Silence fell at Johnnie's hard words and Christopher stared for a moment, his shock hard to miss and matching Mortician's. Kendall sank back against the pillows, her heart turning over at Johnnie's strident defense of her.

"No, Prez—"

Kendall turned towards Johnnie and Christopher at the horror in Mortician's voice and she cried out at the gun shoved against Johnnie's temple.

"You fuckin' move, John Peter, I'm pullin' this fuckin' trigger. You fuckin' listen. Both you and your fuckin' whinin' bitch. If you ain't got the fuckin' balls to tell her to get her fuckin' shit together, I don't give a fuck. But you losin' your balls in this bitch's pussy got Megan hurt. Kendall need fuckin' help. She went through a lot? Yeah, I fuckin' know and I'm sorry. Megan ain't fuckin' stupid, though, but she *is* fuckin' loyal. You her friend, she gonna be your friend no matter what. Now, motherfucker, my wife told your bitch not to fuckin' go. Your bitch told my wife she was goin' with or without her. Nod your fuckin' head if you understand me so far."

The fury in Johnnie's eyes frightened Kendall as much as Christopher's rage and she looked to Mortician, silently asking for help. Instead of giving her an encouraging or friendly smile, he glowered at her.

"I see I ain't tellin' you shit you don't fuckin' know, motherfucker," Christopher continued. "So let's fast fuckin' forward to today. Megan cryin' her fuckin' eyes out cuz the beatin' she took on behalf of *your* fuckin' bitch did somethin' to her. She might not ever, *ever* be able to carry another baby and that's breakin' her fuckin' heart."

Johnnie's eyes widened at Christopher's announcement

and Kendall gasped.

"I thought whiny fuckin' Dinah would cause somethin' to happen to Megan. But your bitch—"

"Kendall didn't cause anything—"

"The fuck she didn't. She a sulkin', miserable cunt that fuckin' manipulate situations to keep herself a sulkin' miserable cunt."

Johnnie shoved Christopher and Kendall covered her eyes when Christopher cocked the barrel.

"Pull the fucking trigger, motherfucker."

"Johnnie, no!" Kendall cried.

"Shut up, Kendall," Mortician snapped. "You fucking caused enough bullshit."

Whirling away from Christopher as if the man didn't have a gun on him, Johnnie's face twisted in rage. "You don't have a fucking right talking to her like that."

The door handle jiggled and Kendall realized Mortician had locked it. "Security!" an authoritative voice called. "Open this door."

Glaring at Johnnie, Christopher shoved his nine into his cut and nodded to Mortician to open the door.

Two uniformed men strolled in and looked at the three big bikers.

"City boys on the way." The mustached one addressed Christopher. "Looks like you three spending time at the County Hotel."

"Jail," the other guard clarified and snickered.

Christopher shrugged, Johnnie rolled his eyes, and Mortician scowled.

"Do they have to go?" Kendall asked, close to having a breakdown. The last thing she wanted was to see them arrested. "Please? They were having a disagreement and it got too loud. I just lost my baby." She pointed to Johnnie. "And he's the father and I need him with me. I'll be even more distressed if he—and the other two—are hauled away." She couldn't care less about Christopher, but she wouldn't single him out.

The nurse sidled through the crowd and administered the shot to Kendall. She patted her hand. "We'll restore peace and order so you can rest, Ms. Miller,' she soothed. She turned to Mortician. "Sorry," she muttered. "They were making too much noise."

Mortician nodded. "I feel you, babe."

An hour later, Kendall found herself alone. They hadn't been able to stay and the hospital security hadn't taken Kendall's words into account. They were on high alert, one of them explained, because of a bombing that had taken place at one of the Portland MCs.

Oh, God! And, Kendall knew, while she'd been leading Meggie on a suicide mission, Johnnie had been bombing the Torpedoes' clubhouse.

Chapter 27

Merriweather Lewis and William Clark had camped in the area over two hundred years ago, speaking of the thick fog, the quawmash flowers and the array of birds. Familiar rivers and land masses had completely different names during their expedition. It would be another ninety years before the city of Camas came about and a just over one hundred years before Washougal and Hortensia were incorporated ten years apart.

Johnnie fucking swore the Hortensia city jail had been built somewhere between Lewis and Clark's expedition and the town's incorporation, waiting for inhabitants to fill it. He could see no other goddamn explanation for the holding cell inside an airless fucking building containing a few battered desks and rickety chairs. The fucking jail was a throwback to another fucking time because it certainly wasn't modern.

Fucking worse? The fact that the fucking cell felt overcrowded with Christopher as a cellmate. Those fucking apes in uniform being so near kept Johnnie from killing Christopher with his bare hands.

Christopher paced back and forth, his anger so palpable it almost jumped the fuck up and bitch slapped all of them. Mortician sat on the bench, his eyes closed, leaning his head against the crumbling concrete wall.

Mortician rubbed a hand over his face. "How long it's

been since you been in the tank, Prez?"

"I don't fuckin' know, Mort. You fuckin' tell me. At this point, I don't give a fuck. I just want out of this motherfucker."

"Hey, Caldwell," the arresting officer called, smirking. "Know anything about the bomb that took down the Torpedoes' MC?"

Gripping the bars, Christopher glared at the portly officer. An older man with salt and pepper hair framing his shiny bald head. "Them Portland MC motherfuckers?" he called with a confused frown. "What bomb? What the fuck I'm supposed to know about them?"

"Tell me," the officer said. "Whoever brings in the fuckers responsible for that will have their fifteen minutes of fame."

"Good fuckin' luck with that, motherfucker," Christopher snarled in low tones. Louder, he said, "Jackpot goin' to somebody else because I don't know fuckin shit."

The cop stared at Christopher. "That so? You three fucks had more than enough guns and knives on you." He rocked back on his heels, smug. "Maybe, I should obtain a search warrant? Check your fucking compound. See what I'll find."

Christopher chuckled. "Do that, motherfucker. First of all, you ain't findin' fuck all. Second, we have permits for the weapons we carry, bug fuck."

They did—thanks to Boss and his big, fucking payoffs.

"Third," Christopher continued, "I hate to fuckin' think of your shitty ass precinct without the fuckin' benefit of my money. When the county boys walk the fuck in here, I guarantee, me and my boys fuckin' walk."

Copper gave Christopher a crooked smile. "We'll fucking see." He pointed to Mortician.

"What about Blackie?" he asked, laughing at his own joke.

"The only motherfucker between us who ain't ever been to fuckin' jail," Christopher commented a little too nice.

"Prez," Mortician whispered from behind him. "Motherfucker jerking your chains. He got a Black fucking wife. A little bitty thing who'll pistol fucking whip him if she heard him."

Christopher nodded and chuckled. "I know. He ain't fuckin' with *me,* motherfucker. He fuckin' with you for fuckin' his wife."

Johnnie stared in incredulity, sure he'd misheard. "Mortician, you didn't fuck a cop's wife?"

"Bitch got a pussy too," he said with a shrug. "She wanted to give it to me, so why shouldn't I have fucked her?"

"Because shit like that puts you on a cop's most hated list, fucker," Johnnie snapped.

"I don't believe he's never gone to jail," the cop called, trying his best to keep his cool but failing. He stood and lumbered to the cell.

"Don't give a shit if you believe it or not, son." Mortician pulled out the cigarettes the fucker had allowed them to keep when he didn't hide the fact he'd pocketed the money he'd found in their belongings when he'd confiscated everything else. "It's the truth."

"Put those away." He pointed to a *no smoking* sign any schmuck could purchase from a hardware store.

Safely behind bars, they couldn't choke the fuck out him for being a thieving motherfucker. Johnnie knew Christopher had considered it, even though Officer Prick had had a partner with him during the arrest and lockup. Allowing them to keep their cigarettes was just a false fucking peace offering to save his own ass from a fuck-up for stealing their cash.

Ass-fucking-hole.

"I'll tell my daddy to pray for your fucking ass if you let me light one up," Mortician offered, breaking into Johnnie's thoughts.

"Shut the fuck up, Mort," Christopher said with a laugh. "I ain't gonna be able to deal with fuckin' Sharper. Hear Mortician? Keep him the fuck away from me."

"Don't worry, Prez. I don't want anywhere near his girlfriend-stealing, baby-claiming ass."

Christopher clapped Mortician on the back. "Char still married to him and you got Bailey."

"And another baby on the way," Johnnie reminded him.

"I might have another baby on the way but I *don't* have fucking Bailey."

"Mortician, motherfucker," Christopher growled. "If you fuckin' pushin' Bailey away cuz of that fuckin' slut, I swear I'll fuckin' castrate you."

"Do it," he snarled. "Please. Motherfucker don't do right by me anyway. Always leading me to pussy better left untouched."

"Your dick don't lead you anywhere, fucker," Johnnie yelled, snatching his cigarette and taking a drag before handing it to Christopher. "Your brain has to be in on it, too."

"My dick and my brain don't always get along. With Char and Bailey, my dick won."

"I'm beginning to believe you, Caldwell." Copper frowned. "You boys aren't equipped to plan a bombing."

"Nope," Christopher agreed, taking another drag. "I just have a ninth fuckin' grade education. The only one of my boys who didn't at least graduate from high school." He nodded to Johnnie. "My brother here got a college degree." Then he jabbed a thumb in Mort's direction. "This motherfucker grew up in fuckin' unimaginable wealth.

Walked the fuck away from it cuz his pops such a flamin' dickhead."

"True that, Prez." Mortician threw the cigarette butt on the floor and stomped it out. "Not a penicillin been discovered to cure him, neither."

Christopher and Mortician snickered and bumped fists and Johnnie stared, wondering if he could walk away from them and the club. As his anger abated, though, he felt betrayed. As long as Christopher felt justified in defending Megan anyway he saw fit, there would be no peace. Not every girl got along with their brother-in-law's woman. That was life, but he and Christopher did too damn much together, worked *too* closely together for their women to cause friction between them.

"Brooks."

Christopher's voice drew Johnnie back to his surroundings in time to see the lawyer striding in, along with the county boys, who looked nervous as hell.

While Mutt and Jeff from Hortensia PD was on the club's payroll, the *county's* sheriff was also on it. If they ended up in the fucking County Hotel, there'd be hell to pay.

Johnnie stuffed the last bit of his clothes into his duffle bag, ignoring Mortician who sat on the bed and monitored Johnnie's every move. They'd bailed out of jail a few hours ago after being there for nearly a day with all types of bullshit questions thrown their way.

Of course they were suspected in the bombing, and so much other shit, if they ever went to jail, they'd get a couple thousand years along with ten life sentences. Whatever game the sheriff played with Christopher, Johnnie didn't know, but the man had just earned a mortal enemy.

Even as Johnnie packed, Val was scoping out the sheriff to report to Christopher why they'd spent hours in jail and been interrogated when the club sent Gs every month in cash to keep heat away from them.

From the time they'd been transferred to county, Johnnie hadn't spoken to Christopher and Christopher hadn't spoken to him. The easing of his rage returned full force, just by Christopher's silence. While Johnnie expected it, it enraged him that Christopher wouldn't offer one word of mollification. After that motherfucker shoved a gun to his temple and insulted his woman, Johnnie doubted he'd *ever* speak to Christopher again. The moment they'd gotten to the clubhouse and Christopher ordered Brooks to wait for him so he could be driven to the hospital where Megan and his bike were, Johnnie had shrugged out of his cut and thrown it to the floor.

Time had stopped, his entire life flashing before him as if the cut had been the thing keeping him alive. Christopher was a cold-blooded motherfucker, though. He'd stared at Johnnie for a moment and then spat at him, "you have sixty fuckin' minutes to get the fuck off premises." Not a word more. No apology. No *let's talk about this*. Nothing.

Fucking nothing.

Then he'd stalked off, not looking back.

"John Boy," Mortician began quietly.

"I don't want to hear one fucking word from you."

"Too fucking bad," Mort snarled back.

Johnnie stiffened. "Get the fuck out of here."

"Or what, motherfucker. You intend to fucking kill me?"

Clenching his jaw, Johnnie snatched the duffel bag and started for the door.

"You going to just walk the fuck away? That's fucked up, brother."

"I don't belong here anymore. You. Christopher. Megan. *None* of you ever gave Kendall a fair chance."

"Bullshit and you know that. Kendall didn't give Meggie a chance. In her ass the moment Meggie walked in."

"My fault—"

"So fucking kind of you to notice, motherfucker. But it still set Kendall off and, in turn, it set Meggie off. No matter what else Meggie might be, she not rolling over and taking bullshit."

Johnnie turned back to Mortician, furious he had to explain any of this. "My fucking point exactly. All she needed to do was open her fucking month and tell Kendall 'no'."

Mortician released harsh laughter. "Meggie girl couldn't win. Kendall went by herself and something happened, she would've been blamed. She *went* with Kendall and got hurt just like her. Instead of embracing both of those chicks, fucking war starting. And I hate to fucking break it to you, but this shit is Kendall's fault."

Johnnie growled and balled his fists.

Mortician got to his feet and glared at him. "I wouldn't fucking do that."

"Then shut the fuck up with blaming Kendall. She has enough fucking problems. Everyone has been comparing her to Megan—"

"Bullshit!" Mortician yelled. "Kendall been comparing herself to Megan. You want to go off half-cocked, then fucking jet. But go off with your fucking facts straight."

Johnnie didn't want to listen to this. Kendall *wasn't* to blame for any of this. Another reason why he had to leave. Everyone was against her, which was unfair. No one recognized her pain. "I can't stay here, Mortician. None of you want to help Kendall."

"Fuck, brother, she have to want to help herself. We'll protect your girl with everything we got, John Boy. She went through some intense and fucked up shit. But the more she give in to it, the more it's gonna beat her. Prez don't have the best fucking delivery all the time. He just give it to you straight."

Scrubbing his hands over his eyes, fatigue settled into Johnnie. He felt hollow inside, but he wouldn't allow Kendall to suffer additional torment. He didn't know what his life would be like without the club and his brothers, but, if he had to choose Kendall or the club, Kendall won now. She was suffering and, now, added to that, she'd lost their baby. He owed it to her to do the very thing he'd always sworn he wouldn't.

"Christopher doesn't care for Kendall and I do. I refuse to stay with all the bullshit." His club. On that floor, when he'd thrown his cut, he'd left part of his soul. But Kendall didn't deserve blame and hostility.

"Give Meggie a chance to get better. She'll talk to Prez. Make him see reason."

"*She* shouldn't have to talk to him," he snapped, his hackles rising again. "He should come to me himself without any prompting from her."

"Get your head out your ass. If you was in some type of similar situation for whatever reason before Meggie got here, Prez would've blown you the fuck away."

"He's my brother," Johnnie rasped, feeling like a pussy and a dickhead at once. Christopher's attitude not only pissed him the fuck off but it hurt him. "He should value me as much as I value him."

"Why you think he went to *her* and not you. Prez want you happy. He didn't want to start no shit with you."

"And going to my girl wouldn't start shit?"

"No! Red don't open her fucking mouth when she could divert a lot of fucking heartache if she did. She keep shit about Spoon to herself. She could keep shit Outlaw rightly told her to herself."

"I'm going. Christopher was out of line doing what he did. He owes me an apology—"

"You waitin' the rest of your fuckin' days for one from me, assfuck," Christopher growled from the doorway. He walked forward, his hair still damp from the shower he must've taken. "Let me get this shit fuckin' out, John Peter. I don't want you fuckin' leavin' the club. You fuckin' belong here as much as I do. We belong here together. But, if you stay, get your bitch straight. If you go, get your bitch straight. She a fuckin' lawyer. She gotta have a head on her shoulders to do that. Tell her to fuckin' use it."

Christopher looked at him and sighed, already seeing the determination Johnnie felt to leave. Christopher glanced beyond Johnnie and, for the first time, Johnnie saw his hurt and regret. "Have it your fuckin' way," he said, recognizing that Johnnie wouldn't budge. "I'll see you around." He swallowed, then nodded to Mortician. "Come on, Mort. I gotta talk to you about somethin'."

Mortician clapped Johnnie on the shoulder. "Take care, brother," he muttered and walked past Johnnie.

Neither of them once looked back, leaving Johnnie to his future with Kendall and outside the loop of the club.

Chapter 28

Four weeks later

Kendall sniffed the red gravy she'd just scooped from the pot and into the wooden spoon. Poking her pinky into it, she licked it. Maybe, it needed a little more basil. Whatever it was, she knew it was almost time to add the fish.

She glanced at the clock as it inched to six-thirty. Any minute Johnnie would walk through the door, looking like a million dollars in his designer suit. He'd be hungry and he'd be nice. He'd be complimentary. But he wouldn't be happy and he wouldn't be sexual.

Each day that passed, Kendall's heart broke a little more. She'd been out of the hospital for over three weeks, going straight to a small house in a quiet neighborhood. When she'd asked about the club, he'd merely said, "I'm out."

For the first couple days, Kendall had been elated because she finally felt she was the most important person in Johnnie's life. She'd even thought their relationship would survive the loss of Baby Biker. All along she'd felt she didn't have Johnnie because he was only trying to make a relationship work because of his baby. Granted, that was more than some men did but neither should children be the foundation of a marriage.

Marriage? Not to Johnnie.

His attitude told her such a life-long commitment wouldn't ever be possible. She'd been right to turn his proposal down in the cave.

"Something smells real good," Johnnie commented, sauntering in, his suit jacket thrown over his shoulder and his tie hanging loosely around his neck.

Kendall smiled and accepted the kiss he placed near her lips. Not on them anymore. "Courtbillion," she explained, pronouncing it in the French way: *Coo-be-yon*. "It's a New Orleans recipe I found on my iPad food app."

He grunted a response and walked away.

He'd purchased the iPad for her so she could read the legal thrillers she loved. She'd read one book because her concentration had been worth shit. She'd kept reliving the exact moment Spoon had gotten her and Meggie. She'd thought she'd gotten them killed and, sometimes, she thought she'd lose her mind. That she'd never be normal again and her uncontrollable tears would flow until she had an awful headache.

Her baby was gone, but she had her life. So empty, though. She'd ended up calling Brooks and asking for work-from-home projects. He'd assigned her a couple of simple tasks. Nothing too taxing, and she didn't know if she was grateful or disappointed.

As hard as the loss of her baby had been, the event had served as a painful eye-opener. She knew she needed *help*. Because she couldn't do this on her own. She didn't know how to overcome her terror and shame. She didn't know how to overcome her love for Johnnie or how to make herself want to do anything other than stay inside and keep house.

Maybe, she'd never be a practicing attorney again. And, maybe, once she got help, she'd be itching to get back into a courtroom. Right now, though, she wanted her life back. She wanted Johnnie. She wanted his babies and his name. She wanted his love.

He strolled past the kitchen, heading outside like he usually did in the evening until she prepared their meal.

Burned tomatoes assaulted her nose and she frowned, scowling when she realized she'd scorched her gravy. The sound of Harley pipes made her rush to turn off the stove and run outside just in time for her to see Mortician and Johnnie do a quick embrace and a mutual fisting on the back.

Although they hadn't invited her, she hurried to Johnnie's side, wanting to greet Mortician. "Hi," she murmured the moment she reached the two men.

Mortician gave her a two-finger salute. "What's up, Kendall?"

Her smile faltered at the cool greeting. She shifted from foot to foot and swallowed. "Do you want to join us for supper?"

"No, he doesn't," Johnnie responded, shoving his hands in his pockets. The humor and glint in his eyes had flickered out days ago. If possible, the silver-gray seemed a little duller. "He stopped in to tell me they're going on a run."

Guilt rose in Kendall and she wrung her hands. "H-how's M-meggie?"

Two pairs of eyes widened and stared with incredulity at her.

"You for fucking real, girl?" Mortician snapped.

"Don't," Johnnie growled.

Mortician nodded and turned away. "I'm out, John Boy." He mounted his bike. "See you round, Kendall." Not allowing either of them a chance to respond, he started the big Harley and sped away.

For long moments, Johnnie stood still, staring in Mortician's wake. He thrust a hand through his hair and turned to her. "I'm going out for a drink, gorgeous. Don't wait up for me."

He gave her a near-lip kiss and sauntered away.

Twenty minutes later, Kendall sat on the bed she shared with Johnnie, wondering where he'd gone. Maybe, he would visit the club. Or, maybe, he'd finally go to another woman. She had so many maybes and what-ifs running through her head, she didn't know which to address first. Most of all, though, her regret and guilt ran deep.

She'd pressed him to leave the club and she'd demanded he place her above Meggie. For that matter, she'd demanded Meggie risk herself to show her friendship when Meggie had made so many overtures since their first meeting.

Kendall had been so bitter and it had taken her losing nearly everything to realize she'd caused some of her problems. Just as Mortician had tried to explain to her. And Meggie.

And just as Outlaw had demanded of her to recognize.

Just as Johnnie had. He'd been patient and frustrated, loving and exasperated, protective and possessive. Each time, she'd shot him down either through words or deeds.

Going to her purse, she picked up her cellphone and stared at it, debating on whether or not to text Meggie. Kendall had no idea if she'd healed or not. She had no idea if Meggie hated her.

Kendall knew Johnnie was worried about her. The fact she was still alive cued her that Megan was alive. She didn't have a doubt in her mind that Outlaw would've hunted her down if Meggie had passed away.

How many truths had she ignored, wallowing in her pain? She hadn't wanted to believe *anything.* Or recognize the importance of the dynamics of Johnnie's life.

It took additional heartache and unimaginable tragedy for her to understand what a mean, selfish bitch she'd been. She'd become the bully and Megan the bullied. She'd played well at being the victim—and, yes, she was—but none of the people at Johnnie's club meant her any harm.

Until she'd fucked up a month ago. Johnnie's treatment of her might've left a lot to be desired, but she'd hurt him. The very thing she hadn't wanted to happen had anyway. She'd lost him.

A sob escaped her and she covered her face. She hated to see his defeat and misery. She'd caused both because she'd forced him to choose. He'd patched out because of the argument with Outlaw, but, Kendall suspected they could've overcome it if she hadn't been so insistent he leave the club.

She thought of Megan again. Maybe, contacting her was a bad idea, but Kendall had never gotten rid of the other woman's cellphone number. Weeks ago, Johnnie had put Meggie's number on speed dial for Kendall and demanded she call her for anything she'd need that Johnnie couldn't provide.

Her fingers shaking, she pulled up Meggie's information and pressed the button to begin a text.

Hi Meggie

She'd keep it simple. Several minutes passed and Kendall decided she wouldn't receive a response. Then, her phone beeped.

Kendall?

Her heart picked up speed that Meggie recognized her

number.

That's me

No response. Kendall bit down on her lip, staring at her phone, wondering if she should pursue the conversation or just let it go.

I'm sorry

A moment later, Meggie responded with a punctuation mark. *?*

For everything. *4 the baby*

An apology seemed so small in comparison to the pain Meggie must've suffered. Kendall's only consolation was she knew what that pain was because she'd gone through it, too.

Ok

Loneliness pierced her and Kendall didn't know what to do. She bowed her head and gripped her phone tighter.

How r u? Have u healed? How's Johnnie? Feels so diffrnt w/o him.

Johnnie is fine. Kendall halted her fingers and backspaced. It was no good in lying. *Johnnie is sad*

Christopher is 2

She'd never meant for this to happen—

Holding back her tears by sheer determination, Kendall drew in a breath.

Is this my fault?

Although Kendall expected an immediate answer, a full ten minutes went by before Meggie responded again. When the alert came though, Kendall hesitated to even read the message.

We r both 2 blame

No long paragraph. No accusations.

And Kendall finally got what everyone saw in Meggie. She could've blamed Kendall for everything. For that matter, she didn't have to respond to Kendall at all. But Meggie faced whatever burdens she had and embraced everyone she came across. While Kendall would never trust many people enough to be so friendly, she appreciated Meggie's attitude.

Have a good eveng got 2 c Christopher off

She didn't want to lose the connection to her right now. She had no idea how long it would take Meggie to tell her husband goodbye, but Kendall would close with something for Meggie to respond to if she felt like it.

Mortician angry w/me Johnnie hardly talking 2 me how can I fix evrythng

Kendall laid back on the bed, thinking about how she'd respond if the situations had been reversed. Knowing she wouldn't have been nice, she cringed. After getting what she'd only ever dreamed of—friends—she'd been so very hateful. She pressed a hand against her belly and grief stole into her. Turning on her side and drawing her knees up to her chest, she curled into her favorite position.

She didn't move until she heard another alert. Glancing at her phone, she saw she'd been still for almost an hour, another pocket of time she'd wasted on nothing. She unlocked the screen and read Meggie's message.

What do u need fixng

Her life. *Make Mortician like me again & have Johnnie luv me*

Johnnie already luvs u

She wanted to believe Meggie. She wanted that switch in her head to snap on and remove all her self-doubt and self-pity.

I think 2 late 4 us He misses the club

Tell him 2 come back

How can I tell him anythng

Open ur mouth

He might not listen

U'll never kno if u don't try

He was very angry w/Christopher
I know. Christopher was very angry w/him Never wanted him 2 leave tho
He went out 4 evenng Said not 2 wait up
Y textng me

Kendall counted to three and told herself Meggie didn't mean it as an insult. She wasn't like those mean girls she'd grown up around. She wasn't hard and cruel like the women who'd hung around the Torpedoes' clubhouse.

What u mean
Text him *call him, maybe LOL a certain popular song just came 2 me*

Kendall laughed, a real laugh. She knew exactly the song Meggie referred to and the beat went through Kendall's head, too.

All right will do
Cool Kendall ttyl
Bye Meggie

Kendall waited a few minutes longer to see if Meggie would text again, but she didn't. Shoring up her courage, Kendall pressed the number 2—Johnnie's speed dial numeral—because '911' was used for number 1.

It went straight to voicemail and Kendall's heart dropped. She had to talk to him and tell him how much she loved him and, as long as he was happy, he could go back to his club. If he wanted, they could move back there.

She just wanted him to smile again and look at her with his smoldering silver gaze.

Johnnie signaled the bartender for another shot of whisky, wondering what the hell he'd done when he'd walked away from his MC and his brothers. He didn't think love was supposed to defeat a man, but that's how he felt.

At the time, when Christopher had been such a dickhead to Kendall, Johnnie's only thought was rising to her defense. Then, the man had pulled a gun on him and Johnnie had lost all reasoning.

He'd believed walking away from the Death Dwellers was the right thing to do for Kendall. The loyal move. God knew he had so much to make up to her. Somewhere deep down he'd considered handing over his patch partial reparation for how much of a jerk he'd been to her.

Before she'd been released from the hospital, he'd secured a house for them and got it furnished. The reasonable rent allowed him time to figure out where he'd buy a house for them. For a week after her release, he'd stuck close to the place to be available for Kendall. He'd purchased another car for her and installed tracking software on her telephone before he remembered he no longer had enemies. Thanks to Christopher and his bombs, most of them were blown to bits.

The bartender slid the filled shot glass to Johnnie. "Last one."

"Get the fuck out of my face." Johnnie squinted to see the time. Close to midnight. He'd been gone for hours. But seeing Mortician and hearing about the run they were all going on to Canada cut through him. He hadn't even thought to question Mort about how he knew his location.

The entire situation had angered him and he hadn't wanted to snap at Kendall since his anger was directed at *her*.

Because of her, he'd had to choose when he should've been able to have her and his club.

He shoved his fingers through his hair and thought about the engagement ring he had in his pocket. He'd bought it a week ago and hesitated to propose. Now, he knew why. He resented all he'd given up for her when she seemed so indifferent to him. Tossing back half the contents of the glass, he sighed and unclipped his phone from his belt. Still off. He cursed, powering it up.

Several beeps told him he had voicemail. Instead of listening to her, he'd leave and go to her. He'd chosen to live his life with her and he loved her. Eventually they'd come to a sweet spot in their relationship and—

"Hi."

The feminine voice reached Johnnie's ears and he turned to his left where a dark-haired girl with small tits and big, brown eyes sat. She was staring at him as if she wanted to swallow him whole. He smiled at her. "Hi."

"This seat taken?"

Johnnie contemplated her, recognized her lust. She was a coed, out for a good time. He knew her type, had had more than his share while in college. She'd be a quick, easy fuck and he'd have the relief and warmth of a female body. Kendall's features rose in his head and he sighed, finishing his shot. "No, sweetheart, it isn't taken."

Her smile widened and she slid on the stool next to him, his dick hardening when she shifted her position and opened her legs to show him her bare pussy peeking through crotchless panties.

Standing, he pulled out his billfold and called the bartender to him. He handed the man three Benjamins. "For my shots and for whatever she'd like to order."

He nodded and took the girl's order.

"You're gorgeous," she murmured, licking her lips.

Johnnie's gaze fastened onto her red mouth. Sucking wasn't fucking. Per se. His nostrils flared at the thought. Licking wasn't sticking, either. "What's your name?"

"Peyton. Yours?"

"Johnnie," he responded, his head flipping back and forth between taking her somewhere and using her until she couldn't walk, bringing her to his Navigator so she could suck his dick, or walking away.

"Do you want to go somewhere with less noise?"

With the minimal crowd, the noise level wasn't bad. A Jason Aldeen song serenaded them at an acceptable volume. Kendall might enjoy an evening with him here.

Kendall.

He wanted to fuck. Not make love. *Fuck* hard and dirty and fast. Something Kendall didn't need but the girl next to him could provide.

The ring weighted his pocket and he closed his eyes, Kendall's face haunting him. Her long, strong legs around his waist as he thrust into her. Her vulnerability for so many different reasons.

He thought about Megan. *Megs*. And smiled. He missed her friendship. Zoann had called him and told him what *really* set Christopher off. Megan had started to bleed, so rapidly her blood pressure began to bottom out.

Zoann, his scarred, fragile cousin, had been almost hysterical. Because she liked Megan, who looked past Zoann's hard outer shell and made her be part of the family.

Johnnie had felt sick to his stomach. K-P's and Caroline's funerals had been enough to deal with. Burying Megan…Christopher had lost his shit at how close he'd come to having to do just that.

He would've been without his anchor. Little Man would've been without his mother. And Johnnie would've been without his friend.

He could share none of this with Kendall. She would've lost it because she wanted to hear nothing about Megan.

All fucking fingers should point to him for this cluster fuck, the hell of it being he didn't know how to rectify it. He remained mired between Kendall and the club he missed like fuck.

A hand grasped his cock and he jerked, his balls tingling. "You wanna leave here?" she asked in a breathy voice.

"I do, sweetheart," he rumbled and she squirmed in her seat before getting to her feet. He shook his head. "You misunderstand," he said quietly. "I'm going home to my girlfriend."

Disappointment pulled down her features, but she shrugged. "Okay."

He turned and started to walk away, running smack dab into Christopher. The girl's eyes widened when she glimpsed Outlaw in his leathers, a cigarette hanging from his mouth and his wedding band glinting in the dimness as he flicked a lighter.

"Bout time you turned your motherfuckin' phone back on, assfuck."

"What—" Suspecting the reason for the importance of his phone being on, Johnnie stiffened in outrage. "You put fucking tracking software on *my* phone?"

How the fuck…Christopher didn't even pay the goddamn phone bill.

"Yeah, why?"

As remorseless as ever. "Because that's some fucked up shit, Christopher," Johnnie barked.

"Tell me that if I ever need to find your fuckin' ass. I only track the phones for you, Mort, Digger, Val, and Stretch."

"And Megan."

He puffed on his cigarette and squinted as the smoke rose between them. "That's a fuckin' given. I also have it on her car in the event her fuckin' phone off."

Mortician chortled. "Yo', Prez, why don't you just have something implanted under her fucking skin?"

"Don't give Mr. Stalker no fucking ideas, Mort," Val called.

"Aren't you all on a run?" Johnnie asked slowly, watching as Stretch and Digger joined the group.

"Are you all real?" Peyton breathed, standing beside Johnnie and contemplating all of them.

Christopher smirked at her. "As real as my fuckin' wife," he responded, releasing more smoke and dismissing her with a nod. "As for you, John Boy. Stop bein' a stupid motherfucker. It look like we on a fuckin' run? I ain't a fuckin' hologram, you know?"

Peyton giggled. Stretch and Digger shifted so they could better see her.

"We going, John Boy," Mortician swore. "We just been waiting around so we could find you."

Puffing out more smoke, Christopher added, "We miss you, motherfucker. Shit ain't the same without you."

Johnnie kept a steady gaze on Christopher. "I don't...I'm going to propose to Kendall."

Christopher shrugged. "Figured you would. Who you fuckin' marry ain't got shit to do with me." He cocked his head to the side, holding his cigarette between two fingers. "Kendall's who you need. Bitch cautious and tight-lipped like a motherfucker. I understand why, but you ain't fuckin' puttin' up with no girl tellin' you every fuckin' thing."

Like Megan did. Johnnie hadn't ever considered if he'd be able to deal with that or not, but Christopher was right.

"Her traits admirable but that fuckin' shit have a place too." Another puff. "Let's stop with this epic fuckin' War of the Bitches, okay? Yours perfect for you and mine fuckin' perfect for me. Our stupid fuckin' asses made it fuckin' worse between them two." Tamping his cigarette out in an ashtray Peyton held out to him, Christopher waved Digger forward and grabbed the cut from the man's hands, then held the leather out. "Take it. I'm leavin' for three days. Think about patchin' back in. If you can't come back, I understand."

The same feeling he'd had when he'd first patched in took root inside him. He grabbed the cut, then remembered Kendall. But how could he be true to her when he couldn't be true to himself? He had to find a way to make her accept his biker lifestyle.

Clapping him on the shoulder, Christopher turned, frowning at Digger who'd taken Peyton aside the moment Johnnie took the cut. "I've already lost fuckin' road hours." He signaled to the rest of the men. "Let's fuckin' ride."

Mortician waited until only he remained in the wake of Christopher's departure. No doubt to provide answers at this sudden turn of events. Before they delved into that, Johnnie wanted to know about the sheriff who'd fucked over them and any ramifications from the bombing.

Since he was out, Christopher wouldn't have allowed any blame to touch Johnnie. It had been headline news for two weeks, fading into the background as other stories came about.

"Brooks worth the money Prez shelling out. We officially cleared of being suspects. Outlaw fucking wild," Mortician chortled. "Motherfucker got the American Scorpions fucking knee deep in it."

"Cee Cee's MC?"

Mortician nodded. "A final fuck-you to your old man."

"Big Joe would be so fucking satisfied."

Johnnie didn't speak—or think—about Joseph Foy much, but he'd taught them all. On rare occasions he wondered what the club would be like if Boss still led. He'd always said when smoke and bullshit cleared, the strongest fucking man would still stand. Like K-P, Big Joe had had their backs. He'd been in with Logan's business, though. That could be the only reason why Big Joe had survived some of the shit he'd done and why he'd spared

Logan's life.

If Johnnie ever met up with Boss in hell, he'd demand fucking answers. Ask him how the fuck he demanded they not hurt women while he sold girls for profit.

"Boss fucking somewhere kicking it with Lucifer and Logan. He taught us what we needed. He knew we'd eventually have to clean up his and Logan's fucking mess, so let's leave it the fuck at that. I'm still fucking celebrating the fall of the Scorpions. Feds taking them motherfuckers down."

"Don't get too relaxed. No one blew up their MC, so motherfuckers can regroup."

"True but Outlaw had this shit planned like a fucking general on the battlefield."

Johnnie laughed and bumped fists with Mortician. Christopher had done them proud.

Them?

Yes, them. First, Johnnie needed to know a few things.

"What the fuck is this about?" Johnnie asked. "I saw you five hours ago and you were leaving then. Now, Christopher comes in here and tells me he's been waiting for me to turn my phone back on. It was on at that time."

Mortician pulled on his leather gloves. "What the fuck you think happened that would have Prez turn the fuck around to come and get you, motherfucker?"

Only one person Johnnie could think of. "Megan?"

"Meggie, brother. Your woman reached out to her and whatever the fuck Red told her, Meggie got to Outlaw and put a fucking bug in his ear, so here we are."

"Kendall called Megan?" he asked stupidly, not quite catching up to what the two of them had orchestrated.

"I wasn't fucking there."

He turned Christopher's words over in his head and

scowled. "Christopher came only because Megan demanded him—"

"Don't be a dumb ass, John Boy. Has Meggie been upset about what went down with you two? Fuck, yeah. She loves your dumb ass. But Prez been meaner than a fucking rattlesnake and the only one keeping him from going completely psycho on all us motherfuckers is his girl, man. He misses you. We all do."

"So—?"

"Does it fucking matter why the fuck Prez came? If he didn't want you back, he wouldn't have turned around."

"Of course he would have." Dickhead alert. Fuck. He didn't want to go back to the same fucking bullshit that had caused him to leave in the first fucking place. It would defeat the fucking purpose. "Because Megan told him."

Sighing, Mortician gave him a hard stare and placed a hand on his shoulder. "Look, brother. Yeah, Meggie got him wrapped around her little finger. She drive him. That bullshit when she tried to knock his fucking rock off with that bottle? Just made him hotter behind her. Crazier about her. He's the first to admit he's pussy-whipped." He stopped and glanced over his shoulder. They all knew one of Christopher's golden rules included not mentioning Megan's pussy in any way, shape or form. He dropped his hand and stepped back. "Anyway, part of his stalkery, pussy-whipped, obsessed, crazy fucking in love shit is he'd either tear anybody who hurt her a new asshole, or he'd just fucking bury them. Tearing of the new asshole is rare and reserved only for a special few. Me, you, Val and Zoann. Possibly Digger and probably not Stretch. Since *you* now encompass Kendall, he taking that approach with her."

"When she was still recovering—"

"Check your bullshit, John Boy and put blame where the fuck it belong. Meggie got placenta something. Abrupt placenta…I don't know what the fuck it was. But she's healing. Prez can't give her no more babies for about six months. She's not my wife and it fucking killed me watching her cry over the baby she lost and the babies she might never get to have. That fucking day at the hospital? You was lost in your own pain. As it should be because your girl was hurting, too. Outlaw was...fuck, me, too...Val, too. Meggie was *dying*. I'm so fucking tired of trying to get you and Kendall to understand this bullshit."

"About that...you don't have to get Kendall to understand fuck all. Keep your counseling to yourself."

"Glad to, assfuck. Not like Red listened any-fucking-way. So I'll tell *your* motherfucking ass. Meggie earned her place at the club. Not by fucking impossible demands, either. She let us get to fucking know her and she got to know us. She tell Outlaw *almost* everything. The rest the motherfucker figure out on his own. He stalk her too close not to. But me and Val and Stretch and Bunny and Gypsy and...fuck, a roll call of fuckers, know if we got a fucking problem or *whatever,* we can call or text Meggie and shit ain't going no fucking further. What the fuck we knew about Red except the bitch came to fuck with Outlaw and spy for Spoon? Kendall a beautiful chick and a smart chick, too, but she one of the dumbest motherfuckers I ever fucking saw."

Balling his fists, Johnnie growled. "Say that again to me, motherfucker," he snarled.

"Fucking Spoon aside, Red need to do some growing up herself. No smart bitch can think to come in and have motherfuckers just trust her like that or move another chick out cause her dumb ass man loved her. If Red knew how many bitches you stuck your dick in who still around the club, she'd make you fucking miserable. I understand Red got issues. I'm not apologizing me and her talk or are friends because you was a low down motherfucker the way you treated her, so go blow your own fucking dick."

"Mortician, for someone who calls me a fucking sociopath, you don't fucking mind pissing me the fuck off."

He laughed. "True that. Luck of the fucking draw, motherfucker."

"I could use my blade."

"And? I *could* have your fucking ass shot the fuck off before you pulled it."

"Stop calling Kendall stupid and stop calling her a fucking bitch and we won't have to put it to the test."

"Okay. Fair enough. I call you fucking stupid then. Your college education affected your common fucking sense."

"Mortician—"

"Last thing about Red. I almost told Meggie and Bailey to revoke her fucking chick card. I asked Bailey about Aunt Flo and *your* bitch asked if that was Arrow's wife. Ain't *no* bitch alive don't know who the fuck Aunt Flo is."

"Kendall doesn't use slang," Johnnie bit out, considering putting a hole somewhere in Mortician.

"Maybe not street slang, but pussy slang? No excuse not to fucking know, whether she *say* it or not." Mortician scowled at him. "That shit's in the past, though. I don't know what the fuck Red did this evening. She made the first move and Meggie took care of the fucking rest. Meggie and Kendall did their parts. Prez did his. Now, the ball's in you court, brother. Use it wisely."

Chapter 29

Johnnie stared at the house he shared with Kendall, wondering if she'd fallen asleep and thinking about all the events of the past two and a half months. He honed in the eventful day when Kendall had gotten the bee up her ass to get Spoon's USB. No matter what, she'd done everything with good intentions. No matter what, she'd lost as much as Megan and deserved the same treatment.

He hated to admit, even to himself, but Kendall had been the catalyst for their shared tragedies. What Mortician had been preaching was wise advice. And Christopher's talk with Kendall in the hospital? Kendall had told Johnnie the part of the conversation he'd missed. Christopher's words had been harsh and out-of-line, but…real. They'd been true, too.

Just like tonight. He had made it worse, seeing only Kendall's need for acceptance and nothing else. Her arrival at the club had been under the wrong circumstances. The brothers wouldn't have so readily trusted her.

Johnnie had set aside his suspicion about her and

expected everyone to fall right into place behind him. Even Megan, who'd had more than enough reason for her wariness toward Kendall.

As it was, Megan had been the one who'd gotten Christopher to allow Kendall to stay. The day Kendall revealed her association with Christopher, he'd told her to leave. In spite of everything, Megan stepped up on *Kendall's* behalf because of him, Johnnie.

Had he ever fucked up more in his life than he had with both of them? He'd lucked out and kept his head on his shoulders, although Christopher almost blew it away more than once.

He'd apologize to Megan. First, he had to fix everything with Kendall.

Swallowing, Johnnie flipped on the overhead light to better see his cut. He wanted Kendall and the club. He hated this fucking house. It was small and quiet. Kendall needed quiet. Maybe, he did, too. He'd lived his entire life around chaos and anarchy.

Fuck. He hated fucking peace and quiet.

Christopher, Zoann, Ophelia, Nia, Avery, and Bev were the only family Johnnie had and he didn't want to lose them. Nor did he want to be out of Mortician's and Val's fucking confidences.

Once upon a time, it had been K-P, Rack, and Big Joe; and Christopher, Johnnie, Val, and Mortician. Johnnie scowled. And fucking Snake...

Fucking hell.

K-P? No. No.

K-P couldn't have known about the little girls Logan and Boss peddled. Rack? Yes. Even Snake. K-P, though? No, never.

He had to have known, though, and participated. He was amongst the core of the club, even before he'd become an officer.

Motherfucker. Johnnie hoped he was rotting in fucking

hell with the rest of them.

Five minutes later, he'd pushed aside his lingering grief over a motherfucker who didn't deserve it and was inside the house, heading to his and Kendall's bedroom. Light shone from the cracked door and hit the floor of the little hallway. He walked into the room and halted, his heart sinking.

Kendall sat on the chair near the bed, fully dressed. His duffel bag gaped open on the bed, and filled with her things. She was leaving him.

"Kendall?" He didn't know what else to say, the scene too shocking for him to form quick responses.

She sniffled and swiped at her tears, then glanced at the digital clock. 1:24AM.

He stepped forward. "Kendall—"

"I can't do this anymore, Johnnie."

More tears slipped from her eyes and her lips trembled. She shoved a short strand of hair behind her ear. It hadn't grown back much and she'd cut it evenly after her release from the hospital, styling it into a bob. Long or short, the vibrant red color fascinated him.

"I...you...I can't share you," she continued.

He stood in front of her, staring at her bowed head, the silvery tear tracks on her cheeks. Unmatchable fear sliced into him and he reached out to touch her. She flinched away and he dropped his hands, balling his fists at his side. "You don't have to share me."

"I tried calling you. Your phone was off. Since I've met you your phone has never been off."

"I needed time alone," he began, not sure how to explain himself, but knowing he had to attempt to do so. "When I saw Mortician—"

"I know," she whispered. "I saw your face. How much

you miss them." She blinked away her tears. "I thought if I got you away from them, you'd be mine. I thought you'd finally love me."

"I do love you," he managed, his heart beating fast and painful in his chest.

She shook her head. "Once I lost Baby Biker, I knew we were done. I held onto hope and—"

"Kendall, I swear to you. You own my heart. You're my everything. With or without a baby." She threw him an accusing stare and he knew it was because of the way he'd referred to their lost baby. But Baby Biker humanized it too much. Gave it a name. Made the loss so much more real. "You can't leave me."

Her nostrils flaring, she stared at him and then licked her lips. "I texted Meggie earlier," she began quietly. "I wanted to know how to fix everything."

"Kendall—"

"No, Johnnie. It's okay. I finally got everything all of you had been trying to make me see about her."

Her heartbroken sob tore through Johnnie and he crouched in front of Kendall, a hare's breath from dropping to his knees.

"I realized so much. The fact that I need help to get through this. An inkling that I might never want to practice law again on a full-time basis. How much I loved you."

Hearing her use past tense to describe her feelings for him made him drop one knee. "I love you, Kendall. I swear to you."

"You've shut me out. You plant perfunctory almost-lip kisses to me. Before, you were distracted. Now, you're just uninterested."

The other knee went down and, in the back of his mind, he knew he appeared to be on the verge of begging. And, maybe, he was. "Kendall, I'm so, so sorry," he croaked, desperate for the right words. "I'm not disinterested in you. I didn't fall in love with you right away—"

"Did you fall instantly in love with Meggie?"

"Instantly in lust," he admitted. He didn't want to talk about Megan, but Kendall deserved to know everything. They'd discussed everything while angry or while despairing over some fucked-up event. Taking a chance, he thumbed away her tears. "I want to be able to tell you I *didn't* love her at some point, but this is real life, sweetheart, and I'm almost thirty-four-years-old."

"I'll be thirty-one in a few months and, before you, I'd never been in love."

Johnnie nodded. "I can tell you I've never loved anyone the way that I love you. When you're near me, I only see you. When we're apart, I think of no one but you."

"Oh, Johnnie." Her face crumpled. "You left me tonight. I...you have to make up with Outlaw—"

Johnnie took her hands into his own and kissed her fingertips. "Outlaw? I thought he was Christopher."

"Not anymore," she admitted with a smile, reclaiming one of her hands and gliding her fingers through his hair. "I understood why he was called Outlaw that day in the hospital. He was..." She closed her eyes and shuddered. "Brutal."

"I know. That's why I got out. He'd always do that to you and Megan—"

Kendall shook her head. "Stop. He was right. What I've seen of him, I know he is unerringly honest and oddly fair. He wouldn't have lit into me without good cause."

Johnnie sighed.

"You know I'm right."

Instead of answering, he gave her a reluctant nod. "He wouldn't have known if Megan—"

"If Meggie what? Hadn't told him? He's ruthless where she's concerned. She was sedated when he questioned her."

"Sedated or not, she would've told him." And how the hell did she know anyway? "Megan is—"

"Still the delicate, gorgeous girl you met," she interrupted. "I've been so unfair to her and I've made you be unfair to her."

"No. Never."

"You can't talk about her now without being so judgmental toward her. At first, I felt vindicated and satisfied. But her only crime was being the embodiment of those girls I dealt with in high school. In looks. In personality, though, she's worlds apart."

Johnnie drew her closer and wrapped his arms around her. "I'm tired of having her stand between us. Can you give me a chance? Can we—"

"That's just it, Johnnie. You miss Christopher and—"

"I love him," he admitted slowly, "but if it means losing you…" he allowed his voice to trail off.

"He isn't the cause of me leaving and neither is Meggie. It's you. Us." She tensed. "Your cheating." Her voice broke at that last. "You haven't made love to me in about six weeks. It bothered me, but, that was before tonight. Before I called and got your voicemail. I could make excuses for everything else."

"There was a girl," he rushed out. "Tonight. Her name was Peyton. She offered herself to me but I declined, sweetheart."

"You haven't touched me."

"You're healing." Emotionally and physically. He hadn't known how to approach her before the miscarriage. Now, he didn't want to hurt her.

Despite the hold he had on her, she stood. The jeans she wore hugged her hips and long legs and the green summer sweater with the V-neck made her tits outstanding.

"Can you take me to a hotel? I can't stay here any longer, Johnnie. You don't…you're not happy here. With me."

She slipped past him and went to the bed, zipping the duffel bag with trembling hands. What could he do to convince her how he felt and stop her from walking out on him? Although he deserved just this for all the times he'd taken her for granted. She started for the door.

Johnnie jerked around, the coins in his pocket jiggling. *The ring.* "Kendall, wait. You've got to listen to me. If you stay, I promise you I won't ever treat you as if you're a second thought. Never again. I swear. When you get pregnant again, I'll attend every doctor's appointment. I'll take you shopping for maternity clothes. Whatever."

She glanced over her shoulder. "W-will y-you go back to the club?"

"Kendall, gorgeous..." His voice trailed off and he felt like bellowing at the top of his lungs. "It's me. The club is who I am," he admitted quietly. "I can't...I want to be able to...*Fuck.*"

"You can't leave it," she said softly.

He slid into the chair she'd vacated and hung his head, sick inside. He could tell himself all he wanted that he'd walk away for Kendall, but it would come between them. His departure had already come between them. "I'm sorry."

She turned a little more. "Do you want to live there?"

He nodded. "I can compromise on that. Live wherever you want if you stay."

Her gaze inscrutable, she studied him. "I...will I be able to get counseling? Have time to figure out where I want to work?"

"Whatever you need, I'll support you."

"You won't think I'm weak for not being able to overcome this on my own?"

"It takes strength to ask for help."

She gave him a tentative smile and lowered her lashes.

"Do you really love me?"

"Yes," he said hoarsely and shifted to shove his hand in his pants pocket and pull out the ring. He placed it in the palm of his hand and held it out to her. "I've had this for a week, trying to figure out the right time to give this to you. The right way."

Gasping and dropping the duffel bag, her hand flew to her mouth.

Encouraged by her reaction, Johnnie dropped to one knee. "Kendall Miller, my gorgeous, brave lady, would you do me the honor of becoming my wife?"

"Johnnie," she breathed, taking another step closer and closer, until she stood in front of him again.

He sensed her hesitancy. "Please," he added. "Trust me when I tell you how much I love you. Trust me to give you everything your heart desires and everything you won't know it wants until I give it you. Say yes."

"On two conditions."

If it had something to do with his leaving the club..."They are?"

"I want to decorate our room when we move back to the compound."

Sure he'd misheard, he blinked, the sparkle in her eyes that had been missing for so long flitting into her gaze.

Stepping into his arms, she urged his head against her belly. "The other condition is I want a cut like Meggie has. Mine will say *Property of John Donovan*. That way, the world will know you own my heart."

Johnnie broke out into relieved laughter and hugged her before taking her hand and slipping the ring on. "You got it, gorgeous."

"Take me to the compound," she said. "I know the guys are on their run. Catch up to them."

Johnnie rose to his feet, excited at what his future held. Kendall. The club. His brothers. His *brother*. "I'll sleep there tonight and leave when I wake up."

The smile Kendall gave him was worth every plea he'd made to her tonight. His Kendall. Strong, brave and beautiful. Even though she had many more hurdles to overcome, she'd come so fucking far.

Johnnie was proud to call her his and even prouder to be hers.

Epilogue

Six years earlier

Joseph Foy considered the house in front of him. The place where his little girl lived. Where the only woman he'd ever love resided. Earlier, Dinah had ripped his heart out and banned him from visiting his Meggie again.

Without being told, he knew Thomas Fucking Nicholls was behind this shit. If only Meggie would fucking talk. The girl needed her brain re-fucking-wired. *Someone* needed to fucking teach her to speak the fuck up.

But Meggie believed she protected Dinah by staying silent about whatever went on behind those fucking doors of this perfect ass house with the upstanding fucking couple.

Twilight had fallen and the night animals were on high alert, sensing a predator in the midst.

Joe smirked. *Him.* The wooded area behind this house made for perfect fucking burial grounds. He'd gut fucking Thomas Nicholls, bury him, and take his baby girl and his Dinah back to the clubhouse.

Better yet, he'd cut him the fuck up and send him to

Logan so that asshole could use *this* asshole as hog feed.

His cellphone rang, cutting into the plan forming in his mind. He'd have to make Meggie and Dinah go before the bloodshed. But asshole would fuck with Joe's patience and he'd end up blowing Nicholls the fuck away in front of his daughter and her mother.

Not something he wanted Meggie to see.

His phone rang again. Obviously, brain dead motherfuckers didn't get the message that Joe didn't feel like being bothered.

Glancing at the name on the screen, his mood worsened. K-P.

Motherfucker whined like a pussy over shit. *He* wasn't all that fucking happy about fucking Logan Donovan, but, whereas *he* got a pass, K-P topped Logan's most wanted list.

If Logan *ever* unexiled himself...K-P was dead meat. He'd refused to go to Columbia with Logan. Strike fucking one.

Stealing fucking files and shit was strike number two.

And confronting Sebastian fucking Caldwell strike number fucking three.

Resting against his parked bike, Joe lit a cigarette. The third strike saved K-P's life. Logan ordered him killed in a most gruesome way. Joe refused and warned Logan to back the fuck off.

Dirty, perverted motherfucker. It wasn't enough Cee Cee had had both of Logan's daughters. No, the motherfucker had allowed the asshole to rape Zoann.

K-P had gone absolutely ape-shit crazy. All kinds of bad shit would go fucking down if he'd succeeded in killing fucking Cee Cee.

Not that fuckhead didn't deserve it.

After Meggie and Dinah, Joe's main concern was Christopher and Johnnie. He sucked on his smoke and snickered. Joey, too. Psychotic pussy-fuck. One day, Joe might get his son help. Who the fuck knew?

Truth be told, he wasn't all that concerned about Johnnie, either. *He* already knew almost everything. If he discovered his old man assaulted Bitsy, he'd just find a motherfucker to slice and dice and get the anger out of his system.

Christopher, though. He had a fucking conscious a mile fucking long. Motherfucker didn't know he did, though. He'd beat the fuck out of himself for the rest of his fucking life if he knew his father had raped his little sister while he'd been on a run.

More than that, if he knew Joe had forced her to take that abortion pill a couple days later to be on the safe side, Christopher might very well kill him. Or fucking try to. One of them would kill the other, eventually, anyway.

Christopher was big on fucking loyalty and Joe had betrayed him in too fucking many ways to count. Sins had a way of catching up with motherfuckers.

Fuck him, if his phone didn't start fucking ringing again. Fuck. Mortician.

Another motherfucker he wouldn't talk to tonight. Mortician's old man, Sharper, was as fucking dirty as the rest of them. Dirtier because he'd taken the one person besides Digger Mortician valued the most.

That fucking slut, Char. Gave birth to Mortician's son but married fucking Sharper and claimed the baby to be his because Sharper paid her the fuck off.

Mortician had gone fucking wild with his grief and anger. But K-P had handled him. K-P loved the fuck out of Mort.

Maybe, K-P had called earlier *because* of Mort.

Bunch of grown motherfuckers had more fucking problems than a pussy parlor.

A light flickered on and Joe's gut twisted. One of them had come to the living room. Meggie? Dinah? Thomas?

He did *not* like that motherfucker.

If only Meggie fucking talked.

Maybe, after she graduated from college, Joe would let her meet Christopher. Test the fucking waters with those two.

Johnnie wouldn't know what the fuck to do with her besides fuck her. Mortician didn't seem inclined to let go of Char anytime soon. And Val wanted Zoann.

Light flickered off and Joe sagged in defeat, an ache in his chest. He deserved this, he supposed. He'd continued to hurt Zoann after Cee Cee had mauled her. He and Rack had held her down and forced the pills into her mouth before stripping her naked and watching her bleed for the next few hours.

If anyone ever hurt his Meggie, the way Zoann had been hurt, he'd fucking kill them in the worst way possible.

Bleakness settled into his soul. Dinah had been right, keeping Meggie in Seattle and away from the club. Meggie would be vulnerable to all of those swinging dicks—friend and foe alike.

Even now, at thirteen, she was fucking gorgeous. None of the boys would touch her until she became of age, but, the moment she did, he'd have a fucking free-for-all on his hands. His guess was Meggie would choose one of the bad-ass young fucks in the club. Christopher or Johnnie. So be it. That wouldn't happen until after she graduated.

Besides, he was fucking proud of her. Sooner or later, he'd tell Joey about his sister, introduce them, and show her off at the club.

Look, fuckheads, but don't fucking touch.

"Joe?"

Dinah's soft voice startled him back to the present. He hadn't heard her approach. She stood in front of him, a blanket wrapped around her arms and body. Her blonde hair fluttered in the cold evening breeze.

"You have to leave," she whispered, the tracks of her tears catching a ray of waning light. "You can't come here anymore."

Joe gritted his teeth. "You fucking told me already, Dinah. A few fucking hours ago."

"Why are you still here? You should be almost back to Hortensia."

"I'm fucking leaving in a few."

"Leave now," she ordered.

"I'll leave when I'm good and motherfucking ready."

"I'm doing this for Meggie." Her tone wheedled, startling and annoying the fuck out of Joe. "You can't come here again."

"You're doing this for that fuck you're married to."

She looked so pale. Fuck *Meggie* talking. *Dinah* was the adult. She should speak the fuck up. He pulled her into his arms and hugged her tight, a premonition that this would be the last time he ever held her stealing the joy of the moment.

"Leave with me. Get Meggie and come back to the club."

She shook her head, as he knew she would. "No. I can't. I couldn't handle the women then. And, now, Meggie is growing up. I can't have her around all those men."

"I'll buy you a house. Big. Little. Small." *Whatever*. Just as long as he had them with him.

He'd demand Logan find another fucking source of income. Enough was enough anyway. He couldn't fucking take it anymore. Every time he saw Meggie, he thought about one of those girls he and Rack helped transport for fucking Logan.

At Logan's suggestion, he'd started shooting up just to

deal with this bullshit. Joe was moving the club away from
Logan's form of money making. He was starting to run
guns. Christopher had begun a hydrogrow operation.

Before Christopher, Johnnie, Mortician, or Val ever
found out—before K-P did something stupid—Joe would
make this right.

"Dinah—"

She turned away from him. "Leave. Meggie has been
crying all night. If she sees you, it'll only make it worse."

"How can you stand watching Meggie cry? Whatever
else I've done, I've always loved her."

"Meggie is going to grow up one day and leave, Joe. I
can't put my life on hold for *her*. My husband requested I
stop your visits—"

"Fuck your husband!" He'd never fucking wanted to
wallop Dinah. *Ever*. But he did just then. "Meggie's my
baby girl. I'm going to fucking fight you for her."

Whirling around, Dinah sucked in a breath. "Go ahead.
Who do you think will get her? Me? Her mother? This
stable home life she has with me says it all," she sneered.
"Or do you think your money will get her away from me?
Having a hormonal thirteen-year-old at a biker club isn't
the smartest decision. No court in the world would give her
to *you*."

Her derision cut through Joe. He'd always held her
sweet words close to his heart. But, fuck, it worked with K-
P. Didn't matter he had his daughter's mother with Bailey
in a house in Hortensia. He still made it work. Fuck, Joe
wasn't too fucking proud to ask for advice about how to
manage that shit.

"All you'd do is spoil Meggie. She doesn't need that.
She needs to learn responsibility."

"She's fucking thirteen. She should be spoiled."

"I wasn't spoiled at that age. And she's almost fourteen I refuse to allow her—"

"I spoiled you once we met."

"Years later." She started to cry. "Please. Just leave. Don't make trouble. You have your club to run. Your son to look after. Your precious Christopher."

"Shut up. You never met Christopher, so your dislike is misplaced."

"Blood in, blood out," she charged. "When you fall, I don't want Meggie anywhere around the fall out."

Joe wasn't a superstitious motherfucker by any means, but Dinah's words sounded like a fucking curse. Bitch wasn't known for fucking prophecies, but all women could hex a motherfucker.

Dinah ran across the street and back into the house, her words floating in the air.

If he ever fell, he wondered who the fuck would be left standing?

Years later, as his life flashed before him, and his finger squeezed the trigger to end Christopher's life, Dinah's words exploded in his head the very same moment Christopher's bullet did.

THE END

Playlist

Perfect	Pink
Just The Way You Are	Bruno Mars
All of Me	John Legend
Sex on Fire	Kings of Leon
Say Something	A Great Big World
True Colors	Cyndi Lauper
Love Bites	Def Leppard
Eternity	Robbie Williams
Skinny Love	Birdy
Careless Whisper	George Michael
I'm Still Standing	Elton John
This Is How We Roll	Florida Georgia Line
The Man	Aloe Blacc
Drunk On You	Luke Bryan
Afterlife	Avenged Sevenfold
Almost Easy	Avenged Sevenfold
Been To Hell	Hollywood Undead
Better Than Me	Hinder
Wanted Dead or Alive	Bon Jovi
I Wanna Sex You Up	Color Me Badd
Sex and Candy	Marcy Playground
Wild Ones – feat. Sia	Flo Rida
Stay	Rihanna
Suspicious Minds	Elvis Presley
Get Up Offa That Thing	James Brown
You Are the Best Thing	Ray LaMontagne
Sexual Healing	Marvin Gay
Free Fallin'	Tom Petty
Free Bird	Lynyrd Skynyrd
Son Of A Preacher Man	Dusty Springfield
Born To Be Wild	Steppenwolf

Mary Jane	Rick James
Until You	Billy Currington
Like The Way I Do	Melissa Etheridge
Mustang Sally	Wilson Pickett
We Will Rock You	Queen

THE DEATH DWELLERS MC

AN EXCITING NEW SERIES BY KATHRYN KELLY

STEP INTO THE WORLD OF CHRISTOPHER "OUTLAW" CALDWELL, THE MEN HE CALLS BROTHERS AND THE WOMEN THEY FALL IN LOVE WITH.

DEATH DWELLERS MC

MISLED

KATHRYN KELLY

Preface

In each of us lives good and evil. The conundrum we face as a society is recognizing those we pigeonhole as evil and those we applaud as good. That's the grossest mislabeling in the world, the greatest injustice. Have we not heard of the fable of *The Wolf in Sheep's Clothing*? Do we yet misunderstand how deceptive appearances can be? The sun casting a golden gleam upon us doesn't shield us from the rain. Good and evil are wrapped in illusions we're determined to create.

The man society views as acceptable…you know the one…? He gives up his seat to little old ladies. Attends church. Sings carols with good cheer. Gives a hand out and a help up. That man, too, has evil lurking in the depths of his soul. Perhaps, he's more evil. This man has the ability to charm and smile and manipulate the world to see his goodness. When, in fact, he's the scariest of all.

He's a wife beater and a child molester. He tears down under the pretense of building up.

I know him well.

He's my stepfather.

Chapter 1

"No! Please. *Stop!*"

The crack of a hand connecting with flesh tore through the tension. Meggie jumped and wrapped her arms around her middle, her sob competing with her mother's pleas. She sat on the edge of her bed, body trembling, praying her mother would survive this latest beating.

Another lick. Dinah wept and Meggie's belly roiled at the tormented sounds.

"Please, Thomas," Dinah cried. "You've got to stop!"

Meggie nodded vigorously. Yes, he had to stop. One of these days he'd kill her mom.

Glass shattered and furniture banged. Dry heaves wracked Meggie at the heavy thud. She knew that sound, knew it meant her mother was careening to the floor. Dinah screamed and Meggie doubled over, sweat popping off her skin, her mother's pain her own.

Surrounded by her white bedroom furniture and pastel green décor, she wondered how her home life was such a nightmare. On the outside, everyone saw the perfect family—a woman, an assistant high school principal, finding happiness in her second marriage with the teddy bear of a middle school math teacher who'd stepped in as a father-figure to the woman's daughter.

Dinah's scream coupled with tearing clothes. Though not in the den, Meggie had seen the situation play out enough to pick out the sounds and their meanings.

"Please," Dinah sobbed. "I don't want to."

She didn't want to have sex, she meant. Meggie bowed her head into her hands, wishing for the strength and fortitude to take it upon herself to kill her stepfather.

"Let's go in the bedroom." Dinah's breath caught around a moan.

Thomas grunted. "I'm fucking you right here. Right out in the open."

Embarrassment competed with Meggie's fear and anger.

Her mother's next sob burned through Meggie and she covered her face.

"Don't. Not in the den. I don't want Meggie to hear."

"Think she's not fucking?"

No. Meggie bit into her wrist, barely feeling the injury but tasting metallic blood.

"No," Dinah echoed through tears. "She's a virgin."

"No. She's not," Thomas sneered. "I should know."

Oh God. Oh God. Oh God. Meggie stared at her bite mark, oozing red, and shook her head in denial.

Silence met Thomas's lie and he took advantage of the stunning insinuation by taunting, "she's been coming on to me for months. I thought it best to keep it in the family."

"Wh-what?"

Meggie wasn't sure if she wanted her mother to believe Thomas or not. Dinah was too broken to attempt to defend her. She hadn't even allowed the police to haul Thomas away a week ago when Meggie had called 911. Instead, she'd blamed her injuries on something asinine and stupid. For Meggie's attempt to defend Dinah that night, she'd gotten her bedroom door removed.

"You lying bastard," Dinah screamed.

Meggie drew in a sharp breath, her already aggravated pulse and heart rate throbbing in her ears. She spread her blood over her skin, attempting to refocus.

Thomas yelped and, for a few blessed moments, it sounded as if Dinah asserted herself and inflicted serious damage.

"You fucking bitch!" he snarled. "I'm going to kill you."

"Big Joe is coming for her," Dinah persisted in a wild, unrecognizable tone. "I called him! And I'm going to tell him. I'm going to tell him you've violated his baby. I'm going to tell him and he's going to kill you. He's going to chop your dick off and feed it to pigs."

Meggie cheered at the thought. Her daddy was coming. She'd been trying to reach him for weeks. Left so many messages, it surprised her his voicemail wasn't filled to capacity. She knew how busy he was, so the fact he hadn't answered wasn't real surprising. Sometimes, it took her months to get a response from him. Before, he'd just blaze into town on his bike, the pipes of the Harley rumbling in the quiet suburb blocks away. He took a lot of trips, something he called runs.

Ever since Dinah had barred him from visiting at Thomas's insistence, two years ago, Meggie always imagined going on the road with him and his boys.

"You know how hard your fighting makes me, huh, baby?" Thomas crooned.

"Y-yes."

"I'm not letting Megan live with him. When he comes, tell him she's not interested in going with him." He groaned and gasped. "Tell him she doesn't want to see him. Ever again."

Dinah moaned. "Right there, Thomas. Harder."

Meggie's cheeks burned and her stomach churned at Thomas's filthy response. And so the cycle continued, she thought, humiliated. She stretched to her pillow and retrieved the little knife she kept hidden under it. Pressing the sharp blade against her forearm, she sliced down, sucking in a breath at the brief burn and pain. Blood rushed from the wound and her tension and fear seeped away with it. The respite lasted a moment. The satisfaction dwindled in the amount of time it took the pain to recede.

Sniffling, she tightened her mouth and slashed again. Meggie swiped her tears once more and slashed at the wrist she'd bitten.

"Ah, God!" She'd gone deeper than she intended and had to grab the sheet to staunch the flow of blood, the sounds from the den both sickening and infuriating. She wasn't sure if her mother truly liked Thomas's attention or if she just accepted it. In the end, no matter what Thomas said or did, Dinah gave him sex. Meggie didn't want to see her mother as a weak, pathetic woman because it went deeper than that.

Dinah had tried to run in the early days of their marriage. Both times Thomas had found her and beaten her to a bloody pulp before using his fists on Meggie. Her mother had just given up and given in. She knew her mother refused to risk Meggie being hurt again because of her escape attempts.

"Meggie?"

She raised her gaze at the sound of her mother's whimper. Dinah stood in the doorway, her face swollen and bloody, bruises covering her naked body. She clutched the wood molding, trembling.

The sight tore through Meggie and she shoved her knife under the bloody sheet. She stood and swallowed; her chin wobbled. Both she and her mother were wrecks but she couldn't add any stress by allowing her injuries to show. She stepped forward, arms behind her back. "Momma."

Dinah went sprawling and Meggie hurried to the door. Thomas stood inches away, naked, too, and smelling of sweat and alcohol. Unable to stop it, Meggie glared at him, her cheeks burning at the sight of his flaccid penis and hairy testicles. Not that she hadn't seen him nude before but the sight always repulsed her.

The back of his hand shot out. Meggie didn't jump out of reach fast enough. Stars danced in front of her eyes at the slap.

"Please. Not Meggie," Dinah whined, prone on the squeaky clean linoleum.

Thomas kicked Dinah's thigh and she whimpered again. Meggie growled and launched herself at Thomas, buoyed by the thought of her father coming for her, not caring if Thomas beat the crap of her. She'd learned to cover her pain and bruises but she wouldn't have to. She could show each little hurt to her daddy and he'd find a way to make them go away. He'd make *him* go away.

Her fingernails dug into Thomas's cheek and she drew them down, drawing blood just like he drew her mother's blood and sometimes hers. He grabbed her upper arms and slammed her against the wall. Meggie bounced and stumbled onto Dinah, who lay silent and still, but warm, the rise of fall of her back assuring she lived. Thomas yanked Meggie to her feet by her hair. She kicked, connecting with his penis and he dropped to his knees.

Meggie blew out puffs of air, not having much time. Steeped in drunken insanity, Thomas's meanness and strength rivaled a dozen men. She doubted he'd even feel a bullet.

Stupid bull of a man.

Ignoring her pain, she scrambled to her mother and latched onto her hands, pulling her forward. "Come on, Momma. Help me."

She needed to get them to Dinah's bedroom. Just until Thomas drank himself into a stupor and passed out. If she couldn't convince Dinah the wisdom of leaving while Thomas slept off the vodka and bourbon, then, at least, the latest danger would pass. Thomas would be sick for a day and sober for a couple more. Sometimes, he even went a week without drinking. Sober, his hits lacked so much viciousness and murderous intent.

Meggie pulled Dinah another inch and her mother groaned. Thomas roared to his feet. She didn't want to leave her mother but her sense of self-preservation took over. Dropping Dinah's arms, Meggie stumbled toward the nearest door, the half bath right next to her bedroom. His arms encircled her waist. He lifted her off her feet. Meggie screamed, struggling in his arms.

He stepped over Dinah, keeping a firm grip on Meggie, and walked into her bedroom. Reaching her bed, he slammed her down. She sprung up and barreled into him, the maneuver useless. When his hand neared her, somehow she dodged it and, instead, sunk her teeth into the fleshy side.

"Bitch!" he yelled, crashing his fist on the side of her head and her world went black.

CHAPTER 1

"I don't think this is a good idea," Megan Caldwell said. She glared at the three men surrounding her after listening to their suggestion that she go away so her husband, Christopher "Outlaw" Caldwell, could enjoy the bachelor party they'd planned for him. They'd waylaid her on her way from meeting with the lady she'd hired to help her decorate her and Christopher's house. Meggie only had time to open the door to the room she shared with Christopher at the MC, thank her mother for babysitting, and watch Dinah scoot through the wall of men Meggie now faced. "CJ and I will stay in the room and—"

Mortician, Enforcer of the club and the man with a variety of handy skills, folded his arms, muscles rippled on his dark brown skin, while the skull ring he never seemed to remove leered from his middle finger. Though cold outside, he wore short sleeves under his cut. "C'mon, Megan," he persisted. "You think Prez'll enjoy himself knowing you and his kid right down the hall?"

She glanced back at her sleeping son. Judging from her achy breasts, his feeding time was approaching. Only six and a half months old, he was the size of a baby eight or nine months and already a smaller version of Christopher with the blueness of his eyes changing to a deeper shade of green with each passing day. *Her* hair might've been golden, but her son's was just as black as his daddy's. A daddy who didn't let him very far out of his sight. Besides, she didn't have time to just leave with the near completion of their house and their church wedding ceremony coming up in a month. Not to mention, Valentine's Day was *two* days away. "Christopher isn't going to like this. He won't want us—"

"Is it *him* or you, girl?" Digger, Mortician's *real* brother, asked, cocking his head to the side.

All right so maybe it was *her* a little as well. But they wanted to throw her husband a bachelor party, complete with the Bobs—those women paraded out for special occasions and their exceptional oral skills.

"We're already married," she pointed out, jabbing Digger in the chest. He was taller than his older brother, a little less broad in the shoulders, arms, and chest. Mortician was *ripped*. Digger was muscled but...she frowned. Was she actually sizing up her husband's officers?

"Why does he need a bachelor party?"

"Right, Megan," Val, the bald-headed RC, grunted. His mouth kicked up in a smile, revealing the sexy dimple that made him irresistible to so many girls.

Umkay. Yes. Yes, she was sizing these men up. Men she'd known for over a year and thought of as friends and older brothers.

"Why you need some big fucking church wedding?" Val went on in the steely voice he adopted for intimidation. "You already married, huh?"

She'd walked right into that one. She stepped farther into the hallway, so their voices wouldn't prematurely awaken her son. She'd be so glad when their house was finished because she was sick to death of living day-in and day-out at the MC. "Where am I supposed to go all of a sudden?"

"I'm with Megs," a voice to the right of her said. Johnnie, Christopher's cousin, and the club VP, leaned against the wall next to her.

Meggie looked at the ankle boots she wore, not wanting to stare at Johnnie. The one glimpse she had seen of his chiseled face, when she'd glanced between the space created by Mortician's head and the wall, proved enough for her.

"Christopher will have your balls if he knows you're pressuring his wife to leave," he continued.

Johnnie's blond hair, longer on top than on the sides, made his silver-gray eyes stand out. The heat of his gaze lasered her profile and she shifted her weight beneath his scrutiny. She didn't have to look at him to know he studied her. He always did. And not in a brotherly way.

"I'm suggesting you asswipes back off," he said lazily.

Meggie rocked back on her heels, satisfied at his defense. "He's known about this bachelor party all along. He's never once said he didn't want me there. Or, at least, on the premises."

"Prez wouldn't want to upset you," Mortician went on. His dreads had grown even longer in the fourteen or fifteen months since she'd met him. Today, they were queued and his strong neck flexed with his movements. "But we gonna have associates, hangers-on, and brothers from our support clubs as well as dudes from our out of town chapters. You know if you're here Prez's either gonna want you out there with him or he's gonna be in here with you. How's that gonna make him look to the other brothers?"

"Like he loves and respects his wife," she snapped.

"Who the fuck are you?" Johnnie snarled, drawing everyone's attention to a man who'd just walked out of the main room and into the hallway where only members and their guests were allowed.

Sardonic green eyes studied them and Meggie frowned when she caught a brief glimpse of him as Mortician shifted and turned to the side. A blue bandanna covered the man's head and he wore a cut with unrecognizable rockers.

He raised his hands. "Sorry, brother. Looking for the shitter."

The men now hid her, their backs to her in a semi-circle of towering, muscled protection. Behind them, she stood on her tiptoes to get another look at the interloper, placing her hands on Digger's shoulders to balance herself.

"This ain't the fucking way," Digger growled.

"Yeah, fuckhead. Public shitters in the other direction," Val added, raising an arm.

Meggie guessed it was to point toward the public *shitters*. They were on the other side of the main room, in the area of the pool tables and dart boards.

"Sorry," the man said again, though something about his mocking tone told Meggie he wasn't sorry at all.

"You forgiven this fucking time," Mortician called. "Make a mistake like this again and we not responsible for where the fuck parts of you end up."

Meggie poked Mortician in the back at the threat, though she knew the score. She sighed and thought of Christopher's bachelor party. Men like the stranger would overrun the place and Christopher's well-earned reputation as a bad-ass meant everything to him. At the thought, her defenses crumbled. Mortician was right. To her, Christopher was everything she could ever want--a wonderful father and a very dedicated husband. To everyone else…he was both feared and respected because of the way he carried himself and the way he handled things. She wouldn't want him to lose face because she couldn't allow him to enjoy his bachelor party without her around.

They turned back to her and she knew the man was gone. She heard the first stirrings of her son. On cue, her breasts opened like a faucet. "Fine," she said before they started in on her again. "I'll call Farrah and Lacey and go to Seattle."

"Seattle?" they chorused, glancing between one another with consternation. She hadn't seen her friends since forever, so, maybe, this would be a good time to visit. At least, they'd serve as a distraction about her husband's bachelor party.

Digger recovered first. "Meggie girl, well, I guess that'll be cool. We know you won't change your mind and decide to come back during the party with you being so far away."

"Seattle, huh, babe?" Val rubbed his jaw, his mouth downturned. "Just don't call Prez every ten minutes, telling him you miss him. That'll be just as bad as you being here."

Meggie shook her head. "I won't call him every ten minutes, but I *will* call him—"

"No, girl," Mortician insisted. "No calls at all 'til the next day. If he hears your voice, he won't have fun."

"What planet have you three been living on?" Meggie bit out, tapping her foot in agitation. "I won't like not being able to talk to Christopher at all after just deciding to fly out of town, but he *really* won't like not hearing from me."

Johnnie cleared his throat and pushed off the wall. He reached in his cut for a cigarette, his gaze falling on her swollen breasts. Meggie lowered her lashes and gritted her teeth, flushing to her toes at the lust in Johnnie's eyes. He didn't light his cigarette, just held it between his fingers and used it to emphasize his words.

"The woman sleeps next to him every night. She knows him better than we do. I say you three idiots listen to her."

"You've known him all your life, John Boy," Val said in defense of his argument.

"My point exactly," Johnnie said. He pointed between the three of them. "And you fucks have known him ten, fifteen years."

Meggie backed out of the doorway and a little farther into the room. "One call to let him know we've gotten there safely."

"Meggie, c'mon," Digger said with frustration, "that won't fly. He's not going to die without hearing from you for *one day*. And neither will you."

She had no time for this. CJ was making his little baby babbles. "Fine."

Not wanting to hear anymore, she turned, finished talking, needing to get to CJ so she could nurse him. Right before she closed the door, she heard Johnnie mutter, "Don't say I didn't warn you bozos."

Preface

I've looked around and envied others the solid ground on which they grew up. Because, I know, as with all shaky foundations, eventually the walls come tumbling down and secrets are brought to light. I feel the tick-tock of the clock, the sands of time slipping away granule by granule. Miniscule time bombs awaiting detonation. Finally, the day I've feared arrives. The explosions rocks our world.

Now, everyone will discover I'm not the perfect, easy-going man I project myself to be. They will see that evil lurks from within—my family and my heart.

Because my family is different.

We are founded and forged in heartache and betrayal.

Unless I intercede, so will we be destroyed by the same.

Chapter 1

A sound awakened Kendall Miller and she sat up, blinking, before stretching her arms above her head. A blond man stood in the center of the room, his silver-gray gaze never leaving her as he withdrew a cigarette from his cut and lit it.

She studied the burning tip, the flame consuming the paper and tobacco, before it dwindled down to a fiery glow. Smoke plumed into the air and Kendall stared at the evaporating curlicues, transfixed at the tangible metaphor of what her life had become. Despair washed through her and everything rushed back. Her failure tonight made her ache inside and undermined the sliver of peace she'd somehow acquired a little while ago, when she'd first stepped into this room.

She didn't want to think of the consequences if she didn't get to the bed of the Death Dwellers' president.

Hugging her arms around her waist, she thought of another MC leader. Her ex-lover. Days ago, she'd gotten over the pain of his multiple betrayals, a blessed numbness consuming her. She'd thought she'd finally found a man who understood her and would protect her at any and all costs. But, no, Spoon had cheated on her, lied to her, and stolen her heart and soul—her little sister—and handed her over to *him*.

Kendall clasped her fingers together, biting the inside of her cheek to prevent more gut-wrenching sobs from pushing through. She *had* to get Caroline back. Their mother, Marie, doted on her. Besides, just the thought of her sixteen-year-old sister's predicament clung to Kendall's soul, unleashing deep desperation inside of her.

She'd experienced Spoon's unsympathetic beliefs firsthand. Compared to Logan Donovan, though, her rat-fink-bastard-ex could've been canonized one day. Logan Donavan, a man she'd spoke to over the telephone but never met face-to-face, epitomized a monster, plain and simple. A web of nerves, unease and anxiety tangling though her, Kendall lifted her gaze to the beautiful man watching her.

Another chill slithered down her back, her thoughts exploding with the repercussions if she couldn't correct her mistake. Repercussions not only for herself, whom she barely cared about anymore, but for Caroline.

She *had* to get her little sister back.

"H-hi."

A brow lifted and heat rushed to Kendall's cheeks, his lingering glance and overwhelming presence unnerving her.

"Hello," he responded, his voice full of dark temptation.

Her hair must've been a mess. Considering everything

else, the innocuous thought surprised her. Coiffures should've been the last thing on her mind. In this life or death situation, the need to have him find her attractive felt ridiculous. Before tonight, she'd never met the man and, more than likely, he'd forget her the moment she escaped him.

She combed her fingers through her hair, arranged the entire length over one shoulder, covering a breast.

He folded his arms and crossed one ankle over the other, leaning against the desk holding the stereo system.

His arrogant nonchalance and golden beauty enhanced her appreciation of him. Judging by his slow perusal and remembering how he'd calmed the club president a little while ago, she suspected the twinkle in his silver-gray eyes hid his fathomless depths.

Waiting for her, contemplating her, he displayed surprising patience. He didn't yell. Or insult her. His all-consuming gaze burned into her and she licked her lips, the hard knot in her belly dissolving into tingles.

Needing to reclaim her rapidly failing senses, Kendall noted his sparse furnishings. A bed. A chest of drawers. A desk. That was about it. He swallowed the space, though, filled it with his presence

She lowered her lashes, flustered. Tall and chiseled, his build screamed strength and power. His forbidding jawline and full lips were pure artistic refinement. She'd never seen a more gorgeous man. His lips curved into a devastating smile, revealing white, even teeth. Ever so slowly, the smile changed to a frown. She hadn't uttered another word since their greetings.

She licked her lips, her body responding to his virility.

Focus, Kendall. Focusing would be the only way to get herself in the *right* man's bed.

Even before he'd snatched Caroline, Spoon hadn't touched her in weeks. She shoved aside her humiliation at his reasons. Although *he* didn't want her, he'd sent her to another man rather than touch her himself, as she'd offered, in exchange for her little sister.

The man he'd sent her to knocked her flat on her ass because he'd been furious that someone would send another woman to him knowing he had a wife.

Kendall wished for such loyalty.

The big biker straightened, his movements and withdrawal catching her attention. If he no longer wanted her, she'd be free to find the president again and complete the job she'd been sent to do. She didn't want the other man, though. From the moment the blond biker jerked her to her feet and placed his body in front of hers, Kendall had felt something she hadn't in a very long time. *Protected.*

For a few, brief minutes, her mind had been blank of her ruined world and her ravaged sister. When he'd directed her to his room, she'd obeyed without thought, fatigue consuming her. Heavy makeup covered the dark rings around her eyes, proof she hadn't slept in days.

So, instead of attempting to find the president's bedroom when she had the chance, she'd come in here. And fallen asleep. After weeks—months—of turmoil, she'd walked into this stranger's room, laid on his bed, and found comfort.

Certifiable. Selfish. Bad.

Kendall grimaced at Spoon's labels. A man was out there, waiting to get photos of her and the Dwellers' president in bed together. Her little sister, Caroline, was being held and used until Kendall delivered what had been asked of her. Going to the police was out of the question— if she wanted Caroline to survive. And, yet…*YET*…desire was pooling in her belly and tightening her core. For a stranger. The *wrong* stranger.

That stranger roamed around, his movements a

coordination of agility and strength. He pulled out the drawers in the chest, eyed the inside, before rubbing his fingertips against every inch of the wood, then repeated the process at his desk and the headboard of his bed. Ignoring their close proximity, he went through the bewildering process all over again.

Unable to stop herself, she followed the path of his hand, imagining his fingertips skimming over her body. His heat surrounded her, the different smells emanating from him zinging to her head. Alcohol. Marijuana. A hint of spicy cologne. Sweat. And *him.*

She chewed on her bottom lip as *With Arms Wide Open* began to play and he stilled, frowning and backing away from the bed. Though he looked in her direction, Kendall doubted he actually saw her. He scrubbed a big hand over his face at certain lines and sighed with heartfelt emotion. Towards the end of the song, his nostrils flared, the bleakness in his eyes calling to her.

"Are you all right?"

He narrowed his eyes. "Who the fuck sent you?"

The hairs on her nape stood at the harsh question. One, he'd asked it and, two, she'd somehow given herself away, leaving her with no good answer. She wanted to shout, *bad men,* the simplest explanation. The truth had isolated her for five, miserable days with Kendall no closer to getting Caroline back.

Unless she got this right. On the other hand, this motorcycle club had gotten on Logan Donovan's bad side, too. Otherwise, he wouldn't have been going out of his way to destroy the president.

Another lift of that imperious blond brow made her scramble for a credible response. She had to say *something.* She hadn't slept enough to be at the top of her game. With the exhaustion clouding her mind and delaying her responses, she wasn't even hovering near the bottom.

"Whoever sent the others. I'm not sure. I'm a freelancer and one of the other girls couldn't make it, so my friend called me. Asked me if I wanted to take the chick's place. And here I am."

"So no one hired you to fuck Outlaw?"

No. Truth. Nothing as mundane as monetary compensation orchestrated this life or death, do or die, situation. "Why would someone hire me for that?"

"To fuck with his relationship with his wife."

Tread with care. The biker's brain matched his brawn. "Seems silly," she got out in a strong voice. "She's not here, is she? How would that interfere with their marriage?"

The question sounded ridiculous even to her stressed-out, overwrought mind. If she ever got married and her husband slept with another woman, *her* marriage would be interfered with, too.

What was Kendall thinking? This entire evening had the makings of a disaster. She'd left herself open to rape when she'd walked into the clubhouse in only a jacket, her clothes discarded in her car. When she walked in, she'd discarded her jacket on a table and headed directly for the club president, then proceeded to gyrate her naked body on him. He'd gotten an erection, but Kendall was experienced enough to know he hadn't appreciated it. Someone, mainly *her,* could've gotten seriously hurt if the president had fired his gun.

Shoving the thought aside and determined to brazen it out until she escaped, Kendall continued.

"Besides, she's a biker's wife. I'm sure she understands infidelity and betrayal." She spat the last word because she'd been suckered into believing different. "I was on his lap. I felt his erection. He wanted to fuck me and would have if there hadn't been all these people here."

"If you think that, then you're a goddamn fool. He couldn't help but get a dick stand with the way you were grinding your pussy against him. But, if he wanted you, he would've fucked you and not cared who was here."

Not knowing how else to stop her rioting emotions or what else to say, Kendall laid back on the bed, opening her legs. Music filled the room and she touched her clit, feeling the bare lips of her pussy. The impulse to ignore her wetness, her hard nipples, almost overcame her. But she'd already made a terrible muck of things tonight and she needed...she needed a moment of peace. A smidgeon of comfort.

She'd blame herself later, figure *something* out. She didn't have a law degree for nothing.

She enjoyed sex immensely and would've responded to the president, but something about *this* man made her want him. *Really* want him. If she wanted to, he'd allow her to walk out. He hadn't made a move toward her until she began to rub her pussy. Like the whore she was supposed to be.

Not saying a word, he removed his cut and pullover, baring his chest. Kendall's eyes nearly crossed. *Ripped* was too tame a word to describe his broad shoulders and bulging arms. His six-pack. Long fingers attached to massive hands. She swallowed as he removed his pants. What...her mouth watered when she saw his cock and she had to rearrange her thoughts. What was the rumor about men with big hands and big feet?

Before she remembered, he'd gloved his cock in a condom and climbed on top of her, settling between her legs.

Surprise broke through the trance the sight of his body had put her in. "We aren't going to kiss?"

Kendall waited for his reply. She wanted to taste his lips—his entire body. He thumbed her clit and she groaned. Bending his head, he licked her nipple and she grew wetter and hotter. He inserted two, thick fingers inside her body, massaging her inner walls and sucking in a breath. She arched against him and moaned, rocking against his hand. He bit her nipple, increased the pressure of his thumb on her clit, the in-and-out speed of his fingers. A keening wail began to escape her but she bit down on her lip, catching the sound in her throat that his kiss could've captured.

Holding her hips in place, he sank into her, filling and stretching her. She brushed her lips against his chest and wrapped her legs around his waist, clutching him tighter to her body, and tilting her pelvis to take him deeper.

"One kiss," she whispered. "Please."

Nuzzling her hair, he slid in and out of her, in long, deep strokes. His cock stretched her and trembles pulsed through her. She sighed, forgetting her overwhelming need to kiss him and reveling in his movements inside of her. He skimmed his tongue over her neck, raining kisses down the column of her throat. Small moans of pleasure escaped her and matched his masculine grunts.

Gripping her hips and raising her body for deeper drives, he pushed against her pussy, hitting internal and external points of ecstasy, continuing until her orgasm broke over her and she cried out.

He shuddered and groaned then went still, his breathing hard and heavy.

A few moments later, he lay next to her, his eyes covered by his forearm. As if he wanted nothing else to do with her now that they'd fucked. And, maybe, he didn't. She'd seen enough of how men treated club ass at the Torpedoes' MC.

Indecision tore through her. But, damn it, he'd gotten what he wanted from her. She'd get what she wanted from him. If she never saw him again, she'd regret not tasting him. He'd refused her the opportunity to feel his mouth against her but she wouldn't leave until she sucked him off.

Turning to her side, she removed the condom and laid it next to her on the bed, not knowing what else to do with it. Then, she leaned over and wrapped her mouth around his dick, immediately relaxing her throat to take him deeper, satisfied at his grunt. He moved, raising up on his elbows. The thought of him watching her while she pleasured him sent another rush of wetness between her legs. Her cheeks hollowed, so she could suck him hard, for her and himself. She wanted to give him a performance worth watching— worth repeating—and she wanted to swallow every last drop of cum he had to offer, so she suctioned him without mercy. He fisted her hair and wrapped it around his hand, pulling on her head. Her scalp tingled from the tug, but the moves prompted her to harder and faster sucks, while he pumped his hips to her deep slurps.

"Ah! Fuck!" Tightening his grip on her hair, he held her head in place, thrusting into her aching mouth as cum jetted from him. His dick remained in her mouth until his breathing slowed. Only then did he pull away and release her hair.

Kendall sat back on her haunches and licked her lips, dizzy from the salty-sweet taste of him. "Now will you kiss me?" she whispered.

Though she hadn't expected those words to fall from her lips, she didn't want her time with him to end. She wanted to stay in there, protected and safe. But that couldn't happen as long as Caroline was away and would never happen even afterwards.

Hands behind his head, he popped an eye open and smirked at her. "You want a kiss, baby?"

She nodded.

"Come here."

Too aroused to be ashamed of her body, she crawled next to him, her breasts hanging, hovering near his mouth. He sat further up and sucked a tight nipple into his mouth while guiding her onto her back. She moaned at the gentleness with which he handled her.

He raised his head. Kendall had never seen a man wear a combination of mirth, arrogance and certainty so well. "If you want a kiss, gorgeous, I'll give you a kiss you won't forget."

Her breath caught and her mouth tingled in expectation. Until she realized the direction he was going. Down instead of up. The first couple times she and Spoon had been together, he'd used his mouth on her and never enough for her to get any real enjoyment. Only enough to get her wet.

Now, though, her blond god ran his tongue along her feminine seem at the same time her spread her legs wide, exposing her pussy to him completely. He tongued her sensitive outer lips, then used his rough fingertips to open them. He licked his way around the inner folds, circling her clit but never quite touching it. Fire singed her nerve endings and she trembled, goose bumps marching across every inch of her skin. He speared his tongue into her pussy and she screamed.

"My God," she groaned, shivering, moving against his mouth. "Who taught you to eat pussy like this?"

He didn't answer her, not that she really wanted one. When he removed his tongue from her, she had to bite her own to keep from begging him to continue. Just as the thought crossed her mind, he pushed the hood of her clit back, exposing the most sensitive part of her and gave her what she'd asked for—a kiss. He pressed kiss after kiss against her before lapping. This wasn't what she'd meant, but she'd take it. Jesus, yes, she'd take this type of kiss if that's what he wanted.

Kendall's womb tightened and she hissed in a breath.

She thrashed against him and tugged at his hair, her legs trembling through her orgasm. Explosions rocketed through her being, shooting her to the moon and back.

Before she recovered completely, he blew on her clit and spread her ass cheeks. He inserted a finger in each part of her and began swiping his tongue over her clit, massaging the thin membrane separating her pussy and ass, keeping her in place by pressing his other hand against her belly.

She screamed and cried and shivered, the pleasure he inflicted upon her body sweet torture. He refused her any mercy, removing his fingers not his mouth, allowing her to fuck his face, sucking and licking her until she couldn't take anymore.

"Stop! Please," she begged and moaned when he pulled away, relieved and disappointed too. Falling back against the pillows, she closed her eyes, hearing his movement.

He rolled onto her and she opened her legs, weak and completely submissive to him. He positioned her feet upon his shoulders and slammed into her over and over again. She was too soaked for his massive size to cause her any pain with his deep, powerful thrusts into her. He shifted, allowed her to lower her legs and wrap them around his waist. She tried to kiss him, but he bent his head and rested it against her shoulder. Kendall wrapped her arms around his sweaty back, running her fingers along the curvature of his spine, squeezing his hard ass as he pumped in and out of her. She couldn't stop the little noises in the back of her throat, couldn't stop herself from fingering his damp hair. She wanted to touch every part of him, remember this beautiful man forever.

He bit her ear, fingered her clit until she reached her orgasm, then emptied into the condom.

After a few moments, he got up and disappeared into the bathroom. When nothing else in the world had broken her, tonight, in a stranger's arms, he'd brought her to the brink of collapsing. She had to hold it together, though. Just until she left here. As she sat up, the thought made her shiver because he was finished with her. He'd make her go back out there, where all those lusty bikers were, with the scent of sex clinging to her body. She wasn't claimed by anyone, though, leaving her fair game.

He sauntered back into the room and she realized she'd get no more than she deserved for coming here in the first place. *She'd* made the choices leading her to this point in her life. She never should've come there with the intentions she'd had. It might've solved her problems, but it would've devastated another woman. He got his cigarettes and offered her one but she shook her head. She didn't smoke.

"I-I need to leave," she said quietly.

He nodded.

"I...my clothes are in my car and my jacket is somewhere out in the main room," she said, a gentle way of reminding him if he stayed in his room she'd have to walk back out there naked and with everyone thinking her a whore sent out for the bachelor party.

He sucked on his cigarette, considering her. Not saying a word, he reached for his jeans and pulled them on. When he yanked open a desk drawer, something stopped him in his tracks and Kendall would've killed to know what had put such longing on his face. Probably, another woman, she realized with a pang. No way a man who looked like him and treated a woman whom he believed a whore with such overwhelming regard for her pleasure, remained single.

He swallowed, his strong throat moving with the motion. He closed the drawer and faced her. Kendall's blood ran cold when she saw his gun. God, what was he going to do to her? Her imagination running wild, she made a sound of distress. Sighing, he shoved the weapon into the waistband of his pants.

"I don't kill or hurt women. Who the hell knows what's going on out there by now? I might have to pistol whip some asshole or shoot the shit out of them as I escort you to your car."

The relief inside her almost made her sag. She wanted to tell him *thank you* and ask for his permission to see him again. She knew it would only be for sex, but, right now, in the haze of her orgasms, she couldn't think clearly. She couldn't think beyond the fact that, once she left him, it would be the end of this magical night.

As if to illustrate his view on women, he handed her a shirt and a pair of shorts. Once she'd put them on—and exalted in the fact that they were slightly big on her—he led her out of the room. When they reached the entry point to the main room, Kendall swallowed. Tonight, her salivary glands were working overtime but writhing bodies and women on their knees servicing men and…the entire situation had spiraled out of control. She glanced around the room, unable to stop herself, and saw no sign of the black-haired, green-eyed president who was a dream to look at himself. He…

"Hey, babe," a female voice said, drawing Kendall's attention to two naked girls. They were average sized and had absolutely no regard to her presence. "Ready to have some fun with us like we talked about last time we were here?"

He winked at them and they both giggled. "Not tonight."

Of course not tonight. He was a biker. Women threw themselves at these men and they happily accepted.

They started moving again, then paused a moment later.

"She's with me, Bowlie," he said, placing his big body between her and the other biker, confusing her all the more.

She had to remind herself she couldn't look at this situation from a female mindset and misconstrue this one-night stand as the beginning to something lasting. Sex and love were two different things, which Kendall was old enough to remember without blurring the lines between the two.

"Th-thank you," she said the moment they left the moans and groans and filthy words of the clubhouse behind and reached the outdoors. She breathed in the fresh air, not even caring it was cold and foggy.

They stared at one another when they reached her car.

"Are you sure you're going to be all right to drive?" he asked, further drawing her to him. The moment she drove away from him, her senses would return. It had to. "We can go back to my room. Spend the night together." He shrugged. "Talking. Drinking. Having sex. Your choice."

Her choice. Those words sounded like heaven to her. Yes, with him, he'd allowed it to be *her* choice. Not because he was an asshole bent on control. Spotlights glimmered around them and burned through the low fog, silhouetting his chiseled features. His tempting lips. "Kissing?"

The wind howled and cold blasted her skin. She only wore shorts and a t-shirt and it was freezing. She hugged her arms around her waist.

"No," he answered. "I'll kiss your pussy. The lovely globes of your ass cheeks. I'll lick you from your toes all the way up to your thighs. But kiss you? No. That I won't do."

Her nipples hardened and her pussy readied for him to put action to words. Remembering the intensity of the orgasms he'd given her, her lips parted, the cold air burning her cheeks. She wanted to kiss him, though. Why? She wasn't sure. She licked her lips, hoping he'd bring her back inside once she pointed something out to him.

"Not even to keep me out of this weather? Keep me here and safe?"

He lifted a brow. "It's your life, gorgeous. If you want to gamble with it by attempting to manipulate me into giving you your way, that's your business."

Raising her chin and chastened by his response, she thinned her lips.

"I want you safe," he reiterated.

She bit down on her lower lip, trying to hide her shock. Not too many people concerned themselves with her safety and no one saw beneath the surface of the career woman she showed the world to her inner vulnerability.

Before she processed it all and told him she'd return inside with him, he pulled her into his arms and hugged her, kissing her temple. "Thank you, gorgeous," he whispered, caressing her cheek. "I had a wonderful time with you."

She nodded, not missing the dismissal in his tone. "Same here."

Using her keyless entry, she unlocked her door. As if they'd been on a date, he opened the door and held it until she got in. She smiled at him, not knowing what else to do.

He gave her a two-fingered salute and Kendall drove away, saying a silent goodbye to that beautiful man.

ABOUT THE AUTHOR

Kathryn Kelly is living her dream and writing books. Everyone who follows Kat on Facebook is well aware of her relationship with her mother. For those of you who are unaware, the following will offer you a taste. To live in peace, Kat acknowledges she is a mom, but prefers to keep her personal life private. In spite of her momma. Kat has always been an avid reader and still devours books in her spare time. She also enjoys football, socializing, music, eating, and jokes. In her head, she's the ultimate biker babe. In reality, she's an ordinary girl-next-door and a native New Orleanian.

Kathryn Kelly Social Media Links:

Facebook: https://www.facebook.com/kathryn.kelly.336717

Goodreads:
https://www.goodreads.com/book/show/19397862-misunderstood

Twitter: https://twitter.com/katkelwriter

Blog: http://kathrynkellyauthor.blogspot.com

Amazon Author Page:
http://www.amazon.com/KathrynKelly/e/B00H4BM862/ref=ntt_athr_dp_pel_pop_1

Google Plus:
https://plus.google.com/115819834470166817540?hl=en